Julie Miller is an award-winning *USA Today* bestselling author of breathtaking romantic suspense—with a National Readers' Choice Award and a Daphne du Maurier Award, among other prizes. She has also earned an *RT Book Reviews* Career Achievement Award. For a complete list of her books, monthly newsletter and more, go to juliemiller.org

By day, **Maggie Wells** is buried in spreadsheets. At night, she pens tales of intrigue and people tangling up the sheets. She has a weakness for hot heroes and happy endings. She is the product of a charming rogue and a shameless flirt, and you only have to scratch the surface of this mild-mannered married lady to find a naughty streak a mile wide.

Discover more at millsandboon.co.uk

PROTECTING THE PACK

JULIE MILLER

CATCHING A HACKER

MAGGIE WELLS

MILLS & BOON

First Published in Great Britain 2025
by Mills & Boon, an imprint of HarperCollins*Publishers* Ltd
1 London Bridge Street, London, SE1 9GF

www.harpercollins.co.uk

HarperCollins*Publishers*
Macken House, 39/40 Mayor Street Upper,
Dublin 1, D01 C9W8, Ireland

Protecting the Pack © 2025 Julie Miller
Catching a Hacker © 2025 Margaret Ethridge

ISBN: 978-0-263-39699-7

0225

This book contains FSC™ certified paper and other controlled sources to ensure responsible forest management.

For more information visit: www.harpercollins.co.uk/green

Printed and Bound in the UK using 100% Renewable Electricity at CPI Group (UK) Ltd, Croydon, CR0 4YY

PROTECTING
THE PACK

JULIE MILLER

For my husband, my dear friend Kim McKane and so many other dedicated social workers who have laboured tirelessly—often with too little credit, a surprising degree of danger and endless stress—to help families in need and children in the foster care system. It's a high-burnout job, and most social workers I've met move on to second careers. It's not a perfect system, but sometimes, they work miracles.

Prologue

"Oh, yeah, he's a fine-lookin' boy."

Gio Williams stood in front of the door to the bedroom he shared with his little brother, Tyrell. Through the thin wood partition, he could hear Tyrell sniffing away tears, just like their mother, who was shaking in her shiny high heels beside their late-night visitor.

The man in the double-breasted suit looked the part of a well-to-do businessman or doctor or something—just like the dads of some of his classmates at the magnet school where Gio and Tyrell went on scholarship. But Vaughn Trask wasn't his dad, or Tyrell's. He wasn't even dad-like, whatever that meant. And this visit to their apartment near downtown Kansas City had nothing to do with acting like a dad, and everything to do with scaring their mom into paying him money she didn't have.

Gio knew because the twenty-dollar bill he'd stolen from one of the rich kids at school to buy groceries for himself and Tyrell was missing from the gym sneaker inside his book bag where he'd stashed it. Since Tyrell was a good kid and wouldn't break a rule to save his life, that meant Toy Williams had stolen the cash from her eleven-year-old son and gone out to buy a hit of crack cocaine or whatever drug she could afford.

Usually from the reputable-looking man who was currently twisting her arm at a painful angle.

Trask smiled in a cold, creepy way that commanded fear and respect across the city. "I can see he's got attitude. I could make some money with him. Pay off the thirty-six thousand you owe me in no time, Toy girl."

Gio Williams raged inside—not so much at the sick words coming out of Vaughn Trask's mouth, but at the way Vaughn's tight grip on his mother's arm made tears roll down her cheeks. Gio remembered that Toy Williams had been a fun, energetic beauty when he was younger—younger than Tyrell was now. Toy wasn't even her real name. It had been Mary until this loser had gotten his hands on her and dubbed her his *toy*. If Gio was bigger, older, maybe part of a gang, he'd be able to punch the man's lights out—or stab him or shoot him or something—and make Vaughn get his grubby hands off his mother and leave them alone.

The only thing holding him back from flying at his mom's boyfriend was knowing that if he got sent to juvie, then Tyrell would be alone. Or if Trask did put him to work for him, then chances were he'd come after Tyrell next. Their mom wasn't going to protect them from Trask. It was up to Gio to take care of the family.

"He's not turning tricks for you." His mother finally found her voice between sobs and shivering.

For all the good it did her. Trask released her just long enough to slap her hard across the face, driving her to her knees before he wrenched her to her feet again and yelled in her face. "I say what happens with this family. Not you. I own you."

"They're my boys," she protested with a whimper.

"Yeah? You win any Mother of the Year awards lately? Are you sure you even know who their fathers are?" He released his grip, and she tumbled to the floor with a gasp of pain. "You're tweakin' so bad, you probably don't know that you haven't fed them for days. You want something from me? Somebody's going to have to earn it."

Toy crawled over to Gio and grasped his arm to pull herself to her feet. "Maybe he could just make some deliveries for you. Make a little money that way."

Gio's stomach churned with conflicting emotions. He wasn't something she could trade for a fix. Yet he knew just how scared she was of this man.

Protect the family. He wasn't sure he could, but he was going to try.

Trask moved closer, and Gio fisted his hands down at his sides. His mom flinched away, but Gio stood his ground as the man grabbed him by the chin and twisted his face up to study it. Gio swung his fists, aiming for the man's belly or farther down where it would hurt. But Trask easily evaded the attack. When Gio kicked out and connected with the man's shin, he cursed and lifted Gio right up off his feet.

"You've got fire in you, kid." The words sounded like a compliment, but they didn't feel like one. "Too bad your mama doesn't have that kind of fire anymore."

"Vaughn, please, baby," his mom begged. But what was she begging for? "We can work something out."

Not for the first time, Gio wondered what it'd be like to have an adult stand between him and a threat, instead of the other way around. Despite dangling like a fish from the big man's bruising grip, Gio twisted his body, aiming his next kick where it could do some damage.

That was when the door behind him opened.

Trask tossed Gio toward the couch and smiled down at Tyrell's tearstained face. "Well, what have we here?"

Tyrell had their mom's cell phone in his hand, and he shoved it toward the unwelcome guest. "I called 9-1-1. We learned about it in school."

"Did you now?" Trask's smile disappeared. "Let me see that phone."

"Don't you touch him!" Gio shouted, grabbing Tyrell and hiding him behind his back.

"What did you do, Ty-Ty?" their mom protested, trying to grab the phone for herself. "How'd you get that?"

Trask was about to laugh when his own phone buzzed inside his suit jacket. He pulled out the phone to read a text while Toy tried to dodge around Gio to reclaim the phone they'd easily borrowed when she'd been passed out on the couch, right before Trask had broken in and roused her by dumping a pitcher of water in her face.

Trask nodded at the message, probably from one of his goons he'd stationed outside the apartment door and on the street below, then tucked the phone back into his pocket. He turned and strode for the door as the man waiting outside opened it for him. "Gotta go."

Toy Williams scrambled to her feet and ran after the hateful man. "What about me, Vaughn? I need something to get me through tonight, baby. You know I'm good for it."

When she grabbed his arm, he shoved her to the floor, brushed the wrinkles from his jacket and stepped over her. When she lunged for him again, the bodyguard stepped between them, blocking her while Vaughn Trask disappeared down the hallway.

As soon as he closed the door behind them, she scrambled to her feet and pulled it open. "Vaughn! Vaughn, I'll do anything…"

But the visit was over. She slammed the door shut and whirled around on Gio and Tyrell. "Why'd you do that? Vaughn ain't never gonna give me my stash now. He's my ticket out of this dump." When she tried to push Gio aside to get to Tyrell, he stood his ground. She was still taller than him, but he was stone-cold sober and willing to fight anyone to protect his brother, even their own mom. When the sirens sounded outside the building and she couldn't reach Tyrell, she smacked her hand across Gio's cheek. "You boys are nothing but trouble."

Gio's cheek stung, and his jaw hurt from where Trask had grabbed him, but no way was she getting past him to vent her frustration on Tyrell. "You want me to make you some coffee, Mom?" Gio asked. Sometimes, the nasty bitter flavor and caffeine could satisfy her cravings for a bit. "I saved you some from yesterday."

Tyrell echoed his attempt to calm her down. "Mama, he's gone. We're safe now."

"You ungrateful little—"

"KCPD. Open up." She was caught off guard by banging on the door. "I need to know everyone's safe in there."

An hour later, after Gio and Tyrell both had talked to the cops and their mom was being led away in handcuffs, Gio hugged an arm around his little brother's shoulders. "Stop your crying, Tyrell, and go pack your bag. They'll be moving us into foster care again."

Chapter One

One week later

Stella Smith had no business climbing the ladder in the barn at K-9 Ranch.

She was forty-eight and a half years old. And yes, she included the half. Unlike when she'd been a child and had wanted to appear older, she now added the label to remind herself that she hadn't hit the infamous forty-nine yet—that her body was as young and content as her heart and brain were most days.

She really had no business climbing up to the loft to retrieve the dog toy her new adoptee, Jasper, had tossed up there. She was certain the big black Newfoundland dog's strategy in their game of fetch was to keep Stella busy long enough for him to mosey over to the closest stall lined with hay, where the big brute could stretch out for a few minutes and dry off after their training session in the pond with the ranch's owner, Jessie Caldwell. He'd give her those soft brown eyes and act all innocent as to the trouble he was causing her.

Stella glanced down at the wet black dog, who watched her ascend the ladder from his sphinxlike position in the hay. "You know, big guy, you're the one who's supposed to be fetching, not me. How did you toss it all the way up here, anyway?"

His answer was a big yawn.

Stella smiled, shook her head and climbed up another rung. "You'd better nap now. I'm siccing the kids on you when we get home."

Not that that was any real threat. Jasper and her foster kids adored each other. If they wanted to run around in the backyard, he'd be right there with them. If they wanted to use him as a big pillow and watch TV together, he'd like that even better.

Jasper was a one-hundred-forty-pound couch potato at heart. Although she'd initially come looking for a small dog to adopt for her kids—to help them learn the responsibility of caring for others and grow closer as a family unit—Jasper had immediately taken a shine to the children. He was both a nonjudgmental set of ears to listen, and a gentle caretaker who had proved to have a calming effect on the children when one of them had a particularly trying day.

After several weeks of training on basic behavior skills, they were now focusing on developing his water rescue instincts, since Stella's home was a lakeshore property. Even with the fenced-in backyard and continued reviews about swimming and boating safety, she was glad to have a dog who not only kept a close eye on the children when they were outside, but also was a strong swimmer in case there was an emergency of some kind. Of course, getting Jasper to obey her commands in and out of the water was a matter of exposure and repetition, keeping him interested in the process and keeping him in shape.

That was why Stella was supposed to be playing with him now after an intense training session with her friend Jessie Caldwell, who ran K-9 Ranch. The big guy needed his exercise so that he didn't become overweight. Plus, the activity was good for Stella, too, who had never been able to shed the extra pounds she'd carried on her five-foot-eight-inch frame since childhood. She was healthy, according to her annual wellness exams, and enjoyed kayaking and swimming in the lake where she lived. But she'd never be skinny.

She'd raised foster children for nearly twenty years now, and stayed in contact with most of them, even after they'd aged out of the system. She lived in a beautiful home nestled beside a beautiful lake on the outskirts of Kansas City, Missouri. She had good friends like Jessie Caldwell, and she woke up happy most days. Stella sighed at the realization. Maybe she and Jasper had more in common than she'd given the dog credit for.

He was the gentlest, most loving and patient dog Stella had ever met, and both she and her three current foster children had immediately taken to him. Her youngest girl, Ana, who rarely spoke and wasn't in school yet, treated him like a giant teddy bear, hugging on him and speaking to him in the gibberish language she'd come up with to survive her failure to thrive after months of neglect. Harper, the intelligent fourth grader with big glasses who reminded Stella so much of herself at that age, was obsessed with researching every last tidbit of information she could find about Newfoundland dogs, which led to more research about the island of Newfoundland and Canada, as well as dog training, pet care, German dog commands—which Jasper ignored—as well as all the nutritional components of healthy dog food and the treats the lumbering black dog consumed like candy if given the chance. Her foster son, Colby, was simply thrilled to have another male in the house and was happy to chase or be chased in the backyard or to sit with Jasper and practice his reading skills.

Stella had reached the edge of the loft when her phone rang in the pocket of her jeans. Bracing herself at the top of the ladder, she pulled her cell out, checked the name of the incoming call on her screen and swore under her breath.

The easy thing would be not to answer the unwanted call. Or to block the number. But she'd learned a long time ago that Preston Alan Jeffries III, who went by the cutesy nickname of Trey, was relentless when he wanted something. If she didn't talk to him now, he'd just keep calling. And if he couldn't reach her by phone, he'd show up at her house or her family's charitable trust management group, where she worked part-time, and then she'd have to deal with him in person. Or worse, he'd wheedle an invitation to a public event and approach her where she'd either have to politely play along or risk the pity of public embarrassment again.

Better to get this over with now. Let her true feelings fly. Find out what Trey wanted and move on.

She answered the call and put the phone to her ear. "I'm busy. What do you want?"

Not the friendliest of greetings. But then, it had been twenty years since she'd considered Selfish McJerkface any kind of friend.

That cultured, polished voice answered. "Stella? Is that you, darling?" Ugh. She hated when he'd dropped endearments into their sporadic conversations over the years—as if he had the right to call her at all. "It's Trey, dear," he identified unnecessarily. "I hope you're well. I was wondering if I could ask you a favor."

Stella knew she had absolutely no business whatsoever climbing the ladder to the loft while she was on the phone with a man she'd once loved, then hated, and now…well, she could honestly say she would never be fond of Trey Jeffries. Especially if he thought he could worm his way back into her life after humiliating her so thoroughly and painfully the night before their wedding twenty years ago.

Stella didn't hold a grudge like she once had. And she'd

gotten over being heartbroken years ago, once she'd figured out it was her desire to love and be loved—not love itself—that had been crushed all those years ago. But the humiliation, the fear that there might be a grain of truth in any of the cruel things he'd said to her, still stung the lonely little rich girl buried deep inside her. However, she was also a grown woman who'd made a successful life for herself and many others. She didn't need any emotional grenade like the one she suspected Trey was about to lob at her. "What do you want?" she repeated.

Spotting Jasper's toy, she leaned over the edge of the loft to grab the hard rubber ball by its attached rope.

Trey nattered on in her ear. "Come on, Stella. We've been business associates and have run in the same social circles for a number of years. We can at least be civil to each other."

Um, no. He'd been a business associate of her father's. Made a point to woo the boss's daughter and tie her to him so they'd both inherit Robert Smith's real estate and investment empire. They'd never worked together except to appear at charity functions. And he no longer worked for her father's company at all, not since she'd inherited everything and converted most of the business into charitable trusts benefiting children, education and service animal organizations like K-9 Ranch. Plus, her social circles ran more to PTA meetings and playdates for her foster kids than gala fundraisers and debutante balls these days. She certainly had no desire to be civil to a man who only saw her as a bank account.

She tossed the toy down into the hay next to Jasper. The big dog raised his head, sniffed at the KONG, then lay back down. "You're welcome, you big galoot." Jasper chuffed a breath out between his heavy jowls and closed his eyes. "I live to serve."

"What does that mean? You're willing to help me?"

He'd heard that? Help with what? She needed to nip that

miscommunication in the bud since she had no intention of lifting one finger to help her ex-fiancé. "I'm talking to my dog, Trey. Now, tell me exactly why you're calling or I'm hanging up."

"I wanted to see if we could have lunch, or if you'd let me take you to dinner. I'm free tonight."

Stella frowned, even more suspicious of Trey's intentions. "Why?"

He laughed. "I'll tell you all about it tonight. Capital Grille on the Plaza?"

Steaming at his relentless assumption that she'd say yes, she took a step back down the ladder. "Tonight doesn't work for me." *Never* was the only time that worked for her when it came to Trey.

"I'm back in town." He went on as if she hadn't spoken. "And I heard there's still no man in your life." Wow. She'd really been a fool—so desperate for a man to love her, to get away from her parents' cold, sterile world—to ever think this opportunist was the man she wanted to spend the rest of her life with.

"Seriously? I have no desire to reconnect with you. You were a mistake, Trey. I returned your ring. I fired you from the company. I moved on ages ago. I don't know why you can't do the same. Besides, there *is* a man in my life. He has four feet and beautiful black fur and probably outweighs you."

"Four feet?" He laughed. Stella hated that sound. It was so practiced and false. He'd probably never belly-laughed in his life. "Your new man is a dog? That is so sad."

She palmed her forehead and silently berated herself. If she hadn't been so preoccupied with enjoying her time with the dog and putting up a wall between her and Trey, she would have picked up on the clues sooner. *Back in town?*

Free? Hinting at her lack of a love life? "Oh, my God. Did another woman dump you?"

"No one dumps me." The charm bled from his tone as if she'd flipped a switch. That was the tone that had called her a fat cow and a spoiled little rich girl in the foyer of a restaurant where all the waitstaff and family and friends at their rehearsal dinner could overhear. "Francine and I have been legally separated for nearly a year. The divorce was finalized last month. I'm a free man."

She'd say *sorry* about the divorce, but she wasn't in the habit of lying like this man was. "Yeah, well, I'm not interested in picking up the slack."

"Excuse me. I'm looking for Stella Smith?" A deep male voice with a slight Ozark twang called from the open barn doors.

Stella whirled around from her perch on the ladder to see a uniformed police officer walking toward her. "Huh?"

"Are you—" The compactly built man gripped his utility belt in one hand and held the other up in apology. "Sorry. I didn't realize you were on the ph—"

"Oh!" Startled by the unexpected guest, her balance shifted. The ladder swayed away from the loft, and she threw herself forward to keep from tipping back. Her sneaker slipped off the rung and she was falling. Her arms windmilled around her head and her phone went flying. Muttering a distinctly unladylike curse, Stella tried to dive toward the cushion of hay rather than the hard-packed dirt in the middle of the barn.

She didn't hit either one.

A pair of thick, muscular arms slammed around her and spun her. Momentum carried them into the stall of hay a few feet from where Jasper lay, and she sprawled on top of the man. She squeezed her eyes shut against the dizzying

aftermath of whatever maneuver he'd used to avoid the con-
crete-hard dirt and land safely in the hay.

"Oh, my gosh." She apologized through squinted eyes,
hanging on to a pair of sturdy shoulders while her brain and
stomach sloshed around inside her. "Are you okay?"

"Are *you* okay?" he countered, his voice deep with concern. "I hit the soft hay. You had farther to fall." A warm
hand cupped the back of her head, pulling a few strands of
hair loose from the messy topknot she wore. "Can you open
your eyes for me?"

Stella was aware of something on his belt poking into
her hip. His holstered gun? And while the rest of his body
branded her with heat, she became aware of the cold, hard
void of warmth where their chests smooshed together. Was
he wearing a protective vest beneath his uniform?

She opened her eyes to a swirling blur of cool colors,
blinking rapidly until her vision cleared and she was looking straight down into her rescuer's face.

Although it was sprinkled with a dusting of brown stubble flecked with gray, the man had the kind of jawline that
gave the word *chiseled* its definition. The shape of his face
was equally angular, perhaps a shade away from being truly
handsome. But wow, he had beautiful green eyes. The points
of his short, silvering hairline were receding, but that made
him seem somehow more masculine to her. Like he was
wiser, more confident, fully at ease with his own appearance and the world around him.

"I need you to talk to me," he ordered gently, lightly probing her scalp. "Did you hit your head or twist an ankle or
anything?"

She continued to stare. So very, very green.

"Stella?" She nodded. "I'm Joe Carpenter. My pal Garrett
said he and his wife, Jessie, plan to set us up."

Stella frowned, transfixed by the rich, mossy green of his eyes. "Set us up?"

"Blind date?" He lay flat on his back in the hay, his hands now resting at her waist while she propped her elbows between them and clutched his shoulders. Even horizontal like this, she realized he wasn't that much taller than she was. And yet she felt...dwarfed by his dimensions. "Didn't they mention that to you?"

"Oh, yeah. Garrett has a cop friend. Said they served together back in their Army days." Right. She briefly squeezed her eyes shut. She didn't need to state what this man already knew. "That would be you?"

"Guilty as charged. You *are* Stella Smith?"

She sought out the green eyes again and nodded.

Joe Carpenter shifted beneath her, the muscles of his thighs brushing against her own, making long-ignored parts of her anatomy sit up and take notice. "I'm not a fan of surprises. I just got off shift and drove out to the house. Jessie said you were in here with your dog. I thought I'd break the ice and introduce myself first. Save us an awkward moment later."

"Right. Because we're having that awkward moment now."

He laughed, and she bobbed up and down on his chest and stomach. A belly laugh. An honest-to-goodness belly laugh. *I could fall for a man like this.*

Wait. She already had. Fallen hard and flattened him at the edge of a barn stall.

Embarrassment warmed her face as she realized she'd been documenting every feature about the man lying beneath her without even properly introducing herself or making sure he hadn't been injured breaking her fall.

She curled one knee into the hay beneath them and scrambled off him. "Oh. I am so sorry."

"It's okay." She caught her foot on his thigh and stumbled. He grabbed her hand and pulled her upright as he stood to steady her. "Easy. I thought maybe you were dazed, or you couldn't move for some other reason."

Dazed was right. She hadn't been that up close and personal with a man like that in weeks. Months? Oh, wow. Had it actually been years? And she'd just sprawled her body all over his fit, muscular self as though she had the right to familiarize herself with his brawny arms and thighs and the heat of his skin. She felt a blush warming her cheeks as they faced each other.

He was one, maybe two inches taller than her five-eight height. But she liked being able to look straight into those rich, deep green eyes.

"Stella? Stella?" Trey's voice shouting from some distant place jarred her from the hazy, hormonal mood she'd been caught in.

She finally released Joe's steadying hand and looked all around her feet. "Oh, no. My phone." Sometime while she'd been lying on top of her rescuer, Jasper had pushed to his feet and was nosing around in the hay. When he raised his head, he had her cell phone clutched in his mouth. "You silly boy. Give that to Mommy."

Joe reached the dog first. "Drop it," he ordered. He caught the phone when the dog opened his mouth and pushed his head into the rewarding stroke of Joe's hand. "Good boy." Joe's face curled up in an icky expression before he wiped both sides of the phone on his pant leg and handed it to her. But not before reading the name on the screen. "It's a little slobbery, but…" He frowned. "Trey the Troll?"

"Pet nickname for someone I don't want to talk to." Stella snatched the phone and cleaned the dog drool and clinging bits of hay with the hem of the untucked blouse she wore. "Thanks."

When she turned away, she put the phone back to her ear. "Are you still there?"

Trey yelled at her. "Who the hell is that guy? I thought you said your new man was a dog. You lied to me. You aren't even giving me a chance?"

"I can't talk right now, Trey. Gotta go." She disconnected the call and turned back to Joe. "Sorry about that."

The dent of a frown between Joe's eyebrows never shifted. "Everything okay?"

"Just a blast from the past trying to charm his way back into my life. Ain't gonna happen." Her attempt to make light of the call failed when her phone rang again. She dismissed the call and stuck her phone in the back pocket of her jeans.

Gripping the front of his belt on either side of his buckle, Joe rested his elbows on the holster of his gun and another leather box clipped to his uniform belt. "Is that him again? He won't take no for an answer?"

Why did she feel that was the same stance and serious look he used when he pulled over a driver at a traffic stop or responded to a disturbance at someone's house?

"It's all right, Officer." She glanced at the chevrons on his sleeve. "Sergeant."

"Try Joe."

"Okay, Joe. Don't get your boxers in a twist. I've been dealing with Preston Alan Jeffries for twenty years. Dumped me the night before our wedding, and every four or five years, he tries to reconcile. Apparently, wife number three just divorced him, too. Or maybe it's number four. I don't keep tabs on him the way he does with me."

"He hasn't taken no for an answer for twenty years? What's his hold on you?"

Twenty years without any other long-term relationship? She'd devoted her life to her kids and her charities and her friends and was happy with her choices. But Joe's probing question made her think. She was uncomfortable to realize that, in some ways, she hadn't moved on. Maybe it was simply an inability to completely trust another man with her heart. Or maybe a tiny part of her still believed the horrible things Trey had said to her that night. That she was unlovable. That he'd been kind to take her to his bed and ask her to be his wife.

Joe's insight was as discomfiting as it was spot-on. Her ex had lived in her psyche for a long time. She needed to be done with that. She wanted to be.

As she became lost in her thoughts, her gaze drifted to the hay beneath her feet and the giant black dog who sat beside her and leaned against her thigh. She stroked her fingers through Jasper's thick hair. The Newfoundland might not be the most excitable dog, but he was definitely a cuddler. Stella needed a good cuddle right about now.

"Sorry. That's none of my business."

Her gaze snapped up at Joe's deep, almost musical voice. "No. It's a legit question if you want to know me." She clutched Jasper's fur and took a deep breath. "I'm fairly well-off, thanks to a generous inheritance and good money management in my own right. That's what Trey likes best about me. Did Garrett and Jessie tell you I'm…wealthy? I'm one of the biggest benefactors to K-9 Ranch. Do you have a problem with me having money?"

He considered her admission, one that made most men's eyes light up with opportunity or darken with intimidation. But Joe's beautiful green gaze remained steadfast. "Are you going to act like you're better than me or anyone else because of that money?"

She frowned at the insulting scenario. "No."

"Then no."

No? Why did that word sound so positive when Joe said it? She might as well lay out all the issues that had kept men from pursuing a relationship with her in the past. "Do you like kids? Some men don't. They see them as competition for my time and affection, or a nuisance. I'm a foster parent. I'm proud of the work I do. I love it. There are always two or three kids in my house at any given time."

He considered her words before nodding. "I'm okay with kids. Don't have any of my own. I've never been married. But I do some teaching at the police academy. I've mentored some high school kids over the years. Some of them seem pretty young to me. Barely in their teens or twenties."

Stella smiled. "My current charges are much younger than that. Two fourth graders and one four-year-old."

"So, apparently we're listing grievances that have kept a partner from committing to us in the past?" The frown that had marred his angular face finally disappeared. "Do you have a problem with me being a few inches shy of six feet?"

Some woman had dumped him for being short? The nerve. Could they not see how much man there was here? "You're taller than me."

"Not by much."

"That just means I don't have to wear high heels when we go out."

He chuckled. "So, you think we're going out?"

"Isn't that the idea of a blind date?"

"It is." Then the serious expression returned. "Do you have a problem with me being a cop? It's a dangerous job, sometimes with unpredictable hours. Some people don't like me just because I wear this badge."

"I don't do jerks, abusers, misogynists or ex-fiancés. Cops and well-built short men aren't anywhere on my do-not-date list." Stella ticked off the list on her fingers. "Do you want to go out with me sometime?"

When he grinned at her impulsive invitation, she knew she was smitten with the man. "Yes."

The dogs in their kennels outside the barn raised a ruckus at the sound of the door closing on the Caldwells' back deck. Even Jasper trotted outside the barn to share the excitement of the ranch's owner, Jessie Caldwell, striding toward them. A white-muzzled German shepherd padded along beside her.

With that much of a plan in mind, Stella and Joe exchanged numbers. After he'd clipped his phone back onto his belt, Joe held out his hand to shake hers. "Nice to meet you, Stella Smith. Talk to Jessie and Garrett. They'll vouch for me. I'll call you soon." When he pulled away, he pointed to her phone. "You won't give me a nasty nickname and ignore my calls?"

"I don't know. I haven't gone out with you yet."

Joe laughed and strode away. "Fair enough. Talk to you soon." At the barn door opening, he stopped to greet Jessie, trading a quick hug and a kiss on the cheek. "Garrett around?"

"In the kitchen. Go on in the back door. There's fresh coffee in the pot." With one last smile for Stella, Joe headed up to the house. Jessie curiously watched Joe move past the kennels before she shook her head and hurried over to Stella. "Sorry, I got caught on the phone with Nate's school. They want to test him for the gifted program."

Stella could tell her friend seemed unnaturally nervous. "That's awesome. I can tell he's a bright kid."

"This parenting thing is scary sometimes. What if we make the wrong decision? He could feel ostracized from his classmates. Or maybe it's too soon after his adoption and settling into life with us to throw something else big at him."

"Take a breath." Stella squeezed her friend's hand. "Talk to Nate about it. Find out what he thinks about being a supersmart kid. Then you and Garrett discuss it, too. Go through all the pros and cons. Make your decision together."

Jessie exhaled a deep breath. "You're so good at this parenting thing."

Stella waved off the compliment. "Nah. I've just been at it longer."

"Thank you so much for guiding us through the fostering and adoption process."

"My pleasure."

Now that the immediate cause for concern had been tamped down, the overly perceptive Jessie she'd known for years came out. "I see you and Joe have already met. The stinker. I knew he'd find a way to get out of it truly being a blind date. How did it go?"

Stella shrugged and realized she didn't feel stiff or sore from the jarring fall. She wondered if Joe could say the same. "I fell off the ladder and he caught me. I believe we're intimately acquainted now."

"You fell off...? Stella!" Jessie circled around her to the ladder that lay across the floor, and they both set it upright again. "Are you okay? Is Joe? When Ben gets back from his honeymoon, the first thing I'll have him do is mount braces on the ladder to secure it. I don't want the kids or anyone else falling out here."

"The only thing that got bruised was my dignity."

Stella recognized Ben Hunter's name as the disabled Army veteran who worked as a trainer and caretaker on the ranch. He'd been very good with her kids when they'd gotten curious about his prosthetic arm. But she suspected that had more to do with the shy young woman he'd just married than with his level of comfort with curious children. Besides, Ben Hunter might be a badass former Special Forces soldier who oozed testosterone, but she was more interested in an older, shorter, stockier man. She smiled as she watched Joe climb onto the back deck and disappear into the house.

She knew her friend Jessie was almost a savant when it

came to matching a dog to the right person. Maybe that talent for knowing just what someone needed extended to her matchmaking skills, as well. "And Joe seems very okay. Did you see the arms on that guy? He's a little alpha and overprotective—he has a hard time getting out of cop mode. But he's a gentleman, and he has a great laugh. And a very nice tushy."

Jessie laughed. "I'm glad there's a physical attraction there. But you and I both know the substance of a man means more than his looks."

Stella's phone vibrated in the back pocket of her jeans. It was probably Trey again. She'd just ignore it. Oh, yes. She knew all about the value of substance over flash. She'd lived that cautionary tale. "Joe didn't point out that I was a klutz. Or that I have hay in my hair. Or that I'm a little fragrant after working out with Jasper and perspiring." Stella plucked the cotton of her blouse away from where it clung to the skin above her cleavage. "Is it just me? Or does it feel like summer already? It's only May."

"You know Missouri weather. It'll change soon enough. But can we get back to your first impression of Joe?"

"A little overprotective. Especially when he asked me about Trey."

Jessie propped her hands at her waist. "That jerk is pestering you again?"

Stella didn't deny it. Nor did she answer her friend's question. "Joe made me feel good about myself, like I was important."

"You *are* important."

Stella nodded. "Men don't always see that. They see the big house and the big bank account, or they see the woman who never did outgrow being a chubby girl."

"That's Trey talking. There is so much more to you than

any of that. Any man worth his salt will get to know you and see you for the treasure you truly are."

"Thanks." Stella appreciated Jessie's unwavering support. She linked elbows with her friend, and they started back toward the house, with both their dogs falling into step beside them. "Now. Joe said you could vouch for him. Tell me more about sexy Sergeant Joe Carpenter."

Chapter Two

Joe Carpenter popped the cap off his dark Irish beer and swallowed a long drink, savoring the bitterness on his tongue and the chill sliding down his throat as he looked out the window to the balcony and the city lights glowing in the night sky. He wondered if he'd be able to sleep tonight or if his insomnia would wake him up after a couple of hours. Shutting down his brain and relaxing had never been his best thing.

The clock on the microwave over the stove said it was ten o'clock. But it might as well be high noon with the way his thoughts were revving. He needed a hobby to take his mind off work. He needed to take a class and learn a new skill. He needed something to look forward to so he could shake off the loneliness that was creeping in more and more with each passing year and making itself at home.

His friends were all married—some of them had even married two or three times. They had kids. Some had grand-kids. They had lives outside of the military or police work. And while he had always been made to feel welcome at family gatherings or social events, he still felt like an outsider. He wanted the love, the belonging, the intriguing unpredictability of a life well lived for himself.

He took another drink before walking back out to the

living room of his condo. He had a good life, but it was an empty one. His place was comfortable and insulated well enough to keep from hearing the street noises and other residents in the remodeled historic building near downtown Kansas City. The two-bedroom, one-bath layout was small, but since it was just him, the size was fine. The decorator he'd hired had appointed it in a sea of neutrals—browns and grays with touches of black. *Bachelor chic*, she'd called it. Joe called it boring.

Sure, it was nice. And if he really wanted to shake things up, he could buy a lamp or pillow or piece of artwork to add some color to the decor. But since it felt more like a hotel room than a home, he'd never made the effort. It served its purpose to give him a place to eat, sleep a few hours each night and relax away from work. But even with the TV on low, playing the news, it was hauntingly quiet. It was one of the reasons he'd been considering adopting a small, city-friendly dog from K-9 Ranch. He could use the companionship, the noise, another spirit to liven up his boring, quiet life.

He'd bet good money that Stella Smith's house wasn't neutral and boring. It would match her colorful personality. She was a bit of a klutz, but she had a funny, quick wit and a hidden vulnerability behind her smart mouth and big heart that had sneaked beneath his body armor this afternoon and tempted him to learn more about the woman. Gray-green eyes the color of a storm cloud had stared down into his gaze for several intriguing seconds. Porcelain skin flushed with a rosy combination of heat and embarrassment had begged to be touched. He'd discovered subtle turquoise and lavender highlights in her tousled ash-blond hair. Definitely not a boring woman.

Her place wouldn't be quiet, either, since she had three foster children and that massive beast of a dog living with her. He wondered if she was a neat freak like him, cleaning everything up at the end of the day. Or if she was more like the free spirit she resembled, taking every mess in stride—eliminating anything that might be a hazard or health risk, but letting chores that could wait...wait. She'd said she was rich—testing him, he suspected, to see if he was a reverse snob or intimidated by her. Maybe she had domestic staff on hand, or someone who came in on a regular basis to keep her home looking like a spread from *Architectural Digest*. But somehow, he hoped she was more hands-on than that. That she and her kids cleaned up after themselves and the dog, maybe even made a game out of it—and that they learned responsibility and gained self-confidence by contributing to the quality of their home.

Yeah. He suspected there was little that was boring or quiet about Stella's home—or about the woman herself.

He'd been worried about Stella's safety when he saw the ladder rocking and her foot slipping, and he'd run to help. He'd never expected the most intriguing woman he'd ever met would fall into his arms and cling to him while she regained her equilibrium. Hell. He was still working on regaining his own equilibrium after that tumble in the hay.

He smiled just thinking about Stella. Then, almost as quickly, that smile was replaced with a frown.

Joe pulled out a coaster and set his beer bottle on the walnut coffee table in front of the brown leather couch. He picked up his laptop, where he'd been reading some police reports and news articles, and skimmed the short list of pertinent notes that he'd made on one Preston Alan Jeffries.

Relaxing in sweatpants and a faded green T-shirt from his time in the Army, he leaned back against the couch's brown leather cushions and stretched his legs out to prop his stockinged feet up on the coffee table. He pulled the laptop onto his thighs. Fifteen years in military intelligence, and another fifteen working investigations and training new investigators at the police academy, pinged his things-are-not-what-they-seem meter all the way into the red zone. There was something up with Trey the Troll that was bothering Stella. Maybe Jeffries was just a guy who wouldn't take no for an answer, which was unacceptable in itself. If she wasn't interested in him, the guy needed to move on. But he suspected there was some painful history there, and that Stella had made light of whatever she feared Trey the Troll might do to her again. Blind date or not, Joe wasn't going to let that happen if he could do something about it.

Stella might see it as prying. But it was hardwired in his DNA to know everything he could about a situation before stepping into it. And clearly, this guy's calls had upset her. Joe reviewed the three things he'd typed on his list. Trey Jeffries liked making society and business headlines, and he couldn't keep a wife. Still, the main cause for concern was the restraining order that had been filed against him by Stella eighteen years earlier. But the order had expired. Why hadn't she renewed it? He wanted the scoop from Stella. Even though he could attempt to unseal court records as needed for a case he was working on, he wouldn't go behind her back.

Who was he kidding? He just wanted to talk some more with Stella Smith. She was adorable. Funny. Had curves for days that fit perfectly against him. He'd been dreading the concept of a blind date, no matter how well-intentioned his friends might be. So, once he'd found out that she would be there, he'd shown up at K-9 Ranch thirty minutes before his own appointment to look at potential pets, in an effort to take the unknown element out of the dating equation.

He set aside the laptop and leaned forward to take another swig of his beer. Not that he needed courage, but he did need to school his patience and have a plan to let Stella know that he wanted to do some investigating on her ex. He had to do this right because he had a feeling he'd be wanting to spend a lot more than a few minutes literally in the hay with Stella Smith.

Despite a few good, if not long-term, relationships, he'd never found the *one*. His career had demanded his attention. The timing had been off. He hadn't been ready, or the woman hadn't been interested in a commitment to a man in uniform. Sure, he was lonely. But Joe had been a bachelor for fifty years, and he could admit that he'd gotten pickier in the prime of his life about any woman he went out with.

Stella was the first woman in a long time he'd felt an instant connection with. And he couldn't help but want to get to know her better. He took one more sip, then leaned back against the buttery-soft leather cushions, pulled up her number on his cell and typed in a text.

Hey. This is Joe from this afternoon. Is this a good time? Am I texting too late? Sometimes I get insomnia and forget that other people go to bed at a decent hour.

Barely a minute passed before he got a reply.

Hey, Joe from this afternoon. Everything okay?

Only if I'm not keeping you awake too late.

It's fine. I got the kids to bed and just put the dog out one last time. I've kicked off my shoes and I'm relaxing for a bit on the couch. What's up?

Joe smiled at the image she described. He wiggled his own toes inside his white socks and imagined her doing the same as she sat on the couch beside him while they enjoyed relaxing conversation and winding down at the end of the day. But he thought it best to get business out of the way and typed.

I wanted to be up front and let you know that I'd like to do some research on Preston Alan Jeffries.

The Third. That's why Preston goes by Trey. So, you want to snoop into my background? Dig into my past? Using your cop skills is an unfair advantage, Sergeant Joe. All I know about you is that you're good at playing catch.

He chuckled at her snarky response, even as he read between the lines and imagined that she wasn't comfortable with him prying into her history. I assure you I don't run around the city catching women falling from ladders. You were my first. But I am a cop. If this guy is threatening you in any way, it's my job to do something about it.

If you find out something you don't like, will it keep you from going out with me?

He hated that she thought that for even one second and hastily responded.

Oh, I'm going out with you. I'm looking forward to it. More than anything I have in a long time. I just wanted to know if I need to wear my sidearm, who I should be on the lookout for, and plan the safest places where I could take you. I don't like that you blew off his harassment when he was clearly upsetting you. He strikes me as the kind of man who'll try again.

The long pause that followed had him shifting uncomfortably in his seat. Damn. He'd probably offended her by following his suspicious instincts. He didn't know her well enough to pry. And she didn't know him well enough to trust that he wouldn't be intrusive or controlling, that he was only interested in making sure she wasn't caught up in a potentially dangerous situation. He picked up his beer and tried to decide if he needed to say something more to reassure her.

When the three dots indicating she was typing suddenly reappeared, he exhaled a breath he hadn't realized he'd been holding.

I don't understand why you're interested in me. I sound like I'm a lot of work.

I have a feeling you'll be the easiest woman I've gone out with in a long time.

Easiest?

Joe spit beer down the front of his shirt. He cursed, wiped his mouth, set down the bottle and quickly typed. That came out wrong. Sorry.

He sent his apology, then stared at his phone for a few seconds while he figured out the best way to explain what he'd meant—that *being* with her was easy. Not that he expected her to fall into bed with him on the first date. He had a few years on the chassis, and the hair he wasn't losing seemed to grow a little grayer every day. But he kept himself in good shape, and no woman—as far as he knew—had ever given him an insulting nickname like Trey the Troll.

Stella's reply came through before he could say any of that.

Relax. I know what you meant. During our brief meeting this afternoon, I found you easy to be with, too. I wouldn't have asked you out if I didn't feel the spark of something that intrigued me. Her kind words, touched with a little humor, calmed the panic that he'd just blown any chance at seeing Stella again. Before he could respond, another message came through. It's just that I've never had a guy do research on me before a date unless he had an ulterior motive. Makes me wary.

His fingers curled into a fist atop his thigh at the idea that she'd had to deal with some man who'd used her like that. But he couldn't lie and pretend to be someone he wasn't. My ulterior motive is to keep you safe. I can't shake fifteen years in the military and another fifteen as a cop. It's in my DNA to look out for the people around me and to protect the ones I care about.

He appreciated that she could be honest, too. I don't mind you protecting me. But controlling who I can and can't talk to? Making decisions for me? It's going to be a very short date if that's the case.

Understood. You're in charge of you and your choices. But I also need you to understand that if I perceive a threat I'll let you know and try to protect you.

Hopefully it won't come to that. But thanks for catching me when I fell off the ladder. I could have squished you.

I wasn't complaining. I prefer a woman with curves.

I've got EXTRA curves, Joe.

Even better.

Joseph Carpenter! (Trust me, I would have used your middle name, too, if I knew it.)

He laughed. It's Thomas. Joseph Thomas Carpenter. Named after both my grandfathers. Called J.T. as a kid. In the Army I became Joe. My drill sergeant didn't like cutesy nicknames.

Thanks for sharing something about yourself. I've enjoyed our conversation, Joseph Thomas Carpenter.

He loved that she stood up for herself and joked with him and was the kind of beautiful that made him want to be the man who stood beside her. He wanted to see her again. Are you free for dinner on Friday or Saturday?

It'd be easier for me to get a sitter on Saturday.

Saturday it is, then. Pick you up at six?

We're really doing this, huh?

Yes.

Okay. Saturday at six works for me.

Looking forward to it. See you then.

He set his phone on the sofa cushion beside him and leaned back against the pillows, feeling equal parts content and excited about getting to know Stella Smith better. Finally, something to look forward to. He had a feeling that an evening spent with Stella would be filled with the kind of *unpredictable* he craved.

Chapter Three

Saturday night came around far too fast for Stella's liking. Not that she wasn't looking forward to her first date with Joe Carpenter, but quite the opposite. She was looking forward to it too much. And that triggered a whole new set of emotions she hadn't felt in a long time.

She hadn't been this nervous about meeting a man since... when? Her first date in high school or college? And she couldn't even say it would be like meeting a stranger in the next half hour or so. They had talked or texted every night since their first lengthy text conversation. They'd laughed. She'd shivered at that deep-pitched voice with the slight twang to it that sounded like a caress sliding across her skin. She'd shared a bit more about her life, and she'd gotten to know Joe better, too.

He preferred dark beer over light beer or mixed drinks. He loved all kinds of sports, although Kansas City Chiefs football was his favorite. He wished he'd been built bigger so he could have played college football, but he'd been happy with his decision to enlist in the Army after high school instead. He grew up in Rogersville, Missouri, a tiny town outside of Springfield—a town which he'd jokingly claimed was known as the Raccoon Capital of the World. Like her, he was an only child whose parents had both passed. He preferred Kansas City–style smoked barbecue over St. Louis–style grilled barbecue. And after fifteen years in the Army, where he'd worked mostly in intelligence, gathering and distributing information to Special Forces teams, he'd moved to Kansas City to start his second career in law enforcement. He'd never married, and the one time he'd asked, the woman had turned him down. He seemed genuinely happy to share that she'd gone on to marry someone else, have kids and settle down on a farm outside of Springfield. But he had sounded wistful—not that he missed his ex-girlfriend, but that he hadn't found the same long-term happiness for himself.

Stella understood his regrets. It wasn't a man, in particular, she missed, but the deep, whole-heart commitment of a real relationship over the years. She'd had male companions who'd escorted her to society functions. A steady boyfriend in college. Even one friend-with-benefits relationship that had soured her on the whole idea of a casual fling. And Trey… The greedy, narcissistic charmer she'd fallen in love with and foolishly believed would love her forever in return.

Now she was older and wiser and unwilling to settle for something that wasn't real. This evening, she was prepping for a date with a man she really liked—a good man who got her jokes, listened when she spoke and seemed to think she was pretty. A muscular, mature hottie who was so effortlessly male that she felt feminine and cared for whether they were talking on the phone late at night or she was standing by his side. Did she really think that Joe was her best shot at finding love at this stage of her life? Was he the *one* she'd been hoping for?

"That's a lot of pressure for a first date, Stella Evangeline Smith." She straightened the collar of her lime-green blouse, ran a brush through her freshly-washed hair, flipping up the colored tips around her shoulders, and studied her reflection in the mirror over her dresser. "Do you really think he likes plus-size women? Has he overstepped my independent boundaries by researching my past with Trey? You did give him permission, but still…"

And yes, Trey the Troll had called and asked her out again. She'd told him to stop calling and had blocked his number—more than once when he'd resorted to calling from another number.

Her nerves about going out with a man she was genuinely interested in was undermining her self-confidence. It had to stop. She pointed the brush at her reflection and gave herself a version of a speech she'd often used with her kids. "You are a gorgeous, accomplished woman. You are interesting and funny. You have friends. You've raised a gaggle of foster children who have turned out to be pretty damn awesome. You head up two charities and run a busy household. Why the hell wouldn't he be interested in you?"

And that was when she saw the child standing in her bedroom doorway. Harper Klein was a ten-year-old whose single mother couldn't stay sober long enough to even know where her daughter was, much less take care of her or support her endless curiosity and intellect. Harper's dishwater-blond hair was pulled back in a messy ponytail, and her green eyes held a blend of wisdom and uncertainty behind the glasses that rested on her chubby cheeks.

"You cussed," Harper pointed out. "Two times. You used the *D* word and the *H* word. Who are you talking to?"

Stella smiled and extended her hand to invite the girl into her room. "I'm giving myself a pep talk. Come here." When Harper joined her in front of the mirror, Stella pulled out the band holding part of the ponytail in place and took her brush to the girl's hair. She brushed Harper's hair and pulled it into a proper ponytail before picking up a ribbon from her catchall tray and tying a big bow around the base. "That's better. Now you're all dolled up for the night, too."

Harper rarely missed a word that anyone spoke. "Why do you have to be peppy?"

"*Peppy*'s not the right word."

"What is?" the curious girl asked.

"I'm nervous about my date."

"Don't you like Mr. Carpenter?" She'd told the children about her date over dinner last night and explained that they'd have a sitter—a former foster child of Stella's who lived with them as a part-time nanny. Sophie Martin was now in college, and to help with those expenses, Stella paid her a salary and let her live in her old room rent-free. In exchange, Sophie helped with the kids and babysat when she didn't have class, school activities or a date. Sophie was more of a big sister than a babysitter, and the kids were all comfortable with her.

"I think I like him too much," Stella admitted. She sat on the edge of the bed and put an arm around Harper when she climbed up beside her. She thought of an explanation her brilliant young charge might understand. "It's like when you want to ace a test at school. You study hard. You do everything you're supposed to do to get ready for it—get a good night's sleep, eat a good breakfast. But you still get a little nervous and worry you won't do as well as you hope."

Harper thought about the example before nodding. "I aced my math test yesterday, and I knew all the words, plus the bonus words, on my spelling test."

"You are my smart girl, and I'm so proud of you." Stella squeezed her in a sideways hug before pulling back to meet her gaze. "But didn't you tell me your tummy was upset when you went to math class?"

Harper frowned. "That was because the fifth graders don't like me. Cindy told me I needed to go back to class with the other fourth graders, and Derrien said I was too fat to be smart."

Stella schooled her reaction to the bullying that Harper endured and squeezed her in another hug. "That just shows you what little he knows. I bet Derrien didn't get a hundred on his test like you did, did he?" Harper shook her head. "And Cindy's not your friend, is she? So, you don't care what she says. It's not nice and it hurts your feelings, but you have other friends. And they like having you around, don't they? They're the ones you need to listen to."

Harper pushed her glasses up on her nose and sort of smiled. "I played jump rope with Daphne and Adina at recess. And Colby's nice to me." Colby Sullivan, her red-haired foster sibling who was in the same fourth-grade class, better be nice to her, or Stella would be having a conversation with the boy in a few minutes. But Harper, bless her curious heart, was still wondering why Stella would be nervous about going on a date. "Are you worried that Mr. Carpenter is going to be mean to you?"

"Heavens, no." She hurried to reassure her. "He's a good guy. But I really want to ace this date, so he likes me and wants to keep being my friend and go out with me again."

That was when Stella's ten-year-old mini-me stood up and pointed a finger at Stella. "If he doesn't like you, I'll be your friend."

Stella gave the girl a big smile. "You *are* my friend, Harper. And you just proved it by making me feel better about going out with Joe." She stood and smoothed the wrinkles that sitting had put in the hem of her tunic blouse. "Do I look okay?"

"Pretty as a picture. Just like me."

"That's right." Stella nodded toward the red and turquoise pashmina shawls she'd laid out on the bed before she'd gotten dressed. "Do you want to wear one of my shawls?" At the girl's answering smile, she added, "Which one?"

"Red." Stella shook out the long, wide scarf and wrapped

it around Harper's shoulders. The pashmina dwarfed the little girl, but Harper popped out her chin and admired herself in the mirror.

"Beautiful." Happy to see the girl having fun playing dress-up rather than worrying about Stella's date, she grabbed her purse and the turquoise shawl, and held out her hand to the girl. "Walk me downstairs?"

Harper slid her hand into Stella's, and they headed down to the open living room, kitchen and dining area together. Harper released her to dash over to pick up a book off the large square ottoman she used as a coffee table and wrapped herself up in the corner of the couch to read. Stella set her purse and pashmina on one of the wing-back recliners and continued to the kitchen.

Jasper raised his large head to acknowledge her before lying back down on the floor beside the tiny girl with long black hair who was still seated at the table.

Sophie Martin, the twenty-one-year-old nanny for the evening, was wiping down the end of the table away from where Stella's youngest foster child, Ana Garcia, pushed her macaroni and cheese around her plate with a spoon.

Sophie's bouncy brown ponytail bobbed at the back of her hair as she straightened and glanced from Stella over to studious Harper and back. "Aren't you two ladies looking fine tonight."

Harper snorted without looking up from her book, and Stella mouthed a "Thank you" for helping to boost the girl's self-esteem. Then she picked up the empty salad bowl from the middle of the table and carried it around the center island to the sink. She leaned back to spy her lone boy, Colby, playing a video game in the adjacent den. "Everybody eat?"

Sophie set another serving bowl in the sink and reported on her three charges. "Harper's done, as you can see. Colby wolfed down two helpings of mac and cheese and four hot dogs. I told him he couldn't play his game until he finished off his green beans, too. They disappeared pretty quickly after that."

Glancing back at the lazy Newfoundland, Stella asked, "And we're sure the dog didn't eat them?"

"Nope. I sat there and watched the whole feeding frenzy. I swear that boy's about to grow another foot, the way he puts away calories."

Smiling indulgently at Colby's latest growth spurt, she shook her head at the gangly, long-limbed redhead sprawled over both arms of the recliner, focused on racing his cartoon cart over obstacles of all kinds to get to the finish line first. "Yep. I've already got it on the schedule to take him shopping for new jeans and tennis shoes this week."

Sophie opened the dishwasher before she glanced back at the table and winked. "I've got this. Maybe you could help Ana?"

Stella returned to the child still at the table. She pulled out a chair beside Ana and encouraged her to actually put the food she was playing with into her mouth. "Jasper is waiting very patiently for you to finish eating so you guys can go watch your show." Ana tilted her big brown eyes at her before lifting a spoonful of noodles to her mouth. She'd been diagnosed with failure to thrive syndrome, and it was often a challenge to get the girl to eat. But Stella had discovered that she'd do just about anything for Jasper, whom she treated like a giant teddy bear. "That's my girl. Did you remember to put fresh water in Jasper's dish?" The little girl nodded and pointed to the mudroom, where the dog's feeding station and one of his dog beds were located. "And did you give him a treat after he did his business in the backyard?" Again, all Stella got was a nod. "It's your job to remind Sophie to give him a treat the next time he goes out."

"Colby cleans up," Ana whispered, wrinkling up her nose.

Stella laughed. Getting any words out of the four-year-old girl was a triumph. "That's right. It's Colby's job to pick up his big potty, isn't it? He's a brave boy for doing that for us, isn't he?"

The girl nodded and scooped another bite into her mouth. Stella stood and kissed the child on top of her head before pulling Sophie aside and running through the babysitter checklist with her—bedtimes, snacks, exercising the dog and making sure each of the children completed his or her chores before they all put on their pajamas and settled in to watch a movie together.

It was ten till six when she heard the powerful engine of a truck or SUV pulling into the driveway. Jasper's sharp bark of alarm bounced through the house, and Stella's nerves belly flopped inside her.

"He's here!" Harper announced, leaning over the back of the sofa and lifting the blinds to see their visitor.

Ana scooted away from the table and ran to the sofa with Jasper at her heels. The dog immediately jumped up to look out the window and didn't so much as whimper or shy away as the little girl grabbed handfuls of his thick hair to pull herself up onto the couch beside him. "He here," the little girl echoed.

"Jasper… Girls…" Stella was trying to break the dog of the habit of getting on the furniture, but that was what the upholstery covers and blankets were for, she supposed. And if his presence gave Ana the confidence she needed to run and play and indulge her curiosity, then she could forgive the dog just about anything. Although Harper and Ana both turned and looked dutifully to Stella, she shook her head. "Never mind."

With both girls plastered to the windows behind the big sectional couch, Stella went to the sidelight on the left side of the front door and peeked out to see Joe park in the driveway behind Sophie's car. Sophie was drying her hands on a dish towel as she hurried over to peek through the windows on the other side of the door.

Even Colby had paused his game and wandered out to the living room to see what the excitement was about. His headphones dangled around his neck, and his freckled face was squinched up in a worried frown. "Is he here?"

"Yes, Colby, it's Mr. Carpenter. No need to worry. We're expecting…him."

Stella's voice caught as the man they were all anxious to meet climbed out of his black SUV. For some reason, she had imagined Joe showing up in his navy blue police uniform. Instead, he was buttoning a gray tweed sport coat over a crisp white-collared shirt, emphasizing thick shoulders and a flat stomach, as he surveyed the yard and street that circled around the lake behind the houses before striding up the front walk.

"Whoa." Sophie hugged the damp towel to her chest and grinned. "That's him?"

Stella touched the silver-and-turquoise necklace she wore, feeling a mini panic attack rising up her throat. "That's my date."

"Girl-l-l. He's a hottie. For an old guy."

Joe Carpenter was a hottie at any age.

And Stella wasn't. She was literally shaking as she turned away from the window. "I am not dressed for this."

Sophie grabbed her wrist, keeping Stella from bolting back up the stairs. "Come on. You look fine."

"He's dressed up. I'm not."

"He's wearing jeans, just like you." She pointed to the chair where Stella had set her purse and pashmina. "Throw that pretty turquoise shawl around your shoulders if you want to fancy it up a little." Stella nodded. She did. She would. Sophie continued with the pep talk. "It matches your necklace and brings out the cool highlights in your hair. Trust me. He's not going to be looking anywhere except those pretty gray eyes."

Stella pulled the younger woman into her arms and squeezed her in a hug. "Thanks for talking me off the ledge. I guess it has been too long since I dated."

Sophie held the hug for a few seconds before pulling away. "There it is. That beautiful smile. He's going to notice that, too."

Ding-dong.

With another deep woof, Jasper jumped down and lumbered over to the door to greet their visitor.

Stella mentally talked herself out of her next panic attack now that Joe was actually at the front door. She reminded herself that she was a mature, professional woman with many accomplishments in her life.

She inhaled a deep breath, squared her shoulders and opened the door. Joe's handsome green eyes instantly met hers, and she smiled. "Hey, Joe. Come in."

He stepped across the threshold and quickly took in the curious crowd gathered around them as she shut the door behind him. He was still smiling as he leaned in and kissed her cheek. The brush of his lips against her skin was firm, warm and triggered an answering rush of heat to the spot he'd touched. "You look nice."

Too late, she realized her fingers had drifted up to touch her cheek. She quickly curled her fingers into her palm and dropped her hand to her side. Oh, well. He'd learn soon enough that she wasn't cool and elegant when it came to the physical side of dating someone. "Thank you. You clean up really well, too."

"Thanks." His gaze drifted from the top of her head down to her navy blue ankle boots and back up to her eyes. "I love that you love colors."

She wouldn't tell him that the last fashion consultant who'd tried to dress her for a charity event had told her she should dress in neutrals and dark colors to downplay her figure. Needless to say, she hadn't hired the woman again. Stella had her own ideas about what looked good and flattered her. But it wasn't every man who appreciated her eclectic sense of style. She gestured around the main open area of the house, hoping he'd take in the brightly-colored picture frames, throws and furniture, as well as the dark teal cabinets in her kitchen and the colorful rugs on the hardwood floors. "Color makes me happy, so why not?"

He took in the layout of her home, then pulled his gaze back to the menagerie of children and dog surrounding her. "Is this the gang?"

"Sorry about the welcoming committee."

"Why?" He seemed genuinely confused as to why she was apologizing for the curious kids pressing in around them.

"We don't get a lot of visitors. I may have talked you up a little bit, and they're curious to meet the mighty Joe Carpenter."

"I'm jealous that I didn't have anyone to talk *you* up to. Introduce me?"

"Jasper, sit." The big dog immediately sat beside her. Maybe he remembered Joe from the ranch, or maybe he wasn't enough of a guard dog to care about someone new coming into their house. "You remember our dog, Jasper. He's our gentle giant."

"Sure. Hey, Jasper." He petted the big brute around his head and ears. The dog's mouth dropped open, and he panted with excitement at being the center of attention for a few moments. "You're bigger than I remember."

"Come here, kids." Stella rested her hand on the dog's head as she invited all her charges to step forward and meet Joe.

"This is my friend Joe Carpenter. Harper Klein."

The little girl tossed her pashmina behind her shoulders with a dramatic flair. "Hi."

He gently grasped the girl's hand with just his fingers. "Harper. Nice to meet you. I like that red with your hair."

"Thank you." Harper squeezed Joe's fingers and held on, even when he'd tried to keep the handshake gentle. "Stella tells us to say thank you when someone gives us a compliment. The book I'm reading is red, too. Not the inside where the words are—that would be hard to read. But the outside is red. Red's my favorite color."

When she finally paused for a breath, Joe asked, "Is it a good book?"

"Yes. It's about demigods going on a quest. I read a lot. Do you read books? Do you have any red ones?"

"Harper," Stella gently chided, squeezing the girl's shoulder. "Why don't you give everyone else a chance to meet Mr. Carpenter?"

"Nice to meet you. Stella tells us to say that, too." As quickly as she'd taken over the introduction, the ten-year-old girl released Joe and climbed back up onto the couch, where she immediately buried her nose in her book again.

Joe chuckled and smiled at Stella. "She's…a lot. Keeps you on your toes, I bet."

Stella rolled her eyes. "You have no idea. Thanks for being patient with her. She's extremely smart and starving for positive attention." A pair of tiny hands wrapped around Stella's thigh. She reached down to smooth her hand over the top of the little girl's dark hair. "This is Ana Garcia. She's shy. Can you say hello?"

Ana shook her head and hugged herself more closely around Stella's leg.

She appreciated that Joe didn't move any closer, or even extend his hand toward her, but he did crouch down to the little girl's level. "Nice to meet you, Ana. I'm one of the good guys, I promise."

Ana's eyes were big and dark in her face as she stared at their male visitor. Then she whispered, "Nice t' meet you."

"Thank you for making me feel welcome."

The little girl smiled at his praise.

Sophie reached behind Stella and scooped up the little girl. "I've got her."

Stella didn't quite know how to handle the shiver of desire she felt at seeing how good Joe was being with her kids. The logical part of her brain reminded her that the long-time bachelor was probably putting on his best behavior to impress her. But even that argument proved a little unsettling because it had been a long time since a man had cared enough to want to impress her. Shaking off her unexpected reaction to all things Joseph Carpenter, she turned to continue the introductions. "This is Sophie Martin. She's finishing up her junior year at UMKC. She's a former foster I've stayed in touch with. I'm helping her with room and board by letting her live here with us. She's watching the kids for me tonight."

"She stays in touch with all of us." Sophie shifted Ana onto her left hip before extending her hand. "Nice to meet you, Mr. Carpenter."

Joe smiled and shook her hand. "Same here, Sophie. And it's Joe."

"Are you taking her someplace nice?"

His green eyes darted to Stella before he smiled at the younger woman. "We both agreed we didn't want to go too fancy for our first date." He arched an eyebrow at Stella, perhaps questioning whether that was still the case.

She immediately reassured him. "He promised me Kansas City barbecue, and I believe Joe is a man who keeps his word."

"I am."

The ten-year-old boy standing on the opposite side of Jasper and clinging to the dog's collar cleared his throat. Stella combed her fingers through Colby's shaggy red hair and smoothed it off his forehead. "And this young man, who's growing like a weed, is Colby Sullivan."

"Colby." Her lone boy stared at Joe's outstretched hand for a moment before ducking his head and focusing on petting the dog. Joe pulled his hand back and turned a worried expression to Stella. "Sorry. Is that a trigger or something I shouldn't have done?"

"Not that I know of." She squeezed the boy's shoulder. "Colby, it's all right. Joe's my friend."

"Shaking hands is what men usually do when they meet each other," Joe explained. "We can do a fist bump, too, if you prefer. Or just say hi."

Perhaps unknowingly, Joe had said the magic word. *Men.* This child was a dear, but he desperately needed a good male role model. Colby's chin came up, and he thrust out his hand. Joe captured it in his much larger grasp. The boy glanced up at Stella with the hint of a smile on his face before giving Joe's hand an enthusiastic shake. "Nice to meet you. Sir." He quickly added the last word and tugged his hand away to dig his fingers into Jasper's fur.

"That's pretty formal for me, Colby. Since you're a friend of Stella's, you can call me Joe, too."

"Thanks. Joe." With the transformation from wary to excited, the red-haired boy looked up at Stella. "Can I take Jasper outside now? You said we could play out back when everyone was done eating."

Stella glanced all the way down at his big, bare feet. "Only if you put your shoes and socks back on."

"'Kay." He clicked his tongue to get the dog's attention,

and the big creature immediately pushed to all four feet and lumbered after him. "Come on, Jasper!"

As the girls scrambled out of Sophie's arms and off the sofa to dash after them, Stella turned and called out her usual warning. "Make sure the back gate stays locked. I don't want the dog or any of you to go down to the lake or the boathouse. The life jackets are packed away, and there aren't any adults to supervise you down by the water."

"'Kay!" Colby shouted from the den and instantly popped back out with his tennis shoes shoved onto his feet—and a dog and two foster sisters on his heels, calling out dibs on a swing and the slide and tossing a ball to Jasper. They disappeared through the mudroom off the kitchen before she heard the back door open. She heard a drumbeat of footsteps across the deck and squeals of excitement and laughter before the door slammed shut.

The sudden quiet inside the house was almost startling. Stella felt a blush heating her cheeks. Now was about the time her last couple of dates had either joked about finally getting rid of the kids or curiously asked how she could deal with demanding children who weren't even hers.

No wonder she didn't date a lot. Her kids were her calling. They were her family, her heart. They gave her the love she'd missed growing up and a purpose that gave her more satisfaction than any high-powered career or ruined engagement ever had.

She studied Joe's expression for a second, expecting him to say *Whew!* or *Finally!* Instead, the line of his mouth softened with a gentle smile, and he gestured to the door. "Ready?"

She couldn't help but exhale a sigh of relief. "Could you hold on for a second longer?" She turned to Sophie for some last-minute checks. "You're sure you're okay doing this tonight? You said you had your final in anatomy on Monday. Do you need to study?"

"I'll study," the young woman reassured her. "Harper's already finished with her homework. She can watch Ana while I pop the popcorn for movie night. I'll have Colby help me and drill him on his multiplication tables. Then they'll all sit down and watch a movie. I can study then. Or after I put them to bed."

Stella frowned. "How long do you think I'll be gone?"

Sophie grabbed Stella's purse and shawl off the nearby chair and pushed them into her arms before turning her toward the door. "Long enough to enjoy yourself, I hope. Don't worry about us."

Stella planted her feet and refused to be pushed out of her own home. "This is our first date. I'm not staying out all night, young lady."

"Go. You'll be late for your reservation. Don't worry about us. I'll head outside to keep an eye on them. I know the rules. Bedtime is ten. The lake is off-limits until Memorial Day weekend. I'll remind them. I've got things covered here."

Joe held the door open for her. She took a step toward him before twisting her mouth up in a rueful frown. "One more thing." She spun back to Sophie once more. "You'll have to put Jasper out before bedtime. He likes to climb into bed with Ana, and I don't want to wake her up by getting the dog out. His drool towel is hanging on a post by the back door. If you need a clean one, they're in the bottom drawer beneath where we hang jackets and book bags in the mudroom."

"I know. It's all on your list." She propped her hands on her hips and looked beyond Stella to Joe. "Get her out of here, will you?" Joe stepped out onto the porch, and Sophie grabbed the door, shooing Stella out, too. "And take good care of her? She's the only mom I ever had."

"I will." Joe's hand settled at the small of Stella's back.

Maybe he was keeping her from stumbling over the welcome mat, but his touch infused her with warmth and support.

His touch also distracted her long enough for Sophie to wave and close the door in Stella's face. The locks engaged and the porch lights turned on before Stella could come up with an appropriate response.

She faced Joe, who was waiting more patiently than she deserved. "I don't know how she can tease me mercilessly, then turn around and say something sweet like that."

Joe's hand fell away, and she missed his warmth. "She loves you," he answered simply.

Stella looped the strap of her purse over her shoulder, then reached for the hand he'd rested at her back. She could feel the calluses of a workingman's hands as she squeezed his fingers. Was there anything about this man that didn't ooze masculinity? She might be anxious, but she wanted Joe to understand that she would always be honest with him. "I'm not very good at this. Sorry if I made it sound as if I was putting off spending time with you. I admit I'm nervous. My dating skills are pretty rusty. I suppose there's a part of me that's worried you're going to regret saying yes to going out with me. But I'm excited to spend some one-on-one time with you and get to know you better."

He shrugged. Oh, those shoulders. They were so dang distracting. "It sounded as though you're a good mom who just wants to make sure her kids are okay before she leaves them for the night."

"Foster kids."

Taking both of her hands in his, Joe stepped into her personal space and locked his green eyes onto hers. "Maybe you were making a point, trying to show me what spending time with you is really like—a little chaos, a lot of caring. But one thing I observed is crystal clear. Those are *your* kids, Stella. From shy little Ana all the way up to Sophie.

You may not have given birth to them, but you care. And they trust you. So, they're your kids."

Some of the tension that had her nerves so tightly wound tonight dissipated with the adamant tone of his words. She squeezed his hands and smiled. "You're a smart, perceptive man, Sergeant Carpenter."

He turned to link her arm through his and walked her down the steps to the passenger door of his SUV. "When I'm on a date with someone as pretty as you, it's Joe."

"Thanks, Joe."

She climbed inside, and he handed her the seat belt before closing her door and circling around to climb in behind the wheel. Joe started the engine, unbuttoned his jacket and backed out of the driveway before he spoke again. "Some man's hit that boy in the past, hasn't he? When I moved my hand toward him, he flinched."

Turning slightly in her seat to face him, she nodded. "Colby came from an extremely abusive situation."

Joe's knuckles turned white where he was gripping the steering wheel. "He was sizing me up. Trying to be the man of the house. Maybe making sure I wasn't going to hurt you, even though he was scared himself." He muttered a curse. "I bet he's only sixty or seventy pounds soaking wet."

Stella understood his anger. "I try to give them a space where they can just be kids, and not worry if they're safe or where their next meal is coming from. Of course, they all need a little extra help. I try to make sure they get that, too."

He glanced across the seat as they waited at a stop sign. "I hope I didn't scare any of them or make things worse."

Stella reached across the center console to rest her hand on his leg, just above his knee. "You were great with them. They went back to the business of being kids as soon as they met you. They wouldn't have done that if they didn't feel safe with you."

Joe dropped his hand over hers, capturing her fingers in an enticing sandwich of heat between his hand and thigh. "Thanks for introducing me. I know part of doing that is teaching them manners, but I think it also made them feel better about you leaving with me." He released her hand as he moved forward into traffic. "I gotta admit, I'm not used to being around kids. Most of the ones I run into at work see me as an authority figure, or even an enemy. But I'd like to get better at reading them, relating to them better."

"Well, if you hang around me, you're going to end up interacting with kids, too."

A smile spread slowly across his interesting, angular face. "Then I guess I'll be interacting with kids more."

Smiling at his unspoken promise, Stella leaned back in her seat, truly relaxing for the first time that evening.

She had a feeling that impulsively asking Joe Carpenter out would be one of the smartest things she'd done in a long time.

Chapter Four

Joe had wondered if he and Stella would run out of things to talk about in person. After all, they'd phoned or texted every night over the past week. But after the drive into downtown Kansas City to the old freight depot that had been converted into a barbecue restaurant, and now sitting at their table enjoying drinks and an appetizer of burnt ends, the conversation still felt new. Funny and fresh, sometimes serious and thought-provoking—but Joe was getting the feeling that there would always be something new to discover with Stella.

He was also getting the feeling that he needed to kiss those full, articulate lips to find out if they were as sweet and soft as they looked, before the night was done. Stella's beautiful mouth smiled easily and made her points succinctly. And the anticipation coursing through his body made him quite certain that this date wouldn't feel complete if he didn't get to taste her at least once before he took her home and they went their separate ways.

She was familiar with the restaurant, and just as much a fan of their food as he was.

But mostly he was hoping they could have good conversation. Really he was looking for a woman who could push him out of his comfort zone and make him laugh, make him think, make him feel like a man just by holding his hand or touching his leg. And he loved being with a woman who made him strategize just how he was going to get his lips on hers before the end of the evening.

Stella Smith seemed to do all that and more.

He stabbed the last burnt end and popped it into his mouth while she dabbed a drip of barbecue sauce off her chin. "Are you sure you're fifty?" she asked, abruptly changing the topic from which sporting venues in Kansas City they had been to.

He swallowed the tasty bite of smoked meat and set down his fork, wondering where she was going with that question. Did she wish he was older? Younger? "Yeah."

She leaned back in the seat across from him and smirked. "And you're in that great of shape? What's your secret?"

He grinned at his own suspicious nature. She was just getting to know him better—and paying him a nice compliment in the process. "There are certain fitness demands for the job, so I work at it. Got used to getting up and training every day in the Army. Never lost the habit." He reached beneath the table to pat his knees. "I may have a few more aches at the end of the day than I used to, but I can hold my own with the young bucks. For a little while, at least," he admitted, knowing he'd lost some of the speed and endurance he'd had back in his twenties. He shrugged and wondered why her pupils dilated, shrinking the striking green-gray color of her irises. "How old are you? If I may ask."

"Almost forty-eight and a half. I'm not on the downside heading toward forty-nine yet."

He chuckled at her witty, if unnecessary, defense of her age. "Forty-eight and a half? And you're in that great a shape?" he echoed, purposely sliding his gaze down to the generous curves hidden by her colorful cotton blouse. Yep, there was some serious cleavage there, and he was man enough to notice.

"Joe... I need to lose thirty pounds. But I love food and I hate exercise, except for swimming or kayaking out on the water. And that only happens when the weather—"

"When a man gives you a compliment, the correct response is to say thank you." He sat back, crossing his arms over his chest, daring her to deny his appreciation of her lush figure. "Are you happy?"

"Most of the time, yes."

"Then you be you. I'll be the stick-in-the-mud who's set in his ways, and you be the bright, beautiful, bighearted light—with a seriously decadent figure," he added, to emphasize his attraction to her as she was, "who I am drawn to like a moth to a flame."

He held her gaze, daring her to dismiss his compliment now.

After considering his words long enough for a beautiful blush to warm her cheeks, she smiled. "Thank you." Leaning toward him, she braced her elbows on the table and linked her hands together, resting her chin atop her fingers. "And if I tell you that every time you flex those shoulders and arms, I find it distracting? Or that your eyes are the most beautiful, calming shade of green I've ever seen? You would say thank you, too?"

"Distracting?"

"Mmm-hmm."

"Not too much gray on the roof?"

Her gaze swept along his hairline before dropping to his mouth. Her lips parted with a breathy sigh that made things swell behind the zipper of his jeans. If she made that deeply satisfied sound after a really good kiss or making love, he'd be a goner. "Uh-uh."

Joe covered the blush he felt heating his cheeks by taking a drink of water. It was nice to know that she was lusting after him a little bit, too. He bowed his head, graciously acknowledging her argument. "Thank you."

He supposed this was real flirting. He could admit he was just as rusty as she'd claimed to be earlier when it came to his dating skills. But he had to admit he was having a lot of fun getting back on the horse, so to speak, and discovering how well the two of them seemed to click together.

They discussed his work with new recruits at the police academy, as well as some of the scarier calls he'd been on. He answered some of the questions he could about his service with Army intelligence. And she shared some of her stories, both amusing and heartwarming, about her foster children and her training experiences with Jasper.

Their waiter had just come by to refill their water glasses and clear their appetizer dishes when Joe circled back to his concerns about Trey Jeffries.

Stella drank some water before setting down her glass and settling against the back of the booth. "Uh-oh. That's your serious look."

The woman was reading him already, just as he was learning some of her tells about when she was nervous or happy or even turned on. He didn't hesitate to be honest with her about his concern. "Is Trey Jeffries a threat to you?"

She closed her eyes for a moment before meeting his gaze again. "More of an annoyance." She explained about their engagement and humiliating breakup at their rehearsal dinner, and how he'd drifted in and out of her life in the twenty years since.

Joe was silent for several long moments. What kind of idiot talked to a woman like that? Especially one who'd claimed to love her.

When he'd been quiet for too long, she prompted him to explain his reaction. "Joe?"

"Sorry. I guess I'm old-fashioned. It steams me to hear anyone treating someone as nice as you like that. Why haven't you reported him for harassment? Gotten the police involved?"

She shrugged. "I got over Trey a long time ago. I've been on my own ever since. I'm just used to dealing with whatever I have to by myself. I do pretty well."

"I'm sure you do. But I'm a veteran. A cop. As much as I want to shake up my life a little bit, it's impossible for me to turn off my need to protect someone when they're threatened. And that's exactly what harassment is. He's trying to force you to do something you don't want to."

"And you want to fix that for me," she correctly assessed. Resting her elbows on the table, Stella clasped her hands beneath her chin again. "Maybe we can retrain you to handle that need to take care of things in a different way."

"Retrain me? You got an idea how to make that happen? Because I guarantee you, if I meet this ex of yours in person, and he puts his hands on you in any way without your permission—"

"You'll what? Punch his lights out? Take him down? Arrest him?"

He didn't bat an eye. "I'd do whatever is necessary if he threatens you. Or one of your kids."

Stella reached across the table to grasp his hand. Her skin was soft and warm and instantly soothed some of the protective fury roiling through him. "Okay. Let's get a couple of things straight. If he would hurt me in any way, *I'd* want first crack at punching his lights out. If that didn't go well, at that point you'd be welcome to intervene. And I will always accept someone stepping in to protect my kids if I can't. But…" She stroked her thumb across the back of his hand. "If he's not being a physical threat, then another option that wouldn't include you going all cop slash super soldier on him would be to put your hand on my back, so I feel your support while *I'm* putting him in his place. Or let me handle any confrontation, and then, after the fact, because I'll probably be upset or angry, and certainly wired with stress, you could listen while I vent, or hold me, or bring me chocolate, ice cream or a glass of wine to console me. Comfort me. Make me feel better."

He gently switched his grip, so that he could slide his thumb across the back of her hand now. "That's what you'd retrain me to do? Step back? Support you? Comfort you? You know that goes against the alpha man code."

"I know." Her teasing grin quickly disappeared. "An independent woman can be strong when she needs to be. But it can take it out of her. Just as I'm sure it does you when you have to step in and take care of business as a police officer. It'd be nice to have a safe space to regroup."

Right. Stella Smith wasn't a naive, codependent woman who needed a man to fight her battles for her. But she did need someone to take care of her every now and then. He could relate to that kind of personality. He was perfectly capable of taking care of whatever he needed to by himself. But it sure would be nice to have a partner who offered a respite from being the alpha protector 24/7—to share a bond with someone who could have his back and nurture his soul in the way she described.

It suddenly occurred to Joe that, while they were very different people, he and Stella seemed to have a lot in common in terms of values and needs. And it didn't seem odd at all that their attraction to each other had been almost instantaneous, and that he trusted their ability to talk about serious things and feel this close this quickly. He wasn't a fanciful man by nature, but he wondered if he and Stella had possibly known each other in another life—that catching her in the barn at K-9 Ranch and sitting here together was an extension of a relationship they'd shared in the past.

But he wasn't going to talk about fanciful ideas like reincarnation or being soulmates out loud. That would be moving a little too fast and a little too far out of his comfort zone, even though he did want to change things up in his life. Instead, he lightened the mood by seizing on something she'd said a moment earlier.

"You know how to throw a punch?" he asked.

She laughed as if she sensed his thoughts had taken a deeply retrospective turn and was glad to have something less intense to talk about, too. "I've taken two self-defense training classes. One in college and one the last time Trey made his move on me. I got picked on as a kid in school. Fatty-Patty. Klutzy the Kid. Someone jealous of the poor little rich girl. So, yeah. Much to my parents' chagrin, I learned where to kick and how to throw a punch."

"I didn't think a bloodthirsty woman could be such a turn-on." She was beautiful when she smiled like that. "As much as I'd love to see you punch his lights out, I also like the idea of holding you, supporting you and spoiling you when you need it."

Stella wagged her finger at him. "Chocolate, wine and ice cream are not spoilage. Neither is a good hug. They're all necessities."

They both laughed.

"Noted." Joe captured her hand between both of his and went back to a fact she'd quickly glossed over. "So...*the last time* Trey made a move on you? He's harassed you before?"

"You just can't turn the cop off, can you?" She sighed, not the sexy, satisfied sound she'd made earlier, but one filled with exasperation. "Not counting our engagement, this is the third time he's tried to charm me or blackmail me into taking him back. Generally, it coincides with his latest divorce and a sudden need for an influx of cash. The first time, I tried to give him a job at my education charity. I knew money was what he was after. And I guess I thought it would show that I'd forgiven him. But what I thought was a generous salary wasn't enough. He wanted to control all the money I had access to after my parents died. That's why he dumped me in the first place. I didn't get access to the Smith wealth until I inherited it after they died in a car accident. That's when things got ugly, and I filed the restraining order. He said he was my only chance at love and a family. That no other man was ever going to want me for anything except my money, so I should make the smart business decision and settle for a familiar friend and lover. Namely, him."

Yeah, he *really* didn't like her ex. "You didn't believe that, did you?"

She reassured him with a shake of her head. "When I turned down that charming proposal and rescinded the job offer, he started doing crazy stuff, like setting up accidents or awkward social situations. Then he'd swoop in to rescue me." She pulled her fingers from Joe's grasp and gestured emphatically. "Like I'd be so grateful, I'd forget how badly he hurt me? He'd already blown any chance of trusting him again. And I could never give my heart to someone I didn't trust."

"Hence your aversion to being rescued."

Her flare of temper quickly dissipated. "I suppose. I didn't have a great childhood. I wasn't abused or neglected. But I wasn't really loved, either. My parents were older when they had me, so they weren't really involved in a lot of my day-to-day life. I was more of a trophy? An accomplishment they could show off to their friends and investors? Dad made sure I understood business so I could take over the company one day. But I'd have traded my MBA and on-the-job training for a bedtime story or a family vacation that wasn't also a business trip. I guess I learned at a young age that if I was going to be happy or successful or anything, it was on me." Her head slowly moved back and forth. "I got swept up in the romance of falling in love with Trey. It was the first time I'd ever felt wanted. Important to someone. I thought letting him be my knight in shining armor and taking care of me meant he loved me. But he was just playing the long game to get at my parents' money."

"Right up until he realized he wasn't getting any of that money."

"Exactly. After that, I learned to do for myself. I made enough of my own money to live comfortably, so that my inheritance was a boon, not anything I needed. I bought a big, family-friendly house on a beautiful property. I invested well. I converted most of my dad's businesses into charitable foundations. I found love with my foster kids. I make a difference in the world with my educational and service animal charities, and with every child who has come into my home. I have friends. I have a lazy, but gentle, devoted dog. There may have been some lonely nights over the years. But it's been enough."

"And you're okay with...*enough*?"

"No." The vehemence of her answer surprised him. "I want to find some gorgeous man I can trust who makes me laugh and makes me feel safe and cherished. Who respects me and takes me seriously. Who's okay with the kids and chaos in my life. Who isn't threatened by my money. Who treats me like I'm the best thing he ever—" Her impassioned speech was interrupted by her phone ringing in her purse beside her. She held up her finger, asking for a moment to pull her phone from her purse. "Sorry. I just want to check who this is in case Sophie's calling about one of the children." When she had the phone in her hand, she looked down at the screen and frowned. "Hmm."

Joe muttered a curse. "Please tell me that's not Trey the Troll."

Stella shook her head. "It's a friend of mine from Family Services. A foster care placement coordinator. I really need to take this."

He relaxed a fraction, though not entirely. Was there an emergency with one of her kids? "Not a problem. Do you need privacy?"

"No. Please stay." Her fingers sneaked across the table and tangled with his again after she answered the call. Whether she thought she needed to calm him down—she didn't—or she was seeking support herself, he squeezed her hand and unabashedly listened to her side of the conversation. "Hey, Helen… I'm fine, thanks. How are you?… Uh-huh… No, Saturday-night calls usually aren't good news. What's up?" She looked across the table to Joe. She probably wondered if he was truly being patient or if he was quietly seething beneath his calm facade. He'd taken her request to heart and tried to convey that he was supporting her while she dealt with whatever unpleasant news she was hearing. "Why would they split them up?… Oh. Is that why you're at the police station? Did the family press charges? Is he a threat to his brother?" *Police station? Threat?* Now Joe really tuned in. "Well, that's something. We can work with that… No, I have the room for both of them. That's not a problem… You'll start the paperwork? Fourth Precinct?… I'll be there as soon as I can." Stella ended the call and immediately began to gather her things. "I'm so sorry. We haven't even been served our main course, and I have to go."

He signaled the waiter. "Something with work? Why the police station?" When the young man returned to their table, he gave a succinct explanation. "We've had a family emergency come up. We're going to need our meal packed to go. Here's my card to run the tab. Thank you."

Stella had pulled her wallet out and set it on the table. "I asked you out. I was going to pay."

"No."

"Just *no*?" She pressed her lips together in an adorable frown. "Joseph Carpenter..."

He answered with a wicked grin. "Should I tell you I get excited when you chastise me with my full name?"

He could tell she was flummoxed by that admission. Her mouth opened, then closed, then opened again. "You should stay. Enjoy what's left of your evening."

"I'm here for the company, Stell, not the food. I don't want you to think for one second that I'm with you because of your money. Yes, you made the first move, but I took the invitation and ran with it. *I* brought you to my favorite restaurant, *I* made the reservation, *I* will pay. There will be plenty of chances for you to plan the evening and for you to pay. If that's what you want."

"Plenty of chances? You want to try this dating thing again?"

"Yes." Now her lips parted with that soft, sexy sigh that settled like a caress against his eardrums. He rested his hand over hers where she clutched her wallet, drawing her attention back to the importance of the phone call. "You mentioned the Fourth Precinct? Why are you going to the police station at this time of night?"

She tucked her wallet into her purse and matched his more businesslike tone. "It's an emergency foster placement. Two brothers. If I don't take them, Family Services will have to split them up. My friend Helen said they've got plenty of takers for the younger brother. But they might have to send the older one to juvie if they can't be placed together."

"Not a group home? Why juvie? That usually indicates violence or chronic criminal activity. What did he do?"

"Helen said he's a behavior challenge. Apparently, he

acted out when his current placement wanted to send him back but keep the little brother."

"So, he took a swing at somebody."

She zipped up her purse and unfolded her turquoise shawl. "I can't imagine how angry that must make him feel. To think he's not wanted? To be separated from the only family he has left?"

"How old is he?"

"Eleven. Fifth grade. The younger one is seven."

"And he's already being threatened with juvie?" He knew taking care of foster kids was her area of expertise, not his, but a fifth grader being threatened with juvenile detention didn't sound like the safest youngster for her to be around. "Is it dangerous for him to be at your home with the other children?"

"I don't know. I haven't met the boys yet. I don't know the whole situation. I imagine he'll be calmer if we can keep them together. That's what Helen is hoping."

When the waiter brought the food, Joe signed the check and added a big tip to the balance. "All right, then. Let's go." He slid out of the booth and grabbed his sport coat.

Stella stood up across from him. "You don't have to come with me. I'm sorry I ruined our date. I'll call a car service and you can head on home."

"You're not taking a car service by yourself. Too many things can happen if you're alone with an unknown driver. I'll take you. Besides, the Fourth Precinct is where I work when I'm not at the academy. I know the people. If there's something I can do to help out, I will." He reached over to take her hand in his. "And just so you know—I'm going to be asking you out on another date. I was enjoying myself."

Her mouth curled into a wry frown. Hell, he wanted to kiss that version of her lips, too. "This is kind of what being with me is like a lot of the time. Noisy home life. Interruptions and busy schedules. You said you were set in your ways. You may not want to get involved with me."

He closed the distance between them, locking his eyes onto hers. "FYI, I don't *want* to be set in my ways. It's boring. You're not. I've got a job I love, and I think I'm good at it. But that's only half my life. I'm tired of going through the motions of living without feeling truly alive. The few hours I've spent with you have given me a taste of what I've been missing." He glanced down to where her fingers clung to his, liking even that simple connection. A lot. "Were you enjoying yourself tonight?"

"Yes."

He lifted her hand and kissed the back of it, letting his lips linger against the warm, velvety texture of her skin. "Then I will be asking you out again."

"I asked you out, remember?"

"Best decision I ever made was saying yes." He draped the shawl around her shoulders and picked up the take-out bag. He laced his fingers together with hers again and pulled her into step beside him. "Let's go."

Chapter Five

Stella watched the two boys in a Fourth Precinct interview room through the one-way window in the room next door. At seven, Tyrell Williams was an adorable child, maybe small for his age, with short black hair and light brown eyes that kept following his older brother, Gio, as the eleven-year-old paced in circles around the room.

When the uniformed officer sitting at the table with Tyrell pushed a fast-food wrapper that held the last of the french fries the boys must have eaten for dinner across the table, Tyrell immediately shifted his attention to the young man, nodded, then picked up two fries. He took a bite of one and held the other out to his brother.

Gio Williams seemed as different from Tyrell as two brothers could be. With short dreadlocks sticking out in every direction, and eyes and skin that were several shades darker than Tyrell's, the eleven-year-old seemed spring-loaded with energy. He was at least five feet tall, with long, gangly limbs he was trying to grow into. Still, it warmed her heart to see Gio grab the fry and thank his brother. He popped the whole thing into his mouth and resumed pacing like a hamster spinning around his wheel in a desperate effort to get out of his cage and run free.

Those two were close. Gio and Tyrell were obviously used

to sharing food and looking out for each other. She wished she couldn't imagine all the possible reasons why two boys would rely on each other for survival like that.

Stella turned to the woman who was almost the same height standing beside her. She'd known Helen Graves from the first day she'd gone into the Family Services offices to apply to become a foster parent almost twenty years ago. Although Helen was now a supervisor who rarely worked with the day-to-day intake and maintenance of individual case-work, she'd intervened to take care of the Williams brothers tonight. Maybe because it was the weekend and their office was short-staffed, or maybe because this wasn't the first time Gio's and Tyrell's names had crossed her desk.

"Has Gio been violent before?" Stella asked.

"Not with a family. Now that I've removed him from the house, they said they wouldn't press charges. But he hasn't talked to me about it or given anyone a hint as to what's going on." Helen's hair was frosted with gray curls now, but her eyes were sharp as she assessed the boys' behavior through the window beside her. Joe perched on the edge of the table behind them. His stern reflection in the glass showed he was wary about the situation, but she appreciated that, other than assigning one of the rookie officers he'd trained to be in the room with the boys while she and Helen discussed details of the case, he was staying back and letting her handle the emergency foster placement. "Usually, they're on their best behavior the first few days because they don't know the rules of the house and they're worried they'll get in trouble. But he hasn't been a model child this week. He got into an altercation at school, and the foster parents called me, wanting to send him back."

She glanced over at her friend. "But not Tyrell?"

Helen nodded. "That's when Gio started breaking things.

He scared the mother and made their birth daughter cry. The dad said he was finished with him."

She could understand a parent wanting to protect his family. But he'd barely given the boys a chance to settle in before calling Helen and telling her the placement wasn't working with Gio. Helen had worried that Gio would run away to get to Tyrell if the two were separated.

"What was the fight at school about?" Stella asked.

"Another boy teased Gio about having ill-fitting pants." Helen released a weary sigh. "I'm convinced something bigger is eating at that child. The teasing was just the straw that broke the camel's back and made him act out."

"Where is their real mother in all this?" Stella asked. She knew many parents made the sacrifice to protect them from violence or poverty or whatever threat kept them from being able to take care of a child, or even themselves. "Is Gio hoping they'll be returned to her?"

"Not gonna happen." Helen crossed back to the table and opened her leather carryall to pull out a thick file folder. She opened it to show Stella the document on top. "She's a repeat offender. Drugs. Prostitution. Criminal neglect. Their mother finally signed away her parental rights when they were removed from the home last weekend and she was hauled off to jail. Said they were too much work and too much money to take care of. Neither of the fathers has ever been a part of their lives, and there are no other relatives in the KC area. She was worried about her boyfriend getting stuck with the boys. It sounded like she didn't want to upset him."

"The boyfriend have a name?" Joe asked, inserting himself into the conversation for the first time.

Helen seemed comfortable discussing legal matters with the off-duty cop in the room. "Toy Williams—their mother—hasn't said. The boys mentioned the name Vaughn when I interviewed them."

"Is that a first or last name?" Stella could see that he already had his phone out to type in the name. She was quickly learning that Joe Carpenter liked to have all the facts about any situation. Maybe it went back to his service in military intelligence, where information was key to the success of any mission. His steadfast determination to be thorough probably made him a good cop, too. He waited patiently for Helen's response.

"I don't know," Helen answered. "I waited for her to dry out and make a rational decision before discussing her termination of rights. But I still got the feeling Toy was more afraid of losing this Vaughn guy than she was her boys. Maybe he's her dealer."

"Maybe she's just afraid of him, period," Stella pointed out, closing the file and returning it to the social worker. "Maybe she believes giving up her parental rights is the only way she has to protect them from him. Do the boys show any signs of abuse?"

"They both have fading bruises on their arms," Helen said. "They're both malnourished. I don't know if Gio has undiagnosed ADHD or if he has anger management issues based on past trauma and emotional abuse." Helen turned to Joe and shrugged. "I couldn't tell you if the bruises are from their mother, this Vaughn person or someone else. Gio was fighting at school, but that doesn't explain the same marks on Tyrell."

Joe nodded. "I'll run a general search. See if we get any hits on a Vaughn—first or last name—related to Toy Williams."

"Toy isn't her real name," Helen corrected. "She's in the system under Mary Williams."

"Got it. Thanks." He stepped out of the room and crossed to a desk where he woke up a computer screen and typed in the information he was looking for.

"We need to get those boys talking." This had clearly been a long day for Helen. "You worked a miracle to draw Colby Sullivan out of his shell. Will you try to work some of your magic on Gio? See if you can find out what's bothering him before I release him into your care?"

"I can try." Stella draped her arm over her friend's shoulders and pulled her in for a sideways hug. "First, we need to fill their stomachs with something nutritious, then get them into a warm, comfy bed where they can catch up on their sleep. And you need to go get a good night's sleep yourself."

"Amen to that." Helen leaned her head against Stella's and returned the hug. "You ready to go meet them?"

Stella followed Helen out of the observation room. While the other woman softly knocked at the door, Stella turned to see Joe looking up from the computer screen and tracking her movements. She smiled her thanks for staying in the background while she did her thing, even though the Fourth Precinct building was *his* space, while she was the visitor here.

He'd shed his jacket almost as soon as they'd stepped off the elevator, tucked his badge onto his belt and gotten her checked in quickly at the front desk. There was an air of an elder statesman about him, according to how the other officers jumped to do his bidding, although he was friendly with every one of them. He said he'd trained or mentored a lot of them on the late shift. She found his easy confidence and the obvious respect he'd earned from his coworkers to be supermasculine and very attractive. She wanted... Well, she wasn't sure exactly what the tingling parts of her anatomy wanted. But whatever nerves she'd felt at the beginning of the evening over diving back into the dating pond had completely dissipated. Now all she could feel was a buzz of purely feminine awareness at having all that male energy and attention focused on her.

She liked Joe.

She wanted Joe.

Although their dating life had gotten off to a rocky start, Stella knew that she could get used to having Joe Carpenter keeping an eye on her and supporting her like this. She'd have to make the ruined evening up to him somehow, and crossed her fingers down at her side, hoping Joe would give her that chance.

Ignoring her fully awakened hormones for the moment, when the interview room door opened and the police officer came out, Stella turned her attention back to the task at hand.

"Ma'am. Ma'am." The young man held the door open and greeted them as they entered, and he stepped out.

"Thank you, Officer Hawley." Once the young officer left the room, Joe got up to exchange a few words with him. The younger cop nodded. Stella followed Helen inside and stood in the open doorway while Helen made introductions. "Gio, Tyrell—I'd like you to meet a friend of mine, Stella Smith. She's an experienced foster parent, and I'd like to send you to live with her for a while. I hope it will be a better fit for both of you than your last placement."

Gio had stopped his pacing near the observation window while Tyrell looked up from the wrapper, where he was divvying up two piles of the remaining french fries.

"Hello, Gio, Tyrell." She smiled at both boys and pulled out the gray metal chair across from Tyrell. "Did you boys get enough to eat?"

Tyrell absently munched on what was probably a cold fry by now and shrugged.

Gio mumbled, "Yeah," without unclenching his teeth.

Supposing that was enough of an introduction for now, Helen gestured to Tyrell. "Should we see if we can find you a hot chocolate? Or a candy bar for dessert? Stella needs to ask your brother some questions." At the mention of candy, the little boy scooted off his adult-sized chair and hurried around the table, reaching for the social worker's outstretched hand. "Good luck," Helen mouthed, leading Tyrell out the door.

"Where is she taking him?" Gio charged the door, intending to slip past Stella. "Bring him back!"

Putting her hands up in a placating gesture, Stella urged him to sit down. "He's just fine. And so are you. You know Helen," she reminded him. "She's just taking him down to the lounge to—"

"No!" With his path effectively blocked, Gio lashed out. A small fist came flying at her. But it was big enough to do some damage. She shifted to deflect the blow, but his fist connected with her face, snapping her head to the side.

Pain blossomed across the side of her jaw, and she tasted the coppery tang of blood in her mouth where a tooth cut into her cheek. Even though she cupped her hand over the tender skin she could feel swelling, she managed to keep her tone calm. "It's all right, Gio. I swear they aren't leaving."

"Get out of my way! Ty!"

The boy cocked his arm back to throw another punch, but it never landed. Joe was there right now, filling the doorway and nudging Stella aside as he easily captured the boy's forearm in his grip. When the boy kicked out, Joe did some twisty thing and spun Gio around, pinning his arms behind his back and turning the boy's head as he pushed him against the wall, trapping him between the wall and his chest. "Easy, son."

"I'm not your son!" Gio's narrow shoulders jerked back and forth, and he hopped from one foot to the next, knocking his knees into the wall without landing one kick against Joe's legs. "Ow! Dude! Let me go. This is child abuse."

"No, *dude*. This is a completely safe hold. No one's hurting you and you can't hurt anyone else. I'm even preventing you from hitting your head as you thrash around." Joe's tone was deeply pitched and matter-of-fact. He was so calm and authoritative as he controlled the eleven-year-old's struggles that Stella mentally shook off the shock she'd felt at being struck and listened, too. "You need to understand. I don't care if you're eleven years old, a hundred or somewhere in between—I won't allow anyone to hit a woman. Especially this one. I won't allow them to hit a child, either. You're safe here. Do you understand me?"

Gio still squirmed, although his feet were glued to the floor now. His brown gaze darted over to Stella, and she could see a sheen of tears there. Her heart constricted. What was this child so afraid of? "She your girlfriend?"

"Understand me?"

Gio finally went still. "Yeah."

"Did you mean yes?"

"Yes."

"Yes what?"

Her heart wanted to go to the boy and wrap him up in a tight hug. But as he pulled away from Gio, she could see that was practically what Joe had been doing—hugging him tightly. He was giving the child firm boundaries, both physically and verbally, allowing him a safe place to purge his temper until he could get himself under control again. Why Joseph Carpenter wasn't a father was beyond her realm of understanding. "Joe…"

Joe spared her a quick glance, asking her not to interrupt yet. When she nodded her understanding, he spoke to the boy in his arms again. "Gio?"

Gio's narrow chest heaved in and out with deep breaths, and he blinked away his tears. "Yes, sir. Don't hit the lady. I get it."

"You okay to sit and talk calmly to Ms. Smith for a while?" His tone had softened, too. Although Joe was still clearly the voice of authority here at the police station, there was a kindness there, too.

Gio nodded. The tension had eased out of his limbs. In fact, he looked exhausted, as if he'd been fighting his unseen enemy for a lot longer than the hour or so he'd been at the precinct offices tonight.

Joe moved his hand to Gio's shoulder and circled around the table to pull a chair out for him. "Sit."

Gio plopped down in the chair beside his brother's. Either his temper was spent, or he was trying to put Joe off guard so he could strike out again. Fat chance of that. Joe's eyes never left the boy's face. "Okay. I'm going to go get an ice pack for Ms. Smith. Can I trust you to stay in that chair and be respectful until I get back?"

Already sulky and slouched in the chair, Gio crossed his arms over his chest and dropped his chin. "I bet that other cop is on the other side of that window watching me."

"He is. But he won't intervene unless you give him reason to." Joe put a little more distance between him and Gio, letting him know he wasn't going to do anything as long as the boy minded his manners and stopped lashing out. "Just talk. Stella's a nice lady and a really good listener. She's funny and caring. Give her a chance. And be honest."

Gio checked Joe's position next to Stella, then tilted his warm brown gaze to hers. "You gonna keep Tyrell and me both? I have to stay with him. It's the only way I can protect him."

"Protect him from what?" Joe and Stella asked in unison.

She reached out to squeeze Joe's hand, trading her appreciation for his concern for the warmth and strength he provided.

Gio took note of the connecting gesture before asking again, "Are you keeping us both?"

When Joe started to push for an answer to their question,

Stella tugged on his arm and stopped him. She righted the chair that had been shoved aside and sat, keeping him standing beside her. "That's the plan. At least for the rest of the weekend. Then we'll take it day-to-day while Helen works out the final placement. It might be with me. It might not. But I have plenty of room for you both to stay as long as you need to."

"If you're lyin' to me, I'll cut you."

Joe's fingers vibrated with tension around hers. "You make another threat like that, and I won't leave."

He didn't lean across the table and physically threaten Gio in any way. But the kid was smart enough to realize he was pushing the wrong people here. "I couldn't really hurt her. I don't have anything to cut her with," he argued lamely.

"It doesn't matter," Stella explained. Her patience with children, even ones as troubled as Gio seemed to be, was a big reason she'd been a successful foster parent for so many years. But she had limits. And there were hard-and-fast rules in her home she expected everyone to follow so that every child felt physically and emotionally safe. "It's still a threat. I don't like threats. They frighten people and make them feel small. And I won't tolerate them being said to anyone in my home, including me. We build each other up. We don't tear each other down."

The boy considered Stella's words and Joe's stoic demeanor for a few seconds before nodding again. "I'll be good."

"Thank you." Then she tilted her head up to Joe. "Thank *you*. I've got this."

"This is the retraining part, right?" he whispered, obviously reluctant to trust Gio to do what he promised. "Stand back and let you do your thing instead of charging in to save the day?"

"His attack startled me. So, I appreciated you charging in

and keeping both of us safe. But like I said, I'm good now. I've got this." She smiled to back up her claim, and immediately winced as the raw skin in her mouth scraped across her teeth. "I bit the inside of my mouth."

"It's already starting to bruise here, too." He gently brushed the back of one finger across her jawline before he bent down and kissed the crown of her hair. "I'll go get that ice pack." He slid his hand around to cup the back of Stella's head. "You'll be okay till I get back?"

She nodded. "I'll be okay."

He spared a look at Gio. "*You'll* be okay?"

The eleven-year-old seemed surprised to be included in Joe's concern. He jerked his head up at the question, then nodded. "Yes, sir."

"I'll check on Tyrell while I'm out here, too."

Gio's shoulders visibly deflated with relief, and Stella wanted to hug Joe for saying just the right thing to lessen the tension that had Gio Williams wired with fear. Then he propped open the door and strode from the room. She watched Joe a few seconds before turning around to face Gio. She smiled gently and kept her voice calm.

"How are you doing, Gio?" she asked, suspecting he wouldn't open up to her right away. But she had to try. "I mean really. You've had a lot happen in the past couple of days—in the past week. You doing okay?"

He watched where her hands were clasped together on top of the table before tilting his gaze to hers. "Your boyfriend didn't hurt me, you know. If you were worried about that."

"I imagine he *can* hurt someone if he has to. But I know he wouldn't hurt you." She liked thinking of Joe as her boyfriend. After one interrupted date, she wasn't sure she could stake that claim, but she was already certain of one thing. "He's a good man."

She was going to ask Gio who *had* hurt him and his brother when Helen and Tyrell came back in with two candy bars.

Helen propped her hands on her hips while Tyrell trotted around the table and climbed up into his chair. "Sounds like we missed the excitement. Sergeant Carpenter said he didn't think you'd be pressing assault charges. But…" When Stella looked up to listen to her friend, Helen eyed the mark on her face and groaned. "What do I need to document?"

Stella squeezed her friend's hand to reassure her. "We were just laying down some ground rules. I think Gio and I understand each other better now. He certainly understands Joe."

Helen rolled her eyes and ended up looking at Gio. "I bet he does."

The older boy nodded. "I won't hit Miss Stella again."

Helen took in the expressions of everyone in the room before sighing and shaking her head. "I'll be in the next room whenever you're ready to go. Or if you change your mind."

"I won't," Stella stated firmly.

With a nod, Helen exited the room. Tyrell gave one of his candy bars to Gio, and Stella waited for both boys to open them up and take a bite. They'd eaten about half of their candy bars when Gio pulled the paper back around the uneaten portion, wrapped it up and reached behind him to unzip the side pocket of his backpack to tuck it inside. Tyrell, who seemed to take every cue from his big brother, quickly did the same.

Taking a chance that Gio wouldn't go ballistic again, she reached across the table to touch Tyrell's hand and stop him from hiding his snack for later. "Go ahead and finish your chocolate. I have plenty of food at home. When we get there, I'll show you where I keep snacks. Most are healthier than candy, but you can help yourself whenever you're hungry. As long as you brush your teeth afterward."

The gap-toothed smile he gave her in return lit up his face and loosened the fist squeezing her heart at the obvious hunger and food hoarding these boys were used to. Never again. Not on her watch.

Although Tyrell quickly unwrapped his candy bar, it wasn't until he glanced over at Gio, and his big brother nodded and pulled out his own candy bar, that the little boy took a big, messy bite and savored it.

Hiding her enjoyment at watching the boys indulge their sweet tooth, she decided to put off discussing their injuries and whatever had them so frightened and talk more about what a placement with her would look like. "Are you boys okay to sleep in bunk beds? You'd be sharing a room with another boy named Colby. But you each have your own dresser to put your things. You have your own desk, although most of my kids like to sit around the kitchen table to do their homework. I'm there to help if they need it. Or my foster daughter Harper is supersmart. She's good at helping with homework, too. I have a younger foster daughter named Ana. She's not in school yet, but she likes to sit at the table and draw or practice her letters and numbers with the other kids." She paused, wondering if either of them would have questions about her house or the other children. When they just kept chewing, but apparently listening, she continued. "I have a dog. Are either of you afraid of dogs?" Tyrell shook his head, then shrugged.

Gio stuffed the last bite into his mouth and quickly swallowed it. "We never had a dog. Does he bite?"

Curiosity, at last. Stella pulled out her phone and searched through her photos for one of Jasper.

"No. But there are certain rules we all follow in the way we treat him, so that he doesn't become aggressive. We all share the duties of taking care of him, and, in return, he takes care of us." She turned her phone to show them a couple of images—one of Jasper at a K-9 Ranch training session, standing at attention as if he was a show dog, and one where he'd just come out of the lake and was shaking water everywhere. "This is Jasper. He's a Newfoundland. He loves the water. My house is right next to a lake. We'll talk about the lake and water safety rules tomorrow."

Tyrell's eyes rounded. "He's big."

"Bigger than you, I imagine. He weighs one hundred and forty pounds." She pocketed her phone after they had looked their fill. "But he's very gentle and loves children. Ana uses him as a pillow sometimes."

Gio's expression tightened with thought. "Can he bite someone if he has to?"

This child. Always thinking about perceived threats and protecting his brother. She had her work cut out for her to get Gio to relax his guard and be a child again—and still feel safe.

"Do you mean, is he a good guard dog?" Gio sat up straighter in his chair and nodded. "He has a scary, deep bark. And he'll see or hear anyone at my house who shouldn't be there long before you or I would."

She glanced up at Joe as he reentered the room. He set a glass of water in front of her and placed the ice pack in her hand before guiding it up to her injured cheek. She thanked him for his kindness, then paused to swish some water around in her mouth to rinse away the blood there. She invited Joe to sit in the chair beside her, hoping to make him appear as less of a threat so that the boys would keep talking.

"Are you afraid of someone, Gio?" she asked. "Are you worried about being in danger? Or someone hurting Tyrell?"

"Someone named Vaughn?" Joe added.

Both boys snapped their heads to him at that question. Bingo. They were closing in on at least part of the threat.

Tyrell pushed the last of the chocolate bar into his mouth before innocently stating, "Vaughn's mean."

"Do you know the rest of Vaughn's name?" Joe pressed.

Tyrell licked some melted chocolate off his fingers. "Mom just calls him Vaughn."

"Hush, Ty." Gio shushed his brother. "We don't know these people yet. Or how long we'll be with them. Her other kids might not like us, and we'll have to go."

Feeling sad, though not surprised, that they expected to be sent away again, she reached over to rest her hand against the denim of Joe's thigh. His muscles quivered beneath her touch, but he quickly dropped his hand beneath the table to hold it against the warmth and solid strength she felt there. "As long as my other kids are safe, and you boys learn and follow my house rules, and don't do anything to get yourselves hurt, no one will have to leave."

Tyrell turned to Joe. "Do you ever hurt Miss Stella or make her cry? Vaughn makes Mom cry."

Joe's fingers curled tightly around hers at the innocent question. "No."

"He made me cry. But I'm little. Gio doesn't cry." Tyrell's tone might sound innocent, but there was nothing innocent about the clues he was revealing. She recalled the sheen of tears in Gio's eyes a few moments earlier but said nothing to undermine Tyrell's hero worship of his big brother. "Do you ever hurt her kids?"

"Don't make him mad again," Gio warned.

"I'm not mad—at either one of you. I'm mad that you think you have to ask that question." Keeping his right hand anchored around hers, Joe rested his left forearm on the table and leaned toward the boys, putting himself at a more equal level with them. "I've never been lucky enough to have kids of my own. But that doesn't mean I don't like them. Or that

I wouldn't like to have some friends your age. And I sure as hell wouldn't—"

"Joe." She quietly reminded him that he was talking to children, not hardened criminals. She shifted her grip against his thigh and turned so she could thread her fingers with his, supporting him just as he'd supported her when she'd been upset earlier.

He squeezed her hand in return, visibly rewinding before continuing. "I'm a protector by nature, not just because it's my job. I would never hurt Stella or any of her children because she's important to me, and they mean the world to her. Hurting one of them would make her incredibly sad, and I'd hate that. And finding out that someone else had hurt one of her kids? I'd be so ticked…" He angled his head toward Stella. "Are you sure I can't cuss?"

Tyrell snickered at the question. All heads turned to the little boy, whose soft laugh had instantly defused the tension in the room. "You are in so much trouble."

"You think big boys can't get in trouble?" Joe teased.

Tyrell laughed out loud and Gio snorted through his nose. It wasn't a pleasant sound, but hearing him laugh like a child triggered something warm and maternal inside of Stella. She joined in the secret joke among the males in the room. "I do have a swear jar at my house."

Joe groaned. "Do I need to put a quarter or a dollar in it?"

She shook her head. "I don't collect money. There are strips of paper in it with different chores on them. If I catch you swearing, you have to draw one out and do that job."

"Let me guess. Now I have to clean the toilets or pick up dog poop?"

Tyrell and Gio both laughed out loud at the words *dog poop*, encouraging Stella that they remembered how to be children. And despite the ice pack, she felt anticipation warming her cheeks at Joe's heated stare. He wanted to be at her house, interacting with her and her children. He intended to be with her long enough to make her children laugh and to become a denizen of her swear jar.

But her excitement at that revelation faded instantly as Joe turned on cop mode again, probably using the light-hearted mood of the room to catch the boys off guard. "Is there someone who wants to hurt you? Is there someone who could hurt Stella or one of her children? I can help. But I need to know the facts."

Their amusement at a grown man getting into trouble with her vanished, and the boys exchanged a meaningful look. But neither answered Joe.

Right. Interviewing the two boys in a police station interrogation room wasn't part of their date. She needed to focus on them, and not the sudden, hopeful awakening of her lonely heart. So, she pressed for answers, too. "Is that why you got in trouble at school and were so angry when you got home? Did someone threaten you? Or Tyrell?"

Tyrell bowed his head and Gio sat up straight.

"Will we be going to a different school?" the older boy asked. "The kids at our school don't like us."

The abrupt change of topic caught her off guard for a moment. Surely, the Williams brothers wouldn't be this upset over a school bully who made fun of their clothes that didn't fit. "Yes. I live in a different district from where you were last week. It's still the Kansas City public schools, though. So, what you're studying should be the same."

Gio reached over to grab Tyrell's hand and squeezed it before looking up at Stella. "We're really tired and we'd like to go home now. To your home. I promise I'll be good. We won't get in Colby's way in his room, and we won't pick on the girls."

"Can I pet the dog?" Tyrell asked.

"Of course you can. He'll come to the door to greet us.

I'll show you how to hold your hand and let him sniff you before you pet him. He'll like knowing that you're friends." Joe wanted to push, but Stella stopped him. They weren't getting any more answers tonight. She set down her ice pack and stood. "Will you boys be okay in here for a few minutes? I need to tie up some loose ends with Helen."

Joe stood beside her and pushed in their chairs. "I'll send Officer Hawley back in to sit with you."

"Yes, sir."

"Yes, sir," Tyrell echoed. "And we won't cuss, either," the little smarty-pants added.

They stepped out the door, and Officer Hawley went in to help the boys clean up and gather their things. Joe stopped her with a hand on her arm. "What do you think that was all about? Flying off the handle and punching you? Laughing one moment, then locking down like Fort Knox the next? Any idea what they're hiding? Because they *are* hiding something."

She agreed. "Clearly, they're afraid of something. Or someone. Probably that Vaughn character. You don't think he approached them at school, do you? Maybe with a message about their mother? Isn't she still in jail? Wouldn't the principal have reported that to Helen? Could this guy have been masquerading as a parent or staff member or someone else who'd have access to Gio or Tyrell?"

"I don't know. I can talk to school officials on Monday."

"And you can find out who this Vaughn guy is? Even if the boys can't or won't help?"

"I'll find him." Joe's curt nod and decisive tone did more to reassure her than the squeeze of his fingers around hers. "And then I'm going to pay him a visit."

Chapter Six

Stella tossed in the middle of her king-size bed, fluffing up her pillow and rolling onto her side to read 2:13 a.m. glowing from her clock on the bedside table. Annoyed with her inability to fall into a deep sleep, she flopped over onto her back and stared up at the shadows on her ceiling, processing the thoughts spinning through her mind and keeping the sandman at bay.

The kids were all asleep. After getting Gio and Tyrell settled in and introducing everyone, she'd decided it was too late for baths and just had everyone brush their teeth, put on pajamas and climb into their respective beds. Although the boys had talked for a few minutes, they were all out by the time she'd made bed checks. Colby was starfished across his bed and impossible to cover up. Gio had fallen asleep with his arm dangling over the edge of the top bunk, and she wondered if he'd held hands with his brother until Tyrell had fallen asleep. She'd gently tucked his arm beneath the blanket and smoothed her hand over the top of Tyrell's soft, fuzzy hair. The girls had been curled up beneath their comforters, with Harper hugging a stuffed animal to her chest. Jasper had stretched out on top of the covers in Ana's bed, taking up more room than the little girl did. He'd raised his head when Stella had entered the room, and she'd petted him around his ears and kissed the top of his head, feeling reassured that the house was secure since he was so relaxed. She knew he'd make rounds sometime through the night, checking on her and each child, either climbing into bed with them or stretching out on one of the rugs beside each bed. Even Sophie had fallen asleep in her room after their late night. Stella had set the heavy textbook the twenty-one-year-old had been studying on the bedside table, tucked the covers around her and turned off the lamp. Although Joe had checked everything before he left, she'd made sure the doors were all locked and the alarm system on the house was set. Then she'd fallen wearily into bed herself, expecting to pass out from exhaustion.

But her brain refused to shut down. She cocked her head to the right, seeing the light of the nearly full moon glowing around the edges of her window shade and curtains. Maybe it was just that the room wasn't dark enough. She really should invest in black-out shades for the bedrooms. On nights like this, when the moon was bright and the lake surface was still, the light reflected across the landscape and made it feel like it was almost dawn outside.

Suspecting that getting her thoughts out of her head was the only way she'd ever get to sleep, she reached over to the nightstand again and turned on the lamp there. The soft, warm glow canceled out some of the cool moonlight from outside. She kicked off the covers that had twisted around her legs and sat up before opening the drawer in the nightstand and pulling out a pen and notepad. Scooting back against the upholstered headboard and pillows, she crossed her legs and jotted a list.

1. Black-out shades
2. Pj's/Clothes that fit G & T (Ditto Colby)
3. Water rules tomorrow

4. G & T intro to Jasper training
5. ____ Vaughn? Vaughn ____?
6. ~~Text Joe~~ ~~Call~~ Kiss Joe

The notepad dropped to her lap as her to-do list finally turned to the man she'd been through so much with tonight. She absently stroked the bruise on her jaw where he had touched her and tended to her injury and made note of all the things she liked about him. Joe Carpenter was tall enough for her. He was muscular. Protective. Those arms and shoulders? Pure masculine perfection. Green eyes—sharp one moment, caring the next. Easy to talk to. His efforts to be *retrained* were endearing. That seductive, deep-pitched laugh.

Even without any covers over her T-shirt and lounge-pant pj's, her body warmed, and her nipples pearled into tight little buds that rubbed against her cotton-knit top. If all the hand-holding and chaste kisses left her feeling this edgy, she wondered what a full-blown kiss with Joe would be like.

When she felt her own tongue sneak out to trace the curve of her sensitized lips, imagining him there, she mentally chastised herself. "Good grief. You're worse than a petulant teenager bemoaning the fact you never got a good-night kiss." Knowing she needed a good night's rest to get through acclimating everyone to their new routine tomorrow—well, later today—she shoved the pen and notepad back into the drawer and straightened her covers. "Go to sleep already."

She was leaning over to turn off the lamp when her cell phone rang. "What the…?"

The screen lit up with an unknown number, and whatever warmth she'd been feeling was chased away by a sense of dread. A call at this time of night couldn't be anything good. An emergency foster placement. A break-in at the building where her charities were headquartered. A misdialing drunk. Or heaven forbid, the mysterious Vaughn had somehow tracked the Williams brothers to her home. She unplugged the phone from its charger and lifted it to her ear. "Hello?"

She heard Jasper climbing out of bed and padding down the hallway to investigate the disquieting noise of a ringing phone and conversation in the middle of the night.

She heard a huff of breath on the line and what sounded like a moan of satisfaction. "You're awake."

Stella hadn't recognized the number, but she recognized that voice. "Trey?" The nerve of that jerk. Anger poured through her system. She sure as hell wasn't sleeping now. "Do you have any idea what time it is?"

"I see the light on in your window, darling. I know you're up."

The light? Stella traded worried looks with Jasper, paused to stroke his long, heavy flank to take the edge off her anger, then hopped out of bed and hurried to the window. At first, she tugged the blind down another inch past the windowsill and unhooked the tiebacks to release the drapes and shake them out over the window, covering it from wall to wall. But needing to arm herself with knowledge more than she wanted to hide from that jerk, she moved to the side and pulled back the curtain and shade to peek out into the back-yard. The moon was bright enough that she could see almost everything from the house to the swing set to the back fence. Although they were separated by an acre or more, she could even make out the two closest lake houses on either side of hers. No movement there, either, but the trees between the homes offered plenty of places to hide. "Where are you? What do you want?"

"To take care of you. To be with you again."

Her temper spiked, but with the dog leaning against her thigh now—maybe seeking reassurance that nothing was wrong, maybe offering his own reassurance to her—she managed to keep most of the emotion out of her tone. "I don't need taking care of, you creep. I don't need you. Nothing you can say or do will ever make us a couple again. Leave me alone."

"Are you aware that there's a man outside your house tonight?"

Trepidation chased away her anger, and she curled her fingers into Jasper's thick coat. How did Trey know about her bedroom light and an intruder unless he was out there, watching the house? And what man was he talking about? Himself?

"Is this another one of your games?" She released the dog and pulled aside the curtain again. "If you're making up some story to scare me, so you can rescue me and play hero, trust me, I'd rather face the boogeyman…"

Her words trailed away as a shadowy movement beyond her back fence caught her eye. Down by the boat dock. Had someone just ducked into her boathouse? She squinted to sharpen her vision and leaned closer to the window. A beam of light slashed across the slats of the dock and then disappeared.

Was that Trey? Had one of the kids sneaked out of the house? No. They would have tripped the alarm opening any of the doors. Sophie knew the alarm code. But why would she…? The light flitted across the window in the back of the boathouse. The damn thing was supposed to be locked. Had a thief broken in? Would a homeless person looking for shelter come this far out of the city?

Stella released the curtain and turned away from the window.

"Do you want me to come over?" Trey offered. "Check things out for you?"

She hung up without answering. She grabbed the hoodie she wore for a robe, slipped the phone into the pocket and stepped into her flip-flops before hurrying down the upstairs hallway. "Jasper. Come."

Her phone rang again, and she quickly silenced it so it wouldn't wake the children. And so she didn't have to deal with Trey's harassment.

The dog stayed right by her side as she peeked into every bedroom. Good. Sophie was sound asleep. All five children were still in their beds, as well.

Her sigh of relief was short-lived. Her charges were safe. But that didn't explain who was down at the boathouse. Or where Trey Jeffries was right now. "Stay with me. Good boy."

She curled her fingers around Jasper's collar and headed down the stairs to get a closer look through the ground-floor windows. But when she got to the bottom of the stairs, she looked through the sidelights on either side of the front door and saw the vehicle parked in the shadows on the street in front of her house. Was that Trey?

Releasing the dog, she pulled out her phone, ready to press 9-1-1. But as she reached the sidelight window, the black vehicle took on a familiar shape. As did the man sitting behind the wheel, his head tilted back against the headrest. "Joe?"

What was he doing here? Was he okay?

Her fingers acted before her brain fully decided whether she was upset that his presence had prompted Trey's call or that she was grateful to see him there. She flipped on the porch lights, disarmed the alarm, swung open the door and ran outside. "Joe!"

The lights must have triggered his attention because he was out of the SUV and jogging toward her before she even reached the driveway. "Stell?"

She was vaguely aware of faded jeans and a rumpled T-shirt clinging to his chest and biceps before she threw her arms around his neck and hugged herself against his strength and warmth. His late-night beard stubble rasped against her cheek, but it felt real, reassuring. "Thank God you're here."

His arms cinched around her waist and lifted her right off her feet, plastering her against his body from chest to hips. With her nose buried against his neck beneath his chin, she could only feel him looking from side to side to see what had panicked her. "Don't scare me like that, sweetheart. What's wrong? What's happened?"

"Why are you sleeping outside my house?" They were climbing the steps before she realized he was carrying her with her legs dangling down between his. "Put me down. I can walk." She scrambled out of his arms.

He didn't let her go far, though. He snaked his arm around her waist and guided her into the house before calling for the dog. "Jasper!" The moment the big dog lumbered in behind them, Joe closed the door and locked it. Then he pulled her into his arms again, cradling her head against the warmth of his neck and holding her close. "I wasn't sleeping. I told you I don't sleep much. I drove back over to keep watch instead of pacing my own apartment worrying about you and the kids. Make myself useful instead of raising my blood pressure. Now, tell me what happened. Is everyone okay?"

"You have insomnia? Don't you have a sleeping aid you can take?" She loosened her grip on the back of his T-shirt and leaned back against his arms. "Once you get home, of course. I don't want you taking one and trying to drive."

"I'm not going to chemically put myself to sleep and not be able to protect you if I need to. You're not answering my questions. Why did you go running outside in the middle of the night?" He reached up and caught a tendril of hair that had fallen out of the messy topknot she slept in and tucked it behind her ear. She loved the feel of his warm hand cupping the side of her neck. "Stell? I love that you're worried about me. I'll be supportive and follow your lead on almost anything. But if there's any kind of threat, then *I* need to be in charge. You can't train that out of me... Talk to me."

Feeling guilty that she'd been distracted by finding him here, the feel of his arms surrounding her and his gentle touches, she slipped out of his embrace and pulled her phone from her pocket. "Trey called. He said—"

"In the middle of the night? I thought you blocked his number." Joe's curse was vehement and precise, and described her opinion of Trey Jeffries to a tee. He pulled his phone from the back pocket of his jeans and scrolled through his numbers.

"Yes, and I did. Anyway, I went to the window—"

"Where's the damn jar so I can find out what chore I have to do because I am not watching my language?" He strode into the kitchen, assuming the swear jar would be in there.

She hurried after him. "What are you doing?"

"I'm reporting the harassment. We're getting that restraining order reinstated."

"That's not what spooked me."

He paused his search for the number he wanted. "Then what did?"

"Trey called and asked why some guy was outside my house."

"Me? How does he know I'm here? *You* didn't even know I was here." He glanced back toward the street and muttered a curse. "He's watching."

"That's what I thought, too. So, I looked out my bedroom window—"

He swore again and spun toward the door. "I'll be back. Turn on the security system—"

"Joe." She darted in front of him, caught his face between her hands and forced him to look at her. "I need you to listen to me. Yes, Trey is creepy as all get-out. But more important, I saw someone out by the lake on my dock, going into my boathouse."

His eyes were hard and narrowed. A beat of time passed before he blinked. She could see that something inside him had shifted, cooled. Frankly, she found that sudden transfer of emotion from his expression a little scary. She imagined the bad guys did, too.

But he reached up to pull her hands from his face. He gave them a reassuring squeeze and kept hold of one as he pulled her into the kitchen with him. "Back door?"

"Mudroom off the kitchen. I couldn't see the person clearly, but I'm pretty sure it was a man. It could have been Trey, right? Pulling some stunt like he used to?"

But Joe wasn't interested in speculation. "Flashlight?" She dug one out of the junk drawer while he pulled a gun from his ankle holster and hooked his badge onto the front of his belt. "Lock this behind me. Reset the alarm. Leave the lights off. Keep the dog with you. Don't let anyone in but me."

"What are you doing?"

"I'm going to go be a cop."

Then he was gone.

Chapter Seven

Stella locked the door and pushed the security code. With the moonlight reflecting on the lake filling the air with a hazy glow, she watched Joe holding the gun and flashlight in front of him as he checked either side of the house before quickly crossing the yard. Her hand fisted beneath her breasts as she stood in the dark mudroom and watched. Good grief. Was this ball of worry knotting in her stomach what it was like being a cop's wife?

Not that she was Joe's wife. Or even officially his girlfriend yet. But she wanted to be. She wanted that good, interesting, funny, sexy, caring man to be hers.

And to get some sleep.

And to not get hurt.

She forced herself to take a deep breath and turn away from the door. Joe Carpenter was a grown man, an Army veteran and an experienced cop. If she truly wanted to be his partner, she couldn't stand here worrying herself into a useless ball of fear. That wasn't how she got through her childhood. That wasn't how she survived the humiliation of her relationship with Trey. That wasn't how she had raised, shielded and loved so many children over the past twenty years. Stella Smith took action. She was too busy to be lonely, upset or afraid. She needed to do something.

Instead of watching or imagining worst-case scenarios, she knelt beside Jasper and hugged him around his thick neck before petting him on the flank, taking comfort from the dog's presence. Then, with the dog at her side, she went upstairs to turn off the light in her bedroom and checked on all five kids and Sophie again. She was relieved to find them all sound asleep and blissfully unaware of the fears she was facing tonight.

She was equally relieved when she heard Joe's knock on the back door, and she hurried down to let him in and locked the door behind him. Jasper snuffled a greeting, already recognizing Joe by sight or scent and accepting his presence there. Joe spared a moment to pet the dog, and Jasper pushed his head into his firm caress. "Good boy." When he was done roughhousing a bit with the dog, Joe headed into the kitchen. She could see that he'd holstered his weapon and was carrying something wrapped in a blue plastic glove. "I saw when you turned off the light upstairs. I checked the sight lines. He had to be in your backyard or out on the lake with binoculars to know that you were awake with the light on. Otherwise, the trees block the view."

Stella hugged her arms around her waist. "I'm not going to live in the dark, just so he can't spy on me anymore."

"Of course you're not."

"I've told him no every way I can think of. Why doesn't he leave me alone?"

"Obsession doesn't work that way. It doesn't have to make logical sense. He's fixated on you as his meal ticket. Or someone he can control."

"That's never going to happen." She raked her fingers through her hair in frustration, pulling several strands loose and shifting the bun on top of her head.

Joe's look was almost sympathetic. "He can wear you down until you give him whatever he wants."

"No. I'm stronger than that."

"Hell yeah, you are." He reached out and brushed a strand of hair away from her eye and tucked it behind her ear.

If Joe believed that, then so could she. Nodding her thanks for his support, she inhaled a calming breath. "So, whoever was out there is obviously gone, or you'd have the guy in handcuffs and a squad car out front. What did you find out?"

He grinned at her accurate assessment of his actions. "I'm assuming you keep the boathouse locked?"

"Of course. It's still offseason, and I don't want the kids messing around there unless I'm with them. Harper and Colby are the only ones who've had swim lessons. And that's just the basics. I don't know about the Williams boys yet."

"You'll need a new lock." He held up a broken padlock for her to see, then set it on the island countertop, still wrapped in the sterile glove. "Looks like it was removed with bolt cutters. Whoever was out there is long gone."

"Is it okay to turn on the lights now?" When he nodded, she turned on the light above the stove and a lamp out in the living room, giving her enough illumination to see the shiny steel cross sections of the lock's shackle without touching it. "Did they steal anything?"

Theft hadn't been Trey's MO in the past. But he might be staging a scene to make her so afraid that she'd turn to him for comfort and welcome him back into her life.

Joe moved to the edge of the island to stand beside her. Although she was drawn to the warmth of his body, she resisted the urge to lean against him and hugged her arms around her waist instead. "It's hard to tell. The place is a mess. Either they got interrupted, or they didn't see anything they wanted and left. Could just be vandalism." He pulled his phone from his back pocket and typed a message into a text to himself. He was taking notes on the crime scene, she supposed. "Do you keep anything valuable there?" he asked.

She shrugged. She supposed there were some things there that could be pawned for profit. But she would have seen a man hauling away a boat, wouldn't she? "Mostly equipment. Kayaks, a rowboat, life jackets, fishing gear, deck chairs. A few sentimental tchotchkes I put out for decoration in the summer."

"How big a guy is your ex?" Joe sent the text, then pulled up his photos.

"Around six feet. Heavyset. The last time I saw him, anyway, a few years ago."

"He have big feet?"

"I suppose."

He scrolled through several pictures he'd taken. The broken door lock. Evidence that the intruder had jimmied open storage lockers inside the boat shed and left a mess for her to clean up. New grass trampled underfoot beside the shed. And numerous footprints in the dirt near the end of the dock. "I don't know if a CSI team can get anything usable. These footprints are all mushed together. Either there was more than one person out there, or the perp purposely sabotaged any chance of tracking him."

"More than one…?" she echoed, hating the possibility of Trey bringing backup with him to terrorize her, or worse— that she'd had unknown enemies on her property tonight.

"Did the Troll ever do anything like this before?"

"Not exactly. But I wouldn't put it past him. Since reasoning and begging aren't working for him, maybe he's trying to scare me into getting back together with him." Stella was already tired from a full day and a lack of sleep. But now she felt utterly weary. "Do I need to go down there and see the damage for myself?"

The cop in him finally retreated beneath the caring man. He tucked his phone back into his jeans and tugged her hands away from the grip she held on herself. "Sorry. Sometimes,

I forget the rest of the world doesn't keep the same hours I do. You can check it out in the morning. If anything's missing, I'll file the report then." When he pulled her along toward the front of the house, she willingly followed. "Will you walk me out?"

"Are you leaving?"

"I'll be right out front."

Stella halted in her tracks, forcing him to stop. "Will you stay with me?"

"I was planning on it anyway, after Gio took a swing at you down at the police station. Now that someone has trespassed and broken into your property, I'm definitely staying to keep watch." He nodded over his shoulder toward the street. "Maybe next time, though, you can text me if you need something, instead of running outside by yourself. When I saw you, it scared me. I don't want to do that again. Okay?"

No. That wasn't going to work for her. She felt raw and vulnerable, and Joe Carpenter seemed to be the only thing making her feel secure right now. She'd asked him out— she'd ask this of him, too. "I mean, will you stay in the house? The couch is roomy enough to make a nice bed, or you can take the last guest room upstairs. You can't be comfortable in your SUV, and I... I'd like you closer."

He studied her expression for a moment before stepping into her space and settling his hands at her hips. "You sure? I might not worry so much if I was closer to you, too."

He slipped his thumbs and a finger from each hand beneath the hem of her hoodie and shirt, and she felt his calloused fingertips slide against her bare skin. Goose bumps prickled along her skin at the intimate touch, and she gasped at the surprise of how good his touch felt on her, how comforting and arousing at the same time.

"I'm positive." Resting her palms on his chest, she barely

had to tilt her head to look him in the eye. But his shoulders were so broad, and his hands were so warm and faintly possessive around the curve of her waist, that she felt surrounded by him. Yes. This was exactly what she wanted—or close to it. "I'm sorry that you have to sleep in your clothes. I'd offer you a T-shirt, but I doubt I have anything that would fit the rest of you."

"That's all right. I have a go bag in the back of my car—emergency change of clothes, a few toiletries, stuff like that. I'll run out and get it. Before I come back, I'm going to walk around, see if I can spot your ex sitting in a car anywhere."

"If that was who I saw at the boathouse, he's probably long gone."

"I don't care. I'm still checking the perimeter. Too many weird things are going on around you, and I don't like it. It doesn't feel safe."

She shook her head. "No, it doesn't. I can't protect my kids if I can't even protect myself."

"That's why I'm here. I've got your back. You've got theirs." His hands tightened at her waist, pulling her close enough for her thighs to brush against his, and for him to press a kiss to her forehead before he released her. "While I'm outside, can you find a paper bag to put that lock in? Be sure not to touch it with your fingers. I want to take it to the lab to see if they can get any prints off it." He nodded toward the living room. "The couch works for me. I'd like to be between the points of entry and you and the kids upstairs."

"Okay. Be safe." She followed him to the door and locked it behind him.

She kept herself busy until Joe came back. She wanted to hear about anything else he'd found that was suspicious, but she also wanted to make sure he was safely back inside the house with her before she retired to her bedroom upstairs. Heeding his request, she put the broken lock inside a paper sack and stapled it shut. Then she got out a marker and labeled the bag with the information she thought was pertinent—the item, where it had come from, the date, time and Joe's name. After setting that aside, she prepped the coffee maker and set the timer for later that morning. She wasn't certain whether or not Joe was a die-hard coffee drinker, but she knew after a night like this one that she would be. Finally, she pulled sheets, a blanket and a pillow from the linen closet and set them on the couch.

A full half hour passed before Joe pulled his SUV into the driveway and she heard his soft knock on the front door. Jasper raised his head from his bed in the kitchen. But once he saw it was Joe and that Stella was fine with him being there, the dog laid his head down on his front paws and went back to snoozing.

"I didn't see anyone out there," he announced as he set his go bag just inside the door and waited for her to set the security system. He settled his hand at the small of her back and followed her back into the kitchen. "Could you spare a man a glass of water?"

"Of course." She pulled two clean glasses from the dishwasher and filled them with ice and water from the panel on her refrigerator. "Are you hungry? I could reheat our dinner."

"No, thanks." He pulled out a stool at the island and waited for her to sit before he downed half his glass of water, then sat beside her. "You look like you're about to drop."

She liked that he kept his arm draped over the back of her stool. The gesture felt protective, familiar. "Well, unlike some people, I need more than an hour or two of sleep to function in the morning." She sipped her water. "But I wanted to hear your report. Did you find Trey or anything else to explain what's going on?"

"Other than the break-in, everything's clear and quiet." He slipped his hand up to the nape of her neck and massaged

the tension gathering there. "You're wound up pretty tight."
Stella closed her eyes and literally moaned at his gentle touch
and leaned back against his hand. When she opened her eyes
again, he was smiling at her. "Better?"

"Uh-huh." But Stella was already beginning to learn the
nuances of Joe's expressions. And though he was tired, she
could see the sharp focus in his eyes. "You want to ask me
something?"

The massage stopped. "Are your neighbors to the east
home?"

"I don't know. They're both retired now, so they travel
a lot. But if they're gone for more than a couple of days,
they'll let me know. If it's longer than that, they'll hire a
house sitter."

"And you haven't heard from them?" he clarified.

Shaking her head, she reached into her hoodie for her
phone. "I can call them to find out."

Joe pushed her phone down to the countertop. "That can
wait until morning, too. There was no car in the garage or
out front. No signs of movement inside the house. But the
screen on the back door had been cut, and it looks like someone tried to jimmy the lock to break in."

"Another break-in?" She reached for her phone again.
"Should I call the police?"

He caught her hand in his and pulled it down to his thigh.
"I *am* the police." His grin reminded her of just how tired
she was. "I already called it in. They'll send a unit out to
do a wellness check if anyone's home, and they'll write up
a report on the attempted break-in."

"Thank you." She squeezed her fingers around his. "I'll
call the Roes tomorrow—er, later today—to find out where
they are and let them know." His green eyes still had that
sharp, focused look. "There's something else?"

"It looked like someone had recently parked in their driveway. There was a fresh oil stain on the concrete, and multiple footprints at the back of the house leading down to their dock." He shrugged, and she could tell his quest for all possible information was frustrating him. "Maybe the thieves were looking for something else to steal when they couldn't get into the house. Maybe they were just checking how secluded the home is so that they could come back later to try to break in again without being detected."

"Or?"

"Or someone could watch your house from there, or easily walk around the lakeshore from there to get to your boathouse."

Stella shivered. Were there any answers to be had? Or just endless possibilities? And frankly, nothing from Gio being afraid of someone named Vaughn to someone breaking into her property to setting up shop at the neighbors' house to spy on her sounded good.

While she was lost in her depressing thoughts, Joe picked up her phone and looked at the call log. "Someone's called you three times in the last hour. The Troll?"

"So, we aren't even bothering to use Trey or Preston as his name anymore?" Her half-hearted snicker held little humor. "I listened to the beginning of each message to confirm it was him, then I blocked the number. But he keeps changing it. He must have a lot of friends willing to let him borrow their phone."

"More likely, he's got a stash of burner phones." Joe handed the phone back to her. "Will you let me file a new restraining order against this jerk? I don't know if he's mentally unbalanced or desperate, but he's hurting you. You're stressed, not sleeping. This needs to stop."

She nodded and pocketed her phone. "I'll go with you to talk to a judge."

"Thank you." He slid his hand over hers where it rested

on the countertop and squeezed her fingers. "Why don't you go on back to bed? You look like you're about to drop from exhaustion."

She turned her hand, her palm to his, and laced their fingers together. "And you don't need sleep, Mr. Insomnia?"

"I'm used to doing without. I grab quick naps when I need them." He stood and pulled the back of her hand to his lips before releasing her and returning to the front room to pick up his bag. "I'll change and see if I can grab an hour or two of shut-eye before morning."

"Sleep in if you need to." He seemed amused by her concern, and she could guess that this man never slept in. "Fine." She pointed past him to the main-floor bathroom. "There's a full shower and tub in there, if that helps you relax. Towels are under the sink."

"Sounds good. I'll be quick." He waved her toward the stairs. "Good night, Stell."

"Good night, Joe."

She was still sitting at the kitchen counter, nursing her glass of water, when he came back out. He'd changed into sweats and a fresh T-shirt after a quick shower. She could see the droplets of water clinging to the short, silvery spikes of his hair and feel the warmth of the hot shower coming off his body as he approached. "Stell? Everything okay? Did he call again?"

Good grief. She was emotionally and physically exhausted, but parts of her body perked to attention at how well the casual clothes clung to every hill and hollow of his compact, muscular body. Protective. Caring. Supportive. Hot. "How has no woman snatched you up before now?"

The words were out of her mouth before her weary brain could temper her thoughts or even realize how random that sounded.

"Uh..." The skin beneath his stubbled cheeks turned a

ruddy shade of pink. It had been more of a rhetorical question, but Joe answered anyway. "I work too much? Couldn't handle being with a soldier who can't talk about his work? Scared to be with a cop? Not being in the same place in a relationship at the same time? I'm short?"

"Seriously? Those things have all happened to you?"

He shrugged. "Tall, dark and handsome was all the rage a few years back."

Uh-uh. Now wasn't the time for humor. "That's as bad as some guy telling me I'm not pretty because I'm fat."

"You're not—"

"Enough." She waved her hands in the air, as if she could erase this whole conversation. "Forget I said anything. I don't want to hear about any other women in your past who had a shot at you and blew it. Or if you're not interested in a long-term relationship—"

"I'm interested." His words were deeply pitched, little more than a whisper against her eardrums. His gaze caught and held hers for so long that she felt his intent deep in her heart. He was talking about her. He was interested in *her*. "But maybe this isn't the best time to have this conversation."

It was on the tip of her tongue to tell him she was already thinking about long-term with him, too, when Jasper stirred in his bed beside her feet. He rolled onto his side, stretched his legs out and snored.

The tension in the air broke, and they both laughed. Stella got up and carried their glasses to the sink. "Well, at least one of us is getting some sleep."

"No deep thoughts to keep him up at night, hmm?" Joe teased. He carried his bag to the main room and set it on the floor at the end of the sofa.

"It's a dog's life." Stella turned off the light over the stove and followed him. "I made up a spot on the couch for you. It's a big sectional, so there's plenty of room."

"It's perfect."

She lingered while he pulled back the covers and fluffed up the pillow. "Could I stay with you for a while?"

"Come here." He sat on the couch and patted the seat beside him. When she joined him, he put his arm around her. She shivered at the contrast of his abundant heat to her chilled body. "You cold?" He rubbed his hands up and down her arms, then reached behind her to free the blanket and wrap it around her shoulders. Then he wrapped both arms around her, blanket and all, and leaned back against the couch. "Better?"

Addicted to his warmth, Stella kicked off her flip-flops, curled her feet beneath the blanket and huddled up next to him, tucking her head against his neck and jaw. "No. I'm mad and I'm scared. I should be able to handle this by myself, but I don't want to."

"Do you know what's going on?" Strands of her hair caught in his beard stubble when she shook her head. "Then you don't know what you have to handle yet. Let me be here to help you, support you, share some body heat, until you do know what you're up against. Then we can make a plan and handle it together." He leaned away, tapping the tip of her chin with his finger, asking her to look at him. "If that's okay with you."

"That's okay with me." She freed one hand from the blanket and cupped his cheek. "One more request?"

"Anything."

"Would you kiss me?" His eyes turned a midnight green as his pupils dilated. "Then hold me for a little while until I can fall asleep?"

He smoothed several strands of hair away from her face and tucked each one behind her ears. "Here I've been plottin' and plannin' since we were at the restaurant, trying to figure out how to get my lips on yours without coming across like some horny lothario taking advantage of the situation."

"We're a mature man and woman, Joe. I don't want game playing. I just want you to be honest about wanting me— the way I want you. If that's something you want." She grimaced, hearing herself repeating the same word over and over. "Trust me, I'm much more eloquent after a good night's sleep and a cup of coffee."

"You *want* me to kiss you?" he teased.

"If you can't figure out the subliminal messaging in what I just said—"

His firm lips covered hers in a blanket of warmth, silencing her words. It was a chaste kiss at first. His lips pressed against hers, retreated, grew more pliant as he tasted her again. She matched him touch for touch, loving his gentle exploration yet groaning in frustration at his endless patience. He chuckled against her mouth, the vibrations moving through her like a burst of light and happiness. It wasn't until he captured her bottom lip between both of his and ran his tongue along the curve that her frustration morphed into full-blown desire.

She ran her palm along the ticklish scrape of his late-night stubble and cupped the back of his head, pulling him closer even as she pushed herself up into the warmth of his kiss. "Joe," she pleaded, wanting more, needing more.

And, oh, how the man delivered. "Right here with you, sweetheart."

His hands slid down to the curve of her bottom and lifted her onto his lap. Then, with her legs splayed across his thighs and her breasts aroused and pillowed against his chest, he opened his mouth over hers and consumed her with heat. His tongue swept across her lips, and she willingly opened to him, welcomed him, chased after him to explore his mouth, too. He must have brushed his teeth in the shower, because the taste of him was minty fresh, intensified with heat and desire.

Stella traced her thumbs across the angles of his cheeks and jaw, then skimmed her hands over those masculine shoulders and biceps. His hands roamed, too, as he continued the tender assault on her mouth. He squeezed her bottom, slipped his hands beneath her jacket and top to caress bare skin. Every place he touched kindled a tiny fire of need that spread through her body, chasing away the chill and uncertainty, leaving nothing but heat and desire in their wake.

Making out like teenagers on her couch wasn't exactly what she'd had in mind when she'd asked him to kiss her. But she wasn't complaining. Had she ever wanted a man this badly this quickly? And felt the attraction and desire she felt for him was genuinely returned?

When he clutched the back of her head and groaned into her mouth, she stretched against him, seeking more, wanting everything. Maybe she should have been embarrassed by the arousal she felt wedged between their lower bodies, but it only reaffirmed that Joe Carpenter wasn't lying when he'd said he was attracted to her just as she was.

A logical spark deep in her brain tried to remind her that this was just their first date, not even really that, since she'd been called to the police station before their evening had barely started. Another part argued that she was a woman who knew her own mind and wasn't afraid to ask for the things she wanted and go after them. It wasn't as if she and Joe were strangers, after all. They'd been talking and texting all week. Friends who knew them both well had set them up in the first place, suspecting they'd be a match. And a third part of her brain reminded her of her current reality, the stress she'd been under and the late hour.

That was the side that won out when Stella pulled away

midkiss and yawned. It wasn't a dainty yawn, either. It was a big, noisy gasp for oxygen that her weary body craved.

"I'm so sorry." She was having a hard time catching her breath, and an even harder time moving away.

Trey would have been angry that she'd yawned in the middle of a kiss. But Joe was miles apart from Preston Alan Jeffries III. Although he was taking deep, stuttered breaths that matched her own, Joe laughed and cradled the back of her head, resting it against his shoulder and the side of his neck. "That's all right, sweetheart. It's late, and I don't want to start something we can't finish."

"It's not the company, I swear."

"I believe you." Joe's fingers tunneled into her hair and stroked her scalp in a soothing rhythm. "If this is a taste of how things can be between us, trust me, I'm more than all right waiting. I love the anticipation of going slow and imagining all the wicked things we can do together next time." He glanced over her shoulder into the shadows of the kitchen. "Besides, your dog is watching us. To be honest, he doesn't seem curious enough to come over here and check us out, but still, having an audience isn't exactly my thing." They shared a laugh. "Also, if one of your kids gets scared by something and comes down here looking for you, I don't want them to find us with your hands up under my shirt and my tongue down your throat."

"My hands...?" Oh. A different kind of heat flooded through her. She had made herself right at home on his body, pushing his shirt up out of the way to explore all those muscles and see how quickly she could turn those male nipples into rock-hard nubs that poked into the palms of her hands. Stella pulled away from the heat of his skin and made a token effort to straighten his shirt before tucking her hands together in front of her and snuggling against him. "Maybe we could continue this another time? I'd hate to miss a single moment because I'm tired."

"Good. That means we'll be doing this again." He lay back on the couch and pulled her on top of him. "I liked it the last time you were like this, minus the straw poking into my backside. I don't have my body armor this time. Now I know I wasn't imagining anything about your lush figure."

"Joe…"

"Stell…" He mimicked the intonation of her two-syllable protest perfectly. "Here. This better?" He shifted her to his side and spooned behind her, adjusting the blanket over them both. "Is this all right? Will you stay for a little while? Just to rest."

She answered by scooting back and cuddling into him. His bicep was her pillow and his free arm another blanket wrapped around her waist to keep her toasty warm. Snuggling in Joe's arms was the rightest she'd felt with a man in…ever. Oh, her heart was in so much trouble here. "Is it too soon for me to say I'm falling for you? We haven't even finished one date, and I'm already worried about how badly it's going to hurt if we don't work out."

"It's not wrong. I'm falling hard and fast myself." He paused for a moment, as if choosing his words before he continued. "I swear it's never been like this for me before. Maybe I see things differently with age. Yes, I am absolutely lusting after your curvy, responsive body and beautiful mouth. But it's like part of me already knows you, recognizes you. I think that restless need to shake things up in my life was about finding *you*. And now that I have, something has settled in me. I'm not sure I can explain how right being with you feels to me."

Stella got what he was saying. She'd been searching for this kind of closeness her whole life, too. She tangled her fingers with the hand at her waist and pulled it up to nestle right beneath the weight of her breasts. "So, staying here tonight isn't just your overdeveloped sense of duty?"

"It might have gotten me here. But that's not why I'm staying." He adjusted to a more comfortable position behind her without pulling away. "I get to hold a beautiful, passionate woman in my arms." He nuzzled her behind her ear. "Smell her hair. What is that, anyway? Coconut?" She nodded. "I know for certain that she and her kids are safe. And I'm actually feeling a little drowsy myself. It'll be a miracle if I fall asleep for any length of time, but I feel like I could."

"Because you aren't worried and on guard now?"

"Because I'm holding you. Now hush. You're spoiling my sleepy vibe with all this conversation."

She giggled, and she felt him smiling against her skin before he pressed a kiss to the juncture of her neck and shoulder. "Good night, Joe."

"Good night, Stell. I'll make sure we're awake and I'm dressed before the kids get up in the morning."

She appreciated his concern about propriety and not embarrassing her or the kids with any uncomfortable questions. "It's Sunday morning. Colby, Harper and Ana will sleep in. Don't know about Gio and Tyrell yet, but they had a superlong day. Jasper will want to go out around seven, though."

"Then I'll be awake for the dog."

She squeezed his hand and closed her eyes. But she stayed awake for a while longer, listening to the sounds of the house and the world outside. Finally, the arm around her waist grew heavy, and like the gentle, rhythmic whisper of waves against the shore, his breathing deepened and evened out, and he drifted off to sleep behind her.

Smiling to know he was getting the rest he needed, she pressed a soft kiss to the arm beneath her head. Soon after, a sweet, dreamless sleep claimed her, as well.

Chapter Eight

"Joe!" Colby charged through the open gate at the back of Stella's yard and ran up the hill to greet Joe with his arm outstretched.

Tyrell hurried up the hill after him, his speed impeded by the orange life jacket and sagging swim trunks he wore. The girls looked up from the lake, where they were splashing in the water with Stella and Jasper, and waved. Even Gio turned from where he was dangling his feet in the water off the edge of the dock. And Stella herself smiled with that beautiful mouth and shouted, "Our hero returns!"

Joe couldn't remember a more enthusiastic welcome, even coming home from a deployment back in his Army days. This afternoon, he'd been gone less than two hours to go to the hardware store, then run by his place to pick up his toolbox and power drill and a pair of swim trunks so he, too, could enjoy the lakeside fun. He quickly set down the toolbox and drill on the patio before he was overrun with boys and held out his right hand to shake Colby's.

"Colby. Good to see you again." The red-haired boy had already shaken his hand this morning when he'd come downstairs for breakfast and found him sitting at the kitchen island, drinking coffee with Stella. She'd been right when she said Colby was desperate for positive male interaction, and he didn't intend to fail the mission he'd been drafted for. "Did you get your face under the water?" he asked, remembering Stella's swimming goal for him after her lessons on water safety.

"Uh-huh," the boy enthusiastically answered. "I helped Stella swim out to put the buoy markers in the water, so we know where it's too deep to go. The water's kind of cold, but I did it."

"Good for you."

"Did you know Gio and Tyrell can't swim? Gio wasn't afraid to try when Stella showed them how to float and 'splained the rules about always having a buddy down by the water, and always putting on a life jacket if you go outside the back gate. I was Gio's buddy. She said we're a family, and we have to look out for each other." Wow. Where was the shy, freckle-faced redhead he'd met last night? This Colby was full of energy and confidence. "Tyrell was afraid to put his face in the water. He's little, like I used to be."

"I am not," the seven-year-old answered, thrusting his hand toward Joe. "Colby said men shake hands."

"That's right." Joe gently wrapped his hand around Tyrell's. "Did you like being in the water, Ty?"

"Uh-huh. Bye."

"Bye," Colby echoed.

"Whoa, there, guys." When the two foster boys started to run back down to the lake, Joe stopped them and put them to work. "Here. Since you're already going that way, will you carry these down to the boathouse for me?" He gave the sack from the hardware store to Tyrell and handed the case holding his power drill to Colby. "You can help me put the new lock on the door if you want. I'll show you how to use the power drill."

"Yes!"

"Gio! We're gonna use the power drill!"

The boys ran ahead as Joe carried the heavier toolbox down to the concrete slab where the boathouse stood. Drawn to Stella in her colorful one-piece swimsuit, which somehow showcased all her curves while looking appropriately modest for swimming with children, he set down the toolbox and moved toward her. "Did I miss all the fun?"

"You missed the lecture and the lessons. Now everyone is doing their own thing until it gets too chilly to go in the water." She ran her gaze over the Army T-shirt, faded jeans and worn leather work boots he wore to do work around the house. "Do you want to swim or take one of the kayaks out before the sun goes down?"

"That's okay if I miss time in the water." Colby and Tyrell had opened the toolbox and were oohing and aahing over the hammer, screwdrivers and wrenches they found inside. They were particularly taken with the level and lining up the bubble between the two lines to show when it was perfectly balanced. "I've got a couple of tool men over there who are anxious to do some manly-man work. I'd better get started before they rearrange everything and I can't find the tools I need."

She waded out of the shallow water, and he had to concentrate on her eyes so he wouldn't fixate on how the water beaded on her skin and caught the sunshine, making her pale skin glow like she was some kind of naiad rising from the lake. She caught his hand and squeezed it. "You've been really good with the kids today. Thank you."

He squeezed back. Even simply holding hands made him feel a deep connection to this woman. "They've been really good for *me*. I don't think I've had a day where I've felt this…relaxed in ages."

She drifted half a step closer, and he could feel the moisture from her swimsuit getting his shirt damp. "Let me guess—you relax about as well as you sleep."

"Not gonna lie. Sitting around doing nothing is stressful for me. But I slept great last night. Four hours straight." Joe leaned in, intending to steal a kiss from those teasing lips. "Because you were with me."

Frowning, she braced her hand against his chest and nudged him back. "That's a good night for you? You need more than four."

"Four beats two."

"Glad I could help, but—"

Joe caught Stella as Jasper ran past and bumped into her legs. The big dog ran the length of the dock up to Gio. "Who's he chasing?"

Jasper skidded to a halt beside Gio, panting with excitement, his eyes laser focused on the fluorescent orange bumper toy the boy had picked up off the dock. Jasper's thick tail swatted the boy with every wag, and he put up his arms to block the furry assault.

"Not who. What." Stella turned in Joe's arms to give the boy instructions. "Throw it, Gio. That floaty toy is Jasper's favorite. He wants to play. Throw it across the water. Say his name. Then tell him to go get it."

Gio tentatively touched Jasper's flank, and that only seemed to excite the dog more. "Okay, big guy." Seeming reassured that the dog wanted to play, not attack, Gio stood up and hurled the toy across the water. "Jasper. Go get it."

The Newfie leaped off the edge of the dock and dived into the lake after the toy, splashing up his weight in water. Gio realized what was about to happen but couldn't move fast enough to escape the deluge that rained down on him. He jerked back from the drenching shower and muttered a curse. "Stupid dog!"

"Gio. Language," Stella gently chastised him.

"Swear jar!" Harper pointed out immediately before bouncing over the rippling wake of the dog's diving entry and paddling her way around the dock, holding on to a boogie board.

"Shut up!"

"Gio Williams!" Stella was in full-on mom mode now, nipping the boy's burst of temper in the bud. She pulled away from Joe and pointed up to the deck and patio. "Five minutes of time-out on the picnic table. Then you're going to apologize to Harper and help Joe with whatever work he needs done on the boathouse." She waved him over as he peeled off his life jacket. She held out her hand when he would have tossed it to the ground, and he looped the jacket over her arm instead. Before he could stomp his way up the hill, she blocked his path. "We talked about how much Jasper likes the water. He's a giant dog, and anyone who's around him is going to get wet. Those are just the facts of life around here. If you're not into that, fine. You can stay inside the fence and play on the swing set." She waited for him to nod that he remembered before she continued. "Besides, you aren't hurt, and you aren't any wetter now than you were when you were swimming. As for telling Harper to shut up? That was mean, and you probably hurt her feelings."

The eleven-year-old shrugged one shoulder at a time. "She talks too much."

"Yes, she does have a lot to say sometimes. But we support her and we're nice to her anyway because she's part of this family, and that's what we do in this house. We don't tear each other down. We build each other up and help each other out." It was Stella's turn to shrug. "You lose your temper easily, which can be scary, especially to someone little like Ana, or Colby, whose dad was really scary. *You're* still part of our family. We still include you and support you, even though you have that temper. Now, you think about that while you're sitting at the picnic table by yourself. You think about your actions and whether you're helping this family or hurting it."

Already processing her words and starting to calm his energy—if not relax the frown on his face—Gio nodded. He took a couple of steps up the hill, then turned. "Does Harper have to keep telling me every time I break one of the rules? It's annoying."

"I'll have a talk with her, too. I'll see if I can help her find a quieter way to support you." Stella hugged the life jacket to her chest. "Now. Five minutes."

"'Kay."

As he trudged up the hill and plopped down on the side of the picnic table, Stella set the life jacket in the bright yellow kayak they'd carried out onto the shore while she'd gone through the interior of the boathouse. Although the place had been ransacked, the kayaks knocked off their hooks on the wall, and the rowboat flipped off the sawhorses where it had been stored, Stella thought that only her binoculars and a fishing reel that had belonged to her father had been stolen. Nothing major, but certainly easy for a thief to grab and worth a few dollars at a pawnshop. Joe had written up a report, and she'd inform her insurance company tomorrow about the stolen items.

Tyrell jumped up to make sure Gio was all right, and she quickly calmed the boy's concern and sent him back to where Colby had pulled out all of Joe's wrenches and was lining them up by size on the concrete. She did a quick check on the girls, too, to find Ana making mud pies at the edge of the water and Jasper, with the orange floaty clutched in his jowls, willingly letting Harper hold on to his collar as he swam them both to shore. The girl blabbered on about lake water and the various life forms living in it every stroke of the way.

"Chaos." Stella mouthed the word and grinned as she

rejoined Joe, prompting him to close the distance between them and plant a firm, quick kiss on that grin. "What was that for?"

"That was a master class in gentle discipline—explaining to Gio what he did wrong and why it was wrong. Subtly teaching him about family and that he's not on his own against whatever is eating at him. Making the consequences fit the crime." Joe crossed his arms over his chest and slanted a glance at her, sharing his observations. "Is the time-out really a punishment? Or are you giving him five minutes to cool off and take a break from Harper?"

"Oh, great." She pinched her lips in an exaggerated pout. "You're on to me. Don't tell the kids I'm a softy, or I'll never get them to mind me."

"Your secret's safe with me. But seriously…" He dropped his voice to a whisper. "There *are* quiet times, right?"

"Occasionally." Stella cupped the side of his jaw in her hand. "For instance, after all this time outdoors, they're going to sleep really well tonight."

"Yeah?"

She leaned in and nipped his earlobe. A trail of goose bumps tickled down his neck before she whispered, "I'll meet you on the sofa tonight after the kids are in bed. We'll see if last night's make-out session was a fluke."

"Woman…"

Joe scolded her for teasing him like that, and he pulled away before he embarrassed himself by getting aroused in front of the kids. He loved that she wasn't shy about voicing what she wanted, but it played hell on his libido when he needed to be in mentor mode right now.

His sexy maternal goddess strolled away to check on the girls and the dog, but she looked back over her shoulder and very practically stated, "I'll send Gio to the boathouse when the five minutes are up."

His.

Yeah. Too soon, perhaps. But that didn't mean the feeling wasn't there, and that his desire to claim Stella Smith and be a part of her life wasn't real. He'd never believed those insta-love stories, but getting to know Stella over the past week, and spending time with her and her kids this weekend, felt more like reuniting with a lost love, like recapturing what should have been all along, rather than dating someone new. Although, he wasn't sure that an afternoon with five kids and a giant dog in tow qualified as a date.

Still, he wasn't taking the speed at which this was happening lightly—they were both grown people, not impulsive new adults or randy teenagers. Their response to each other physically was too incendiary to be anything but real. And he believed the feelings were real, too. They were deep and permanent kinds of feelings of trust and respect, of tenderness and excitement, and...love.

Joe paused and inhaled a deep breath at the revelation. Stella might not be at the same place in their relationship yet. But Mr. Thorough, Set in His Ways, By-the-Book Bachelor Cop was falling in love.

And nothing in his fifty years had ever felt so right.

More than comfortable with that admission, Joe nodded. Then he turned his focus to the boathouse to teach Colby and Tyrell about the different tools and what they were used for.

His purchases from the hardware store included several pairs of safety glasses, along with a new disc lock that would be nearly impossible for bolt cutters to get through, and a new steel hasp. Nearly an hour later, he and the three boys all had their shirts off in deference to the late-afternoon heat, and all sported their glasses like a team of nerdy superheroes. They'd glued together a crack in the exterior where the lock had been forced, then installed a block of wood behind the locking mechanism so they could use longer screws to attach the hasp more securely.

Colby, especially, had caught on quickly, and seemed to enjoy learning how to build and repair things. Tyrell was a true seven-year-old with a short attention span and was currently more interested in piling up the screwdrivers and removing them one by one like a game of pick-up sticks. Gio had acted like he was too good for manual labor at first. But when he saw how much fun the other boys were having, he didn't want to be left out. Some of his questions were surprisingly insightful and a tad disheartening. He'd wanted to know if the lock on any door could be upgraded and reinforced like this. Together, the four of them brainstormed ways to make different types of doors more secure—from installing an alligator pit on one side to the benefits of a steel or hardwood door over a hollow door.

Just like he might during a police interrogation when he needed to get a suspect talking, Joe asked a question here and there, and added enough information to keep the conversation going. But as time went on, he said less and less, and let Colby and the Williams brothers get better acquainted. Maybe he could also learn more about the Vaughn character who had Gio and Tyrell so terrified by just letting them talk.

He heard Stella call the girls out of the water to towel off and put shorts and a T-shirt on over their suits before they got sunburned. Then the girls teamed up with their already damp towels to try to dry off Jasper. Panting, the dog stood patiently, his tongue lolling out the side of his mouth, his eyes at half-mast. He was probably worn out from all the swimming and retrieving, and the brief training review Stella had done with him, but he was enjoying the girls' attention. Stella mentioned going into the house to change and bring out the hamburgers for the grill as soon as everyone had finished their jobs and put the girls to work collecting toys and putting them away in the boathouse. Joe promised the boys would have on dry clothes and be ready to eat when it was time.

When Colby drilled in the first screw that locked the hasp in place, Tyrell popped up from his pile of tools. "Can I do it?"

Gio nudged his brother aside. "It's my turn."

Tyrell nudged right back. "You already did one."

"Uh-uh. No horseplay around the power tools, boys. It's too easy for someone to get hurt." Joe quickly played peacemaker and put the drill into Gio's hands. "There are three more screws. You can each put one in. Just like I showed you. Then it'll be time to clean up. We can't leave the hammer and screwdrivers outside where they'll get wet and rust."

With the boys lined up to finish the installation, Joe knelt and started putting away the tools himself. He had no idea what kind of information he was about to hear as the boys continued with their casual conversation.

"My dad hit me with a hammer once," Colby announced without any fanfare. "Broke three of my fingers."

Oh, hell no. The child did not just say that. Joe's fist tightened around the hammer he held. Should he report that to Stella? Or did she already know gruesome, tragic facts like that about her kids?

Gio took the information in stride before drilling in his screw and handing the power tool off to Tyrell. "That sucks."

"Yeah. I went to the hospital for that one. Dad told them I shut my hand in the car door. I've got steel pins inside me now. If I ever get to fly on an airplane, I'll set off the alarm at the airport."

"Sweet."

"Really?"

While Colby and the others seemed to think setting off metal detectors was a cool consequence of what must have been a heinous injury, Joe wanted to track down Colby's father and beat the snot out of him for hurting this sweet, gentle boy. As a cop, he knew that wasn't legal, but the man in him was sorely tempted to risk it. Maybe he should re-think Tyrell's idea about the alligator pit and build one to encircle the entire property to keep Stella and the children safe behind it.

"Did you get a cast?" Gio asked.

"Yeah. From here to here." Colby pointed out the tips of his fingers to the middle of his forearm where the cast had been. "I had some friends at my old school who signed it."

The resilience of these boys awed Joe. But still, they shouldn't even know about the violent stuff he'd worked years on to stop, much less have firsthand experience with it. How did Stella process information like this and still be so patient with the children? And smile so beautifully while she did so? He had a feeling he'd be at the gym, punching the heavy bag every night.

"Can I sign it?" Tyrell asked.

"He's not wearing it now, doofus," Gio chided.

Joe's hands were still clenched in fists in anger as Colby stuck up for Tyrell. "If I was still wearing it, you could sign it, Tyrell. You're my friend." He was a little more hesitant when he added, "You could sign it, too, Gio."

"Whatever."

Colby's overture of friendship got shot down, so he clammed up and knelt across from Joe to help put away the tools. But Tyrell seemed almost empathic about what people were thinking or feeling around him. He drew Colby back into the conversation. "We don't have a dad," Tyrell added, finishing up the screw Gio had started for him. "So, I've never been hit by a hammer."

"That's good." Colby waggled his eyebrows. "It hurts a lot."

"Did you cry?" Tyrell asked, handing the drill back to his brother.

"Yeah."

Joe's nostrils flared as he inhaled deeply and pushed to his feet, fighting to calm his temper. "Dads don't hit their kids with hammers. Nobody should hit anyone with a hammer. Got that? Tools are to work with, to make building and fixing things easier—not to ever use against another person."

"Why did your dad hit you?" Tyrell asked, as if Joe hadn't spoken.

"He was drunk and said I was too loud. I don't think he likes me."

Gio, sounding far too familiar with the evils of the world, nodded. "When you leave foster care, will you have to go back and live with him?"

Colby shook his head. "I'm never going back. He's in prison. The judge said he'll die there." So, his father had committed a capital crime of some kind, in addition to hurting Colby. Unless his abuse had killed someone? Colby never mentioned his mother. But there were lots of ways a mean drunk could get himself into trouble with the law. Joe filed the information away to look up later. Stella might give these boys a home, but he was going to make sure they never had to deal with that kind of violence again.

Tyrell shrugged. "I love my mom, but I don't want to live there, either. She sleeps a lot when she's home and doesn't always remember to feed us. Gio said she used to be nice, but I don't remember. When Vaughn's around, she gets mean. He's mean, too. Remember when he picked you up by your neck?"

"Shut up, Ty," Gio scolded. "We're not supposed to talk about Vaughn. Remember? He'll…"

"He'll what?" Joe asked when the boy hesitated. He was

more certain than ever that this Vaughn had threatened the boys. But the details were still too sketchy to act on. "What will Vaughn do to you?"

Chapter Nine

Gio caught Joe's focused gaze on him and handed the drill off to Colby before shutting down and turning away. "Never mind."

That boy was spooked by something. He was trying to handle the threat all on his own and protect Tyrell in the process. Joe's instinct to hug the tension from Gio's shoulders was as unexpected as the desire to shake some answers out of the boy. But he couldn't afford to act on those feelings right now. This was the information he'd been hunting for since meeting the boys at the Fourth Precinct. And if Gio wouldn't talk, maybe he could catch his younger brother off guard and learn something from him.

"Is Vaughn your mom's boyfriend?" Joe asked, handing Tyrell the hammer to put away in the bottom of the toolbox.

"I guess. He sells her drugs, and she helps him with… his business."

Joe had a pretty good idea what that business might be, though he hated that this sweet little boy had any idea about drugs and the *business* of making enough money to pay for those drugs. "Your mom is Toy Williams? And Vaughn is…?"

Maybe because he'd asked it so nonchalantly, and Tyrell was

distracted by the tools, the boy answered without thinking. "Vaughn Trask. His friends are mean, too. One time they—"

"Tyrell!" Gio's warning silenced his brother.

But Joe had already heard enough to go to work. "That's all right, boys. I won't push. But I do want you to know that you can tell me anything. I won't judge you. I won't arrest you. I want to help. I don't mean to make things more difficult for you. And if you're still not comfortable talking with me, then talk to Stella. She has your best interests at heart."

Gio did that one-shoulder-at-a-time shrug again. "Then she'll just tell you."

"If she or any of you children are in danger, I hope she does. Otherwise, I'm sure she'll keep your confidence."

"Whatever."

Taking his cue from his big brother, Tyrell also shrugged and focused on putting the tools away. "Yeah. Whatever."

Their responses were disappointing, but Joe was all right with that. Gio had just confirmed that there *was* something to tell. They weren't friends yet, but they'd taken a step toward trusting him—at least, a little. Now he could find out everything about Mom's boyfriend-dealer-pimp and make sure he could keep the boys safe. He could even loop in some of his friends from the vice squad to get real-time info on where Trask was right now, and all the ways he could be a threat to Gio and Tyrell. If the boys could speak to the man's illegal activities, that would certainly put them on the criminal's radar as a potential enemy. And it would explain their reluctance to talk to a cop. No doubt Vaughn Trask, or maybe even their own mother, had promised retribution if the boys talked about them to the police. Maybe Stella would have better luck getting them to open up. But for now, his new experiences with family time this weekend had just morphed into a full-blown protection detail.

But before he could pull out his phone and type in the

name, Harper pulled away from Stella and came running toward him. "Joe?" She was slightly breathless as she pushed her glasses up on her nose and tilted her head back to look up at him. "Can girls shake hands, too?"

"Excuse me?"

"You said shaking hands is what men do when they meet each other. I want to shake hands, too."

"Of course girls can. If they want." He paused a moment to pull his T-shirt back on and tuck his phone into his jeans, trying to calm himself. He'd vowed to protect Stella and these children from any threat, even if that threat was a grown-up dismissing this bright girl's curiosity. A rejection from him right now could do more harm than postponing his deep dive for intel on Vaughn Trask and Toy Williams. "A lot of women in business do that. Men or women meeting for the first time might shake hands. Sometimes, they give each other a hug. If they're good friends. But some women don't like to get their clothes wrinkled or mess up their hair or makeup..." He lifted his gaze to include Colby and the Williams brothers. "And a guy shouldn't touch her unless she specifically wants him to." Harper was absorbing every word he said, so he tried to choose his words wisely. "You have to get to know someone, so you know how they like to greet or be greeted. I mean, guys usually go for the handshake because we don't like to get into a lot of mushy stuff—"

"Except with their girlfriend."

He looked beyond the girl to Stella, who had an amused smile on her face as he navigated the tricky waters of explaining boy-girl rules to Harper. He really wondered where she was going with this. "Yeah, if they have a girlfriend, they'll hug her or kiss her cheek."

"Stella is your girlfriend," Harper pointed out, with a logical tone that sounded much older than her ten years. "You kissed her before we ate breakfast. And you kissed her a little while ago, on the mouth. That means she's your girlfriend."

This time, when Joe met Stella's gaze, her cheeks blushed a shade of pink that had nothing to do with the touch of sunburn she had. She quickly turned away to pull shorts on over her swimsuit and add her towel to the impossible task of drying off Jasper.

Yes, he'd kissed Stella before breakfast. Then, when the kids had run upstairs to change into their swim trunks and bathing suits, he'd backed her up against the kitchen sink and kissed her again. Kissed her until they were both breathing hard and gasping for air. After that make-out session on the couch last night, he knew he'd never get enough of kissing Stella Smith. She made him hungry and feverish, and his body reacted to hers like he was twenty years younger. He'd slept for four hours straight with Stella in his arms, and he'd felt better rested and more excited to start a new day than he had in years.

He wasn't sure he could define the connection he felt to that woman. He wasn't sure he wanted to. Joe just wanted to be in her world—to talk to, to kiss, to share mundane tasks with, to claim as his own if she would give him that right.

But that wasn't his right. Not yet. So, he dropped his gaze back down to Harper's green eyes. "Sometimes, there are people who are shy or who aren't comfortable touching others. And there are some people who don't want to be touched at all."

"Like people who've been touched in bad ways?" Gio asked, reminding Joe that all the children were listening to the conversation.

"Right." Joe cringed at the implication. What did Gio know about that? Was that why they were so afraid of Vaughn Trask?

Stella was on her feet again, her eyes narrowed as she, too, listened in.

But Harper was nothing if not persistent. "So, if you like someone, and they're your friend or your mom's boyfriend, girls can shake your hand, too?"

Joe swallowed the urge to grin. Now he got it. This whole conversation had been about one thing. "Do you want to shake my hand?"

"Yes."

He let the grin out and extended his hand to the girl. "Hi. I'm Joe. Nice to meet you."

She squeezed his hand and shook it vigorously. "I'm Harper Klein. I think I'm going to be the kind of girl you can hug once we get to know each other better."

Joe nodded. "I'll keep that in mind. Thanks for letting me know."

And…the conversation was done. She pushed her glasses up on her nose and ran over to her foster sister. "Ana! Stella was right. Girls can shake hands, too."

The younger girl ran over and stuck her hand out without saying anything.

Joe gently took her tiny hand in his. "Nice to see you, Ana."

The little girl beamed from ear to ear and then ran back to the lakeshore to pick up her towel and traipse up the hill behind Harper.

"Joe?" Stella patted Jasper's flank, perhaps using the dog's presence to keep the concern stamped on her face from revealing itself in her tone when she whispered, "Is everything okay? Did the boys say what's wrong?"

He closed the distance between them—first, to keep the children from overhearing, but more so to tuck a damp strand of lavender hair behind her ear and to cup her warm cheek and jaw. After listening to the boys talk, he needed the contact with her to settle the need to take action inside him. "Nothing concrete yet. I've got some more info on the boys I want to follow up on."

She reached up to cover his hand with hers. "Do I need to be concerned?"

"Let me find out what I can first. Then we'll talk."

"Promise?"

"Of course. They're your children—"

Jasper barked, startling them both. It was a single thundering alarm before the big dog charged up the hill, beating the girls to the patio and scratching at the back door. Joe had never heard the dog agitated like that before. "What's he going on about?"

She clutched his hand between both of hers and pulled it down between them. "He must hear Sophie inside. Maybe she decided to join us."

"I don't think that sounds like a friendly greeting." Instinctively, Joe moved between Stella and the door as it opened. "What the…?"

Sophie came out the back door, her sweats, high ponytail and weary eyes making her look like the young woman studying for a big test she was. "Stella? You have a visitor. He says he's an old friend."

A dark-haired man, wearing a wrinkled tan suit with no tie, pushed his way out the door beside her. Jasper must have heard a car door or the doorbell or even unfamiliar footsteps in the house. He plopped down on his haunches in front of the man and woofed again, identifying the stranger on his turf.

Judging by the way Stella's nails dug into the palm of his hand, though, their visitor was no stranger to her. "Preston Alan Jeffries the Third, I take it?"

"Stella, call off your dog," the man yelled. It wasn't that

Jasper was threatening him per se, he was just a big enough dog that he simply blocked his path.

"Right on the first guess," Stella whispered. "Times like this, I wish Jasper wasn't such a gentle giant."

"I'm not gentle," Joe assured her.

But before he could march up the hill and introduce himself and his badge and toss the guy out, Stella tugged him back to her side. "I've got this. Let me handle him. I need to do this."

"Okay." It killed Joe not to help her get rid of this jerk. Especially after hearing the boys talk about the horrible ways they'd been hurt or intimidated, he was antsy to take down any threat. But her shoulders were set, and her eyes had darkened like steel. She'd asked for backup, not a champion to fight her battles for her. He squeezed her hand. "I'm right here if you need me."

She squeezed back before releasing him and heading up the hill. "Girls, wait." Ana stopped and turned immediately. "Sophie, would you please take the girls inside and get them changed for dinner?"

"Sure." She scooped Ana up. "I'm sorry if I shouldn't have let him in. I had my earbuds in, and when the doorbell finally registered, I just automatically ran downstairs—"

"Not to worry. I've got this."

Sophie headed to the door with Ana in her arms, but Harper was too caught up in her newfound discovery. She nudged Jasper aside and stuck her hand out to their unwelcome visitor. "Hi, I'm Harper."

"What?" With the dog out of his path, Trey dodged to one side and strode right past Harper. "Stella. We need to talk."

Harper dashed in front of him again. A little less sure, but always determined. "Girls can shake hands, too."

"Get the hell out of my way, kid," he snapped at her.

"Swear jar. We don't get to say words like that—"

"Shut up. I'm not here for you."

"Trey!" Stella slid a protective arm around Harper and pulled the girl against her. "You don't talk to any of my kids like that. You shouldn't even be talking to *me*."

Harper's lips quivered, but her arm was still outstretched. "You don't want to shake my hand?"

"No! I don't want to shake your damn hand." He swatted her hand away. "Stella? I'm tired of you ignoring my calls. Let's be adults about this. Can we talk? Privately?"

Joe was moving the moment he touched Harper. The other man flinched at his approach, but Stella hit him with a sideways glance, warning Joe back.

Stella jammed her finger in the middle of the Troll's chest. "How dare you touch my child like that?"

"They're not your kids. They're a do-gooder project you took on because you couldn't get babies of your own and you lost me."

Harper, in tears, spotted Joe and ran straight toward him. He scooped her up in his arms and hugged her to his chest. Even if he knew nothing about Trey Jeffries's harassment of Stella, the man was on his hit list for making Harper cry. The boys gathered around him while Stella talked to Trey. Or rather, endured the man's diatribe.

Gio whispered from Joe's side. "He's a bad man, Harper. You can tell by his eyes. He doesn't care about anybody but himself."

"You got that right, G." It was very astute for a child to know what Joe hadn't learned until he'd joined the military and had been in his first firefight. It said a lot, too, that Gio knew an enemy when he saw one. He wasn't surprised to see that Gio had pulled Tyrell behind him, always conscious of protecting his brother from a perceived threat. Without thinking, Joe reached out with his free hand and rested it on Gio's shoulder.

In that moment, when the boy didn't pull away, Joe realized that he wasn't just falling in love with Stella Smith. These children were starting to mean the world to him, too.

Courtesy of his brave, beautiful Stella, there was some fire and brimstone raining down on Trey, not that the other man seemed aware of it. "You're not welcome here. If I don't want to talk to you on the phone, then I certainly don't want to talk to you in person. You are not a part of my life anymore. I owe you nothing."

"But you love me," Trey argued.

"Ego much? I don't love you. I haven't for years." It wasn't lost on Joe how Stella angled her body to keep Trey from seeing and interacting with the children. He was also relieved to see Jasper sitting right beside her, with her fingers curled around his collar. "I've come to realize it was the idea of being in love and feeling loved that I fell for, not you. I tried to help you once, and you didn't want what I was offering. I have nothing else for you."

"Come on, do-gooder. I need a break. Where am I supposed to get the money I need to support three ex-wives?"

"Grow up? Get a job? Be a better husband, so they stop leaving you? It's not my problem." She stroked Jasper's head, as if taking strength from the stoic dog. "Now please leave. You're intruding on our family time and upsetting my children."

"You and I used to be able to talk about anything, Stella." Trey's demeanor changed and his words took on a wistful tone, as if he thought a gentler approach would get him what he wanted better than anger and frustration could. "You would always hear me out. You listened."

For a split second, Joe worried that the change in tactics might work. But she reached back to him instead. "And now Joe will escort you off my property."

"Hold her hand." He didn't give the order to anybody in

particular, but it was Colby who reached for Harper's hand when he set her down. Joe was at Stella's side in three steps. "Just waiting for you to give me the okay."

Trey propped his hands at his hips and shook his head. "I saw him parked out front last night. I get it now. Mr. Muscle is the guard dog."

"It's worse than that, Trey." Stella's snarky tone did funny things to Joe's insides, even as it confused their guest. She wound her arm around Joe's waist. "He's the boyfriend."

Joe wrapped his arm around her shoulders and pulled her close enough to press a kiss to her temple before releasing her and gesturing to the side of the house. "After you, Jeffries. We'll go through the gate. No need to have you in the house again."

Trey tried to get around him to plead his case, but Joe wasn't going to allow that. "If you won't consider rekindling what we once had, what about that job at your charity? You know I can run a business. I need money, the kind of money you have."

"My charities are about children and animals, Trey. I don't think you'd be a good fit." If words were bullets, Stella had just zinged this loser with the skill of a sniper.

Joe couldn't be prouder, more turned on, more eager to get this menace away from this makeshift family. "We're done talking, Stell. It's my turn. Get the kids changed and fire up the grill. I'll make sure Mr. Jeffries finds his way out."

There were no goodbyes. No waving, certainly no shaking of hands. Joe clamped his hand over Trey's upper arm and quick-marched him through the gate and around to his car, parked in the driveway behind Joe's SUV.

Although Trey struggled against Joe's grip, he was no match for his superior strength—or his determination to rid this Troll from Stella's life. When they reached the white luxury sedan, Joe finally released him—only to spin him around and back him up against the fender of his car. "If you ever talk to one of those children like that again, or disrespect Stella, you're going to answer to me."

"Get off me, man." Trey shoved, but Joe didn't budge. That was when the taller man tried to lean over Joe and threaten him. "I'm suing you for assault, Shorty."

"After you smacked that little girl and threatened Stella? I don't think so." When Trey started to protest, Joe grabbed him by his silk lapels and bent him back over the hood of the car. "Once I serve you with the restraining order, I never want to see your face around this family again. Do you understand?"

"I have rights, you know. Stella and I are old friends. I can talk to her."

Joe got in the guy's face. "Did you mean yes?"

"Yeah." Trey raised his hands in surrender. "I mean yes. I'll follow the restraining order. Let go of me, already."

Joe hauled him upright and opened the car door. "If I find out you're parked on the street here or over at the neighbors' house again, I'll arrest you for trespassing and vandalism."

Trey braced his arms on the top of the door and the roof of the car, looking genuinely perplexed by Joe's words. "The neighbors' house? What are you talking about?"

"Where were you when you were spying in Stella's window last night?"

"Not in their house. People were home."

"What did their car look like?"

"Why should I tell you?"

Without a word, Joe dug his badge out of his pocket and held it in Trey's face. "This gives me the right to ask questions."

Trey cursed and finally took his hissy fit down a notch. "Just my luck. She's dating a cop now. Are you going to arrest me?"

"You going to answer my question?"

"Um, a dark sedan? Four doors?"

"You get a make or license plate?" Joe pressed.

"Missouri?" Trey shrugged. "Cars aren't my thing."

Only pricey ones like the one he was hiding behind. He could sell it and make enough money to get on his financial feet again if he got off his lazy, self-centered butt and made the sacrifice.

But Joe wasn't going to offer any helpful suggestions. "Did you cut the screen on the Roes' back porch and try to break in?"

"Who are the Roes?"

"The neighbors."

"I'm not going to break into a house when people are home." Trey shook his head and corrected his statement. "I'm not going to break in, period. The last thing I wanted was for anyone to see me when I walked down to their dock with my binoculars." Joe wanted to doubt every word out of this guy's mouth. But there seemed to be something genuine about his ignorance. "Honest. You ought to be harassing whoever went into Stella's boathouse and stole stuff."

"That wasn't you?"

"No. Hawking a few items isn't going to get me the kind of money I need." He opened the door a little wider, giving himself enough room to climb in behind the wheel. "You're not pinning anything else on me. I've got enough alimony and legal fees to take care of. Just let me go. I promise I'll leave Stella alone."

Joe held the door open. "You think I'm going to trust that promise?"

"I don't care what you do, man. She's yours if you want her. But I warn you, she's more trouble than she's worth." He had the audacity to grin as if he was sharing a man-to-man secret. "Of course, you probably already know what she's worth."

Joe's hand fisted around the door's open window. "Leave. Now."

"Am I lying?" Trey taunted. Then he cursed when he finally read the anger vibrating through Joe. "She was a mistake twenty years ago, and she's a mistake now. Just leave me alone." Trey started the engine.

Joe stepped away as the other man backed out of the driveway. He wasn't buckled in or driving the speed limit, but Joe wasn't inclined to stop him. Even hearing him insult Stella just now, Joe knew that keeping his distance was probably the only way to keep his fist out of Trey's mouth.

He scrubbed his palm over the weekend stubble furring his jaw. Something was off here—something more off than an ex-fiancé jerk who thought stalking was an easier way to make money than knuckling down and working.

Joe followed the white car to the end of the driveway and surveyed the neighborhood. The huge lots separated by pines and deciduous trees that were greening up didn't offer a clear view from one house to the next, but there was little traffic, and nothing seemed out of place.

That was when it hit him. He'd walked right past it.

Or rather, he'd walked right past something that should have been there but wasn't.

An oil stain.

Joe turned and studied the concrete behind his truck. There was dirt and fine gravel, but Trey's car hadn't been leaking oil like the pool he'd spotted in the driveway at the Roes' house last night. Someone else had been there. Someone with a leaky car who'd made Trey think the house had been occupied. But if the Roes were traveling, then who had been at the house?

Jeffries could be the consummate liar, but Joe read desperation and impulsiveness in him, not the calculating watch-fulness of someone trying to take over a house that was empty for the weekend. Did Jeffries have a partner? Although Stella's ex didn't seem the type to play well with others, he did seem smart—and a smart man would probably hire someone who would be less detectable than himself to spy on Stella.

Someone besides Preston Alan Jeffries III had gotten way too close to Stella and the kids last night. What the hell was going on here?

Not that he was ready to take the man at his word. But if Jeffries hadn't vandalized the neighbors' place and broken into Stella's boathouse, then who did?

Chapter Ten

We're a family. We don't tear each other down. We build each other up and help each other out.

Gio made it all the way to Friday without getting into trouble or drawing attention to himself at Lakeside Elementary, where all of Stella's foster kids—except for Ana and Sophie, of course—went to school. But he was going to have to step up and risk getting into trouble now because Stella's dorky words kept playing over and over in his head as he sat in the back of fifth-grade math class and worked on the lengthy assignment the substitute teacher had given them.

The sub had assigned them partners since she claimed she didn't get the math they were doing and had said that as long as they were fairly quiet, they could work together with their table partner and help each other. As the new kid, Gio had been the odd man out. So, he sat at a table in the back by himself, kept his head down and pretended that all the problems made sense to him.

But the class wasn't being very quiet.

The sub was reading a book at the front desk and didn't seem to notice the talking and how some of his classmates had already switched seats to be with their friends.

And Derrien Johnson kept punching Harper in the shoulder every time he walked by her table to sharpen his pencil, or get a cord for his laptop, or ask the teacher for permission to go to the bathroom.

The teacher looked up every now and then, but either that was a really good book, or her eyes and ears were older than she looked. Even with Harper and Derrien seated at a table in the front of the room, she hadn't seen Derrien picking on Harper. In the week he'd been here, Gio had already sized up the kids and knew Derrien thought he was king of the hill at Lakeside. He was paying attention to when he could attack Harper, and he seemed to have a knack for not getting caught. Now he was out in the hallway, taking way too long to go to the bathroom, and probably thinking up some other way to torture Harper or some other kid who wouldn't stand up to him.

The first time he'd hit her, Harper had looked shocked that her table partner would rather pick on her than work on their math problems together. She glanced to the teacher for help, but since she hadn't cried out, the sub hadn't noticed the incident.

As mouthy and annoying as his foster sister could be, in this class, where she had to work with fifth graders because she was smarter than her own classmates, Harper was dead quiet. Her shoulders were hunched, and he thought she was crying, because her glasses were all steamed up.

Are you helping this family? Or hurting it?

Gio didn't trust his new family. Didn't trust Stella not to give him back and keep Tyrell. Didn't trust Joe—who wasn't part of the family, but who seemed to be at the house a lot—not to report him to the police if he lost his temper and hit someone again. Although, he did think that Joe might be able to stand up to Vaughn. He was strong. He didn't put up with stuff. He noticed everything. And he had a gun. One-on-one, anyway, Stella's boyfriend could take him. But if Vaughn cheated and had some of his friends with him, then it wouldn't be a fair fight. Joe would get hurt, and Stella would cry. Probably the girls, too. Then they'd probably take him away for letting that happen, for bringing Vaughn Trask and his mom into their lives. And Tyrell would be alone to face off against Vaughn and their mom.

Gio's stomach hurt. He'd had a hard time keeping his food down this past week, and it wasn't because Stella wasn't a good cook, or she forgot to feed him. Families were complicated. And as much as he'd always wanted one who would take care of him instead of him taking care of them, he sure didn't understand them. Or trust them.

At last, Derrien strolled back into the room. The substitute greeted him and watched him walk back to his table before returning to her book. When he was certain the teacher wasn't watching, Derrien punched Harper's arm in the same place he had before. Harper bent over her paper and whimpered. Three girls, who were sitting at the same table together on the other side of the room, even though the teacher had said they were supposed to work with partners, giggled. They shut up when the teacher glared at them. But then they were drawing pictures and making fun of Harper behind her back, and Derrien was eating up all the attention.

Gio was going to have to do something. And since he was the last person who would rat someone out to a teacher, he scooped up his laptop, papers and book bag and stood.

Looping the book bag over his shoulder and hugging everything else in his left arm to keep at least one hand free, he walked up to the boy sitting at Harper's table. "Move." Derrien smirked when he looked up at him. But when he didn't immediately get out of the chair, Gio channeled Joe's authoritative tone and said, "Move. Now. Go sit with your jerk friends. I'm sitting here."

The substitute teacher finally set her book down and studied the three of them. "Gio, what's going on?"

He'd learned to lie pretty well over the years by watching his mom. Blend in a little bit of truth and talk like you mean what you're saying. "I don't understand everything on the assignment, and Harper's a good teacher. You said you didn't get it, either, so I thought she could help me."

She considered his explanation for a moment, then smiled. "That's a good idea. Are you okay with that, Harper?"

Harper never looked up, but she nodded.

"All right, then. You boys can switch. Derrien, you sit in the back."

"You want to sit with the four-eyed butterball?" Derrien whispered as he pushed to his feet. When Gio pulled his shoulders back and looked him straight in the eye, the other boy shrugged as if picking on Harper wasn't entertaining for him anymore—rather than being rightfully worried about what Gio might do to him. Because even though it had gotten him tossed from his last foster home, Gio knew how to throw a punch. Derrien wisely brushed past him and headed for the back of the room. "Go for it."

Gio sat and set out his paper and laptop. After a quick look behind him to make sure Derrien was where he was supposed to be, Gio picked up his pencil and whispered to Harper. "Don't cry, Harp," he said. "They like making you cry. Makes them feel like they're somebody, and they're not. Don't let them win." She reached up beneath her glasses to wipe away her tears. "Now, how do we do this?"

She sniffed again and pulled up the collar of her shirt to dry her eyes. "Do you really not understand?"

"We didn't do this stuff at my old school. I can do the measurements. But I don't get adding them all together."

She pushed her glasses up onto her nose and finally looked at him. "You don't add. You multiply to get the volume."

"Multiply what?"

"You have to find the area of the base first. Then you multiply that by the height."

"Can you show me?"

She nodded. Gio's stomach felt a little less like he was going to puke—not because he'd stopped the bully, but because he'd asked the right questions to get Harper to stop crying and focus on something besides how bad she felt. She really was a good teacher, too, because she explained the terms and formulas that had been on the computer lesson in a way he understood. And when she showed him how she found the answers, he picked it up pretty quickly. It was the first time he'd finished his assignment before the end of the class period. And that felt good, too.

When class was over, and the sub lined them up for lunch, Gio scooted Harper out the door, so that she could get back to her fourth-grade class before Derrien or the mean girls could talk to her. In the cafeteria, he saw her sitting with some girls from her own class, and then he lost track of her until close to the end of recess, when she walked up to the ball diamond where he and a bunch of other boys were playing kickball. Since he'd just scored a run, and his team was still at the plate, he was leaning up against the backstop.

Harper seemed hesitant to interrupt in the middle of a game, but when he made eye contact with her, she hurried up to him. "Thanks for helping me with Derrien." She fiddled with the ends of her long, dark blond ponytail. "I just wanted to let you know that I won't be a nuisance and try to hang out with you, so you can still be popular."

He supposed he was making some friends here since he was a pretty good athlete, and they wanted him on their team. But Harper's offer still didn't seem right. "I don't care if you hang out with me."

She wrinkled up her face in a frown. "I'm not good at

kickball. Or any other sports. Except swimming. And we don't have that here at school."

"You can say hi to me if you see me. Work together in class if you want."

She noticed a couple of the other boys looking at them, and she started backing away. "That's okay. I don't want to embarrass you. You need to make your own friends. I can still help you with math at home. If you want."

When she turned to go, he saw the big reddish-purple bruise on her upper arm. "You've got a huge bruise. Stella's gonna notice."

She tried to pull her sleeve down over the mark. "I'll tell her I ran into the door of my locker."

"You shouldn't lie to her."

"You're lying to her. I heard you and Colby talking last night when you were supposed to be asleep."

Gio shrugged. "You weren't asleep, either, if you heard us."

"You said your mom and her boyfriend hurt you. Colby's a good listener. Maybe that's just because he can't read very well, but he's getting better and better, and in the meantime, he pays attention to everything people do or say. Like Joe does. But Stella's a better listener. And she can do something about stuff. Like when she got me into the HAL classes. Or when she helped Ana learn how not to walk on her tippy-toes all the time because she's got failure to thrive. That means she didn't get enough food or taken care of when she was little."

He could tell Harper was feeling better, because she was talking too much again. But he was getting used to annoying Harper. Quiet, crying Harper meant something was really wrong. "My problem's different. Stella can't help me."

"Joe can help, too. He's coming to the house to pick up Stella for a date tonight."

"No!" Now he did move toward her to nudge her farther away from the kickball game, so nobody else could overhear. "I don't want any cops in my business. It'll just make everything worse if he tries to help."

"Don't you like Joe? I think he'd make a good dad."

"Sure. He's okay. But he's still…" Gio's words faded away as he looked through the chain-link fence surrounding the playground and saw a fancy white car pulling up to the curb. The car was different, but he knew the man who saluted him from the back window. He nearly threw up the peanut butter sandwich he'd eaten for lunch.

"He's what?" Harper moved into his line of vision. "What, Gio?"

"Shh." He'd learned his lesson about saying *shut up*. But he really needed Harper to be quiet right now. "Stop talking."

"I'm sorry. Now I'm embarrassing you, aren't I?"

"Harper," he begged. Vaughn Trask climbed out of the back seat of the fancy white car with gold trim. He paused a second to smooth his tie, button his suit jacket and make eye contact with Gio before reaching back inside to take Toy Williams's hand and help her out to the sidewalk beside him. "Mom?" This was bad. What was his mom doing out of jail so soon? What was she doing here with Vaughn? Where did she get that fancy dress? It wasn't the kind she sometimes wore when she went with Vaughn to do some work, but one like a lady might wear to church. A pretty blue dress like Stella might wear. It was like she was playing dress-up.

"That's your mom?" Harper asked, sounding just as surprised as he was. "He's not your dad, is he?"

No. The big white dude who had all the money and a mean streak was definitely not his dad. Vaughn looked right at Gio and crooked his finger in the universal invitation to *come here*. He could tell that Vaughn wasn't asking. That was an order.

"There's my baby." Toy Williams rushed the fence, curling her fingers through the links. She was smiling too big for Gio to trust. "Where's Tyrell, honey?"

This was really bad. The driver, probably one of Vaughn's big, muscled friends, stayed in the car. Gio clenched his hands into fists down at his sides. He knew he was breathing too fast. "Go find Tyrell. Make sure he's okay. That he's with a teacher."

"But the first graders don't have recess with us."

"I don't care. Ask if you can go inside and use the bathroom. Go find him. Right now." He turned to the worried eyes behind her big pink glasses. "Please."

Harper seemed to understand the urgency of the situation, because she was already backing away toward the school building. "I can go to his class, say he forgot his lunch."

Sounded like a good idea. "Go!"

Harper took off running, and Gio started walking toward the fence.

He was surprised to see a shock of red hair out of the corner of his eye as his skinny, freckle-skinned roommate fell into step beside him. Colby was slightly breathless when he asked, "Is he the bad man you talked about last night? The one who hurt you guys?"

"Yeah." Gio stopped and warned Colby to go back to whatever game he'd been playing. "You don't have to come with me."

But Colby fell right back into step with him. "We're a family. We stick together. Just like Stella said. Just like when you helped Harper." Gio frowned at his taller, red-haired foster brother. "Yeah. Everybody's already talking about how you made Derrien back off in math class. He's a jerk. That must have been pretty sweet." Colby nodded toward the couple waiting for them at the fence. "That guy reminds me of my dad. Only my dad never wore a suit and tie. But he still looks mean."

That was the truth. "If you come with me, he'll hurt you, too."

"Then he really reminds me of my dad. Joe said we should always be on the lookout for anything that doesn't feel right. This doesn't feel right, them being here. They should check in at the office, not talk to you through the fence at recess. How'd they find you?"

"I don't know. But I can't let them get Tyrell."

"Why do they want Tyrell?"

"Gio!" His mom urged him to hurry.

"Because then I'll have to do whatever Vaughn says. He'll hurt him if I don't." Nodding as if that explanation made sense to him, Colby followed Gio to the fence. "Hi, Mom."

"Hi, baby." The maternal smile he remembered from when he was little distracted him for a moment, or else he would have seen the wild look in her eyes and guessed her intent. She reached through the fence and snatched his wrist, jerking him off balance until he stumbled toward her and crashed into the fence. "I hear you got money now. All those years I paid for you, now you owe me."

She hadn't paid for much of anything besides drugs. Social services, the Supplemental Nutrition Assistance Program—if his mom didn't sell their food card—and whatever Gio could mooch or steal had taken care of the rest. "You're hurting me."

"I'll do worse if you don't get me what I need."

"You're not my mom anymore. You gave us away, remember? I don't have to do what you say."

"You will do exactly what—"

"Let. Go." Her grip pinched. But he was getting stronger every day he got older. He tugged hard enough that she had to dig her nails in to try to hold on to him, leaving painful scratches on his wrist and hand as he pulled free.

When she thrust her arm out to capture him again, Vaughn grabbed her other arm and twisted it behind her back, pulling her away from the fence and warning her to calm down. "Ow. What are you doing?"

"Back off, Toy," Vaughn hissed in her ear. "You're drawing too much attention. I said you had to play this like a society lady. Like you're somebody who belongs here."

"Gio's my boy. I belong wherever he is, no matter what kind of scratchy dress you make me wear or how much he disrespects me."

"Shut up." He twisted her arm higher and higher behind her back until she whimpered. "I've got a bigger prize in mind for this tough guy. Maybe Raggedy Andy over there wants a piece of the action, too."

Colby didn't say a word. He was probably too scared to talk. But it was nice to have him standing close by. That, and the fence between them, made Gio feel a little braver. "I'm not going to come work for you. I have to finish school and get a job. I have to take care of Tyrell."

Vaughn's eyes narrowed. "Your family owes me a debt. An even bigger one now that I got your mama out of jail. You want to take care of your family? Then you need to step up. Your mom's too old to turn tricks for me."

"Vaughn. I told you I can—"

"Shut up." Toy whimpered as his cruel grip silenced her protest. "One way or another, I intend to get paid. Maybe you won't be so brave and mouthy next time if your friend here, or your little brother, or even that rich lady you're livin' with, gets hurt." Wait. How did he know he was living with Stella? The dangerous man leaned closer. "Because that's what's gonna happen. I'll hurt every one of them, one by one, until you do what I want."

Gio felt his threat like a punch to the gut.

"Gio." Colby tapped his arm, and he looked behind them to see the fifth-grade substitute teacher approaching.

Now she was being observant? Or had Harper reported what was happening? He hadn't thought much of her as a teacher before, but he was really glad to see her approach, to have an adult backing up him and Colby. "I'm sorry. If you want to talk to one of the students, you need to go through the office and get the visit approved."

When Gio faced their visitors again, Vaughn had hooked his mom's arm through the crook of his elbow, and they were both smiling. "This is the boy's mother."

"That's my Gio." Toy's smile seemed like more of an ef-fort than Vaughn's, but her words sounded almost sincere. "I've been away and haven't gotten to see him for a while. I just wanted to know how he was doing at his new school."

Gio cringed at the lie. His mom had never been to one of his schools other than to get him and Tyrell enrolled at the beginning of the school year, and sometimes not even then.

"You haven't seen him...?" Clearly, something about Toy's statement put the sub on alert. She put a hand on Colby's and Gio's shoulders and pulled the boys back to either side of her. "Still, you need to go to the office. We have rules in place to keep the students safe. Besides, it's time to go back to class. Come on, boys. Time to line up. Go on."

They ran back as another teacher blew his whistle and ended up at the back of the fourth-and fifth-grade lines. Harper's line walked past him, and she gave him a thumbs-up. "Ty's okay. I gave him my lunch, so it didn't look like I was lying."

Gio returned the thumbs-up and gave Colby a nod as he, too, walked past him into the school. This was the first time in forever that he didn't feel alone against the troubles of his life. It felt...unfamiliar. But good. Maybe Stella was right, that a family helped each other. That they were stronger together.

But the tightness in his stomach didn't ease when he looked back toward the fence. The teacher was walking toward the building, so she couldn't see, but Gio sure did. Vaughn was staring at him over the roof of the white car. He pointed two fingers to his eyes, then turned his hand to point at Gio.

I'm watching you.

Shivering at the unspoken threat, Gio nudged the student ahead of him to get the line moving faster.

If Vaughn *could* get to Tyrell or Colby or Harper, or little Ana, or Stella, he'd hurt them. He knew he would. Because that was what a man like Vaughn Trask did. He hurt people to get them to do what he wanted. If he had a dad or even a real mom, they'd stand up to Vaughn and make him stop. But the only thing his mom had ever done to protect him and Tyrell from Vaughn Trask was to sign away her parental rights and give them to foster care. Tears welled up, and he angrily swiped them away before anyone could see them. His mom wasn't going to help him. He had to take care of his family himself.

Maybe he could find a regular job, mowing grass or something, to make enough money to pay off his mother's debt.

Or… Stella had money. A lot of it, he thought, judging by the size of the house she lived in, the new clothes she'd gotten him and Tyrell, and the plentiful amount of food she kept in the house. She was nice. Nicer to him than he'd been to her. Maybe he could borrow some money from Stella. Or take it.

Because he didn't want to work for Vaughn Trask. He didn't want to run errands for the man. And he sure didn't want any of Vaughn's friends to touch and hurt him the way they did his mom. He wanted to help his mom get away from the man, but the only thing she seemed to want was drugs.

And the only thing Vaughn seemed to want was money—or Gio, if he couldn't pay him.

He had to figure out how to get that money. And he had to do it before Vaughn hurt Tyrell or his mom, or anyone else in his new family.

Chapter Eleven

Stella rubbed at the headache pounding between her eyes and waited for Joe to pick up the phone. While she usually made a point not to call him during work hours, she knew his shift at KCPD was almost up and that he'd be heading to her house to pick her up just as soon as he'd showered and changed.

She wanted to save him the trouble.

Maybe being with her was too much trouble for any man to take on.

"There's my favorite lady."

The rush of excitement she felt at hearing Joe's deep-pitched greeting faded with a heavy sigh. She shoved her fingers through the hair that had been coiffed for a business meeting earlier today and massaged the back of her skull, remembering Joe's fingers there. "Don't be nice to me."

"You don't want me to be nice to you?"

She pulled out one of the stools at the kitchen island and sat. "No."

"I'm not going to be anything *but* nice to you, sweetheart." She heard the change in his tone. The background noise of the call quieted, and she imagined him moving away from the class or friendly gathering around the coffeepot to find a quiet place to speak. "Has something happened? Are you all right? Did Trey violate the restraining order? Talk to me."

"I don't want you to be nice because it makes me feel guilty."

"Why would me trying to be a good boyfriend make you feel guilty?"

"Because I have to cancel our date. Again." She glanced around at the house that was weirdly subdued for a Friday afternoon. Colby and Tyrell were in the den, playing a video game. Harper was stretched out on a pile of pillows in there with them, wearing headphones and reading. Gio had gone up to his bedroom, saying he needed some quiet time. Ana was in the mudroom with Jasper, doing one of her chores, measuring out kibble and feeding the dog. Oddly enough, the little girl who rarely spoke was the only one talking. She carried on a quiet, one-sided, gibberish-sprinkled conversation with the dog. Jasper sat there patiently, watching every nugget that fell to the floor and bounced away, waiting for Ana to retrieve each bit, piece by piece, to fill his dish. "I'm sorry, Joe."

There was a long pause, the closing of a door, then complete silence on Joe's end of the conversation. "I found out more than I wanted to know about Vaughn Trask. I was hoping to discuss it with you. Actually, I was hoping I could discuss it with Gio and Tyrell, too."

Stella knew Vaughn Trask was a conversation they needed to have. But at this moment she only wanted the hammering in her head and the fear that not all was right in her world to stop. "Can I take a rain check? Tonight's just not a good night."

"You sound tired."

"I am. It's been a long week at work for me, presenting end-of-the-year scholarships and going through the first batch of applications for grants this fall. Board business today. And…"

"And what?"

"It was a tough day at school for the kids. I've gotten emails from two different teachers and a call from the principal."

"That sounds serious. What happened?"

"You don't have to listen to my problems."

"I *want* to listen to your problems. Since I'm not allowed to charge in and save the day, I have to find other ways to support you."

Bless this man. Although it was taking some retraining of his alpha personality, he seemed to really get what she needed. An adult to talk to about personal things. Someone to listen. "Harper got bullied again. She has a bruise the size of Texas on her upper arm. Apparently, Gio stepped in and made the boy stop hitting her."

"Someone hit her?" Joe's pitch dropped to an eerily intense pitch. "Is she okay?"

"As far as I can tell, it's just the bruise. She's sitting with an ice pack on it now. But for Harper, she's subdued."

"Did the boy get suspended? What about Gio? Did he get in trouble? Did the boys fight?"

"No. Actually, I'm proud of him. He handled it without throwing a punch." She had a feeling if Joe was here in person, she'd be trying to placate him to ease the tension she could hear in his voice. Maybe she could do the same even if she couldn't look him in the eye or touch him. "I think something you said about never putting your hands on a girl without her permission stuck."

He inhaled a deep breath, obviously making the effort to cool his protective reaction. "Or something you said about taking care of your family registered with him."

Maybe Gio had needed to hear the message from both

of them. "They suspended the other boy for three days, and Gio's up in his room, sulking."

"You didn't punish him for standing up for her, did you?"

"No, I did not." She pressed her fist against the cool granite countertop. "And I'm ticked off that you would even think that." She rubbed her chilly fingers against her forehead. "Frowning at you makes my head pound."

"Headache?"

"Nothing a solid meal, no stress and about twelve hours of uninterrupted sleep couldn't cure."

"I'm sorry, sweetheart. I'd never doubt your parenting skills. But that's a trigger for me—violence against women. Of any age." She wondered if he quieted his tone out of care for her headache, or if his burst of emotion had passed. "Why is Gio sulking, then? He sounds like the hero in all this."

"That would have to do with the other phone call." He waited for her to explain. "Gio's mother showed up at school today, tried to talk to him at recess, without going through proper security procedures. She's a noncustodial parent. She signed away her rights. Helen told me she'd been arrested. How is she even out of jail?"

She could hear the keys of his computer clicking as he typed. His soft curse wasn't a good sign. "She was bailed out yesterday."

"How? She doesn't have any money."

"Looks like her attorney posted bond for her." How could the woman afford an attorney and bail, but not food for her children? "What did she say to Gio?"

"I don't know. The teacher who reported it interrupted the conversation and sent Gio and Colby back into the building."

"Colby was there, too?"

"That's not the worst of it. The teacher said there was a man with Toy."

Joe swore. "Trask. I bet he's behind the bail money."

"Vaughn Trask got close to my boys? The same Vaughn Trask you were researching for me?"

"Gio didn't say?"

Stella glanced around the house again. The only change was that Jasper was happily eating and Ana was sitting on the floor, watching him. "No. The kids aren't talking to me. I think they've made some pact to cover each other's backsides. I wish I'd heard all this from them, and not the school."

"Maybe they're scared about getting in trouble, and you giving them back to Helen at Family Services."

"I am not giving these kids away to anyone. I hate that phrase." She knew Joe was only trying to help. But treating any child as disposable was *her* trigger. "They're mine, through good times and bad. Until a parent or family member proves themselves capable and reliable and steps up to take them in, I want this family. I love them."

"Have you told them that?"

Stella pushed to her feet, suddenly feeling the need to gather the children in her arms and do just that. "How bad is it that Vaughn and Toy Williams got to Gio today? They were directed to check in at the office, but they never did. It seems like their goal was to corner Gio and talk to him."

"It's bad. He has a history of violence. Dealing drugs. Human trafficking."

"Human trafficking? As in children? The boys' mother?"

"Stell, believe me when I say to you that you do not want Vaughn Trask anywhere near the children. Or you."

The headache pounded through her skull as she shook her head. "And I just got Trey out of our lives."

"Vaughn Trask is a whole different level of evil than your ex."

"I need to put eyes on the kids. Right now." She stepped around Jasper and Ana in the mudroom and made sure the back door was locked. After she paused in the archway to the den to find Harper, Colby and Tyrell all engrossed by their chosen form of entertainment and unaware of her watching them, she crossed through the house and checked the front door, too. Her next catch of breath almost sounded like a sob. "Do you really think he wants to use Gio or Tyrell like that?"

"I didn't mean to upset you."

"No. I'd rather know the truth and be prepared than think everything's hunky-dory and get blindsided. I'm just not sure what I'm supposed to do about it."

"Set the security system. Take an ibuprofen. Check on the kids and then go up to your room and lie down for thirty minutes. Nobody's going to starve in that time period, and you aren't doing them or yourself any favors by not taking care of yourself."

She paused at the bottom of the stairs, anxious to check in on Gio. "Can I call you later? After bedtime? I really hate that we still haven't gotten to go on a date."

"You call me anytime, sweetheart. I'll answer."

I love you was on the tip of her tongue. It felt like the truth, and she wanted to say it. But she couldn't even get a break in the threats and work and the chaos of five kids and a dog to spend one evening alone with this man. How could they build a relationship on that? Maybe she'd better not scare him away by dumping anything else on his plate and changing the routine of his life more than she already had. "Thanks, Joe. I'll talk to you later."

"I'm glad you called me this evening. I'd be upset if I found out you were going through this on your own and you didn't reach out to me."

She headed up the stairs. "I've never had anyone I could reach out to before," she admitted.

"Well, you've got someone now. Later, sweetheart."

She found Gio asleep on the top bunk in his bedroom. Although he hadn't yet opened up to the idea of hugs and handshakes, Stella took advantage of his sleeping and reached through the railing of his bed to brush aside the dreadlocks that hung over his forehead. Her gentle caress confirmed that he had no fever, so she was relieved to discover that he hadn't nodded off because he was sick. But her heart clenched at the idea of how poorly he must be sleeping, or how stressed he must be, for a boy his age to fall asleep from exhaustion. "I'll do everything in my power to keep you safe," she whispered. "I promise." The boy stirred in his sleep, and she pulled her hand away. "I love you, Gio. If you'd let me, I'd love you a whole lot."

Then she stepped out of the room and quietly closed the door.

An hour later, Stella was shuffling around the kitchen after a fitful nap, searching for something fast and nutritious she could fix for their dinner. Thanks to Joe's advice, and perhaps his permission to take a break and relax for a few minutes, her headache had reduced to a dull pulse at the back of her head, and she felt better, if not energized. She set a skillet and a large pot on the stove, and was about to pull out the fast, child-friendly favorite of spaghetti and frozen meatballs with a jarred sauce when Jasper woofed from his bed at the end of the counter. "What is it, boy?"

He got up and trotted to the door a split second before the doorbell rang.

Tensing with alarm, Stella glanced at her watch. Someone was here after seven o'clock? Muttering an unladylike curse, she spun toward the door, the skillet still in hand. "I swear, Trey Jeffries, if that's you, I'm coming after you with this frying pan." As usual, wherever Jasper went, Ana was trailing closely after him. Stella quickly set the skillet down, then pulled up the security app on her phone to identify their visitor as she hurried after the little girl. "Hold up, Ana. Let me get it." Although she recognized the familiar outline of those shoulders, the man's face was partially blocked by what looked like a cardboard cube. "What the…?"

Joe Carpenter stood on her front porch, holding a stack of pizza boxes. He doffed a salute to the camera in her doorbell.

Confusion turned to relief, then to excitement, then back to confusion again as she disarmed the security code, turned the dead bolt and opened the door. "What are you doing here?"

He chuckled. "Hello to you, too."

Oh, what this man did for a T-shirt and jeans. If she wasn't so tired and worried about the kids, she'd be a puddle of hormones right now for this silver fox who'd shown up at her doorstep bearing gifts of the best kind.

A shadow of self-doubt flickered through his eyes. "May I come in?"

He thought she might not want him here? Stella closed her gaping mouth and stepped back to usher him through the door. "Oh, sure. I'm sorry. Please."

He'd barely made it over the threshold before Ana thrust her hand up toward him. Balancing the pizzas on one forearm, he reached down and gently grasped her tiny fingers. "Hi, Miss Ana."

"Joe." She uttered the word as clear as day, and the little girl beamed him a smile. Stella's rusty ovaries perked to life at the sweet scene between man and child. Then, with her fingers clutched in Jasper's fur, Ana clicked her tongue in her version of a *Come* command, and the two trotted off to the den, probably to tell the other children of their visitor.

Joe's smile was more pensive as he straightened. "The boys are going to be falling all over her when she grows up."

"Let's not rush anything, please." She'd already had that thought and wasn't looking forward to the unpredictable girl's teenage years. So, she focused on the strong, steady and reliable man in her life right now. "Let me guess. You're moonlighting as a pizza deliveryman now? It smells delish."

"Heard the kids had a tough day at school, and I understand you wanting to stay home tonight. But I didn't want you to miss out on me treating you to dinner. I chose six different toppings. Hopefully, there's something here that everyone will eat."

"It's pizza, Joe. As long as there's plain cheese in there for Ana, they'll eat it."

"There's plain cheese." He shifted his load to both hands. "All meat. All veg. All cheese. And a couple of combinations in between."

"That's very generous and considerate of you." She pushed the door shut behind him. "I'm sorry I had to cancel and you're stuck here again. It's not that I don't want to go out with you—"

"I'm not mad, Stell. I'm happy to spend the evening here with you and your kids." He shrugged. "If I'd be welcome."

"Of course you're welcome. Get in here." Six pizzas for five children and a woman with no appetite? They'd need his help eating it all. She reached for three of the pizza boxes. "Here, let me help you. We'll set them on the island counter and let everybody go through buffet-style to pick what they want to eat."

He locked the door behind them and followed her to the kitchen. "If you need to spend time alone with them, or they need you—"

"No. I'm glad you're here."

"I can leave the pizza and go."

"Stop trying to leave." She set the pizzas on the island a little harder than she intended. By the time he'd set his boxes down beside hers, she'd turned to Joe. Fisting her hands in the front of his shirt, she drew him in for a big kiss. His firm, warm lips quickly parted and took over, demanding everything she had to give him, and giving her everything she asked of him in return. By the time she was finished kissing him and he'd done more than his fair share of kissing her, she was on tiptoe, her arms winding around his neck and his hands gripping either side of her hips in a possessive grasp. He'd backed her against the counter, where she was stunningly aware of the contrast between the cool granite at her back and the disorienting heat of Joe's hard body plastered against her from her breasts to her thighs. They both were breathing in deep gulps of air that pushed them even closer together with every inhalation. And yes, she was more than aware of that most masculine response to their make-out session pushing the zipper of his jeans against the weeping juncture of her thighs.

"I told you they were boyfriend and girlfriend." Harper's objective, know-it-all voice interrupted the impromptu canoodling, and Stella drew her swollen, kiss-stung lips away from Joe's.

Stella was glad he had a strong grip on her, because she wasn't sure she could stand on her own two feet at the moment. She glanced at the five children gathered in a semicircle behind him. Then she tilted her gaze back to Joe's and whispered, "This is more embarrassing than the dog watching us." But, of course, Jasper was there, too, curiously watching the two grown-ups clinging to each other. "Thank you."

Joe chuckled as he rested his forehead against hers. "All of that was just to say thank you?"

She pulled her fingers from his ticklish short hair and leaned back. "Dinner's late and I don't have to cook and you're wonderful. Thank you. This was very generous and very considerate."

He brushed a strand of hair off her forehead and tucked it behind her ear. "You're welcome." He eased his grip on her waist but didn't let go. "I'm going to need a minute to recover from your thank-you."

It was her turn to laugh. "Okay. We can just stand here and hold each other for a little while."

The kids were blessedly unaware of their passionate response to each other, and quickly filled the kitchen up with their normal brand of chaotic energy.

"Look, it's pizza."

"I told you it was pizza. That's what it says on the side of the boxes."

"I can read that, Harp."

"What kind is it?"

"I love pizza."

"I'm hungry."

"Pizza!"

Stella had no idea which child said what. She was too caught up in the deep green forest of Joe's eyes, and the incendiary memory of his hands and mouth on her.

"Did you bring a go bag?" she whispered.

"I always have it in the car."

"Good. Then you're staying the night." Her cheeks heated with a blush. "If you want."

Joe grinned. "I want."

"You good now?" When he nodded, she raised her voice to direct the children surrounding them. "Everybody helps set the table tonight. Joe can sit at Sophie's place. We're eating buffet-style. All we need are plates and napkins."

Harper must've been feeling more like her usual forthright self. "Can we shake hands now that you're finished saying thank you?"

Both adults laughed and moved apart as the kids all lined up to shake hands with Joe. "Hey, there, Harper." Everyone shook hands with him except Gio. Even little Ana went through the line to shake his hand again.

Gio stuck his hands into the pockets of his jeans and came around the island to stand beside Stella while she pulled down seven plates from the cabinet. "Need help?" he asked.

"I can always use some help." She curled her fingers into her palm to stop the instinct to touch him again. Now that he was awake and aware, she doubted the boy would be interested in a hug. "Feeling better?" she asked. He nodded, and when it became clear that he still wasn't going to elaborate about his visit from his mother and Vaughn Trask, she scooted the plates across the countertop. "Can you handle all these? Carry them to the table for me?"

Again, he nodded, scooped up the plates and took them to the table where the others were putting out place mats and napkins. As Gio left, Joe approached from the other side. His face was stamped with concern. "He still hasn't opened up to you about what happened today?"

"No."

"Maybe he just needs some time."

"He's been with me three weeks, Joe. I thought maybe after standing up to protect Harper today, he'd feel like he's one of us now. You think he's ever going to learn to trust me?"

"Long before he trusts me." He leaned in to press a quick kiss to her temple. "He's like a soldier with PTSD. Whatever he went through at home—with his mother, with Trask—it scarred him. He needs time to recover and get used to his new normal. He's already a different kid than the one we met at the police station. You're working your magic on him, Stell. Just give it time."

She captured his hand and squeezed it before he turned away. "Thank you for the pep talk. You really are a rock star when it comes to being there for me and offering support."

"It's what you asked for."

She brushed the tip of her finger across his lips, reliving

every memory of the kiss they'd shared in a single moment. "Thank you."

"You're not going to get mushy and thank him again, are you?" Tyrell tugged on the hem of her blouse. "I'm hungry."

Stella snorted a laugh at his poor, pitiful tone. "It's coming, Tyrell. Have you washed your hands? Make sure everyone else has, too." She pulled out serving spatulas for the pizza and turned to the island. "We'd better feed my tribe."

Joe laughed, too. "Wouldn't want a rebellion on our hands." While he helped her open up the pizza boxes, he asked, "Where's Sophie?"

"She went out to the movies with some of her friends. She had the last of her final exams today, and when they called, I told her to go. Have fun. Relax and celebrate. If I know them, they'll go out for coffee and dessert afterward. Or drinks. I guess she's twenty-one and can celebrate however she wants. Oh, Lord, I'm not ready for that."

"Relax, Stell. You just went from cheerleader to worrywart in the span of two sentences. Sophie seems like she has a good head on her shoulders. She won't do anything dangerous, like drink and drive."

"You're right. Of course you're right." She turned her attention to the five children, waiting with almost painfully polite patience for the pizza. "Tonight, you can have one can of soda with your pizza. You can all go over to the fridge and choose your poison."

The other four children hurried from the table to the refrigerator, but Harper stood in place, her face tilted up with a frown. "Why would we choose poison? That's bad for us."

"Oh, Harper. It's a figure of speech, sweetie." The girl's eyes blinked with unsatisfied curiosity behind her glasses. Stella smoothed her hand over the top of her hair, feeling utterly weary. "I'll explain it later. The sodas are perfectly safe. Now go get your drink."

As the girl dashed off and the others returned to the table, Stella felt a warm, strong hand settle against the nape of her neck. "Headache better?"

She tilted her head back into Joe's firm, yet gentle caress as he massaged the tension at the base of her skull. Her eyes drifted shut. "I dreamed of this earlier."

"You take it easy and eat what you can. I'll keep the conversation going."

She turned to him and blinked her eyes open. "I'm a lousy date."

"If you think a headache and a family emergency are going to scare me off, you're wrong." He feathered his fingers through her hair and cupped the side of her neck and jaw. "If I hadn't met you, I'd be home nursing a beer right now, wondering why my life was so quiet. I'd be resigning myself to boring and lonely, telling myself that I have a good life, that I've accomplished plenty, I'm making an impact on my city and the future—and it doesn't matter if there's no noise and color in my world."

"There's plenty of noise and color here."

He grinned. It was a handsome slash of mouth amid his silver-and-brown beard stubble that she desperately wanted to kiss again. "I wasn't expecting to date a whole family when I said yes to you asking me out. And yeah, it takes a little getting used to for this old bachelor." And then he did press his lips to hers in a chaste, wonderful, all too brief kiss that was full of a promise she wanted to believe in. "But I'm all in. I want to see where this goes between us. Between all of us. On good days and bad ones."

Reaching out, she cupped the strong line of his stubbled jaw. "You'll let me know when you need a break? I'll understand if you need to take some time off from us."

With that, he pulled back, frowning. "You're so sure we're going to fail, and I'm going to walk away?"

"Everyone else has."

Joe leaned in, his face mere inches from hers, as he squared off in front of her. "That's because you hadn't met me, sweetheart. I'm not going anywhere."

Yet. Was she setting herself up for heartbreak to believe that Joe would be here—would be hers—for the long haul?

Maybe for tonight, at least, she could set aside her need to be strong and self-sufficient. Maybe for tonight, she'd let Sergeant Joe Carpenter take care of her and the kids. She'd pretend that they were the family she'd always wanted growing up, that she was loved and that Joe Carpenter really was hers.

THREE HOURS LATER, with full tummies and only eight slices of pizza left, the mood around the house was mellow and surprisingly content. Stella had the children put on their pajamas, and now they were playing games and relaxing. Joe sat at the kitchen table with Gio, Colby and Harper, teaching them how to play poker. Stella had come up with the idea of betting M&M's, with the warning that no matter how many they won, they could only eat ten pieces before brushing their teeth and bedtime. Meanwhile, she sat in the den with Ana and Tyrell, watching an animated movie about a genie and a lamp. Both children had dozed off, wedged into the recliner on either side of her, but since it was one of her favorite movies from her own childhood—and she enjoyed a good cuddle—Stella continued to watch until the end of the show.

She was happy to hear Joe asking about Harper's arm and listening to how Gio had put one of her bullies in his place—along with praising them for how they'd handled the situation and discussing different strategies if something like that should happen again. Joe's experience as a police interrogator was being put to good use, or maybe, she hoped, they truly liked hanging out with him and felt comfortable talking to him. She heard the conversation shift to Gio spotting his mother and the white car through the fence at recess, and how Harper and Colby had teamed up with him to make sure Tyrell was accounted for and that none of them would be on their own against a perceived threat.

But that was where the conversation ended. Stella craned her neck to look over the back of the recliner where she was snuggled with the younger children and saw meaningful glances and ducking heads around the table. Although it hurt her heart to know the older children were keeping secrets, she was pleased to see that Gio, Colby and Harper had bonded over the past three weeks and were supporting each other.

Joe glanced over his shoulder to catch her gaze and shrugged, sharing her frustration and concern. But he quickly livened the children's spirits up again by shuffling the deck of cards and telling them to ante up a red-coated candy if they wanted to learn how to play Omaha Hold'em. Stella exhaled a weary sigh and settled in to watch the last few minutes of the movie. Even if nothing had been resolved tonight, she was grateful for Joe's calming presence. The children felt safe enough to relax and have some fun. And she felt herself relaxing, too.

Stella was singing softly along to the music playing beneath the closing credits when her cell phone rang on the table beside her. Unwinding her arm from around Tyrell, she reached over and picked up the phone. She was frowning at the unfamiliar number when Joe picked up the remote to turn off the television and then waited in front of the recliner.

"You think that's Jeffries?" he whispered.

"I don't know. I don't recognize the number," she whispered back, not wanting to wake Ana and Tyrell.

"Could be another burner phone. If it is him, I'm arrest-

ing his ass for violating the restraining order." Joe copied
the number down into his own phone as it rang two more
times. "It's late. You want me to answer?"

"No. But stay close." With his nod, she pushed the call
button and cautiously answered. "Hello?"

"Stella?" A familiar young woman's voice spoke. But
Stella's sigh of relief was short-lived at the spew of panicked
energy that followed. "Oh, my God. I was worried you'd already gone to bed and wouldn't answer. There are plenty of
police here, but I thought I should call you, so you wouldn't
worry, 'cause I'm gonna be late. Well, I guess I'm calling to
get a ride home, too, because my tires are all flat—"

"Sophie? Sweetie, can you slow down?" Stella tried to
get up without disturbing the children sleeping beside her.
"Are you all right? Tell me exactly where you are and what's
going on. Why are you calling from this number? Where's
your cell? Why are the police with you?"

Joe lifted Ana and held out his hand to help pull Stella
to her feet before gently setting the sleeping girl back
down. Then his hand settled on Stella's shoulder. "Put it
on speaker."

Stella pushed the button and held the phone up between
them. "Joe is here with me, listening in. Now, tell us exactly
what's going on."

"Hi, Joe."

"Hey, Soph," he greeted her, sounding a little exasperated, even though he was smiling. "I need you to talk to us.
Stella's worried."

"Oh, right. Sorry." There was some indistinct conversation in the background, telling them Sophie wasn't alone.
And since she didn't seem overly alarmed, Stella had to assume she was with her friends. "We came to this Irish bar
where Elisa had been on a date one time. I mean, it's nice,
and there are plenty of guys, but these two that were hitting

on us the most weren't exactly our type. We decided we were tired and ready to head home. But when we went out to the parking lot…someone had slashed my tires."

"Slashed?" Joe clarified. "As in deliberately cut with a knife?"

"That's what one of the police officers here said. He said he was going to call it in and sent the three of us girls back inside. Then I couldn't find my phone. We were talking to those guys at one of the pool tables, so maybe one of them picked it up by mistake. Or maybe I just lost it in the dark corner of the booth where we were sitting. I'm using Meiying's phone."

"What's the name of the bar?" Joe asked.

"The Shamrock Bar. Have you heard of it?"

"Seriously? I know it well. It's just around the corner from the precinct offices." His hand went to the nape of Stella's neck to infuse her skin with his heat and the relief he was obviously feeling. "It's a cop bar. That's why there are officers there who've probably stepped up to help her." He turned his attention back to the phone. "Don't worry. Jake Lonergan runs the place now. He's a former DEA agent and a good friend of KCPD. Tell him I said to keep an eye on you. He'll make sure no one bothers you."

"Uh, the scarred-up guy with gray-white hair behind the bar?" That didn't sound like a promising description.

But Joe didn't seem to think the dangerous-looking man was an issue. "That's Jake. Don't worry. He's not as scary as he looks. If it helps, he's married and has two girls. He'll take care of you."

"You'll come soon?"

"I'm on my way," Joe promised. "I'll leave as soon as I get my boots on."

"Okay. Thanks."

Stella ended the call and turned to Joe, already thinking

of the smoothest way to get to Sophie without disrupting everyone's night. "She's not your responsibility. I need to go pick her up. The kids are already in their pajamas. I can just load them into my car. Everybody, get your shoes on—"

Joe grasped her by the shoulders and stopped her from organizing the troops. "*I* will go. You stay with the kids. These two are already out. I'll protect Sophie like she was my own. I promise."

Stella realized the practicality of his offer. Nodding, she reached up to wrap her fingers around his wrists. "Okay. Thank you."

"What's wrong?" Colby asked, startling her when he entered the room. The three older kids had probably overheard the concern in Stella's voice, if not the actual call, and had gathered around them in the den. "Is Sophie okay?"

"I think so," she answered honestly. Her former foster daughter was upset and stressed, but it didn't sound as though she'd been injured in any way. "Someone scared her when she was out with her friends. And her phone's missing. Obviously, she's concerned about that. She called because she was worried about getting home."

"That's why I'm off to get her. She'll be okay, champ." Joe squeezed Colby's shoulder in reassurance, then strode to the front door to put on his work boots.

Stella followed him to the door and turned on the porch lights. "Bring my girl home."

"I will. Lock up behind me." They exchanged a brief kiss before he strode out into the night.

Stella locked the door and reset the security system. When she turned back around, she saw that a parade of three worried children had followed her. Oh, dear. Fun night had been forgotten. The hour was late, and those unsure, mopey faces all needed some reassurance. Sadly, these three were used to crises and the worry caused by late-night calls.

Well, not in this house. Not on her watch. Her job was to provide a safe haven for these fosters—to supply their basic needs, to give them the structure and emotional support that had been missing from their lives before foster care. Her calling was to show them that they were worthy of being loved, that *she* loved them. No child would ever feel the disinterest she'd grown up with. No child would have their value equated with a dollar sign. Her love would not be conditional on how they behaved or what they could do for her.

She draped her arm around Colby's and Harper's shoulders and hugged them to her side. "Okay, everybody. Upstairs to brush your teeth. We can clean up down here in the morning." She felt them perking up as she walked them to the stairs. "How about I read another chapter or two from that fantasy book we've been reading together before bedtime? Meet in my room. Bring your favorite quilt or pillow. It'll take me a couple of trips to get Ana and Tyrell."

Colby and Harper dashed up the stairs to their respective girls' and boys' bathrooms while Stella went to the den to pick up Ana.

"I can carry Tyrell," Gio offered.

"You sure? Up the stairs?"

He nodded and hauled his brother up onto his hip. Tyrell roused a little bit, but when he saw it was his big brother who had picked him up, he rested his head on Gio's shoulder and closed his eyes again. "I've done it before."

She smiled her thanks at his help. "All right. Go up in front of me, then. Set him on my bed. Then you can bring a cover for him when you grab yours."

With a nod of understanding, and a stepped-up degree of cooperation, Gio led the way upstairs.

Two chapters and part of another later, all five kids were cuddled up in the king-size bed with Stella, dozing on her extra pillows, using her for a pillow or lying crossways at her feet. Everyone but Gio had fallen asleep, and even he seemed to be having a hard time staying awake at the foot of the bed. Although she was sitting up against the pillows and the headboard with the quilt pulled up over the leggings and blouse she still had on from earlier in the day, the children were on top of the covers, effectively pinning her in and keeping her from getting up without waking everyone. Even Jasper thought that family togetherness was a good idea tonight, and he was stretched out on the other side of Ana at the edge of the bed.

She glanced over at her cell phone on the nightstand and wondered if she should be worried that neither Joe nor Sophie had called her to let her know that everyone was okay. She reached over to try to pick up the phone and call Joe, but that would involve squishing Harper or rolling her into Ana and knocking them both into the dog.

Perhaps sensing her concern, or maybe worried himself, Gio whispered to her from the foot of the bed. "I think Sophie got hurt because of me."

Stella kept her voice quiet so she didn't disturb the others, either. "Sophie didn't get hurt, sweetie. Someone vandalized her car. Maybe stole her phone. But she's okay."

"But she was scared, wasn't she?" Gio sat up, lines of worry etched on his young face. "That's my fault."

"How? You didn't slash Sophie's tires."

"But I know who did."

"You need to talk to me, Gio. So we can keep our family safe." Stella pushed herself forward as far as she could without pulling the covers taut enough to flip anyone off the bed. She couldn't quite reach Gio, but she needed to. "Do you know who slashed Sophie's tires and scared her tonight?"

Pushing his blanket aside, Gio sat up on his knees, inching closer to where her feet rested beneath the covers, perhaps subconsciously wanting to end his self-imposed isolation at the end of the bed. "Vaughn Trask. He said he'd hurt the people in my new family—he'd hurt Tyrell—if I didn't do what he asked."

This was it. This was the conversation she and Joe had tried to have more than once with Gio. She carefully schooled the *Hallelujah! Finally!* out of her voice and simply said, "What did he ask?"

"To pay him the thirty-six thousand dollars my mom owes him."

"Where…?" She almost forgot to whisper. "Where does he think an eleven-year-old is going to get that kind of money?"

"He said I could steal it from you." Hell, if she thought it would really make him go away, she'd give Trask the money. But she suspected he'd be like Trey and keep coming back for more. "He said I could go to work for him, running errands. I know that means delivering drugs and money for him, because I'm young enough the cops aren't going to be looking at me. Or…"

"Or what?"

"He said he could charge guys money to let them touch me."

Stella nearly threw up at the very idea of how this boy's own mother could allow him to be terrorized like that. But she choked down the bitter bile and managed to keep her demeanor relatively calm. Although fate and time and her inability to trust a man completely after Trey had robbed her of her chance to have children of her own, there was a deep-seated need inside her to be a mother—to love and protect the children in her care with the ferocity of a lioness.

"That's never going to happen," she vowed, gathering him in her arms and pulling him right into her lap to hold him close. She knew he didn't like to be hugged, but she really needed to hug someone right now. And since the boy wasn't squiggling in her grasp or pushing her away, she held on tight and rested his cheek against her shoulder and rocked him. "Tell me everything."

Chapter Twelve

Joe locked his gun in the glove compartment, since there was no place in Stella's house to secure it away from curious children, and closed the SUV door. Then he walked Sophie up to the front porch and waited for her to unlock the door. He turned to survey the quiet street and the shadows among the trees, unable to shake the feeling that they were being watched.

Once he'd been satisfied that things were being properly handled at the Shamrock with a police report and taking care of Sophie's car, he'd driven her friends, Meiying and Elisa, home to the apartment they shared. Since the young twenty-somethings were justifiably rattled by the night's events, he'd walked them into their building and checked to make sure their locks and windows were secure. But the moment they pulled out of the parking lot and turned toward the outskirts of the city, the hair at the nape of his neck had pricked to attention. An unseen sixth sense warned him that something was wrong, even if his eyes couldn't see it. There was plenty of traffic and bright lights in the city to mask any car that might be following them. But even when the traffic thinned out as he drove toward the remote subdivision where Stella lived, he couldn't shake the feeling that they weren't alone. Maybe the incident at the Shamrock had been an attempt to draw Stella out. He wouldn't put it past Trey the Troll to hurt Stella by going after one of her foster kids. Or to try to isolate her away from Joe and his protection.

And maybe he was just a paranoid old buzzard who'd seen and done too much to ever really drop his guard. But he'd swear there were eyes on them, tracking their movements, trailing them to the lake and to Stella.

But there were no cars driving past, no lights on at the Roe house at the bend of the road. He heard the lapping of the lake against the shore in the distance, and the whisper of the wind blowing through the leaves and branches of the woods between the houses. Besides the cicadas buzzing and chirping in the trees, the world around them was quiet, curiously devoid of human sounds. And yet…

"Are you coming in?"

He almost startled at Sophie's question. He'd been so intent on finding the cause for his internal alert. "Do you think Stella would mind?" He pointed to his watch. "It's almost one in the morning."

The young woman smiled. "Joe, she's in love with you. I don't think she's going to mind."

Stella was in love…?

Those words did startle him, stated so matter-of-factly, as if earning Stella's heart was a foregone conclusion. Even as the pronouncement settled that edgy feeling inside him, he still needed time to process how their unconventional relationship had led to the possibility that the dream of love and partnership and family he'd given up on might still come true.

"Did she say that?" he asked.

"Not in so many words. It's that she talks about you so much, and the way she looks at you, and gets nervous and excited when she knows she's going to see you, and…you know." He didn't know. But 1:00 a.m. on the front porch, when the threat he felt was as palpable as the humid air surrounding them, wasn't the place to discuss it. Sophie typed in the security code and pushed the door open. "Come on. She probably heard the car pull in and is wondering what's taking us so long to check in. She'll worry until she gets eyes on me."

"The last thing I want to do is add to her worries." He ushered her inside the house and closed and locked the door behind them. The first floor was dark, and Stella hadn't set out blankets and pillows on the sofa for him. With his suspicions on high alert, he intended to stay, even if she'd changed her mind about the invitation. But a soft light beckoned him from the top of the stairs. "Stell?"

"Up here."

He gestured for Sophie to precede him up the stairs. He'd give his report, then make himself at home down here or in his truck. Sophie already had her fingers to her lips, shushing him when he stepped into the doorway to Stella's room. "I locked everything up, and Sophie set the security alarm."

He was whispering by the end of his sentence, and grinning at the scene that greeted him. Stella sat up in bed, her legs trapped beneath the covers. Gio was curled up in her lap, sound asleep. Harper leaned against one side of her, her glasses in one hand and a book in the other. Ana was tucked between Stella and the dog on the other side. Tyrell had one arm hugged around Stella's legs, and Colby was stretched out across the foot of the bed, softly snoring. The lamp from her bedside table provided the only illumination in the room.

"Did you have a slumber party, and I didn't get invited?" Sophie teased.

"Worryfest," Stella explained. "They felt more comfortable hanging out together. I lost them all before the end of story time."

Sophie frowned. "Worried about me?"

"They'll be fine when they wake up and see our pack is all together again." Stella reached out and squeezed Sophie's hand since she couldn't get up. "You okay?"

Sophie nodded. "Still can't find my phone. Meiying called it, but we never heard it ringing anywhere. Maybe the battery died. But yeah, I'm good now."

"We'll figure out your phone and getting your car fixed and home tomorrow."

"Joe already took care of it. He called one of his rookie trainees, Ezra."

Stella looked behind Sophie to meet his gaze. "Ezra?"

He stepped into the room. "Ezra Hawley. You met him that night at the station? He helped watch the boys."

"Anyway, Joe arranged for the car to be towed. Ezra is staying with my car until it gets to the shop. Then he's going to come out and pick me up tomorrow and drive me to the repair shop once the new tires are on."

Stella frowned. "Aren't repair shops closed now?"

Sophie glanced over at him and smiled. "Joe knows a guy. He called and got it all arranged for tomorrow morning. And he said Ezra's a good guy. That I'm okay riding with him tomorrow. Those big brown eyes don't hurt, either." Uh-oh, Sophie sounded a little smitten with Ezra. He supposed the young cop might be a little taken with her, too, since Ezra had volunteered to chauffeur her around the rest of the weekend.

"I bet not." Stella's smile indicated that she didn't seem to mind whatever little crush Sophie had developed that night.

"Okay, well, I'm going to clean up and go to bed. Don't wake me in the morning unless you need something. I'm finished with classes, and I don't have to work." She headed for the door, but stopped and came back to hug Joe. "Thanks. That was just like a real dad coming to rescue me when I needed help." He lightly returned the hug before she pulled away, looking a little stricken. "I mean, can I say that? That's not an insult, is it? That you did a dad thing? I don't mean you're a dad joke. Or that you're old. Well, you're not that old."

Joe put his hands up to stop the humbling apology. "I'm okay with that, Soph. I don't have any experience in that department, but I'll take it as a very nice compliment. You're welcome."

Her moment of embarrassment forgotten, she turned back to Stella. "Is it okay if Jasper sleeps with me tonight? I kind of don't want to be alone."

"Of course. He'll be happy to snuggle with you." Sophie called to him, and the big black dog willingly climbed down and followed her down the hall to her bedroom.

Stella's relief and amusement at hearing about Sophie's adventure ended abruptly when she patted the bed on the other side of Harper. "You and I need to talk."

Frowning, Joe sat on the edge of the bed. He nodded to the boy sleeping in her lap. "What's really going on here? I didn't think Gio was a cuddler."

Her breasts rose and fell with a big sigh, and tears glistened in her eyes. "Anything you need to know about Vaughn Trask and Toy Williams, I can fill in the blanks. They want to use Gio—abuse him—to work off his mother's debt. And they're willing to hurt Tyrell or any of us to force him to cooperate. He thinks they went after Sophie tonight to prove a point. He's worried about who they'll hurt next unless he goes with them and does what they want."

Joe reached out with the pad of his thumb to wipe away the tears that spilled over onto her cheeks. "Now we know what we're dealing with. You okay?"

She shook her head, and Joe needed to hold her, to erase that sadness tinged with anger that darkened her eyes to stormy shadows. "I will be. But what do we do about this? How do I protect these children from a criminal like Trask?"

"The first thing you're going to do is lean over here." He didn't leave her confused about the request for long. As she stretched herself toward him, he slid his fingers around to the nape of her neck and leaned over Harper to cover Stella's lips in a kiss.

Her sigh of contentment whispered against his mouth and chin in the instant before he claimed her. This woman loved him. This woman was his to cherish and support and protect. With two children nestled between them, he couldn't pull her into his arms. But she held on to his forearm and managed to stretch herself another fraction of an inch to allow him to deepen the kiss. He wasn't sure if she was surrendering or taking what she needed. But he offered comfort, trust and desire. And he silently promised that her feelings for him were returned and that he wanted to end every night for the rest of his life with his lips on hers.

"Better?" he asked when he reluctantly pulled away.

She brushed her nose against his before nodding. Her eyes sparkled like grayish emeralds in the lamplight, all trace of her sorrow gone. "I'm going to need you to stay with me tonight."

Yeah. This was where he needed to be, too. He gave her a nod and stood as she leaned back against the pillows. Joe took off his boots and his belt, and set his badge, wallet and phone on the bedside table.

Then he pulled Harper's glasses from her limp fingers and set them and the book on the table beside his things. He tucked the small red blanket around the girl and lifted her, climbing onto the bed and taking her place beside Stella. When he set Harper down, she stirred a little, rolling away, then turned back to burrow against his side.

Joe held his breath until she settled, hoping he hadn't

awakened her. But he stroked his hand against her soft hair, and she soon grew heavy against the side of his chest.

"I think you've got a fan there."

"It's mutual." He turned to press a kiss to Stella's temple and breathe in her familiar coconut scent before settling into the pillows at his back. "All right. Here's the plan. We're going to get whatever sleep we can. In the morning I'll take Sophie to Precinct headquarters to look through mug shots to see if she can ID the guys from the bar. I know a couple of guys who can stop by to keep an eye on things here while I'm gone. I know you can hold down the fort without me, but I don't want to take chances."

"You know a couple of guys? With the car? Guard duty?" She leaned her head against his shoulder. "You are a man of endless resources."

"It's my job to know how to get things done and make connections. The trainees at the academy can use the hours on their résumé. And the car guy is a friend who'll give Sophie a good deal—and who'll send one of the tires on to the crime lab to see if the sharps guy there can get a match on what kind of knife was used."

"Someone deliberately slashed her tires?" She shook her head. "Of course it was deliberate. A knife in your tires doesn't happen accidentally."

"Jake said the two men chatting up Sophie and her friends weren't regulars. He didn't know them. I don't know if that's a connection or a coincidence. Does she have any enemies? An old boyfriend who might not like seeing her out on the town having fun without him?"

"Sophie's twenty-one years old. The only dates she had in high school were junior and senior prom. In college, she's been so devoted to her studies that she doesn't go out much. Maybe just with friends. Do you think one of her male friends wants something more?"

"You know me. I want all the information before I decide on any answers." It felt a little weird to be talking through a case in whispers. But a late-night chat with Stella snugged to his side felt like the kind of partnership he'd been looking for his whole adult life. "I thought it might even be Trey the Troll trying to hurt you by going after one of your kids. Technically, it's not a violation of your restraining order since you weren't there. Maybe we should refile that, include the children."

"I know. You know a guy. A judge you can call on the weekend to make the adjustment for us." She chuckled and shifted Gio in her arms so that she could squiggle so close that the blanket and their clothes were the only things between them. Then she tilted her chin up to press a kiss to his jaw before tucking her head into the juncture of his shoulder and neck. "I'm glad you're on my side, Joe Carpenter."

"You're my favorite partner I've ever had," he confessed. They sat together for several minutes in peaceful companionship before he reassessed their situation. "Like I told Sophie, I don't have much experience with this. This isn't exactly how I pictured my first time in bed with you. Do we sleep with a pile of kids on us all night? Or do we actually get some grown-up time?"

She chuckled quietly. "We'll carry the little ones to their beds after a bit, walk Colby, Harper and Gio into their rooms. We'll tuck them in, check on Sophie, even though she insists she's an adult, pet the dog and then come back here. Once we close the door, we can have our grown-up time."

She punctuated her directions with a big yawn, and Joe grinned. "We're going to be too tired to do anything *grown-up* by that time, aren't we?"

"Probably. But I can hold you through the night, and you can hold me."

"I'll take that offer."

"And if we happen to end up naked while we're holding each other, so be it."

He laughed and nudged her chin up to kiss her full on the mouth. "Making love to you is going to be so much fun."

She smiled and snuggled in. "I can't wait."

DESPITE THE ROCKY start to her Friday evening, it ended up being one of the best nights of Stella's life. Her family was all together. They were safe.

The lines of stress that had marred Gio's young face had lessened now that he'd shared the burden he was carrying about the threats Vaughn Trask and his mother had made. He still wasn't the most sociable or trusting of children, but she was pleased to see that he was more childlike this morning at breakfast, laughing with Colby and debating the positives and negatives of loop-shaped cereal versus cereal with marshmallows with Harper. He did still make sure Tyrell got his breakfast first and was eating, and he'd given Sophie a quick hug when she'd come downstairs, perhaps still feeling guilty over her getting stranded at the bar. For her part, Sophie was excited about spending the day with Ezra Hawley, after going to the precinct offices with Joe to look at mug shots of the men from the Shamrock.

And Joe Carpenter had made love to her. Despite the late hour, Joe checking the house and grounds after putting the children to bed—reminding her that he was a protector through and through, and he wasn't dropping his guard and putting her family at risk—they'd come together in a passionate, even somewhat demanding way. She never once felt anything but beautiful in his arms.

This was the life she wanted. Minus the stalker ex, her foster children being hurt or threatened and Joe's insomnia. Joe had insisted they throw some clothes back on afterward, in case the children needed her in the night. And it had been a beautiful thing when she'd heard that first knock on the door in the morning, and she had awakened to find Joe deep asleep on the pillow next to hers, his hand still resting possessively at her hip as he spooned behind her.

Tyrell and Ana were hungry, and Jasper needed to go outside. Ana mimicked Stella putting her finger to her lips, warning them to be quiet. She shooed them on downstairs before slipping out of bed. She stepped into a pair of flip-flops, pulled on a hoodie and wound her loose hair into a bun on top of her head and secured it.

"Best two hours of sleep I've had in my life," a deep, drowsy voice murmured behind her.

"Why don't you make it three? Relax for a while longer if you can." She climbed back onto the bed and kissed Joe's grizzled cheek. Remembering that stubbled face against her most tender skin made her nipples pearl into beads of desire all over again. "You've earned it."

"Is that a double entendre? Or are you feeling sorry for the tired old man?"

"I don't see an old man." She brushed a few messy spikes of hair away from his forehead. "I see the stud who gave me not one, but two orgasms last night."

His green eyes narrowed with concern. "Are you all right? Are you sore this morning?"

"A little." She smiled, silently thanking her friends Jessie and Garrett Caldwell for introducing this caring man into her life. "But I'm also deliciously happy. On so many levels. And I have you to thank for that."

"Stella!" Tyrell shouted from the bottom of the stairs, in his very own, pint-size *A Streetcar Named Desire* impersonation. "The milk jug is too heavy to pour on our cereal."

They both laughed.

"Duty calls."

"I understand that." He caught her hand when she pulled

away. His eyes looked at her differently this morning—as if she was more precious to him, as if an unspoken promise had been shared between them last night. "Something about you settles me inside, Stell. Either that or worshipping that lush, sexy body of yours wears me out."

She laughed, feeling some of those extra bits of her jiggle. But with this man looking at her like that, with him touching her the way he had last night, any body-shaming that men like Trey Jeffries had made her feel was long forgotten. "I can't do that every night anymore, not that I ever did."

"I can't, either. But that'll make the next time we come together all the more special."

"I love…" No, she couldn't do anything to scare him away, not when things were still so new and wonderful between them. "The way you think," she finished lamely, although honestly.

He pulled her hand to his lips and kissed the back of her fingers. "I love the way you think, too."

"Stella!"

They shared another laugh. "Better go save our Stanley Kowalski before he wakes the others." He sat up and pointed to her en suite bathroom. "I'm going to borrow your shower if that's okay."

She paused at the hallway door. "Make yourself at home, Joe."

"Home. I like that."

"Me, too. See you downstairs."

STELLA HAD ALREADY gotten a call from Joe that said Sophie had identified the two men who had been flirting with her and her friends at the Shamrock Bar, and that they were known associates of Vaughn Trask. The idea that anyone that evil had gotten that close to one of her kids terrified her. Hearing that KCPD had put out a BOLO for the two men to bring them in for questioning made her feel slightly better. Finding out that Sophie and Ezra Hawley had been making *goo-goo eyes* at each other, to quote Joe, made her smile. Although her tires had been replaced, apparently Ezra wanted to take Sophie out for lunch before picking up her car.

And when Joe had added, "For some reason, I didn't get invited," she laughed out loud.

"That's better," he whispered. "I know you're worried. But we'll get these guys, I promise. We'll get all of them, and your children will be safe."

"I know. Thank you, Joe, for helping us." She was pulling a pair of shorts on over her swimsuit when she heard her five young fosters running downstairs to the kitchen, after changing into their swimsuits and trunks to go out and have some lakeside fun after lunch. "Will you be heading back now?"

"Go ahead and eat lunch without me. I know a guy over in Vice I want to talk to. See what kind of warrants Trask and his minions have out on them, so I can arrest them on the spot if they show up in front of Gio or Tyrell again."

"You sure do know a lot of guys," she teased. "I should have you lead the professional networking seminar we offer to single moms living in homeless shelters who are looking for jobs."

"I'd be happy to help out."

Of course he would. Because that was the kind of man Joe was. "I'm just glad I know one guy, in particular."

"Me, too. I'll call again when I'm headed your way. Be safe. See you soon."

She and the kids were cleaning up the lunch dishes and making last-minute trips to the restroom before heading outside when Stella's phone rang again.

She was excited to think Joe was leaving the city and driving out to her neighborhood already. He'd be able to join them for some time in the rowboat or kayaks and splashing around the dock. When she read the name *Sophie Martin* on her phone, she was equally excited to answer. This had to be good news. "Hey. You found your phone. Where was it?"

But the man who answered was definitely not Sophie. "Ms. Smith? Quaint name, by the way. I believe you have something I want."

Everything inside Stella chilled, and she instinctively swept her gaze around the main floor of the house to make sure all five children were still here with her. "Who is this? How did you get this number?"

"I helped myself to your daughter's phone. I wanted to make sure you'd answer."

Oh, she had a bad feeling about this.

"We're on the way to your home right now to pick up my property. I had to wait until your boyfriend with the badge left."

She had a very, very bad feeling. Instead of asking any more questions, she disconnected the call and ran to the front door to make sure it was locked. "Kids! I need everybody where I can see you. Right now."

They spilled into the foyer from different parts of the house, but they were all here. They were all safe.

"Stella?" Harper ventured cautiously.

Clearly, she wasn't hiding her panic. She needed time to plan the best course of action. She needed time to think. A white car with gold trim pulled into the driveway.

She didn't have the luxury of time.

That was Trey's car. But it wasn't Trey behind the wheel. And the man and woman in the back seat weren't anyone she recognized.

A small hand grabbed hers and pulled her away from the window. Gio shared her panic. "That's Mom and Vaughn. We need to go."

When the first car door closed, Jasper barked. His alert snapped her out of her worried stupor.

"No, sweetie. *You* need to go." She squeezed Gio's hand and caressed the crown of his hair. "I've got an idea."

She turned and slapped her phone into Colby's hand. "Call Joe. Tell him what's going on. Tell him to bring everybody he can to help us. Harper, you're in charge of Ana. Gio, you have Tyrell. Everybody—hide!"

Gio grabbed her hand again. "Come with us."

"No. I have to stall them." She got a better idea. She scooted everyone toward the back door. "Everybody, down to the boathouse. I'll keep them in here with me."

"They'll hurt you."

"I'll be fine. Nobody hurts my children." She wanted to hug him, but she shoved him into the mudroom instead. "Go!"

With a nod, he reached for Tyrell. Colby was on the phone. Harper had Ana's hand and followed Jasper out the door. "You keep an eye on our pack, Jasper. Now go. Hide!"

She watched the kids running down to the boathouse before closing and locking the back door. The doorbell rang and she shuddered. But she inhaled a deep breath, flipped up the collar of the tunic blouse she wore over her shorts and suit, and strolled to the front of the house.

Any polite greeting out on the front porch went by the wayside when she opened the front door and a blond man in a double-breasted suit and a skinny woman pushed their way inside. The other man who'd driven the car took up a position just outside. She was certain the bulge beneath the arm of his suit jacket was a gun. She dodged to the side when he reached in to close the door, effectively trapping her inside.

So, no escape that way.

"Boys! Gio! Tyrell!" the woman shouted, walking around

the living room, touching everything. "It's Mama. You come on out and see me now."

Stella turned and put on her best haughty-heiress persona to greet them. "You must be Toy Williams." She looked up at the heavyset blond man. "And you're Vaughn Trask?"

His smile crawled across her skin. "I see the boys have been talking about us. I hope they're still in good condition."

"Condition?" Was he really talking about Gio and Tyrell as if they were a used car he wanted to buy? And speaking of cars, the white Lexus in her driveway looked awfully familiar. "Where's Trey Jeffries? That's his car."

"He won't be needing it."

Did that mean what she thought? She wasn't a fan of Trey, but she had no desire for him to be a victim of a carjacking—or something worse. "Where is he? What did you do to him?"

Her boys momentarily forgotten, Toy stopped in the formal dining room, in front of the hutch. She opened the door and picked up an antique silver goblet. "I could live like this. No wonder my boys left me for the rich lady."

Stella crossed the room to the other woman, plucked the goblet from her grasp and set it back inside the hutch. "Gio and Tyrell didn't leave you, Toy. You gave them away with the drugs and the violence and this man in your life. You signed a piece of paper and gave them away."

"Well, I changed my mind!"

Stella tried to reason with the woman, tried to remind her that she'd been a real mother once. "You don't want your children. You're going to give them to this man. Do you know what he's going to do to them? How he's going to hurt them? If you ever loved Gio and Tyrell, don't let him take your sons."

A strong hand clamped down on the back of her hair and jerked her backward, sending hundreds of pinpricks across her scalp before Trask pulled a chair out from the dining room table and shoved her down into it. She blinked away the tears of pain that stung her eyes as he braced his hands on the arms of the chair and leaned over her. "You stop talking to her. *I'm* the one you need to talk to."

The man had probably once been handsome. But all Stella saw was the meanness in his eyes and the smirk of amusement on his skinny lips.

"You and I are businesspeople, Ms. Smith." Even a statement sounded like a threat to her. No wonder the boys had been terrified of this man. He sat back on the edge of the table. "Now you and I are going to talk business." He touched his fingertip to her chin and drew it down her neck into her cleavage. She couldn't suck her breath in enough to get away from his vile caress. "I'm not into fat girls. But I am into rich ones. You give me Gio and Tyrell—and a check for fifty grand—and we'll leave."

"Sounds like a lousy bargain to me."

He lightly smacked her cheek and laughed as he stood. "You're a smart one. Come on. Tell me where those boys are before your boyfriend with the badge gets back, and nobody has to get hurt."

"How did you know Sergeant Carpenter was gone?"

"Been watching the house. There's a great view from your neighbors' back porch."

She felt sick to her stomach. "Oh, God. Did you hurt them? Are the Roes all right?"

But Vaughn's attention had shifted back to Toy. She had her purse open and was stuffing two of the silver goblets inside. "I could sell some of this stuff. Get what I need to pay you back and then some."

Stella nodded, knowing she could convince Toy to leave more easily than she could convince Vaughn Trask of anything. "Take it. Whatever you want, it's yours. Just don't harm those children."

Vaughn slapped the goblet out of Toy's hand and knocked her bag to the floor. "We're not hocking anything here. This lady has real money. The land, the house, the things inside." While he'd been distracted, Stella had scooted out of the chair. But she hadn't gotten far enough away to avoid the cruel fingers grabbing her hair. Vaughn forced her head back and practically spit in her face. "You could write me a check for fifty grand right now, couldn't you? A hundred grand? A million? I could take you to the bank and you could get all that for me in cash."

Cautious in answering, she prayed the kids had gotten themselves hidden and that Joe and reinforcements were on the way. And she'd thought Trey had been a money-sucking nightmare. "If I do that, you'll just come back for more. You'll never leave my family alone."

He considered her response for a moment before releasing her. The release of pressure threw her off balance and she stumbled.

He strode to the front door and opened it, ordering his man inside. "Go with Toy. Find those kids. We'll take 'em with us. Then I bet you'll happily write a check for a million dollars to get your family back."

"Kidnapping?"

"Taking what's owed me." She glanced toward the back door. Vaughn was sharp. He saw the furtive movement. He called the others back from their search of the house and moved toward the kitchen. "Check outside in the backyard."

"No!" Stella leaped on his back and clawed at his face to try to stop him.

But she was no match for his superior strength. He grabbed one arm from around his neck and tugged so hard, she felt something tweak in her elbow. The pain was enough to loosen her grip. He pulled her off him and literally threw her into the kitchen island. Her foot tangled with one of the stools, and she went down, cracking her forehead on the edge of the counter before she hit the floor.

Several precious seconds passed before the room stopped spinning and she could reach for the top of the counter to pull herself up. She saw the drops of blood hitting the clean white granite but didn't stop moving toward the back door. "No. Not my children."

She pushed open the back door to see Vaughn and his man and Toy coming back together from the places they'd been searching and heading down to the boathouse.

With the rowboat out on the lake and the two kayaks sitting on the shore beside the dock, she wasn't sure where the children were hiding. She hurried down to the water, ignoring the pain that pounded through her head with every step. And was the sun unusually bright this afternoon?

She made it through the back gate when she heard the door to the boathouse bang open and Jasper's deep, echoing bark. Stella made it to the shoreline before Vaughn came out dragging Colby by the sleeve of his wet T-shirt, while the other man scooted Harper and Ana out of the boathouse ahead of him. Toy stood by, mostly screeching and avoiding the big dog that lumbered past her, keeping a close watch on his children.

"Where are they?" Vaughn shouted to anyone who would answer. He shoved Colby toward Stella, and the girls ran to join them. "Where are Gio and Tyrell?"

Now that she was out of arm's reach, Harper piped up with an explanation that made Stella proud. "They're gone. They ran away and we helped them. We're a family. We have their backs."

Vaughn mocked Harper's speech. "Well, isn't that sweet?

Which way did they run, little girl?" He turned back to the boathouse. "Check it again."

"Did you call Joe?" Stella asked, keeping her eyes on the intruders but talking to the children. She pulled Harper, Colby and Ana to her sides and hugged all three of them.

Colby nodded, understanding the need for subterfuge. "He was already on his way. I called 9-1-1, too. They're all coming."

Wait. Why was the rowboat out in the middle of the lake? Had the children untied it and set it adrift as a diversion? Or... Oh, no. Neither Gio nor Tyrell could swim. "Life jackets?" she whispered.

"There wasn't time to put them on," Colby whispered back. "We threw all of them in the boat. The guys are hiding underneath so you can't see them. I pushed them out as far as I could, and then Gio was going to start rowing."

Vaughn Trask was mad when he strode out of the boathouse and headed straight for them. "They're not here!" She shoved the children behind her before he grabbed Stella and twisted her sore arm behind her back. Jasper barked, and Vaughn kicked at the dog. Ana screamed when his foot connected with Jasper's leg, and Vaughn screamed louder. "Where is my merchandise?"

"KCPD!" Joe stormed out the back door of the house, pointing a gun at Trask. Several other cops, in uniforms and plain clothes, came out behind him and swarmed around either side of her house. "You're surrounded, Trask. You've got nowhere to go and no way out except in cuffs or a body bag. Your choice. Let go of that woman and put your hands where I can see them."

"You get over here and make—"

Bang. Stella jumped at the gunshot. Joe wasn't messing around with any kind of discussion. His bullet hit Vaughn in the shoulder. The man cursed and jerked back, giving Stella enough time to duck out of his grasp before Joe tugged her out of the way and set her behind him and his gun. "Get on the ground, Trask. Hands on your head." Once Vaughn had assumed the position of surrender, Joe holstered his gun and pulled out his handcuffs. He locked one around one wrist, then pulled the other down behind his prisoner. He glanced over at Stella. "He the one who hit you?"

She nodded. "Threw me off his back, actually. I hit my head on the counter on my way down."

Joe tightened the cuffs, and Trask protested how he was being treated. But there were uniformed officers there immediately to pull Trask to his feet and lead him, his driver and Toy Williams up the hill. "Get 'em out of my sight. Call Seth Cartwright in Vice. Tell them we've got some of their people coming in. We're arresting these three on suspicion of assault, making terroristic threats, abuse of a minor and murder."

"Murder?" Stella asked. Had someone died?

"How bad are you hurt?" Joe gently inspected the bump and cut she must have on her forehead. "Two of my guys found Trey Jeffries in the neighbors' house. Apparently, they liked his vantage point for spying on the back of your house but didn't like having the extra tenant."

"That explains why they're driving Trey's car, too. I'm sorry he's gone, but he was never really going to give up—"

"Stella!" She whipped around to where Harper was pointing out across the water.

She heard the splashing before she saw the boy struggling in the water. Gio had fallen overboard, trying to get the oar she could see floating away from him. Yes, he'd put on a life jacket, but he still couldn't swim. Stella was already running down the dock, shedding her blouse and flip-flops as she went. "Gio! Hold on to the side of the boat!" She dived in and swam like hell, cutting through the water with long, even strokes. She heard a second splash behind her and assumed Joe was coming to help, as well.

But she didn't have time to look behind her. She didn't have time to decipher the shouting she could hear from the shore. She had to reach Gio. "Grab the side of the boat!"

But she could see him struggling to do so, and his splashing kept scooting the boat farther away from his grasp. Stella kicked harder and quickened her pace, her sore elbow protesting the effort.

She was in feet of reaching Gio when Tyrell popped up from the bottom of the boat. "Gio, I'm scared." When he spotted his brother in the water, he leaned over the side of the boat, tipping it dangerously close to the surface of the lake, risking the boat taking on water or the younger boy falling in, too.

"Tyrell, no!" she shouted, swallowing a mouthful of lake water. She switched to treading water as she coughed it from her throat and lungs. The effort rang through her scrambled brain and her form faltered. Reaching deep for extra strength, she moved forward again.

She heard Joe yelling from a distance. "Tyrell! Sit down in the middle of the boat and don't move. That's it, buddy. Just like that." And then, "Kids, you stay with me. Be careful, Stell! She's coming for you, Gio! She's coming to get you!"

When she touched Gio's arm, his frantic dog-paddling ceased and he latched on to the promise of rescue. He wrapped his arms around her neck, pulling her down below the surface. But Stella had grown up around the water. She knew water safety. She knew she couldn't afford to panic. She twisted Gio in her arms and kicked to the surface, resting him on her hip as she turned into a sidestroke. "Easy. Easy. Calm down. I've got you."

"I lost the oar. I couldn't get it back. I don't know how to make the boat go without it."

"Where is it?"

He pointed. She gauged the distance. It was even farther away than the rowboat, and she was quickly tiring.

"Stella?" Tyrell was trying not to cry and failing. "I'm scared. Is Gio okay?"

"He's fine. I've got him."

That was when she heard the strong strokes through the water behind her.

Before she could even turn her head, Tyrell shouted, "Jasper!"

"You big, lazy son of a gun. Yes!" The web-footed Newfoundland was doing the job he'd been trained for. Reinvigorated by the dog's unflinching support, she swam with Gio to the boat. "We're going to be okay, boys. Come on, Gio. Let's get you back in the boat."

Once she'd lifted him up out of the water and he'd climbed into the boat, he turned and reached for her. "Come on, Stella. Get in."

Her elbow was throbbing along with her head now, and her vision was a little blurry. "No. I'm not strong enough to pull myself up. I might tip it. But we'll be okay. Jasper's here. This is what he's trained to do." The dog swam up to her. She petted and praised him. "Good boy. That's my good boy." She held on to him briefly, to catch her breath, then pulled herself along the gunwale to the front of the boat. "Okay. We've got this." She felt around to find the bow rope tied there. "Here's what I need. Gio, Ty—is there one of Jasper's bright orange floaty toys in the boat?"

While they scrambled to search for the toy, she focused on conserving her energy and ignoring just how much her head was throbbing from where she'd hit the granite countertop.

"I got it!" Gio stood up to hand it to her.

"Sit down! You'll tip it over." He immediately sat, and she changed her tone from her panicked outburst to Mama's-got-this. "I need you both to sit down in the very middle of the boat. Don't rock it. Don't try to help. You'll help by being very still." She pulled down the rope and tied it to the toy that Jasper was now eyeing like a piece of raw steak. She pulled it taut. "You boys ready?"

She was dragging in big gulps of air now, the physical exertion and ball bearings pinging off her skull exhausting her. But satisfied that this water rescue was going to work just like all their training sessions at K-9 Ranch, she held the floaty out to Jasper, who immediately chomped his big jowls down around it. "Swim, Jasper." She gave him a hand signal to move toward the man who was already waist deep in the water, walking toward her, and the three children waiting anxiously on the shore. The boat jerked ahead with the dog's strong, sure strokes, and she quickly grabbed on to the side of the boat to stay close to the boys and keep them calm before she kicked out herself. "That's my good boy. Swim."

Chapter Thirteen

"Is Stella going to be okay?"

Joe knelt in front of the row of chairs where five children, their twenty-one-year-old big sister and nanny, and a justifiably tired Newfoundland dog sat outside the hospital room while an ER doctor and nurse tended to Stella's injuries. "Yeah, Colby, she's going to be fine. They put three stitches in her scalp where she hit her head, and they're giving her some antibiotics in case any greeblies from the lake got into her bloodstream. We don't want her to get sick." There was a combination of nods and head shakes that indicated different levels of understanding. "They're dressing the wound right now, and then we can go in to see her. I'm going to stay the night to keep an eye on her, to make sure there are no side effects from her concussion."

A couple with a teenage boy on crutches walked past with another nurse, who scowled at the black dog taking up a good chunk of the waiting area. If she or anyone questioned Jasper's presence in a sanitary hospital, he simply held up his badge and said, "Service dog."

Jasper might think he was just going for a swim and playing with his toy, but this dog had saved the life of the woman he loved, and helped rescue two children who meant the world to him. As far as he was concerned, Jasper could go wherever he wanted and have as many toys as he wanted for the rest of his life. The dog was as much a part of this family as any of them.

Joe also carefully explained that Vaughn Trask, Toy Williams and Vaughn's driver had been arrested, along with the two men who had slashed Sophie's tires and stolen her phone on Trask's orders. Neither they nor Trey Jeffries would be coming to the house and scaring any of them again. By the time he was finished reassuring them that they would be safe, that no one was going to take them away from Stella, and that he intended to stick around to make sure everyone understood that this foster family was under his protection, the children were either slumped in their chairs or glazing over.

Right. He wasn't lecturing a classroom full of police cadets. These were children. And while they were brave, smart, resourceful and caring children, the hour was late, and waiting was boring.

Joe pushed to his feet as the doctor came out of the room and announced, "The nurse will let you know when you can go in and see your mom." He held out his hand to shake Joe's. "She's going to be just fine, Sergeant."

"Thanks, Doc."

He watched the man in the blue hospital scrubs walk back to the main desk before he took a seat in the chair at the end of the row of seats. When he turned back to face the others, Gio was standing in front of him, holding out his hand just like the doctor had. Feeling the gesture of friendship and trust all the way down to his bones, Joe shook Gio's hand.

"I always wanted a real dad," Gio said. "Like you."

Joe muttered a curse to fight back the tears as he pulled the boy in for a hug.

"Swear jar." Harper popped up out of her seat. "You said a bad word."

"Yes, ma'am, I did. And I'll pay for it. I just got too emotional to hold it all in. But I'll do better." He released Gio and squeezed his shoulder. "That means more to me than you'll ever know, G. I'm glad you decided to be my friend."

Colby stood up behind Harper. "Are you gonna marry Stella?"

Harper nodded. "We know modern sensibilities say it's okay for grown-ups to live together."

"What do you know about modern sensibilities?" Joe asked, teasing her.

But Harper was serious, and the others had gathered around him to listen. "We don't want Stella to get in trouble with Family Services and then we have to leave."

"I would never do anything to jeopardize your relationship with Stell. You're her kids. She loves you all so much. I love you, too." He looked to each and every child. He gently chucked Ana on the chin, winked at Sophie and petted Jasper. "You guys need to stay together as a family if you can."

Gio crossed his arms in front of him. "If you marry her, you could be part of our family, too."

Joe agreed. "That's a solid plan, G."

Harper tugged on his sleeve to get his full attention again. "Should we ask her now?"

Joe smiled, then hugged her. "Why don't you let me ask her? When the time is right."

"Okay." The intense, grown-up conversation ended, and the kids were ready to move on to looking at magazines, playing games and recounting the events of the long day from each of their unique points of view.

There were more hugs and overlapping conversations when they went in to see Stella resting on her hospital bed. The thing looked damn uncomfortable, but she was covered up again with a dry pair of scrubs from the hospital. Her color was better, other than the bandage that barely covered the bruise in her hairline. Her hair hung loose and damp around her shoulders, the tips of turquoise and lavender curling against the tops of her breasts.

But despite the heated blanket draped over her, he could see she was still shivering from the exertion of her springtime swim. That prompted Joe to stand up and pull out his wallet.

"Hey, Soph. Here's my debit card. Why don't you take everyone down to the cafeteria and get them a snack?"

She smiled and hugged him, too. "Sure. You need some time alone with Stella. How long do you need?"

He smiled at the bright young woman. "However long you can give me."

"Okay, gang. Let's go find some snacks. Joe's treat."

"What about Jasper?" Joe petted the dog, then handed the leash to the kids. "He's going with you, of course. There's nobody I trust more to keep an eye on you and keep you all safe." Jasper lolled his tongue out the side of his mouth and almost looked like he was smiling at the assignment.

Once everyone else had left the room, Joe closed the door. Stella reached for him, and he hurried to the bed to take her hand. "I heard you all talking out there. Now it's so quiet. This is usually where I get worried and track down the kids to make sure they aren't getting into trouble. Everything okay?"

"Yep. They're Sophie's responsibility for a while. They're all fine." He kept right on coming, sitting on the edge of the bed, then swinging his legs up to lie down beside her. The bed was a lot narrower than the king-size bed they'd shared the night before, so he had to cuddle close.

"What are you doing?" she asked.

"I need to hold you. You're cold, and I don't like that. And I need to feel for myself that you're okay. Is this all right?"

She snuggled in, and the weight of her against his side

made him sigh in contentment. "It's more than all right. God, Joe, I was so scared today. I don't think I could have kept it together without you here."

"I was scared, too. When I saw that black-and-blue goose egg on your forehead and saw the blood around the cut, I about lost it. Then seeing you in the water with Jasper and the boat... You were like some kind of Olympic water princess. The most beautiful, powerful, fiercest thing I've ever seen."

"Joe? I love you. I feel like we're doing this relationship backward, but I know my feelings are real. And I realized I'd never told you that. I wanted you to know."

"I love you, too, sweetheart. I feel like I've always loved you. Like— This sounds like a fairy tale, but I feel like I've always known you, like we were together before, maybe in another life, but we got separated somehow. Now that I've found you again, I never want to let you go."

"That's beautiful. And yeah, I get that. I feel that way, too."

"So, we're a couple, right? Even without ever going on a date?"

"Yes, we are."

He rested his elbow and propped himself above her. "Still...um, just to be official... You want to go out with me sometime?"

She pulled him down for a kiss. "Yes."

* * * * *

CATCHING
A HACKER

MAGGIE WELLS

To the best thing I ever scored online—my Super
Cool Party People. From cyber acquaintances to friends
IRL, we've been through it all in the last fifteen years.
You truly are Top-Tier.
My life would suck without you!

*Content Warning: This novel contains discussion of
self-harm and suicide attempts as a result of bullying
that might prove upsetting to readers sensitive to those
subjects.*

Chapter One

"Parker?"

Captain Simon Taylor hadn't shouted her name, but Emma Parker jumped at the sound. She'd been wholly engrossed in studying the data from a series of transactions involving a small florist shop in Eureka Springs, Arkansas. Given the quantity and amounts involved, it was easy to see whoever was sending and receiving the payments was involved in more than simply pushing posies of peonies.

"Sir," she replied, tipping her screen down and hoping the angle was acute enough that her boss wouldn't see what she was studying.

She'd used a backdoor Trojan to bust into the accounts they located. And while it wasn't technically illegal to deploy the silent tracking software when she had cause, it was sometimes hard to make prosecutors believe the information gleaned from legit hacking was on the up-and-up. Her boss hated having to defend their methods to the prosecuting attorney's office. She was hoping to come up with evidence of money laundering so irrefutable, no one would pay much attention to how it had been obtained.

Emma had to blink a few times before her section chief came fully into focus. Though Captain Taylor was under six feet tall, he was powerfully built for a computer jockey.

But his physique wasn't what made him impressive. It was the superprocessor he called a brain.

"I need to pull you away," he said without apology or explanation. He inclined his head toward the monitor she'd been glued to for hours. "You recording the data transfer activity?"

"Yeah—" Second-guessing herself, she turned to look at the screen again. A green light flashed in the top right corner. "Yes, sir."

"Come with me."

He turned and headed toward his windowless office. The Cyber Crime Division of the Arkansas State Police was one of the newer sections created by the Department of Public Safety, and therefore not the most prestigious of postings. But she loved it. And though Emma and her colleagues had all gone through the same training and patrol curriculum as their fellow troopers, they were often looked at askance by the other investigators. Most of their work was done at desks, rather than in the field. She and her colleagues spoke a different language. They looked for different types of clues. Ones rarely visible to the untrained eye. But her eyes were highly trained, and damn good.

Emma swiped a hand over the front of her blouse as she rose. She'd dribbled broccoli-cheddar soup down her front after becoming distracted while eating lunch. She had no doubt the dark trousers she had on were creased from sitting too long, even though she'd purposefully bought the kind purported to be "wrinkle-free." At least her shoes were shiny, she thought, glancing down at the new lug-soled loafers she'd acquired over the weekend.

She rounded the corner then drew up short at her boss's open door. There were people in there. A man with dark hair shot through with silver, and a long-limbed young woman with loose waves of hair pulled over one shoulder and downcast eyes. Emma paused in the doorway, her hand braced on the frame. Her chest tightened as she took in the sight of the three of them sucking down all the oxygen in the room.

"Sir?"

"This is Max Hughes and his daughter, Kayleigh," Simon said, nodding to his guests. "Come in and shut the door, would you?"

Emma took a step to her left, then swung the office door closed, trapping the four of them in the cramped office. She put her back against the wall and forced herself to breathe evenly as she scanned the room, desperate to spot an air vent. Simon started talking, but she was having a hard time hearing him over the rush of blood in her ears. Panic clawed its way up her throat. She tried to catch what her boss was saying, but it was—oh, thank goodness. She exhaled long and loud when she spotted the vent placed high in the wall above her head.

"Agent Parker?" Simon prodded. "You with us?"

"Sir. I mean, y-yes, sir," she stammered. Reassured, she forced herself to play catch-up. Gaze traveling over the people in the guest chairs, she did a quick assessment.

The man was wearing quality clothes. Conservative in style. Nice shoes. Freshly barbered hair. He was clean-shaven and the hand he held clasped in his lap had clipped nails, not bitten. *Manicured?* she wondered. Emma fought the urge to curl her own fingers, with their raggedy cuticles and uneven nails, into her palms as she shifted her attention to the daughter.

"…senior at Capitol Academy. Straight-A honor roll, homecoming queen, chair of the community involvement committee and Harvard-bound this fall," Simon said.

Emma took in Kayleigh Hughes's designer joggers and the cropped-but-still-oversize sweatshirt the girl had on, with white-on-white designer sneakers too pristine to have been out of their box for long. A leather bucket bag in a metallic mint green sat at the girl's feet.

As if she could feel Emma's inspection, Kayleigh looked up. Eyes fringed with what had to be lash extensions were puffy and red. If she started the day with any makeup on, it was long gone. Her lips were chapped and cracked. She'd clearly been biting the bottom one. Emma could see a patch of tender pink where the skin had been peeled away.

"…has been sent home for allegedly bullying another girl in her class."

Emma blinked, her head jerking back. "Bullying?"

She frowned as she studied Kayleigh again, slotting this new information into place and seeing how it skewed the data she'd already taken in. Emma knew all about bullying. She'd been a victim of it herself long ago. And being a victim had driven her into retaliation and self-harm, and ultimately into the career she loved.

Sliding her hands behind her back to keep from clenching them into fists, she asked, "What kind of bullying?"

"Social-media posts, mostly," Simon said, nodding in her direction. "The school is looking into the matter, but Mr. Hughes and I go back a long time. He's asked us to look into these posts—"

"Posts Kayleigh didn't make," her father quickly interjected.

Kayleigh started to cry. Were they tears of guilt or fear? Was she upset she'd been caught, or did the girl feel genuine sadness? The need to know the truth gripped Emma like a vise. And she wasn't going to get to the truth through intermediaries.

Dropping to one knee, Emma watched the startled girl's eyes widen in shock as she reared back. "What happened?"

"Trice—" she began, then broke off on a sob. "I would never— We were friends…you know, when we were kids…"

She fanned her face and Emma could practically feel her pulling herself together enough to get the words out. "We don't hang much anymore, but I'd never... Trice was so sweet."

Startled by Kayleigh's use of the past tense, Emma lifted her head and swiveled a look between Simon and the girl's father. "Trice...?"

"Patrice Marsh," Max Hughes answered, reaching for his daughter's hand to comfort her. "She and Kayleigh have been friends from elementary school on."

"And what happened to Trice?" She turned to look at Simon.

"She took some pills. Her mother found her in time and took her to the ER. She's expected to make a full recovery," he said, his voice gentling on the last part.

Emma cocked her head, realizing she'd missed something in the introduction. Simon knew these people. This girl. And he called her in here to...what? Prove this girl, who obviously was at the top of the social heap, hadn't picked on someone less fortunate than her? Clearly, Simon didn't have much experience in the world of teenage girls.

"Patrice tried to hurt herself?" She directed the question to Kayleigh.

"Yes, ma'am," Kayleigh mumbled between soft hiccups.

"*Did* you post mean things about her on social media?" she asked directly.

Kayleigh looked up, her gray eyes wide and guileless. "No, ma'am. I swear. Someone must have hacked my accounts. I'd never. Trice and I...we're friends."

"Still?" Emma persisted. When the girl hesitated, she nodded. "You're friend-*ly*, but you don't really hang anymore. Am I right?"

Kayleigh nodded emphatically. "Yes, ma'am. She tried

too hard. And could be a bit cringe, you know? But it isn't like she's a total outcast."

"I get it. You don't run in the same circles," Emma concluded.

"No, ma'am."

"And there were posts made by your account about…" Emma paused, unsure if she should use Patrice Marsh's nickname or not. Doing so felt overfamiliar, but on the other hand, she was trying to make Kayleigh comfortable talking about her friend. In the end, she tiptoed around the girl's name. "I take it they were unflattering posts."

"I'd never say those things about Trice. Or anyone," Kayleigh insiste, her bloodshot gray eyes flashing with indignation. "I'm not a bully. I'm not a mean girl, no matter what some people say." She spat out the last few words hotly.

"People are saying you're a mean girl?" Emma asked, holding eye contact.

In her peripheral vision, she saw Kayleigh's father shift in his seat, but resisted the temptation to check him. If he wanted to jump in, he would. She needed to establish a rapport with Kayleigh. Let her know Emma was truly listening to what she had to say.

Kayleigh's chin wobbled, and she drew her poor, abused bottom lip between her teeth. Emma wanted to reach out. Touch her arm. Assure her she hadn't stepped into some empty no-man's-land filled with disapproving adults and Waspish peers, but she had to maintain professional boundaries. So rather than comfort, she offered Kayleigh the consolation prize—attention.

"Can you show me the posts?" she asked gently.

The teen shook her head mutely, then shot a glare in her father's direction. Emma read between the lines.

"You have her phone?" she asked, turning her attention to the thundercloud of a man seated beside his daughter.

He stared back at her with eyes the color of polished pewter and a fierce scowl. "Not because I believe she did anything wrong, but because—"

"Because I told him it was possible her device was compromised," Simon Taylor said, breaking in, his tone stiff and a tad defensive.

She glanced up at Simon, surprised. A straight shooter with a no-nonsense manner, her boss was a cop through and through. Giving people the benefit of the doubt didn't come naturally for him.

She extended her hand. "May I?"

Max Hughes hesitated, but on Simon's nod, he dug into the inside breast pocket of his suit coat. "I saw them earlier," he explained. "Dr. Blanton, the principal at Capitol Academy, had printouts of some posts made on FrenzSpace and Pictur-Spam accounts with Kayleigh's name and photo, but when I asked Kay to pull up her accounts, they weren't there."

Emma nodded as she took the latest, greatest smartphone from the man's hand and turned it over to his daughter to unlock the home screen. The device was equipped with facial recognition and sprang to life the moment the teenager raised it to her eye level.

"Do you have a code, too?" she asked Kayleigh in a quiet voice.

"Yes, ma'am."

"Does anyone else know your code? Your best friend, maybe?"

Kayleigh shook her head. "No. Not on this phone. I changed it when we set it up."

Interesting. Emma eyeballed the array of app icons on the screen. "Is there a reason you changed it?"

She tried to come off as nonchalant as possible. Emma knew firsthand how quickly a kid could clam up if they thought they were violating the rules of "us versus them."

She needed Kayleigh to count her on the side of "us" if she was going to be of any help to her.

"I, uh…" She hesitated, a pale pink flush adding extra color to what Emma could only assume was a spring-break tan. "The old one was from a song I liked, but you know, it was kind of…done. I wanted something fresh."

Emma scrolled from screen to screen. "Were the posts only on those two apps? Nothing on ChitChat or Blabber?"

The question earned her a mild eye roll. "No one uses Blabber anymore. And ChitChat? Really? I'm not, like, thirty," she said, the words dripping with disdain. "Truthfully, I hardly use any of them anymore. I check FrenzSpace sometimes because all the student groups and stuff are on there, but mainly I post pics."

"To PicturSpam?" Emma prompted.

"Yeah." She cast a glance under lowered lashes at her father, then added, "And Foto."

Emma glanced over as Max Hughes's dark eyebrows slammed together. "Foto? What's Foto?"

He directed the question to her, and not his daughter—almost as if he couldn't bear hearing one more surprise from the girl. "It's another photo-sharing platform. More…artistic than social media."

Stormy gray eyes bore into her. "Please tell me *artistic* is not a euphemism."

"I'm not using it as one," she assured him. "But the platform is a favorite of artists, photographers, models and the like." She turned her attention back to Kayleigh. "You posted some photos there?"

After a moment of hesitation, she nodded. "Nothing to get all worked up about. They were some shots Tia and I took at the park. I thought they turned out pretty cool and wanted to, you know…"

She trailed off with a one-shoulder shrug and Emma silently filled in the blanks. Kayleigh was looking for attention—possibly to make contact with someone who knew something about models or modeling agencies. After what had been said about her being Harvard-bound in the fall, taking a detour into the world of clothing designers and cosmetics companies was likely not a part of the plan. But rather than wading into the tangled quagmire of hopes and dreams versus expectations, Emma carefully steered the conversation back to social media and Kayleigh's posting habits.

She tapped on the icon for PicturSpam and held up the phone to capture the girl's face. Before Kayleigh could get a glimpse at the notifications piling up on her profile, Emma took it back and began to check her most recent posts. She flicked through the last twenty or so without finding anything mentioning Patrice Marsh or vaguely resembling bullying.

"Mr. Hughes, did the principal give you screenshots of the posts the school said came from Kayleigh's account?" she asked without slowing her scroll.

"I have them," Simon announced. "You said PicturSpam?"

"Yes, sir," she replied, glancing up at her boss as he thrust two printed pages at her. "Thank you."

She frowned as she took in the image attached to the post in question. It was the same as on the account she'd pulled up on Kayleigh's phone. But the message tagged @SweetTrice by name, accusing the girl of trying too hard to fit in, and mocking what sounded to Emma like normal teenage foibles and fashion choices. On a scale of mean to cruel, Emma would have clocked it on the less offensive side, but she was no longer an insecure seventeen-year-old. She didn't have a tight grip on what passed for bullying these days, but she could see how the critiques could be hurtful. Particularly when coming from a girl who was once a friend and now sat at or near the top of the high-school social strata.

"You didn't post this." Emma looked up and met Kayleigh's anxious eyes.

"You believe me," Kayleigh whispered. Then her gray eyes filled. Tears trembled on the edge of her lashes, threatening to spill, but not quite making the fall. Yet.

"I believe there are lots of ways to manipulate social media," Emma said, tearing her gaze away to check the other posts on the printed pages. The profile picture was the same. She squinted at the handle associated with the account. It took her a full minute to pick out the difference between the authentic accounting and the copycat. The copycat had mimicked the original by changing the *i* in *Kayleigh* to an exclamation point. "See? 'At-kayleigh-hughes-oh-eight' on yours, but this one is 'at-kayleigh-hughes-oh-eight,' with an exclamation point in the middle."

Without looking up to see if the girl's lash extensions were being subjected to another flood of tears, she closed the app. "You said the others were on FrenzSpace?"

"Yeah," Simon responded, thrusting the remainder of the papers at her. "Same kind of stuff."

She switched to the app, with its globally recognized navy blue icon, and turned the screen in Kayleigh's direction. She felt the telltale vibration signaling a successful log-in, and tapped until she was in Kayleigh's timeline. The only posts she'd made on the account appeared to be automatically cross-posted from her PicturSpam account. Photo after photo of teens alternately grinning or pouting for the camera filled the page. Though the content was blatantly self-indulgent not one of the captions could be considered cruel.

"You're positive you haven't shared your log-in information with anyone?" she asked, meeting the girl's gaze directly. "No one? Not even your, uh, bestie?"

She was rewarded with a soft snort of derision. "No, I don't share passwords with my *bestie*," she replied, placing excess emphasis on the last word. "We took all the classes, you know." With a glance in her father's direction, she continued, "I know how the internet works. I got an A in Information Technology."

"Don't get snippy, I'm not the one who almost got expelled today," her father reminded her gruffly.

Kayleigh's face crumpled, and in what Emma could only describe as an act of desperation, she reached out and placed a calming hand on the young woman's knee.

"Hey. Listen. I need to look into this more, but I think you've been hacked." She glanced over her shoulder at her boss. "Hacked, or possibly spoofed." Shifting her focus to Kayleigh's father, she said, "If you don't mind, I'd like to hang on to this. I want to monitor the accounts to see if anything pops once word of the day's events gets around."

He nodded his assent. "Oh, it's getting around," he said gravely.

For the first time since Emma entered the room, Kayleigh Hughes sat up straight in the chair. "What? You want my phone?" She whirled to look at her father. "You can't give her my phone."

"I can and I did," he answered calmly. "You'll survive without it for one night."

"But I—" She gaped at her father, practically trembling with teenage indignation. "I have to tell my friends I didn't do it. I need to tell them I didn't make those posts."

"If they're your friends, they'll know you didn't," he countered evenly.

Emma rocked back to sit on her heels. The last thing she wanted was to get caught in the middle of a daddy-daughter spat, so she redirected. "Do you have any other devices linked to this one? A tablet? Laptop?"

Father and daughter nodded. "Both," Max answered.

"I'd like to take a look at them, too, if you don't mind," she said, directing the request to him.

"I can get them and bring them in this evening," he offered.

Emma considered for a moment, then turned to her boss, hoping he was following the same train of thought she was riding.

"Best to see them on the home network," Simon said gruffly.

He had indeed read her mind. Smiling, Emma inclined her head. She shouldn't have been surprised to know they were in sync. The Cyber Crime Division was small, and they'd worked in teams of various combinations over the years. And all of those teams had one common denominator—Simon Taylor.

Max inhaled deeply and stretched his arms up. He let them fall—one to his side, the other landing solidly on his daughter's shoulder. But rather than flinching away, as Emma thought she might, Kayleigh leaned into his touch.

"It's been a long day, and I think we're both ready for some quiet time."

"How about I monitor your phone this evening, then bring it by your house tomorrow," Emma suggested. "I can take a look at the other devices then, but I strongly caution you not to use them." She turned her attention to the father. "I assume you have an office set up at home?"

"I do," he replied, inclining his head. He turned to his daughter. "You can make a couple calls from my computer. Audio only, no video. And no social media."

"But Da—"

He cut her off with a swift shake of his head. "You can tell your friends you're okay, but then we're both going to unplug for the night."

One perfectly groomed eyebrow rose. "Both of us?" Kayleigh challenged. "How will your clients know when to draw breath?"

The teenager's tone was heavy on the sass, but the underlying current of hopeful wonder was unmistakable.

He shrugged. "I guess they'll have to hope their autonomic systems remain functional for the night."

He pulled another phone from another pocket in his immaculately tailored coat and presented it to Emma with a flourish.

"Whoa," Kayleigh breathed. "What if the house catches on fire or something?"

A laugh escaped Emma as she placed the sleek devices on the corner of Simon's desk and rose to a standing position.

A wicked gleam lit Max Hughes's dark eyes as he stood, too. "If you're really worried, I'm pretty sure I have an old flip phone stashed in the junk drawer."

"Oh, no. I'd rather the house burned down with us in it," Kayleigh replied, and it was tough to tell whether her horrified expression was an act or not.

"Don't say such things," he admonished.

Emma assumed he likely was running on autopilot. She remembered being a teenage girl all too vividly. There was no doubt in her mind Kayleigh Hughes's parents had seen their fair share of hormonal hysterics.

"How should I contact you in the morning?" Emma asked as they gathered their belongings and prepared to leave.

"You can come by. Let's say nine o'clock?" he suggested.

"Sounds good. And Simon has your address?"

"He does. He also has my email if there's an issue." He gestured to his own mobile phone. "I don't know if there's any kind of test you can run to see if there's anything on my—"

Emma nodded. "I'll run some diagnostics and antivirus checks."

Simon handed over a well-used legal pad and pen.

"Let me get your access codes and I'll need handles and passwords for your socials," she said to Kayleigh. "We'll want to reset everything to make sure you're secure, but for now I'd rather not give any indication we think something may be wrong." She gave the girl a sympathetic grimace. "Please don't say anything about our involvement or being hacked to any of your friends. Until we know what's happening and who's doing this, we need to keep things on the down-low."

Kayleigh nodded. "Thank you for not saying 'on the DL,'" she said solemnly.

Emma grinned in response to the girl's deadpan attitude. "I really wanted to," she confessed. Impulsively, she gave Kayleigh's arm a reassuring squeeze. "It all seems bad today, but it will get better. I promise."

"How do you know?" the girl answered morosely.

"I know, because when I was in school, I had something similar happen to me," Emma said bluntly.

"You did?"

This time, Emma was the solemn one as she nodded. "I did. Except I was on the Patrice end of things."

Chapter Two

"What do you think she meant when she said the thing about being like Patrice?"

Max started at the softly spoken question. Kayleigh had been sullen and silent, staring out the passenger window since they pulled away from state police headquarters. She refused his offer of drive-through sustenance with a shake of her head and her jaw locked shut. He couldn't help feeling that she somehow blamed him for the events of the day.

Or maybe this was nothing more than his own sense of inadequacy rearing its ugly head.

"I have no idea," he said, wading into the conversational opening with caution. "Maybe she was bullied in school?"

She gave a soft snort, but didn't look over at him. "Can't see it. She seems cool."

Max couldn't help but smile. Sometimes, the immediacy of adolescence struck him like an anvil being dropped by a cartoon coyote. Everything in their world happened in the moment. The future was too amorphous and somehow the past didn't count. To them, people were who they were today, and would never change. His daughter met a bright, confident woman who knew a lot about technology and the mores of the online world, therefore Special Agent Emma Parker was cool and cutting-edge. She'd grown up in the era of tech billionaires. She couldn't imagine a world where the computer kids were the outcasts.

But he remembered it.

"I'm sure she is cool. Simon is cool." The derisive snort she gave was enough to convince him she disagreed with his assessment of his old college roommate. "Okay, maybe *cool* isn't the right word for Simon," he conceded. He pondered alternatives, but the best he could muster was: "He's always been really smart, though. Smartest guy I know."

The observation must have struck a chord with his daughter. As he slowed for a red light, he glanced over and found her staring at him, the look of perpetual disdain she'd been wearing for the last few years was gone. He found himself looking into the open and curious eyes of the girl he'd adored since the moment they placed the squalling pink infant in his arms.

"What?" he asked, caution making him slightly breathless.

"You know I didn't post those things about Trice, don't you, Daddy?" she asked, her voice hoarse with fear.

He answered with his heart. "I know, sugar." He reached across the console and gave her clasped hands a reassuring squeeze. "We'll get this straightened out."

"What about Harvard?" she asked, panic filling her voice. "I'm not going to graduate. I won't be valedictorian."

He sucked in a deep breath and returned his hand to the steering wheel as the light changed and the cars ahead of them began to move. "One thing at a time. Let's go home. Regroup. I'm going to call Todd Marsh and check on Patrice. Make sure he and Dara know we're thinking about them. Then I'll call Dr. Blanton."

With a tentative plan in place, they lapsed into silence for the rest of the drive home.

TRUE TO HIS WORD, Max started making calls the moment Kayleigh trudged off to her room. He closed his study door behind him, pulled up the contact list synced to his computer, and used the audio-only option on his desktop to dial a number he hadn't used since the days of elementary-school slumber parties. He wasn't surprised when his attempt to reach out was shunted off to voicemail. Undeterred, he left a brief, but heartfelt, message.

"Todd, it's Max Hughes. I don't know what to say. I hope you know Kay is wrecked. She swears she didn't post anything about Patrice, and I believe her, man. Our girls…" He choked up, then cleared his throat. "I know they've drifted apart, but you know Kay. You know she'd never want to hurt Trice." *Or want Patrice to hurt herself,* he thought, scrubbing a hand over his face. "Anyway, I know we're probably the last people you and Dara want to talk to, so no need to call back. Please know we love Patrice and if there's anything we can do… Yeah, well… Take care."

He ended the call and exhaled in a gust. He allowed himself the space of five deep breaths before opening his email and messaging accounts. Twenty-three unread emails. But there were only nine texts, so he started there.

The first two were from his assistant, seeking direction on how to handle tasks on client accounts. He shot back quick instructions, though he knew the ever-efficient Leah had likely figured things out on her own. Two were auto texts from political candidates seeking donations, another a reminder for a dental appointment the following week. But he slowed his scroll when he saw the name *Amy Birch* pop up next on the list.

Amy was the Information Technology teacher at Capitol Academy. She was also an attractive woman he'd met through a dating app the previous summer. They'd enjoyed one-and-a-half coffee dates before they realized she taught at the school his daughter attended. Indeed, she'd been slated to have Kayleigh in her class when the fall semester started. He'd called it quits on their second getting-to-know-you session before they'd finished their lattes and croissants.

Still, he'd liked Amy, even if the possibility of them dating was out of the question. And because it was a nonstarter, he never told Kayleigh about his near miss with one of her teachers. The teen years had been bumpy enough for them. Coming out of eleventh grade, Kayleigh had her sights set on Harvard and it seemed like things were finally starting to even out between them. The last thing he wanted to do was alienate his daughter. Again.

Darting a nervous glance at the closed door, he clicked on the messages.

Hi. It's Amy Birch in case you removed my number from your contacts. I heard, and wow. I'm sorry. For both girls, I mean.

I can't believe it. I never would have thought Kayleigh could do that.

Sorry. Are y'all okay?

Let me know if there's anything I can do to help.

He wiggled his mouse, gnawing on his bottom lip as he toyed with the idea of responding. But what would he say? Everyone at school thought his daughter was a bully. A mean girl so ugly on the inside that she'd post vile things about a young woman who'd once been her best friend. What could he possibly say?

He clicked out of the messaging app and started moving briskly through his email inbox, discarding junk and flagging items he could deal with later. He was pondering the tax implications of a client request when a message from Kayleigh popped up in his notifications.

Can we order pizza? I need cheese.

He was trying to decide if giving in to her dinner request could be considered a reward for bad behavior when another email appeared in his inbox…from Emma Parker.

Please ask Kayleigh to refrain from using her devices. Thank you.

He blinked at it twice. Kayleigh was messaging him from her room. From either the tablet or the laptop Emma Parker wanted to check the following day. He hit the reply button and began typing: You can see her messages?

I have her phone. Her devices are all connected.

Max stared at the screen wide-eyed. He thought he'd been clever, buying his child devices with a shared platform. He wanted to avoid the tragedy of lost term papers and be sure he could contact her any number of ways. It never occurred to him it would also make it easier for one person to access everything Kayleigh had. Then he thought about all the confidential financial transactions he handled from his home office and his heart began to hammer, and he began typing again: Do you think my desktop is compromised as well?

Are they networked or synced to Kayleigh's?

Max blew out a breath of relief. And typed a quick No in response.

His desktop at home was linked to his office computer. He glanced at the message Kayleigh had sent about pizza and let out a breath of relief when he realized it had come though the operating system's built-in messaging application.

Another message appeared almost instantaneously: Best to keep Kayleigh offline. Pizza might help take the edge off.

Will do. Off to be the bad guy.

He clicked over to his browser to place an order from their favorite local place. Knowing it would take the better part of an hour for the delivery and feeling resolute, he pushed back from his desk. His first stop was the kitchen. He was probably being overcautious, but after what happened with Patrice, he wasn't about to take any chances. After grabbing a plastic grocery bag from under the sink, he opened the slim cabinet beside the fridge and stared at the small pharmacy they kept there.

He stared at the mostly untouched bottle of prescription painkillers left over from when Kayleigh sprained her ankle during a volleyball match in PE. It sat on the top shelf and taunted him with its easy access. His heart flipped over in his chest. He attacked the shelves like a dad possessed. Every bottle of aspirin, acetaminophen, antihistamines and cough syrup went into the bag. By the time he was through, the only things left were a bottle of chalky pink antacid, an elastic wrap and a box of adhesive bandages.

He stalked back to his study, then opened the small closet and kneeled to unlock the safe where he kept important papers, their passports and a stash of emergency cash. Once the bag was bolted away, he changed the digital combination for good measure and pushed to his feet with a grunt.

Then he strode purposefully to his daughter's room. Hesitating only for a moment, he raised his hand and gave the door a decisive rap. He'd learned many important lessons since becoming a widowed single dad to a two-year-old, but one of the most important had come when he and Kayleigh were a decade into their life as a twosome. Overnight, his easygoing kid had turned into a screeching preteen. He'd learned not to even touch the door handle until he heard her muffled invitation to enter.

"Come in," she called, her voice raspy.

He turned the knob and found his daughter sitting cross-legged in the center of her bed, her tablet open to an ever-moving social-media feed and tears streaming down her puffy face. Rushing into the room, he all but threw himself onto the bed in his haste to get to his child.

"Shh. Shh," he soothed, as a giant sob racked her slender body. She twisted her coltish leg under her and turned to him. "Oh, baby, no," he murmured, kissing the top of her head and holding fast. "It will be okay. We'll figure out what happened, and everything will be okay."

"It won't be," she groaned, looking wretched. "Trice is going to die and they all think it's my fault."

"What? No," he quickly assured her. "Patrice is not going to die. She's going to be fine. They may have sent her home already."

He had no idea if the young woman had been discharged from care, but when he'd spoken to Dr. Blanton earlier, the man seemed to be under the impression she would not be held in the hospital much longer.

Kayleigh peeled her face from his shirt and used the back of her hand to wipe away some of the moisture. "It's not just Trice. Now whoever is doing this is posting about Carter."

She waved her hand at the tablet as if he was failing to keep up. And maybe he was. He had no clue what she was talking about. Carter? Kayleigh had gone to the homecoming dance with a guy named Carter Pierce. A football player.

Not a boy he would have pegged as his daughter's type. He drove a jacked-up truck and talked as big a game as he played on the field, but under all the bluster and posturing, he'd seemed like a nice enough kid.

Max pulled back, shooting a worried glance at the tablet before looking into Kayleigh's swollen eyes. "What about Carter?"

"They're all talking about him," she whispered, burrowing into him again. "And me. They're saying I told him to do it."

Reflexively, his hold on his daughter tightened. "Do what, sweetheart?"

"But I didn't," she went on, unhearing. "I didn't, Daddy, I swear. You were with me. I don't even have my phone," she insisted.

He pulled back again to look her in the eyes. "Told Carter to do what, Kayleigh?"

Pressing her lips together, she shook her head in adamant denial, tears streaming down her cheeks.

Desperate to find out what was happening, Max reached for the tablet. The feed kept jumping with new posts, so he scrolled down until he saw the handle @kayle!ghhughes08 tagged in a post with a screen capture.

It featured a photo of Kayleigh and Carter Pierce taken at the homecoming football game. She was wearing the short slip dress they'd argued over for hours before she'd bombarded him with picture after picture of her friends modeling similarly slinky dresses and he'd relented. After all, what did he know about teen fashion?

She had on a giant chrysanthemum wrist corsage. Carter was in his football gear, his helmet tucked under the arm. Max had taken the photo himself and shared it and the dozens of others he'd captured with his daughter to be cropped, primped and preapproved for posting.

The post had been generated by the spoofed account, but unless someone was looking closely, no one would ever realize the minor alteration in Kayleigh's screen name. He squinted at the grayed-out timestamp and saw this photo had been shared mere hours ago. Probably not long after they'd left Dr. Blanton's office.

The caption beneath the picture read:

@Kayle!ghhughes08 Framed! OMG I cannot even. As if I'd say mean things about @SweetTrice. We've been besties since birth and ugh! So messed up. @CarterScoresAgain did this. He thinks he can cancel me so he can be #1. TF???? I earned the V. Bruh needs to suck it up and own Salutatorian or go suck on the tailpipe of his swaggin' wagon. IYKYK Amirite? #PrayersforPatrice #besties4eva

A quick scroll up through the feed made it clear many of the commenters believed Kayleigh was trying to deflect blame for Patrice's suicide attempt onto Carter and accused her of encouraging Carter to do the same.

He was opening his mouth to ask what was going on when the doorbell rang. Kayleigh peeled away from him and flung herself into the pile of pillows mounded on the bed. "I don't wanna see anybody."

"Shh," he said, giving her leg a gentle pat. "I ordered pizza, remember? It's probably the delivery driver."

He crawled off the bed, taking the tablet with him. On his way out, he swung past her desk and unplugged the laptop she used for schoolwork. "Let's do what Agent Parker said and stay offline tonight, okay?"

Kayleigh sniffled loudly, and Max decided he would interpret it as assent.

He dropped the tablet and laptop on the hall table, then hurried to the door as the bell rang again. He checked his watch and was shocked to discover less than thirty minutes had passed since he placed their order. Without his phone, he couldn't check to see if it was the delivery driver ringing his bell. Max frowned, annoyed with himself for feeling so bereft without the device. After flicking open the dead bolt, he pulled open the oversize oak door.

"Sorry, I need to grab my wallet—"

He trailed off when he found Special Agent Emma Parker standing on his doorstep, all petite curves and rumpled clothes. The late-afternoon sunlight caught the auburn in her hair. Straight eyebrows drawn down over dark brown eyes, she gazed back at him, her grave expression incongruous with the freckles sprinkled across her nose.

"Sorry, I don't have your pizza," she said in a low voice.

She wasn't supposed to come to his house until the next day, but here she was. Staring at him like he was a puzzle to be solved. Her scrutiny made him want to fidget like a schoolboy. "I thought we agreed—"

He was about to ask if he'd been confused about their appointment when he saw Simon Taylor coming up the walkway behind her accompanied by another man.

Samuel Blanton.

Max's stomach dropped to his feet as he took in the grave expressions the two men wore. Instinctively, he turned back to Agent Parker. "What's happening?"

"There have been more threats made," she began. "Well, posts," she amended. "Other students are reading and interpreting them as harassment."

"Let me guess—they're about a boy named Carter Pierce?" Max asked, directing the question to Agent Parker and ignoring Taylor and Blanton.

"You've seen the posts," she concluded quietly.

"I went up to collect Kayleigh's tablet and laptop, and found her crying." At last, he looked over her shoulder at the men crowding his threshold. "She didn't make those posts. You could see they were from the other account. Even I could see as much," he insisted.

Simon Taylor took a step closer. "May we come in?"

"No." Instinctively, Max raised both hands to stop them from advancing. "I don't… I can't… Kayleigh is already distraught. We can't talk about this anymore tonight."

"Mr. Hughes… Max, I'm terribly sorry to do this," Dr. Blanton said. "Until recently, Kayleigh has been an exemplary student, but these situations can set off a chain reac—"

Max held up a hand. "Please." He heard the edge of desperation in his voice but couldn't be bothered to mask it. "I understand you have to be proactive, but you know something more than what meets the eye is happening here."

He turned back to Agent Parker, willing her to back him up. "You know something is suspicious about these posts."

Her expression softened and she inclined her head in acknowledgment of his plea. "I understand you and Kayleigh are both upset by the events of the day. We know there are duplicate accounts claiming to be Kayleigh, but unfortunately we don't know for certain Kayleigh isn't the one posting to both accounts."

His gaze flew from Agent Parker to Simon Taylor, one of his oldest friends. A man who'd sent congratulations on Kayleigh's birth and condolences when Jennifer succumbed to the cancer first discovered during her pregnancy. "What are you saying? You think Kayleigh is doing this?"

"We're saying we need to rule her out," Simon replied, his tone unaffected.

Max stared at the man as if he'd never laid eyes on him before. How could he even entertain the notion? He knew what they'd been through. He knew how hard Max had worked at being a good parent. Now he dared to stand on his doorstep and imply he'd failed? How dare he insinuate

Max had raised a daughter who bullied and belittled other kids? Couldn't they see what was happening? Didn't they understand it was the real Kayleigh who was being framed, not this mean-spirited imposter?

"We have to take all incidences of bullying seriously. You know this, Max," Dr. Blanton said quietly, but firmly. "We must investigate thoroughly and do our best to mitigate any adverse effect this…situation has had on our student body." He pulled his reading glasses onto the end of his nose and peered at the papers he held in his hand. "Surely you understand. If it were happening with any other student, you would expect me to carry out my due diligence, would you not?"

Before he could respond, a battered hatchback pulled into the driveway, blocking the agents and the principal of Capitol Academy in. Max didn't want to know what was printed on the pages the principal held tight in his hand. He only knew he wanted them gone.

Taking two steps back, he snatched the laptop and tablet he'd confiscated from Kayleigh's room from the hall table.

He thrust them at Agent Parker and his gaze fixed on the older man standing behind her. "There. The police now have every one of Kayleigh's devices in their possession." In his sweater vest and half-moon reading glasses, Dr. Blanton looked like a caricature of a private-school headmaster. Max couldn't help wondering if the resemblance was an accident or a choice. "I only ask you refrain from making any life-altering decisions until the police have had a chance to eliminate my daughter from suspicion."

Samuel Blanton hesitated for a moment, then, glancing at the two agents, gave a slight bow. "Kayleigh will remain suspended indefinitely." He removed the glasses from the end of his nose, folded them and used them to gesture to the electronics Agent Parker held cradled to her chest. "We can discuss her possible return to campus once this matter is resolved."

Max nodded and gestured to the young man carrying a thermal delivery box up the sidewalk. "Now, if you'll excuse me, our dinner is here."

Special Agent Parker and Dr. Blanton turned away, but Simon hesitated, his gaze locked on Max. Impatient with his old friend's awkward social skills, Max waved him off. "Go. Do your job."

But Simon didn't move as the delivery driver edged past him.

"Hughes?" the young man asked, darting the other man a look as he slid the pizza from the insulated carrier.

"Yes," Max responded. He held up a single finger. "Hang tight. I need to grab my wallet for your tip."

"I've got you," Simon said gruffly. Before Max could wave him off again, he pulled his own wallet from his pocket and thrust some bills at the driver. "Keep the change."

The driver handed Max's pizza over to Simon in exchange. "Thanks, man," he said, snatching up his carrier. "Y'all have a good night."

Simmering, Max snatched his pizza from Simon's hands. "You didn't have to."

"You'll pay me back," his friend replied with a shrug. "I put Emma on this because she's my best," he said in his typically blunt manner. "Not only did she experience something similar when she was young, but she's also the best I have when it comes to tracing the untraceable. Trust me. Trust us. We're going to find out who's doing this."

"Whether it's my kid or not," Max retorted, still prickly and defensive.

Simon held his gaze for a moment, then gave a slow nod. "Whether it's your kid or not." He turned to leave, then called over his shoulder, "Eat. Get some rest. If I know Parker, she'll be back here first thing tomorrow."

Shoulders slumping, Max watched as Agent Emma Parker stowed the electronics in the trunk of a nondescript sedan. Simon slid behind the wheel and Max noticed the car had tags declaring the car to be state property. Agent Parker stood back, waiting for the delivery driver and Dr. Blanton to back out before heading to the passenger door. With her hand on the handle, she looked up and their eyes met and held.

She didn't nod or wave. She offered no encouraging smile or other outward sign of support, but once again, he couldn't help feeling she was on their side. Heartened by the thought and buoyed by the aroma of spicy sauce and herbed cheese, he stepped back and swung the door closed before calling his daughter down to supper. When Kayleigh didn't respond, he left the pizza on the dining table and made his way to her room again.

But when he got to her open doorway, he found the room empty, the rumpled bed with its plethora of pillows in complete disarray. His heart hammering in his throat, his gaze flew to the window, as he thought she may have made a break for it. It was closed, the blinds undisturbed.

"Kay?" he called, his voice trembling with the odd mixture of wariness and weariness he'd grown accustomed to feeling when approaching his only child.

No response.

"Kayleigh," he called more forcefully. Making his way down the hall, he peered into the darkened bathroom and found it empty. Impatience warred with worry as he passed the untouched guest room and headed for the primary suite. "Kayleigh, come on. Your pizza is here."

But when he reached the open doorway, he drew up short.

There, on the king-size bed he and Jennifer had bought when they believed they had decades ahead of them, lay their little girl. Kayleigh was all grown up now, curled into a tiny ball on the side of the bed he barely touched, even after all these years. She looked too young for any of this. Too innocent to have her whole future come crashing down during second period. He moved to the side of the bed, then perched cautiously on the edge.

"Kayleigh? Sugar?" he whispered loudly. "Pizza's here."

She didn't move and his thoughts dashed to the bag of over-the-counter medications he'd collected from the kitchen cabinet. Tentatively, he brushed her hair back from her tear-streaked cheek. "Honey? You hungry?"

But his daughter only snuffled and snorted, mumbling something unintelligible as she shied away from his touch, curling tighter into a ball. His heart squeezed as if caught in a giant fist as he rose from the bed. Sleep was probably the best thing for her, anyway, and if she felt more comfortable in his room, she was welcome to it. He pulled the duvet from his side of the bed and wrapped her in its warmth.

"I'll put the pizza in the fridge," he whispered from the doorway. "It'll be there when you're ready."

And so would he, he resolved. No matter how long it took.

Chapter Three

Rather than going home after Agent Taylor dropped her at headquarters, Emma retreated to her desk. She stared at the mobile phones belonging to Max and Kayleigh Hughes, the printed screenshots the school had used as evidence and the devices the girl's frazzled father had handed over at the house. This whole situation stank.

In her tiny cubicle, she checked to be sure the program she'd started running before Simon Taylor pulled her into the meeting with Dr. Blanton from Capitol Academy had completed. Satisfied, she dropped into her chair with a gusty exhale. The scene at the Hughes house struck too close to home. Once, it had been her parents standing in an open doorway gaping at a man flashing a badge identifying himself as an agent with the Federal Bureau of Investigation.

With Taylor gone, the Cyber Crime Division had cleared out for the day. Emma wondered if she should, too. One of the perks of being on the CCD team was they didn't need to work from their desks all of the time. Like most of the other agents in the department, Emma had better, faster equipment at home than the clunky models requisitioned for the Arkansas State Police. Sure, she had to use the laptop to log in to the state systems, but she'd always been a creative person. She found ways to enhance the tools she'd been issued.

She gazed at the detritus on her desk. A pad of paper with the odd note or numbers scrawled at convenient angles. She leaned forward to collect the scattered pens and markers she'd used to mark up a printout someone had delivered from the ancient dot-matrix printer in the basement of the building. Two monitors, turned vertically, were squeezed side by side on the modular desktop. There was a dog-eared square of sticky notes on top of her docking station.

The only personal item in the whole setup was a plastic hedgehog figurine she'd scored ordering a kids' meal at lunch one day. Her cubicle mate, Special Agent Wyatt Dawson, said it reminded him of her. She took it as a compliment. Hedgehogs might appear spiny, but for the most part they were peaceful creatures. Like her, they were simply content to mind their business. When she said as much to Dawson, he shook his head and said it was because she made all sorts of weird squeaks and grunts while she worked and got prickly when interrupted.

Reaching for her messenger bag, she shoved the printed pages into the outside pocket, then dropped both the phones in, too. The tablet Max Hughes had thrust at her sprang to life when she flipped it over. She reached for the list of passcodes and started tapping in numbers, assuming that Kayleigh would prove to be as lazy as 99 percent of computer users when it came to security. Sure enough, the teenager used the same combination for both devices.

Shaking her head, she set it aside and opened the laptop. She pressed the power button to boot it, but when the operating system engaged, the desktop appeared without any security clearance at all.

"Aw, come on now," she muttered under her breath.

"Someone making it too easy for you?"

She jumped, startled by the gruff question. When she turned and saw Wyatt Dawson leaning an elbow against the partition wall, Emma heaved an exasperated sigh. "Yes. For me and everyone else in the world," she said, spinning her chair to face him. "I'm telling you, people never think about getting some kind of antivirus until it's too late."

"And then only during cold-and-flu season," he replied with a smirk. "You're hanging out late."

She raised both eyebrows. Emma hadn't seen Special Agent Dawson putting in a lot of after-hours time since Cara Beckett, America's favorite lifestyle guru, had moved back to Arkansas. "It appears you are, too."

Wyatt didn't bother to hide his smug smile as he moved into the space next to hers and started gathering his belongings. "Not for long." He slammed his laptop closed, grabbed a couple of files and shoved them all into his bag. "Hear you have a new case."

"Yep. Cyberbullying. Some kids at Capitol Academy."

He let out a low whistle of appreciation. "You're in with the big-time players," he commented. "The blue web has it on good authority the boss hand-picked you for this assignment."

The blue web was what she and her fellow CCD officers liked to call good old-fashioned cop gossip. She rolled her eyes. "You mean the kids of the big-time players," she said dryly. "And you know there's nothing more fun than watching teenagers goad one another into self-destructing."

Wyatt sobered as he straightened. "Right. Sorry." He flashed a wan smile. "We've been poking around in so many dark corners lately, I've forgotten how to be a human being."

She returned his smile with a weary one of her own. "Nah. I know how it is." Glancing back at Kayleigh Hughes's unguarded computer, she decided she'd do well to take the whole lot home with her. Sitting on her comfy couch in her cozy apartment would make slogging through hundreds of hateful adolescent social-media posts slightly less…daunting. Maybe she'd treat herself to a pizza for dinner. The one Max Hughes had delivered to his house had made her mouth water, it smelled so good.

Decision made, she closed the laptop and shoved it into her bag along with the tablet. "Hold up. I'll walk out with you."

Wyatt waited patiently as she gathered everything she needed, then motioned for her to lead the way through the warren of cubicles between their tiny island and the exit.

"Sounds like the boss knows these people personally?" he ventured as they pushed through the double doors into the warm spring evening.

"Looks like it." She shrugged as they crossed to the parking lot. "You know Taylor. He didn't offer up much in the way of backstory."

"I'm sure he didn't. One of the guys near his office thinks he heard something about college mentioned," Wyatt offered as they reached her car. "Can you even imagine Taylor being eighteen and shotgunning beers in some dank basement?"

"Uh, no, I didn't think I could, but thanks for planting the visual," she said, clicking the fob to unlock the doors.

He raised one hand in farewell as he started walking away. "Don't stay up all night creeping on the socials. It rots your brain."

"I'm hoping my translation app has a teen-to-adult setting."

Waving goodbye, she opened the rear door of her car and scanned the interior before putting her electronics-laden bag on the rear seat. She slid into the driver's seat as the lights on Wyatt's SUV flashed. After punching the button to start the engine, she gripped the steering wheel with both hands, then drew what felt like her first full, deep breath of the afternoon.

When she joined Cyber Crime, she knew she'd be called

in on cases involving teenagers. She'd hoped to be of more help when it came to sniffing out internet entrapment or thwarting catfishing schemes targeting underage girls. But she wasn't naive enough to think she'd escape without having to confront at least a few cyberbullies. Adolescents armed with keyboards could be some of the most vicious creatures on earth. She knew as much from first-hand experience.

She drove to her midtown apartment on autopilot, her thoughts pingponging between Kayleigh Hughes's predicament and her own past. Her gut instinct was to believe the girl, but Emma knew better than most how duplicitous teenagers could be when they deemed it necessary.

She parked in the designated spot for the condominium she rented in one of Little Rock's mixed use residential-shopping-dining complexes. Her unit was two flights up from one of the many sandwich shops occupying space on the ground floor. With the heavy computer bag digging into her shoulder, she pulled open the door to the shop and was hit with the scent of fresh baked bread.

"Hey, Tom," she called over the chime of the electronic bell.

"Hey, Emma," he answered. "The usual?"

"Yes, please. Extra—"

"Mayo, no tomato, no lettuce," he finished for her. "Gotcha."

She waited near the register while he built her triple-decker club sandwich, selecting a bag of chips and a large cookie in a paper sleeve from the temptations on hand.

"You need a drink?" the man behind the counter asked as he expertly wrapped her dinner.

"Nah, I'm good," she said, presenting him with her second buy-ten-get-one punch card of the month. "Everything going okay here?"

He rang her up, punched her card and bagged her purchases with the brisk economy of movement that robotics specialists dreamed of replicating. "'S'all good. You know, same old, same old."

She waved her debit card at the reader and took the bag from him, waving off his offer of a receipt. "Same old, same old," she echoed. "The way we like it." Turning to the door, she called, "'Night!"

"See you tomorrow," he answered.

Twenty minutes later, she had her sandwich wrapper spread on the antique trunk she used for a coffee table, a cold can of soda and her favorite true-crime series queued up to stream. She took a huge bite of her sandwich, pressed Play on the remote and started pulling devices from her bag as she chewed.

She pulled the laptop from her bag and opened it before setting it aside on the cushion. The tablet was easier to navigate one-handed. Sandwich in hand, she sank into the cushions, half-heartedly listening to the recap of the previous episode as she paged through screen after screen of apps.

Sure enough, Kayleigh Hughes's legitimate account had been tagged in dozens of outraged posts on PicturSpam. She scrolled back a few days in an attempt to pinpoint the moment when the tide of public opinion turned on the homecoming queen and found no hint of the animosity currently running rampant across multiple platforms. Patrice Marsh's attempt to take her own life seemed to have acted as a sort of starter's pistol. In prior posts, the worst she could find was a semifawning comment made by a girl with the handle @DarbyDaBarbie. Kayleigh had posted a picture in which she and two other girls mugged shamelessly for the camera, numbered bibs from a ten-kilometer race pinned to their layered tank tops.

Next to a thumbnail photo of a willowy beauty with long, golden blond waves drawn over one shoulder, DarbyDaBarbie had posted: OMG. Could you stahhhhhp with the awe-someness, @kayleighhughes08? We're getting dewy tryin' to keep up, grrrrl!

Emma clicked open Darby's profile, confirmed the girl was every bit as flawless as the object of her admiration, then checked the timestamp. She'd commented on the pos-trace photo around ten o'clock the previous evening. There wasn't another mention of Kayleigh Hughes in particular until sometime after lunch.

@CapMarkMorgan2026: Wow. Sad to hear about @Sweet-Trice. I hope her parents press charges. I swear, girls like @ kayleighhughes08 think they can get away with murder.

Beneath his comment others chimed in.

@DooodIKR1113: Or not quite murder. Hang tough @Cart-erScoresAgain ! #PrayersforPatrice #TeamCarter

@StacezSpam: So. Sad. #PrayersforPatrice And now she's trying to set @CarterScoresAgain up to take the fall?!?! I hope @kayleighhughes08 gets what's coming to her, but you know her daddy is Mr. $$$

@LindC: You mean her zaddy, rite? Whew! Sry, but srsly. Daddy Hugebucks is fire!

And down the rabbit hole Emma went. She scrolled through all the tagged posts on Kayleigh's account, then read through what seemed like hundreds more she accessed through Patrice's PicturSpam handle and various hashtag searches. When she checked Carter Pierce's account, she found the pile-on happening in full force.

And almost no one was attempting to raise a defense on

Kayleigh's behalf. It looked like the girl had gone from one of Capitol Academy's most popular and admired students to sea-witch-level villain in less than a day.

Looking up, she realized she'd completely lost the thread on the episode she started, so she decided to opt out. But when she leaned forward to hit the power button on the remote, the screen on Kayleigh Hughes's laptop sprang to life.

Assuming she'd done something to activate the touchpad when she moved, Emma didn't think much about it as she scooped up the other half of her sandwich and switched off the television.

But as her teeth sank into the soft bread, she saw the tiny arrow of the cursor skate across the computer screen.

Frowning, she placed the sandwich carefully back on its wrapper, wiped her fingers on the crumpled paper napkin tucked under her leg and turned to look directly at the laptop. She stared at it, unblinking, not daring to move a muscle in case her hunch turned out to be true. She was about to shake off her suspicions when the tiny green light indicating power to the computer's camera came on.

Acting on instinct, Emma shoved the lid of the device open wide, pointing the camera up at the plain white ceiling. Then she held her breath for what felt like an hour. If the camera was on, the microphone was likely activated as well. Her gaze darted from the green light to the cursor, then back again. Max Hughes said his computer was not linked to his daughter's via a network, but it appeared someone was operating the device remotely.

The hacker?

Gritting her teeth in an exaggerated grimace, Emma slowly slid off the edge of her sofa, trying her hardest not to jostle the computer or make any noise. One knee touched the ground, then she braced her hands on the top of the trunk to transfer the rest of her weight from the cushion. She slipped silently to the floor and was reaching for her phone to record a video, when the cursor skated across the screen and the green light blinked out.

Emma counted backward from ten before exhaling in a whoosh.

She slammed the lid of the laptop closed, then pushed to her feet, pacing the small living room as her mind raced with possibilities.

Did whoever cloned Kayleigh's accounts have access to her computer?

It looked like it.

Were they watching Kayleigh through her camera? Recording her?

Emma gnawed her bottom lip as she pondered all the possibilities.

Where did she keep her computer? Did she carry it with her? No. She likely did everything through her phone. The laptop would have been for homework. Did it stay in her bedroom? Was it always open? Could some creep have been watching her?

Anything was possible, she thought with a shudder.

She'd need to go over all her concerns with Kayleigh's father. The minute she got into their house the next morning, she was going to ask Kayleigh to set up her laptop exactly where it would have been.

Lowering herself gingerly to the edge of the cushion she'd abandoned, she closed her eyes and allowed herself to think like the hacker she once was.

"Backdoor Trojan," she murmured, jumping to her feet again. "But how did they get in? File transfer?"

Knowing she thought better when she was in motion, she rubbed her hands together as she stared hard at the sleek computer. She was about 90 percent sure it hadn't awakened in the time she was scrolling PicturSpam, but she couldn't be certain. She'd need to find out if Kayleigh used any cloud services, or transferred data using portable drives. She hoped Kayleigh was smart enough not to allow Bluetooth connections to drop files onto her devices, but given the lack of security measures in place on any of them, Emma couldn't rule out the possibility.

She fired off an email.

Does Kayleigh keep her laptop in her bedroom?

She stalked the living room, tapping the edge of her phone against her thigh as she waited for a reply. Determining the extent to which Kayleigh Hughes's devices were compromised was not the difficult part. Tracking down MAC or IP addresses would not be difficult, either, though Emma assumed whoever was doing this was also clever enough to use public or communal computers, and was likely good enough to put some misdirection in place. But Emma was good, too. Better than good. She could get through whatever roadblocks their perpetrator threw up. The question was, could she do it in time to stop Kayleigh's life from being derailed and other teens from suffering any additional harm?

She glanced at her phone. No response from Max Hughes.

Her mind racing, she wrapped the remains of her dinner and placed the leftovers in the fridge to take for lunch the following day, then wiped down her already clean kitchen countertops.

Still no reply.

After checking her phone again, she stuffed a load of laundry into the unit's tiny washing machine, then returned to the living room to collect all the other devices. She set up shop at the breakfast bar that separated the kitchen from the living area. A power strip loaded with charging cables kept the juices flowing to Kayleigh's phone and tablet.

She carried Max Hughes's phone over to the small desk, where she had a desktop unit with enough speed and power to run circles around the combined forces of every computer in the Cyber Crime Division, and began running diagnostics on his phone. After checking the operating system for flaws and noting the history and condition of the phone's battery, she ran through the downloaded apps, looking for spyware or other vulnerabilities.

The phone was as clean as could be expected. He didn't seem to keep any extraneous apps hanging around and didn't appear to have social media downloaded to the device at all. The number of emails hanging out unsorted in his inbox made her left eyelid twitch, but she knew not everyone was capable of striving for inbox zero. She tweaked a few settings to help improve performance and generally button things up a bit, made notes of the changes so she could let him know what had been done, then set aside his device.

The moment she started running the same tests on Kayleigh's notifications, warnings and alerts began popping up like fireworks. She groaned and rocked back in her task chair, lacing her fingers together to keep from starting in on them before the program had a chance to finish processing.

She picked up the tablet, then tapped on the FrenzSpace icon and waited for Kayleigh's timeline to load. The notification icon showed almost two hundred awaiting attention. The built-in messaging application showed thirty-seven private conversation threads.

She didn't want to open one for fear of sending the correspondent a notice their message had been read, but the idea of private messaging stuck. Emma was curious to see whether Kayleigh's friends might be showing their support in a less public forum.

Opting out of FrenzSpace, where required usernames did not allow for much anonymity, she scrolled until she spotted the icon to open ChitChat. The instant-messaging app was one younger generations preferred because they believed it left no virtual footprint. But they were wrong.

People liked it because they could "arm" a Chit with a time bomb, which would make the message disappear after a specified time limit. Character limits within the application ensured messages were short, but not necessarily sweet. Several of her fellow CCD agents agreed that there were few online arenas as brutal as ChitChat. Worse, they thought they could get away with saying anything and everything thanks to the company's highly touted anticapture software, which made getting clear screenshots of messages next to impossible.

For the average user, that was.

But Emma had always been above average when it came to finding work arounds. She'd figured out a staggeringly low-tech answer to ChitChat's so-called security scrambling while consulting on an extortion case the previous year. She might not be able to keep the message from disappearing when time expired, but she would get what she needed. Grabbing her own phone, she opened the camera app.

After capturing a dozen more incoming messages, she closed the application. She studied a half-dozen photos of messages popping up on Kayleigh's feed before she caught a glimpse of the words *kill yourself* in one of them. Though her breath came in a ragged shudder, Emma forced herself to remain calm as she enlarged the photo of the tablet.

Her fingers trembled as she zoomed in on the next. And the next. The last one she read came from a user with the handle @8675309: Girls like Kayleigh Hughes don't off themselves, but maybe someone will do the job for us.

Someone responded with What a waste, and attached a grainy photo of a young woman clad only in a skimpy bra-and-pantie set.

Emma didn't have to zoom in any further to know it was a photo of Kayleigh Hughes. Most likely a still shot captured by the camera on her own computer. One she likely kept open and on, unaware she might be broadcasting her bedroom for all the world to see. Or, at the very least, for this one creeper to see.

Stomach turning inside out, she switched to her email app. Still no response from Max Hughes. Her stomach sank like a stone when she realized she couldn't call to tell him what she suspected. She had his phone.

Clicking over to the case notes she'd typed up after their initial meeting, she scowled at the blank space where a home phone number would be listed. At the time, she didn't think much of it. People were giving up their landlines. But those people hadn't handed over every mobile device they owned to the police. And now, innocent or not, a young woman was receiving death threats.

She opened an email and pounded out a quick message.

I'm coming over.

A second later, a faint buzzing from Max Hughes's phone confirmed the warning had gone through. Gathering both their phones, the tablet and Kayleigh's laptop, she shoved them all into her messenger bag with her clunky state-issued computer and took off.

Chapter Four

Max was dozing on the sofa in his family room when his doorbell rang for the second time that night. Swinging his legs to the floor, he looked down at his feet. He'd ditched his shoes long ago, but he hadn't gone back into his room to change out of his work clothes. Pushing off the couch with a groan, he tugged at the waistband of his suit pants and rolled his shoulders. The starched white shirt he'd pulled from his closet that morning was now a rumpled mess. He'd rolled the sleeves onto his forearms before extricating a single slice of pizza from the box earlier, and now the cuffs were accordioned in the crooks of his elbows.

The bell rang again, and he traded his concerns about his appearance for whatever fresh torment awaited him on his porch. He tried to remember the last time someone other than a delivery driver had approached his front door and failed. He missed his phone, and the handy app that allowed him to interact with whoever darkened his doorstep without having to appear face-to-face.

"Coming," he called when it pealed a third time.

Crossing the foyer, he felt a telltale spot of smooth cool tile on the ball of his foot and cringed. Time to buy new socks. He closed his eyes for a moment, gathering himself before tipping his head to look through the narrow strip of glass alongside the huge front door. His visitor was a female. One of Kayleigh's friends?

He flipped on the outdoor sconces and golden light illuminated the porch.

But the woman at his door was not one of Kayleigh's friends. It was Agent Emma Parker. She stood and stared at his door, shifting her weight from foot to foot, practically levitating with energy despite the bulging bag she carried.

He twisted the locks, then yanked the heavy door open wide. "What is it? What's wrong?"

"Is Kayleigh okay?" she demanded, matching the urgency in his tone.

"Yes. Why? What's happening?" He stepped back and gestured for her to enter.

"She hasn't been online, has she?" she asked as she brushed past him.

"No. How would she? You have all of her devices," he pointed out, closing the door behind the agitated agent. "What's going on?"

She blew out a breath, ruffling her hair. "Does Kayleigh keep her laptop in her room?"

He frowned. "Yeah. But you have it," he reminded her, waving a hand at her straining messenger bag.

She reached for the strap of her bag, grimacing as she lifted it off her shoulder and over her head. "Can you ask Kayleigh to show me where she keeps it when she's not carrying it with her?"

He blinked. "Uh, she's sleeping." A thump from the other end of the house made their heads turn in unison. "Or not," he muttered.

"She hasn't been in your office?"

He ran a hand over his face, hoping to brush off the lingering dregs of his own exhaustion.

"I'm not sure. I don't think so. I dozed off." He hooked a

thumb over his shoulder to indicate he'd been in the oppo-site end of the house. "She was sleeping when I went in to watch TV." She nodded, but the worried crease between her eyebrows didn't go away. "What's the matter?"

The dull thud of a drawer or door shut with a tad too much force prefaced a disembodied, but clearly annoyed, voice that called, "Da-a-a-ad?"

"She's definitely up now," Agent Parker murmured dryly. "Why do I feel the urge to step in front of you?"

"Part of me wishes you would," he said in a low voice. "But don't worry, I'm used to being the villain around here."

Emma took a small step back as Kayleigh stormed past them, her sights clearly set on the family room and his office beyond. She drew up short in the hall, scenting her quarry and doubling back, her angry gaze fixed on him. "Did you take my computer?"

The parent in him cringed, embarrassed by her rudeness, but he didn't have the energy to open a second battle line in their ongoing power struggle. "I did. We're both staying offline, remember?"

"What did you do with it?" Kayleigh demanded.

"I gave it to Special Agent Parker." He gestured to the woman watching them go back and forth like a couple of tennis players fighting it out on center court. "You remem-ber Special Agent Parker?" he prompted, unable to keep the snarky edge from his voice. "The police officer looking into your alleged hacking."

The moment the words were out of his mouth he wished he could suck them back. If Emma Parker didn't latch on to the underlying tone, Kayleigh certainly would.

He wasn't wrong.

Both women zeroed in on him.

"Alleged?" Agent Parker asked. "You have reason to be-lieve your daughter's devices were not compromised?"

"I knew you didn't believe me," Kayleigh accused. "You never believe me anymore."

Max took a step back, raising his hands in surrender and shaking his head. "I didn't mean it to sound like I didn't believe you."

"How did you mean it?" Emma asked, surprising both him and his daughter with how quickly she leaped to Kayleigh's defense.

"I'm tired and…stupid," he said, giving up on mounting a stronger argument. "I say stupid things when I'm tired. Everyone does."

Without another word, Agent Parker turned to face Kayleigh head-on. "Y'all can call me Emma. I have your laptop, phone and tablet." She darted a glance in his direction. "I came because I also have your father's phone, and it occurred to me you might not have another way to call for help if needed."

"You think we might need help?" Max asked.

"I think there's a lot going on, and neither of you needs to feel isolated," she replied. Emma pulled his phone from her bag, and handed it over to him. "I checked it. Yours is clean."

"Can I have mine back, too?" Kayleigh asked.

Emma shook her head. "I'm afraid not. I have reason to believe your phone has been spoofed, meaning all the applications you use on both your phone and your tablet are likely breached. I also believe your laptop has been ratted."

"Ratted?" Kayleigh repeated. "What's that?"

"I mean someone has installed a kind of spyware. It allows them to access your computer remotely. RAT stands for Remote Access Trojan. Like the wooden horse from Greek mythology, a program sneaks into your operating system by looking like a normal file. Once it's in, it unleashes all sorts of nasty code. Depending on what's written into them, they can tie up or delete files, slow your operating system, infect programs, monitor your online activity, access stored data, clock your keystrokes and basically control the whole thing."

"Someone has been sneaking into her computer?" Max asked, aghast.

"I think so. I noticed some suspicious activity earlier, but I had to shut it down. I didn't want whoever was controlling the device to know someone was onto them." She turned to Kayleigh. "Would you show me where you usually keep it?"

Mutely, the teen nodded and turned on her heel. Max fell into step behind them, his mind racing. Infected files? Spyware? Suspicious activity?

"What kind of suspicious activity?"

Emma shot him a pointed look over her shoulder. He figured he was supposed to know what her glare meant, but he was as clueless as he'd been when Dr. Blanton had called him and asked him to come down to the school. Was it really the same day? Time was both whizzing past and moving at a snail's pace. Deciding the smarter thing to do was to follow her lead, he zipped his lips and stuck close.

"Do you power your laptop down at night?" Emma asked as she stepped into Kayleigh's room.

"No, ma'am," his daughter replied.

"Do you close it, or put it in sleep mode?"

Kayleigh shook her head. "I usually just plug it in. I mean, it goes to sleep after a while, you know."

"I know," Emma confirmed. Pulling the computer from her bag, she handed it to Kayleigh. "Don't open it yet. Set it down in the spot where you usually keep it."

"O-kay."

A tiny furrow appeared between Kayleigh's eyebrows. Max figured there had to be a wrinkle as deep as the Mariana Trench between his. He watched as Kayleigh placed the computer on the desk. His gut twisted as he pictured the laptop open, the light from the screen saver acting as an unofficial night-light for a girl who was too old to admit she wanted one.

"Do you recall noticing any times when your computer woke without you touching it?" Emma asked Kayleigh.

His daughter frowned in concentration, then shrugged. "I guess so. I figured they come on every once in a while, you know, to let you know it has power."

Nodding absently, Emma moved to the desk. She stood in front of the computer and turned in a slow semicircle, her gaze skimming over the dresser, the bed and the door leading to the en suite bath and walk-in closet.

Max stood frozen in the doorway, torn between wondering what she was thinking and fear that he knew where this was heading.

"I assume you video-chat on here sometimes?" she asked, gripping the back of the desk chair.

"I did when I took a remote class or we had to meet for group projects," Kayleigh said, then shook her head dismissively. "But most of the time I use my phone."

"Is it safe to say you don't use your laptop as much as your phone or tablet?" Emma asked, her tone neutral and business-like.

"Yeah, definitely."

Emma opened the laptop, then stepped to the side as she plugged in the power cord. Reaching across the trackpad, she wiped and tapped until a program for the built-in webcam opened and a wide-angle view of his daughter's bedroom filled the screen. Apparently satisfied with what she saw, she clicked out of the program, then gestured for them to leave the room.

The three of them stepped into the hall, but when Max glanced back, he saw she'd left the computer sitting open on the desk. "Are you going to—"

Emma pointed in the direction of the main part of the house. "Let's go in here to talk."

She lifted her bag and strode down the hall, leaving them no choice but to follow. Once in the living room, the heavy satchel hit the floor with a soft *thunk* as she sat on the ottoman situated in front of the sectional sofa, gesturing for them to take seats across from her.

Max smirked, vaguely amused to be shepherded around in his own home. He was used to issuing the orders. He should have been annoyed by her overreach, but he didn't have the energy to work up his outrage. Besides, he couldn't help but admire her confidence. She was clearly in her element.

"I think someone is controlling Kayleigh's computer remotely. Most likely they gained access through what we call a backdoor Trojan. Like I told you earlier, it's a type of spyware that rides in attached to a file or program."

Kayleigh turned to her father, instantly defensive. "I haven't been downloading random apps. I swear."

Emma shook her head hard. Max reached over to place a calming hand on Kayleigh's arm. "It's okay. Let's hear what Agent… Emma has to say."

"It doesn't have to come from a download. If you use any kind of cloud service or share files with other students, a memory stick you might use to save work in the school computer lab, an email. There are all sorts of ways someone can get in." She waved a hand as if to clear the air. "The how isn't as important as the who and what." She leaned in, bracing her elbows on her knees. "My job is to figure out who it is, and what they are doing."

She paused for a moment, then looked Kayleigh in the eye, treating her like an adult. An equal.

"The thing is, for me to figure them out, I need to be as sneaky as they are. And I'm going to need your help."

"My help?" his daughter asked, shooting a worried glance

in his direction. "I don't know anything about this stuff. I mean, I took an IT class, but only because it was required. I've never been too into computer stuff, you know, beyond social media."

"You don't have to worry about the technical side of things. Tech is my job. All I need you to do is be you," she said, reaching into the bag at her feet. "Now, I'm going to show you something and it may be upsetting," she warned. Then, slipping a glance at him, she added, "To both of you."

Max turned to look at his daughter, but she was nodding.

"Okay," Kayleigh said eagerly.

"No, honey, hang on—" he began.

"Daddy, I have to," she said, cutting off his protest at the knees. "No one believes I'm not doing this stuff. You don't even believe me—"

"I do—"

"Allegedly." His baby, the girl he'd dedicated his whole existence to for nearly eighteen years, pursed her lips and arched an eyebrow at him like he was a worm squished on the pavement. She'd drawled the word he'd carelessly used minutes earlier.

Max felt the last of his defenses stripped away. She was right. This was her life they were talking about. And in less than two months, she'd be eighteen and flying the nest. If they could get her through graduation. Turning his attention to Emma Parker, he nodded his acquiescence.

"Do what you need to do."

"Someone posted this on ChitChat earlier tonight."

She pulled her phone from the bag and pulled up a picture. Max grimaced and turned away as soon as he recognized the girl in the grainy screen capture. Someone had posted a photo of his daughter in her underwear. His heart thudded slowly in his chest. Was this really happening?

"How did they…?" Kayleigh cut herself off. "Ew, is that my bedroom?"

"Looks like it to me," Emma confirmed. "I suspect whoever is behind this has been using your webcam to capture footage of you in your room. This has all the signatures of a still grabbed from a video stream."

"You said you got it off ChitChat?" To his surprise, Kayleigh took the phone and squinted at the image. "How? I thought Chits couldn't be screen-capped?"

"Their encryption makes it hard to grab them, but sometimes the easiest way around advanced technology is to go old school." She took the phone back from Kayleigh. "I pulled the app up on your tablet, then took a picture of the screen. Not the best resolution, but I grabbed a bunch before they disappeared."

She flashed an impish smile Max found oddly reassuring. This wasn't just a determined woman, but a clever one. Emma Parker had the will to find a way.

Now he understood why his old friend Simon assigned this agent to the case rather than taking it on himself. Simon was a by-the-book guy. The quintessential linear thinker. He didn't color outside the lines or think outside the box. Max had no doubt Emma Parker would kick her way out of any box she encountered.

"So smart," Kayleigh whispered on an exhale. "I'm totally doing that."

"Anyway," Emma said, shaking off her moment of tech triumph. "I don't want to tip whoever is doing this off, so I want to set the computer up in your room again."

Max saw Kayleigh's eyes widen and opened his mouth to protest, but before he could get a word out, Emma held up a hand. "No, I'm not suggesting you let this creeper go on watching you."

"Then what are you suggesting?" Max asked.

"I think we need to role-play the removal of the computer," she said slowly, as if letting the idea unfurl. "We need to make it look as normal as we can, because we don't know when our watcher will be watching. But first, I need to get more information, so I need to let them pop in a few more times."

"But I can't...ew. You want me to let him watch me sleep?" Kayleigh protested.

Emma pulled a face and Max realized she was holding back from telling them this creep had likely been watching her for some time.

"Obviously, you shouldn't undress or even sleep in there, but I'd like to set it up so we can track it. Once we get what we need, we can make it look like you and your dad got in a fight over being suspended, and he takes it away. The trick will be playing it out when we know they are looking."

"How will we know?" Kayleigh asked.

"We wait for the computer to wake. If it does, we watch for the light indicating the webcam is in use. It'll be our cue."

"I'm supposed to sit there and watch it?"

Emma shook her head. "Nope. Again, the tech is my job."

"You're going to what? Camp out in my room?"

Max caught himself staring at Emma Parker with the same incredulity his daughter voiced. Would she? Sit there all day and all night, waiting for this predator to show themself?

"I don't know if this will work. All I know is I don't want you in there."

"But won't you be all weirded out, knowing someone might be watching?" Kayleigh asked, concern in her tone.

"I plan to stay out of camera range. After we get what we need, I can cue you guys and all you have to do is...fight."

"Well, we can certainly fight," Max said dryly. "But we don't know when or if they will, uh, pop up. It could be days."

"I have a feeling they're going to want to look in fairly often now things are happening," Emma said with a sympathetic wince. "I mean, wouldn't you?"

Max couldn't contain the guffaw. He couldn't imagine purposefully wreaking such havoc in an innocent stranger's life. "I suppose, if I were some kind of cyber stalker," he conceded.

"Listen, I didn't really think all this through until I was on my way over here, but I think it's a good plan." She turned to Kayleigh. "If I get tired, I'll sleep in your bed. My hair is dark enough to pass for brown in low lighting. If I keep the covers pulled up, they'd see nothing more than a lump in the bed, anyway."

She tossed off another one of those shrugs, and Max couldn't help but wonder what drove Special Agent Emma Parker. He couldn't recall meeting any woman so obviously unconcerned with her own comfort or needs. Did she even have a toothbrush with her? Did he have a spare in the house?

"I can do my work from anywhere," Emma explained, gesturing to her bag. Turning to him, she said, "Call Simon Taylor. Ask him if he thinks this is a good idea. If he tells me to stand down, I'll leave."

"Don't leave," Kayleigh interjected, surging to the edge of the sofa cushion as if to intercept the agent. Then his daughter turned to look at him. "I think we need to try."

Max shifted his jaw as he thought the agent's impulsive plan through. He knew he'd give in, but he needed a moment to process it all. If this was what Kayleigh needed to feel safe, he'd do it. If this unconventional approach to investigating this incursion into their privacy was what it took to get his daughter's life back on track, of course he'd do it.

But inviting a strange woman to sleep in his home? In his daughter's bed? He wasn't sure he was impulsive or unconventional enough to agree to this plan.

Zeroing in on the earnest agent seated across from him, he asked, "You don't mind if I call Simon and run this past him?"

Emma's smile was slow, but certain. "Not at all. As a matter of fact, I'll call him myself."

As she tapped the screen to place the call, Max knew it would be a moot point. She placed the call on speaker. Simon answered on the second ring.

"Taylor."

"Chief? I'm here at the Hughes house with Max and Kayleigh, and we want to run something past you," she said in a rush.

"Go ahead," Simon prompted.

"What would you think if I were to stay here and set up a sort of cyber stakeout?"

Chapter Five

Emma awoke in a strange bed the next morning. She blinked at the pale aqua wall blankly, then groaned as consciousness seeped in. She was in Kayleigh Hughes's room. She'd camped out in there, setting up her surveillance in accordance with the plan she and Simon Taylor concocted on the fly. Max and Kayleigh hadn't appeared to be convinced, but they'd provided her with fresh sheets, a slice of pizza and an unopened travel toothbrush bearing the name of a local dental practice.

She'd worked late into the night, as was her habit, relying on the glow from her own laptop and the ceiling fixture in Kayleigh's preposterously large walk-in closet to light the room. Her plan was to stick to the shadows or under the covers, providing enough movement to satisfy whoever was controlling Kayleigh's webcam.

Emma had seen the camera activate twice before she'd become too sleepy to sit propped against the wall. Satisfied her tracking software was running, she'd brushed her teeth in the adjoining bathroom, then crawled into Kayleigh's bed.

Snuggled into the warmth of the covers, she took in her surroundings. The room was the perfect aqua-and-white backdrop for a girl on the precipice of adulthood. There were dozens of photos tucked into a beribboned memory board above her desk and strings of white fairy lights draped from the crown molding.

Emma squinted at the bright sunlight streaming in around the edges of the blinds and wondered if Kayleigh Hughes would ever feel bright and beautiful in this room again. Her privacy had been breached. Her reputation was shredded. And her perception of what her peers thought about her, well, there'd be no putting the genie back in the bottle.

The soft whir of her laptop fan caught her attention. She peered over the edge of the bed in time to see the screen flash to life. Seconds later, Kayleigh's did, too.

"Oh," Emma gasped, pulling the sheet up high enough to cover most of her head, then rolling off the edge of the bed onto the floor.

Had the watcher peeked in while she'd been sleeping? After the sun came up? Had they noticed her red hair?

Emma was lying flat on the floor, her neck twisted so she had a direct view of her screen.

The cursor moved.

She smiled her satisfaction. She'd successfully cloned the clone. Her desktop was now a perfect replica of Kayleigh's… at least on the surface. Now all she had to do was wait to see what their stalker's next move would be.

The waiting was the absolute worst part of her job.

She watched as the cursor moved to the icon for a video-conferencing application popular among teens, postpandemic. Emma was torn between derision and admiration. It was such an obvious place to spy from, and yet, beautifully effective. Almost everyone Kayleigh's age used the application at one time or another. How better to hide in plain sight?

The cursor zipped across the screen to the camera control panel and Emma peered at her screen as the bedroom view filled the screen. Thankfully, the angle was good. She was completely hidden from view on the floor, but had she not bailed from the bed when she had, the slash of sunlight cutting through the blinds and hitting the pillow would have given her away for sure.

She was taking in the view, wondering how long they'd dare to stay connected, when a knock on the door almost jolted a yelp out of her.

Emma clamped her lips shut, then glared at the screen. If she spoke, the person watching may realize she wasn't Kayleigh. She closed her eyes, willing whoever was on the other side of the door to go away without speaking.

No such luck.

"You up?" Max Hughes called through the door.

Thankfully, he hadn't called her by her name. "Don't say my name. Don't say my name," she whispered into the fluffy white chenille bedside rug.

"Uh, there's breakfast if you want it," he said, raising his voice a few decibels.

"Go away. Go away," she muttered.

"Okay, well…" She squeezed her eyes shut, willing him to walk away. "Okay," he said in gruff defeat.

She turned her head. In the sliver of space between the bed skirt and the polished floor, she saw a shadow move past. She exhaled into the preternaturally clean space under the bed. What kind of teenager didn't keep stuff squirreled away under her bed? She puzzled for a moment, then turned her attention back to the computer.

Her screen was back to its replica of Kayleigh's wallpaper. A crimson block letter *H* on a snow-white background.

Harvard.

Kayleigh was planning to go to Harvard in the fall. She was a student leader with perfect grades and a list of extracurriculars like a rap sheet. Homecoming queen.

Did she even have time to wreak havoc on her fellow students? Why would she? Some kind of revenge? She was almost done with high school. The finish line was in sight. Soon they would scatter to their fancy colleges, pledge fraternities and sororities, and move on to law school or med school, or corner offices in Daddy's investment firm. What could someone like Kayleigh hope to gain from tearing down the kids around her? She already had it all in hand.

Wriggling around, Emma pushed up enough to rock back onto her heels.

She looked down at the short shorts she'd borrowed the night before. Her shorter, curvier body pushed the seams of the clothes she had no doubt were fashionably slouchy on Kayleigh's long, lithe teen frame. Glancing over at the navy pants and rumpled, stained white shirt she'd discarded on a chair, she winced. She decided to worry about her wardrobe later and marched into the bathroom.

After splashing water on her face and brushing her teeth, Emma availed herself of one of Kayleigh's hair bands, pulling her hair into a ponytail as she wandered into the massive closet. In the back, buried behind a selection of winter-to-spring coats and jackets, she found exactly what she needed—a long, thick terrycloth robe.

Shrugging into it, she hummed her appreciation as she belted the sash tightly. She'd dash home, change and pack a couple outfits…just in case.

Following the scents of coffee and bacon, she found her way back to the kitchen. She spotted Max Hughes standing at the island, with his back to her. His hair had been recently barbered. She could see the thin line of paler, newly exposed scalp along his nape. He wore dark jeans so perfectly pressed she had no doubt there was an empty dry cleaner's hanger in his closet. His broad shoulders were perfectly encased in yet another crisp white dress shirt, but the sleeves had been neatly folded back to expose tanned forearms. As he lifted an oversize white coffee mug from the marble island, she hesitated, trying to determine the best way to approach, when she noticed his feet were bare as well.

"Good morning," she said, pitching her voice low, not wanting to startle him.

It was no use. His hand twitched and he yelped as hot coffee spilled down the front of his shirt.

"I'm so sorry," she said, grabbing a striped towel from the counter and rushing to the island. She thrust it at him, stopping shy of mopping the mess from his chest. "I didn't mean to scare you."

She was babbling. Of course, she hadn't meant to surprise him, but she had. The best thing she could do was cease and desist. She froze in place, the towel dangling in the space between them.

"Sorry," she repeated.

"No." He shook his head and took the towel from her. "My fault. I was zoning out."

Flashing a wan smile, she nodded to his streaked shirt-front. "Well, at least you haven't left the house. I usually trash my clothes after I get to work and have to walk around wearing my shame for the rest of the day."

His smile came slowly. "Yeah. Thank goodness for small favors." He gestured to a thermal carafe parked beside a coffee maker that looked like they'd lifted it from a high-end café. "I can offer you plain old drip. If you want something fancier, we'll have to get Kayleigh involved. She doesn't like me messing with the settings," he explained as he tossed the towel onto the counter, then lifted his mug for another attempt.

"Drip is perfect," she assured him.

"Mugs in the upper cabinet."

Emma located another one of the big white mugs and filled it halfway with the rich, dark brew. Lifting it to her nose, she took an appreciative sniff. This was nothing like the scorched sludge they called coffee at headquarters.

"Do you take milk or sweetener?"

Her lips curved into a smile, and she shook her head as she wrapped both hands protectively around the mug. If it tasted half as good as it smelled, she wanted to savor every sip. "No, thank you."

They both raised their mugs. She blew across hers to cool it before hazarding a cautious sip, but he drank deeply. She figured he'd been up awhile.

"I have egg bites," he said, moving around the island to her side.

Her eyebrows rose as he slid open a stainless-steel drawer to reveal muffin-shaped scrambled eggs flecked with what looked like red peppers, cheese and bits of breakfast sausage. Their uneven sizes and crispy cheese edges made them almost look homemade. Then she lowered the mug and took a sniff.

"Did you make these?"

He nodded. "They're not anything fancy. Kayleigh goes back and forth on the whole to-carb-or-not-to-carb question, so I try to go protein-heavy in the mornings."

She lowered her mug, her jaw dropping as she took in his nearly pristine white shirt. "You cook?"

He cocked his head to the side, an amused smirk tugging at his lips. "You think I've been raising my child on a steady diet of chicken nuggets and toaster waffles?"

She gave a helpless laugh. "Maybe?"

He chuckled, too. "I cook. I also clean." She pulled a horrified face and he pressed on. "I also do laundry, but not as often since I accidentally shrank one of Kayleigh's sweaters."

"Yes, well, shrinking sweaters is grounds for termination," she said, matching his sober tone.

Max waved an expansive hand around the kitchen. "I'm

not saying I don't have help here and there, but for the most part, I'm fully domesticated."

"I'm both chastened and impressed." Giving him a small bow, she plucked one of the breakfast muffins from the drawer. Emma immediately regretted her impulsiveness. This wasn't the kind of kitchen made for scarfing a quick bite standing over the sink.

"Here." He picked up the towel she'd thrust at him moments before and handed it off. She took it whispered sheepishly, "Thanks."

Grinning, he spun and pulled a small white plate from the open shelf beside the cooktop. "I can offer you a fork and a seat as well," he said as he held the plate under her breakfast.

She widened her eyes. "A fork? Cutlery would mean I'd have to eat two."

Without another word, he pulled a dinner fork from a drawer, speared a second egg muffin and deposited it on the plate.

Her cheeks flamed, but she didn't wave him off. Scooting around the island, she inclined her head toward one of the stools. "Here?"

"Please."

"Thank you," she murmured, pulling the padded stool out so she could slide onto it.

Thankfully, he turned away to top off his own coffee mug while she got settled. "Did anything happen last night?"

She nodded as she chewed. Chasing the delicious egg concoction with a slug of coffee, she used the dish towel she'd co-opted as a napkin. "Yes. Three hits noted. I'll have to check my software to see if they attempted to peek in while I was asleep."

He turned to face her, his mouth thinned into a tight line. A tiny muscle in his jaw jumped and Emma wanted to kick herself for her insensitivity. She wasn't a cop spouting off the facts for a superior officer. She'd blithely told this man some stranger had likely been sneaking peeks at his daughter while she was blissfully unaware.

"I'm sorry," she said gruffly. "I was… I'm sorry."

He pursed his lips so hard the edges of them turned white, then swallowed hard. "I, uh…" He paused to take a ragged breath. "It's done, right? We know now. We're on to him. Her. Them. Whoever," he said with an impatient wave of his hand. "You should be able to trace it? With your software?"

She nodded. "Yes."

Emma shoveled another bite into her mouth before it could run off without her brain engaged. Pinpointing their culprit would be more complicated than a simple trace, but there was no reason to get too far into the weeds with him.

"Listen, I'm at your disposal," he said, shifting gears abruptly.

Her shock and confusion must have shown on her face. He set his cup down on the counter with a clink and ran his hand through his dark hair, ruffling it out of its neatly combed style.

"I, uh—"

He raised a hand to stifle her stammering. "I mean, I'm taking time off work. I can handle any emergencies from here, but this…" He paused, gulping in a breath and looking around the opulent kitchen as if seeing it for the first time. "Kayleigh is my everything. This…situation has my undivided attention."

"I understand, but the best thing you can do is keep living your life and let us do our thing." She offered him a wan smile as she prodded the second scrambled-egg muffin with the tines of her fork. "We might be a small department, but the CCD is mighty."

"Oh, I know." He opened his hands to show he meant no offense. "Simon is proud."

She smiled. "He handpicked each and every one of us."

"I heard."

"I was going to suggest the two of you get away, but Simon thinks it's better if you stay put."

"Nowhere to go, anyway." He gave his head a slow, sad shake. "It's me and Kayleigh against the world."

"Grandparents?"

"All gone," he said with an almost apologetic shrug.

"Simon said Kayleigh's mom passed when she was young?"

"A week shy of Kayleigh's second birthday," he said, a hint of gravel in his voice. "Jen was twenty-six weeks along when she found a lump. Metastatic breast cancer. She had a lumpectomy at week thirty-two and started chemo as soon as she delivered, but…" He shook his head.

"I'm sorry."

Though the words were heartfelt, they sounded small to Emma's ears. Inadequate. But they were all she had. She stared at the large, capable hands splayed atop the marble island, trying to imagine this quietly controlled man attempting to manage the unmanageable. Cancer. A newborn. Widowerhood. Parenthood.

Setting the fork down, she straightened her shoulders and met his gaze. "I'll catch the person who's doing this."

"I'm counting on it," he said gruffly.

After pushing the plate away, she wrapped her hands around the coffee mug and drew it closer. "I have to tell you, whoever is doing this is almost certainly using public internet access. This is someone who knows what they're doing. This isn't television. We're not going to pinpoint an IP address and find some oblivious loner hanging out at a desktop in their parents' basement."

"Simon already told me the cautionary tales," he assured her.

"We have to be smart. Careful. And at times, it's going to mean moving more slowly than you'd like."

"Understood."

"The moment we tip our hand, they could simply 'poof,'" she said, making an exploding gesture with her fingers. "Slip off into the ether, never to be heard from again."

He raised his open palms. "I can't think of any other way to tell you I get it."

"Cool." She nodded and slid off the stool. "Thank you for breakfast." After taking one last gulp of coffee, she carried her plate, fork and mug to the massive farmhouse sink, but he stepped in to intercept her.

Disconcerted, she began to babble. "I'm running diagnostics on last night's activity now. Once I have what I need backed up to my laptop, I'll run home and change, then go into headquarters. I'll meet with the team and put together a game plan. I hope to be back here by about noon."

His eyebrows rose as he rinsed the dregs of coffee from her mug. "Kayleigh and I don't have to stay in the house, do we?" He grimaced. "I mean, we can go out?"

"I'd advise against going out much. Not only are we dealing with a stalking situation, but Kayleigh is getting some pretty upsetting backlash online."

He stiffened, his movements jerky as he turned off the faucet.

She blew out a soft sigh. "I want to minimize her exposure. We both know what a small town Little Rock can be. I'd hate for someone to spot her out and about and use seeing her to spin a narrative about Kayleigh being unfeeling, given what happened with Patrice Marsh."

"Ri-i-i-ght," he said, drawing out the word.

"We're living in a world made of perception, Mr. Hughes—"

"You slept in my house last night. I think you can call me Max," he interrupted, a sharp edge in his tone.

"And perception is the reason we should do our best to observe propriety, Mr. Hughes."

"Fine, Special Agent Emma Parker," he replied mockingly.

She raised her hands as she backed away. "I'm only trying to make this as easy on you as I can."

"Nothing about this is easy, Special Agent Emma Parker," he grumbled. "I'll make sure we place ourselves under house arrest."

Inhaling deeply, Emma counted to three then let his anger roll right off her as she exhaled. "Thank you. Please leave Kayleigh's computer as it is until we have a good bead on our watcher. Remind her to keep an eye out for the green light and assume nothing in her room is private."

"This is a nightmare," he muttered as he slotted the dish and mug into a dishwasher hidden behind a cabinetry panel.

"No, sir," she said softly, but firmly. "This is not the nightmare. I know what's happening to Kayleigh is upsetting, but I can give you a half-dozen ways this could be worse off the top of my head."

"I didn't mean—"

Emma shook her head in dismissal. "This situation is frightening, possibly dangerous and absolutely damaging to your daughter's reputation," she allowed. "But as it stands at this moment, the biggest consequence Kayleigh is facing is the possibility she may not get to attend her first-choice university."

"Now, wait a minute—"

Emma didn't want to hear his attempts at forming a defense. "While such an occurrence would be unfair and possibly a threat to her future, at this time she still has a future. A bright one. Even if Harvard bails on her."

"I'm not—"

She cut him off. "There are photos of your daughter partially dressed out there. Their existence alone could push this case to another level. We need you to be patient. Give us the chance to catch this creep."

He inhaled deeply, but rather than the anger and frustration she braced for, he simply exhaled in a gusty whoosh and dropped his head, nodding his acknowledgment.

"The internet is an amazing place, Mr. Hughes," she said softly. "Things blow up bigger and faster than we ever imagined, but within a day, they are old news. People may dredge something up years from now, but it won't have the same impact as it has in the here and now. Social media is to traditional media what cable news was to the newspaper. Gossip and speculation are the fuel of the online world. Your job is to help Kayleigh keep everything in perspective."

"Right," he said, his voice rough with pent-up frustration.

Emma looked directly into his pewter eyes, smiled and spouted the words her grandmother used to use on her when the world closed in on her. "I promise—this, too, shall pass."

AN HOUR LATER, Emma walked through the doors of the state police headquarters, her laptop bag slapping against her hip. She'd stopped at her apartment long enough to shower and change clothes. Simon Taylor was sitting at her desk chair when she reached her cubicle.

"I hear you told Max Hughes his privilege was showing," he said by way of greeting.

"Not my intention," she replied stiffly.

Simon shrugged. "Eh. It probably was. Max has always had a sort of master-of-the-universe way about him. Even when he didn't have the proverbial pot to use for toilet training."

She slid the computer bag from her shoulder, then placed it on her desk as the section chief rose from her seat.

"I simply reminded him his daughter is a bright, accomplished young woman. Even if Capitol Academy opts to expel her, she won't have any difficulty meeting equivalency requirements and landing a spot at a top-tier school."

"Particularly since her father has deep pockets," Simon said with a brisk nod.

Emma smothered a smile. Simon had a reputation for being abrupt and abrasive. He called things as he saw them and spoke his mind without even attempting to finesse his words. It was a trait she appreciated in a superior, but knew did not serve him well when it came to a smoothing his career path.

"Did you get any hits?" he asked, pivoting to the task at hand.

"Yes. Unfortunately, each one pinged a different MAC address. Three from fast-food restaurants, one a coffee shop and the last the unsecured router of a small upholstery company on the north side of the river."

"Randomized," he concluded with a frown.

"Yes, sir."

"You're going back for more?" he asked with a curt nod.

"Yes. I'm going to copy my data over for Wyatt to poke at as well," she informed him.

"Copy me, too," he said, pushing away from the cubicle wall. "I assume you're staying there tonight?"

Her head jerked up. It took every ounce of her willpower to fight back the blush threatening to flood her cheeks. Knowing she wouldn't be able to hold it at bay if they got into a discussion about her sleeping arrangements, she latched on to the order he'd issued.

"You want me to copy you as well?"

He gave a soft snort. "Don't act so surprised, Parker. It's not unusual for me to look into cases."

True. In the past, he frequently poked his nose into ongoing investigations. And with his ability to slide into some kind of hyperfocus mode, he often proved to be quite help-ful, drilling through mountains of data with laser-like pre-cision. But for the last six months, the boss had become increasingly fixated on the activity surrounding an online smuggling ring they believed to be running out of a small town in the northwest part of the state. It had been a long time since Emma heard him ask for anything more than the most cursory of updates on any other case.

"I'll send it over now..." She turned her head as Wyatt Dawson came around the corner, a laptop cradled on his forearm and his phone clutched in the other hand.

"You sending over your sleepy-time footage?" he asked, flashing a distracted smile at their boss as he sidled past to deposit his computer on the desk behind her. "There's a bet-ting pool on whether you drool in your sleep."

Emma rolled her eyes. She didn't doubt there was such a pool. Cops would bet a couple bucks on just about any-thing. "I do not drool."

"Everyone drools," Simon said in his matter-of-fact way. "It's more a matter of whether your stalker captured the mo-ment or not."

She bit her lip, then turned to face him. "I know *stalker* is the correct word, but for the sake of the Hugheses' peace of mind, I've been using *watcher* instead." His eyebrows and he pinned her with a questioning stare.

"Watcher, huh?" Wyatt repeated, too busy plugging in and arranging his devices to his liking to even glance up. "You've invented stalker-lite. Still creepy, less threatening."

She bit her lip, then shrugged. "I'm trying to keep a sev-enteen-year-old from completely freaking out."

"Good call," Simon said with a decisive nod. "Forward your footage and findings. I'd like you to set up a time to speak with Patrice Marsh's parents, then I need you back on watcher duty."

"Yes, sir," she replied.

"I think it's safe to assume we're looking for someone with Capitol Academy ties, but I'd like to nail down something more specific in the next day or so. You know how the cycles run on these things. If they don't get whatever it is they want from framing Kayleigh, they'll either push harder or find another kid to pick on."

"They're already testing those waters from what I saw online last night," she said grimly.

"We have to keep moving on this. See if you can get Kayleigh to open up more, get her talking about her friends," he suggested.

She gave a huff of a laugh. "I'll try."

"You can do mani-pedis," Wyatt suggested with a smirk.

Before she could retort, the boss stepped in. "You have good instincts for this stuff, Parker. Go down the rabbit holes. We'll be your backup. You can pass off anything that feels off-kilter to you to us, and the team will do deep dives," he said, hooking a thumb in Wyatt's direction. "I want you nipping at their heels."

"Understood," Emma said with a nod.

"Good." Simon thumped the top of the partition twice, then spun on his heel and marched off, already moving on to the next thing on his list.

"Another slumber party at Richie Rich's house, huh?" Wyatt teased. "Hey, does he have one of those miniature trains you can ride all over the house?"

"Sadly, no," she said, all mock solemnity. "But he did make these really yummy breakfast bites made out of scrambled egg, cheese, diced-up peppers and big hunks of sausage. You should get Cara to make some for you…oh, wait. Your guru girlfriend is vegan, isn't she?" She tipped her head in mock sympathy. "Never mind."

"Not vegan—vegetarian," he corrected, but she could hear the sulk in his tone.

"Oh, well, you can have the eggs, peppers and cheese, I guess," she said with a laugh.

"And the meat-alternative sausage is actually pretty good," he said unconvincingly.

"Keep telling yourself you love it," she cooed. "Now, leave me alone. I need to offload some files to my backup so I'm free to go chase bad guys."

Chapter Six

When Emma Parker returned to his house, she blew in like a tornado.

A tornado carrying a plastic laundry basket filled with folded clothes, and the straps of two computer bags criss-crossing her chest like bandoliers. A tall, dark-haired agent crossed the threshold on her heels. "This is Wyatt Dawson," she said breathlessly. "He's on our team."

Max smirked and took the man's proffered hand. "We're a team now?"

"I think she means I'm part of the Cyber Crime Division," Wyatt responded genially. "Our Emma is all about getting things done faster. She forgets to connect the dots sometimes."

"Yep. Connect on your own time. I'm setting some stuff up in Kayleigh's room," she said as she pivoted. "Is she in there?"

"She's, uh, no. She's in the media room," Max answered, his attention following the auburn-haired dynamo marching to the hall leading to the bedrooms.

"What's happening?" Max asked the other agent as they followed in her wake.

"We've identified the locations where the, uh, watcher, routed through, but they're all public hot spots. Not uncommon when someone is familiar with masking software. Unfortunately, we can't trace beyond the relay point unless we get in there while they are active in the software," he explained. "So we're setting some more equipment up so we can hardwire in. We don't want to leave a digital footprint our perp might spot."

"Okay." Max wasn't sure he was following the plan entirely, but it sounded like these people were planning to camp out in Kayleigh's room indefinitely. "So this is something you all have to be here for?"

The agent beside him shook his head as they stopped outside Kayleigh's bedroom door. Emma was already in the room, rearranging items around the desk. "I'm going to help Emma set up and test everything."

At last, Emma straightened, using her foot to scoot her laundry basket off to the side. "If they keep up the pattern they showed yesterday, I think we can get a hit on them fairly quickly." She turned and looked at him head-on, her gaze direct, but wary. "Only trouble is, I will need Kayleigh to hang out in here with me."

"You want to use my daughter as bait," he said flatly.

Her eyes flashed and she looked like she wanted to jump down his throat, but when Agent Parker opened her mouth, her tone was calm and reasonable. "No, I want your daughter to carry on living her life exactly as she was the day before yesterday."

"The day before yesterday, I wasn't under house arrest," Kayleigh said, startling them both.

"Kay." Max pressed a hand to his chest as he turned to find his daughter leaning against the wall behind him. "I didn't hear you."

"You're not under house arrest," Emma said, craning her neck to look past him.

"Virtual house arrest," Kayleigh insisted. She stepped around him to peer into her room.

Wyatt Dawson looked up from the computer and smiled when he saw her. "Hey."

"Hi," she replied. Turning her attention to Emma she asked, "What's up?"

"This is Agent Dawson. He works with me."

"I figured as much."

Unfazed by mild sarcasm, Emma Parker continued. "We're setting up to try to catch them watching live so we can pinpoint where they are accessing from. They use masking software. We'll need to have you in here so they have reason to stay online longer."

"Watching me," Kayleigh said, wrinkling her nose. "So creepy."

"I know, right?" Emma replied.

Max watched the byplay between the two of them like a spectator at a tennis match. This total stranger seemed to have an in with his daughter Max hadn't had in years, and watching them together both hurt and heartened him. He wanted Kayleigh to connect with someone, even if it couldn't be him.

"So I sit here staring into space and waiting for the green light?" Kayleigh asked.

"Well, you don't have to stare into space," Emma replied.

"I don't have my phone. I can't get online. What am I supposed to do?" Kayleigh retorted, her tone edging toward combative.

Emma let out a huff, then pulled a book off one of the shelves over the desk and tossed it to his daughter. Kayleigh caught it reflexively, then sneered as she looked down at the cover of a once-beloved teen romance.

"Seriously?"

Emma rolled her eyes, then returned to helping Agent

Dawson set up. "Stare into space, for all I care. Pretend you're doing a makeup tutorial. Clean out your sock drawer—"

"Sock drawer would be off camera," Dawson pointed out, nodding to Kayleigh's closet-slash-dressing room.

"Good point." Emma turned back to Kayleigh. "Dance party? Yoga?"

"Or get a jump on studying for your physics final," Max interjected. Everyone in the room stopped and turned to him. "What? Midterms weren't great and you can't coast your way into an Ivy League school. You're suspended, not expelled. You still have to keep up."

Kayleigh stared at him, her expression a mixture of pettiness and disbelief. "Daddy, I'm not going back to school."

"What? Yes, you are. They're going to catch whoever is doing this and—"

"She's probably right, Mr. Hughes," Emma said, looking up from her work. "Even if we clear everything up, the school may not want the disruption. Kayleigh could finish out her senior year remotely."

"But...graduation. You'll be valedictorian," he argued. But the words sounded weak and whiny to his own years. Reality set in like a stone sinking in his stomach. "You won't walk at graduation," he concluded, shoulders slumping.

Kayleigh leaned into him, and a lump rose in his throat. He was the father. He should be consoling her, not the other way around. But now... Taking advantage of the moment, he wrapped his arm around his daughter and pulled her close into his side. "I'm sorry, baby. This is all happening so fast."

"I know."

Her whispered response nearly broke the dam holding back the emotion rising inside him. But there were two strangers in the room, and though they were pretending not to watch, their family drama was playing to an audience.

He kissed the top of Kayleigh's head, then loosened his grip before she could wriggle away.

"Okay." Max cleared his throat. "We'll give it a few hours, but we're getting out of the house this evening, even if it's only to go for a bike ride."

The two agents nodded as they worked, and Kayleigh gave a noncommittal hum, but he was banking on restlessness winning out.

"There," Agent Dawson said, rocking back to sit on his heels. "All set."

A laptop running code on a black screen sat beneath the desk, a wire connected it to a dongle attached to Kayleigh's computer. With a few keystrokes and a tap on the trackpad, an exact replica of Kayleigh's desktop appeared on its screen.

Emma nodded and typed in a few commands. A moment later, she nodded. "I'm in, too."

Max shifted uncomfortably from foot to foot. They made it all look so easy. Too easy. "You guys are scaring me with how quickly you can get into all this stuff."

Agent Dawson rose to his feet, slapping his hand across the front of his jeans. "Nah. We do this all the time. Most people wouldn't have a clue, believe me."

Max did believe him because he hadn't had a clue, and he'd always thought he was fairly tech-savvy. The last two days had debunked him of the notion. He hadn't even heard of half the applications Kayleigh and Emma discussed, much less knew what they were for or how to get into them.

The agent looked down at his partner. "You all good here?"

"All good. Thanks for your help." Emma stood as well. "Agent Dawson and rest of the CCD team are going to be helping track down any background information we may need." She turned to Kayleigh. "I'm going to be checking socials on my devices throughout the day. I may need you to clarify some things or identify some of the subjects."

"In between makeup tutorials and sun salutations?" Kayleigh asked, raising her brow to match her mocking tone.

Agent Parker was quick on the uptake. "Exactly. But don't look to me for help with the physics stuff. I lost interest after an apple fell from the tree."

"I guess you could say you're relatively slow," Dawson said, nudging Emma as he walked past.

She groaned in response. "Sheesh, Wyatt. If anyone should be telling the dad jokes around here, it should be him," she said, pointing in Max's direction. "You don't even have kids."

"Oh, don't get him started," Kayleigh groaned. "My dad thinks he's hysterical."

Boggled by how quickly everything circled back to him, Max shook his head. "Hey, wait a minute. How'd I get to be the target here?"

"You're the default dad," Kayleigh said, shooting him a wicked grin.

Max laughed, too happy to see his daughter's smile to care if he was the butt of every joke she ever made. "Lucky me." He turned to Agent Dawson. "Come on, I'll walk you out while these two argue over who gets to braid whose hair first."

"Age before beauty," Emma Parker said as they started down the hall.

"Are you gonna be the braider, or the braidee?" Kayleigh retorted.

He chuckled, shaking his head as he and Wyatt Dawson made their way to the foyer. "Thanks for your help with this."

Wyatt took his hand and gave it a firm shake. "I really am nothing more than backup. Emma's the best with this stuff.

If anyone can figure it out, she can." He paused, as if debating whether he should go on. When he spoke, it was clear he was choosing his words with care. "Emma went through some stuff when she was younger than your daughter. She's a good resource, you know, for someone to talk to."

"For Kayleigh or for me?" Max asked.

The younger man shrugged. "Either." He reached for the door to let himself out. "If you need anything more, have Emma give us a shout."

"Will do," Max assured him. "Appreciate your help."

He watched until the other agent slipped into a nondescript SUV. When he pulled away, Max spotted a silver subcompact parked to the side of the semicircle drive. It was a newer model. Shiny in the afternoon sunlight, but otherwise unremarkable. A car built for fuel efficiency and likely purchased for reliability. A vehicle for people who preferred substance over style, he mused as he engaged the locks on his front door.

A no-nonsense car for a no-nonsense woman.

He puzzled over the laundry basket as he wandered back toward Kayleigh's room. Was it possible she didn't own a suitcase? A duffel bag? The more likely explanation was she didn't want to take the time to pack. He smirked, thinking back to his long-ago bachelor days. Once upon a time, he'd thought nothing about dressing out of a hamper. At least the clothes she'd hauled in looked washed and folded.

The murmur of soft feminine voices drifted down the hall. Kayleigh spent hours laughing, chatting, giggling and squealing with her friends in there, but this was different. His steps slowed. He'd never heard Kayleigh speaking to a woman like this. It was conversational. Easy. Low-key. Stripped of the forced brightness or heightened self-awareness of interactions between teenage girls, the timbre of his daughter's voice was richer. Fuller. A smooth, self-assured alto.

She sounded so much like her mother.

The realization struck him like a physical blow. Leaning against the wall outside her room, he pressed the back of his head into the drywall and gazed at the ceiling, trying to recover the breath knocked out of his lungs.

"So what did you do?" Kayleigh asked.

"I didn't deal well," Emma replied.

The vagueness of her answer likely frustrated his daughter as much as it did him, but to her credit, Kayleigh didn't push. He smiled as his bright, inquisitive girl tried a different approach.

"How'd you get over it?" she asked.

"Who says I did?" Emma returned without missing a beat.

"Is what happened to you why you do this?" Kayleigh persisted.

"Absolutely."

Emma's unequivocal answer startled a laugh out of him. The occupants of the room fell silent, and he knew he'd given away his position. But this was his house, and he wasn't about to be made to feel like the interloper here.

Turning so he stood square in the doorway, he asked, "Can I get you anything?"

"I'm fine," Emma replied, looking up from her laptop. "Thanks."

"What are we having for dinner?" Kayleigh asked then.

Max blinked as she unfolded her long, coltish legs, then repositioned herself like she was animatronic origami. "We ate lunch an hour ago."

"Can we go out?" she persisted. "Maybe get Greek salads from Garden of Paradise?"

Max shifted his gaze to Emma, then back again. "Depends on Special Agent Parker."

"As I said before, Mr. Hughes—"

"Her name is Emma, and his is Max," Kayleigh interrupted with a huff. "Sheesh, it's not like she didn't sleep in my bed last night. This Mr. Hughes, Special Agent Parker stuff is sounding…weird, you know?"

He startled when he spotted the cop sitting on the floor. "Agent Parker?"

"Emma is fine," she muttered, returning her gaze to the computer in front of her. "As for going out, can I convince you to give it one more night?" She looked up at Kayleigh, her expression frank. "I know you haven't been online today, but I can tell you it's still not pleasant."

Kayleigh took this in, her nostrils flaring as she pursed her lips. "I didn't do anything wrong. It's not fair—"

Emma held up a hand to stop her. "I know. It's totally not fair, but it is reality. Perception is reality at the moment. Until we can nail down proof, people are going to believe whatever they read."

"Whatever happened to innocent until proven guilty?" Kayleigh cried.

"It's a nice idea, isn't it," Emma returned without missing a beat. "Unfortunately, it's pretty much only true in a courtroom, and sometimes not even there. The person who controls the narrative, controls the court of public opinion."

Max stood in the doorway, watching the two of them go back and forth. For the first time in nearly eighteen years, he was not the person Kayleigh looked to for answers to her questions. It was both a relief and a knife to the gut.

"I think we should listen to, uh, Emma," he said, inserting himself into their stare-down. "One more night. But maybe we can take the bike ride I mentioned earlier?" He turned to Emma. "We have an extra mountain bike if you want to join us."

She raised an inquiring eyebrow. "You keep an extra bike? I thought the toothbrush was impressive."

Kayleigh snorted. "I have a trail bike and a ten-speed. Dad got really into cycling for, like, a minute and a half."

"Or ten years," Max interjected, feeling suddenly outnumbered. "Still am. Not that you'd notice," he added in an undertone.

Emma caught it, though. She cocked her head as she looked up. "Cycling, huh? Do you wear the funny aerodynamic helmet and the shorts with the padding?"

"It's so embarrassing," Kayleigh groaned, flopping back on her bed, her legs still twisted into a shape he couldn't imagine was comfortable, much less sustainable.

"I wear gear appropriate to the sport," he replied stiffly. "When I was in college, I was a track racer."

"Oh, God, this is where he tells you how cool he used to be," Kayleigh said, speaking to the ceiling.

Emma chuckled. "Did you, now?"

"I think I'll head for the other end of the house. Shout if you need anything," he said gruffly.

"Hey, Max?" Emma called after him.

Startled by the sound of his own name, he stopped in his tracks, then turned slowly. "Yes?"

"Once we pinpoint a location, don't forget I'm going to need you and Kayleigh to be ready to do a I'm-taking-your-computer-away-for-your-own-good performance," she said, dropping her voice an octave in what he could only assume was supposed to be an imitation of him.

"I'll practice my lines." He turned on his heel.

"And, Max?" she called again, and he turned back slowly. He replied in an exaggerated drawl. "Yes, Emma?"

"Oh, now you're going to make first names weird," Kayleigh complained to no one in particular.

"I'd love to go for a bike ride later," Emma said, unperturbed by the teen's mockery. "I think we can all use a break."

He nodded. "Sounds good."

"As long as you don't mind if I skip the spandex," she added, a wicked gleam lighting her eyes.

"Yeah, no uniforms required," he conceded, feeling unexpectedly awkward. Shifting his attention to his daughter, he scrambled for more solid footing. "Maybe we'll ride and get Garden of Paradise to-go. We can earn one of those salads."

"There's no such thing as earning a salad, Dad," Kayleigh said, pushing onto her elbows. "You bike for ice cream or cookies, not salad."

"I don't believe food has to be earned," Emma said, turning her attention back to her screen. "It's ridiculous."

"I know, right?" Kayleigh exclaimed, sitting up again. "I mean, who decided salad was good and ice cream bad, anyway?"

Max chortled. "The FDA, maybe?"

"Dad," Kayleigh groaned, shooting him a look he secretly named the Side-eye of Scorn.

"I'm going," he said, lifting his hands in surrender. "But you blew your chance to score both salad and ice cream," he called over his shoulder as he walked away.

He'd gone no more than three steps when he heard Kayleigh pick up the thread of the woman-to-woman conversation he'd interrupted. "I really hate how everyone is so fixated on food. I try not to be, but it's hard when you know girls who tally up everything on their lunch tray, and then I feel like I'm doing something wrong, you know? I mean, if you're going to feel bad about something, why not focus on something with more of an impact, like recycling, or something."

"I hear you," Emma agreed.

Unable to help himself, Max lingered in the hall. Kayleigh was rambling on about all the things teenagers should be doing rather than obsessing over all the things teenagers have obsessed over for decades when his phone buzzed in his pocket. Kayleigh stopped talking midrant, and a strange stillness settled on the house.

He pulled the device from his pocket and saw he had a text message from Emma. It contained only two words.

Green light.

Within seconds, Kayleigh was up and bustling around her room as if she wasn't moving random objects from one spot to another. Almost a full minute passed before he heard the muffled thump of his daughter flinging herself across the bed.

"You can't keep me locked up forever," she shouted into the hall.

Max flinched, even though he knew she was only spouting lines Emma had suggested. He didn't respond. According to Emma, their watcher might get spooked and ditch if they thought he was nearby. It was better to let them think Kayleigh was bored and restless and pushing back against her confinement. Whoever was doing this was determined to disrupt her life. It was better to let them think they were winning.

Pressing flat against the wall, he listened to Kayleigh muttering and grumbling, every nerve in his body tingling with the need to rush in. To protect her. But he couldn't. If they were going to catch this creeper, they had to be every bit as sneaky as the perpetrator.

Kayleigh got up and started stomping across her room, playacting at living her normal life. But everything was upside down. Her voice grew watery, and soon her complaints were being punctuated with sniffles. Max squeezed his eyes shut and clenched his fists as he listened.

It seemed to go on forever.

At one point, he caught himself holding his breath and had to force his lungs to exchange oxygen at something resembling the usual rate.

He checked the time on his phone. Three minutes had passed since Emma sent the text.

Kayleigh managed to keep going, though. He heard something hit the wall at about the five-minute mark, but the thump was soft. Unlike her gasping sob.

"They can't kick me out of Harvard," she called out to no one in particular. "I've already been accepted. They can't take it back," she insisted with all the forceful naivety of someone who still believed life was driven by absolutes.

He wanted to rush in there and grab her. Put an end to this farce. Three more minutes had passed. Was this reprobate getting their kicks watching a seventeen-year-old girl fall apart?

Max figured it had to be another kid. What would an adult hope to gain from this torment? No, it was probably another student. A clever one, who knew too much about how technology works. He didn't think so at first, but knowing what he did about how Emma honed her skills, he was reassessing.

His phone vibrated.

All clear. Come in.

He rushed into Kayleigh's room and found her crumpled on the bed, her cherished Harvard hoodie balled in a wad beneath her as she cried softly into her pillow.

"Shh, sugar," he whispered, jostling her as he perched on the side of the bed. He reached across to hold her.

Praying she'd turn into him instead of away, he braced

himself for rejection. But once again, she curled into him. He pulled her up, banding his arms around her as she heaved a sob. Resting his chin atop her head, he glared at the agent sitting cross-legged on the floor, tapping on her keyboard.

The lid to Kayleigh's laptop was closed. Relieved to know no one could be spying on them, he exhaled in a whoosh. "I hope you got what you needed, because we're not doing that again," he said, his voice rough with emotion.

"It certainly should have been enough," Emma murmured distractedly, her fingers flying across the keys.

He rocked Kayleigh gently, refusing to loosen his grip even when her sobs turned to hiccups. A series of pings reverberated in the quiet room. He could see Emma's phone on the floor beside her. The incoming messages moved at such a clip he wondered if she was even able to get the gist of them.

Then her spine straightened and she pulled her hands away from the keyboard as if she was afraid to go a keystroke too far.

Her phone chimed again. This time, she glanced down to check the message.

"Got it," she said briefly.

"Where are they?"

She pursed her lips as she read the message again. "It'll take a bit more time to pinpoint a device, but we can confirm the signal we picked up as routing through the Coffee Cup franchise on the six-hundred block of Capitol Avenue originated three blocks north of there."

"Three blocks north?" He frowned as he tried to envision the coffee shop and its surrounding environment.

"Yes." Emma met his gaze as Kayleigh lifted her head from his shoulder. "Capitol Academy. The posts are coming from inside the school."

Chapter Seven

By the time Emma finished giving an update to the rest of the team and an impromptu video conference with her boss, she was more than ready for some fresh air. Kayleigh and Max had decamped the minute the calls had begun.

If the offer of a bike ride was no longer on the table, she'd blow off some steam with a jog on the quiet, tree-lined streets that wound down the city side of the high bluffs above the Arkansas River. Rummaging through the basket of clean laundry she'd brought from her condo, she unearthed a pair of running shorts and a clean T-shirt, then ducked into the bathroom.

Toeing off the thick-soled loafers she wore to work, she tried to recall whether the gym bag with her running gear was still in the trunk of her car. The last thing she wanted to do was to ask the teenager she was supposed to be protecting to loan her some sneakers.

She pulled a hair tie from her computer bag, then slid down the empty hall in a pair of no-show running socks. Reaching for the handle of the large front door, she hesitated. The display panel on the wall opposite the entry showed the security system was armed.

"Crud," she muttered, letting her hand fall.

She'd hoped to slip out and check to see if she had shoes

before letting the Hugheses know she was ready to escape. Biting her lip, she eyed the display, wondering if she could disarm it without a code.

"Hey."

She let out a startled yelp, pressing her hand to her chest to calm her jumpy heart. "Hi," she said, cringing at her reaction as she turned to find Max watching her from the kitchen doorway. "I was, uh—" She hooked a thumb over her shoulder. "I need to go to my car."

"Oh." He moved to the alarm panel and jabbed in a series of numbers. Three beeps signaled the all clear. "There you go."

Glancing self-consciously down at the toes of her socks, she nodded. "Thanks. Left one of my bags out there."

The moment he stepped aside, she yanked on the door handle and escaped. Thankfully, her gym bag was still in her trunk. She also spotted a small bag containing skin-care samples she'd scored when one of the women in the department had an in-home party sponsored by a cosmetics company. She'd forgotten it was there. Unzipping the gym bag, she exhaled a breath of relief when she spotted her battered running shoes nestled inside. She also pulled out the sleeve she wore to hold her phone while she worked out. Back when she worked out, she amended, slipping it onto her forearm so she wouldn't forget it. Sitting on the bumper of her car, she wriggled each foot into the shoes.

Emma was trying to force air into her compressed lungs when a pair of pristine men's athletic shoes entered her field of vision. She twisted her own laces around her fingers to keep from jerking upright.

"You still up for a bike ride?" Max asked.

"Sure," she said, trying to keep her tone casual. "Unless you and Kayleigh would like to go on your own."

He chuckled. "I think at this point, Kayleigh would pay you to go along."

"I'm already being paid," she said as she straightened, planting her hands on her hips. "I'm here to do my job," she said, using a smile to soften the reminder.

"And we appreciate it." Unfazed, he hooked a thumb over his shoulder. "I got the extra bike down and we got it cleaned up. We can grab dinner while we're out."

She bit her lip. "Probably best to call something in. I think we should shield Kayleigh as much as possible. When we get there, I can go in and pick it up."

"Sounds like a plan."

He hovered nearby as she pulled the bags from her trunk. When she turned, Emma was gratified to see him looking as uncomfortable as she felt.

"We do appreciate what you're doing, Emma," he said, using her first name with deliberate care.

"Like I said, I'm only doing my job," she insisted.

"I'm not a fool. If it weren't for my relationship with Simon, I wouldn't have a trained agent staying in my house because my daughter got into some kerfuffle on the internet." He gave her a wry smile. "We both know this goes above and beyond, and I'm aware of our privilege."

"But you're not afraid to wield it," she said, the words popping out before she could stop them.

"No," he admitted, a self-deprecating smile tugging his mouth down. "Not when it comes to protecting my daughter. I'll do anything to make sure she's safe."

"You'll do anything to make sure she's cleared," she corrected. "You didn't go to Simon because you thought somebody was threatening Kayleigh. You went to Simon because you thought Kayleigh was threatening somebody else, and it would reflect badly on her."

She watched the color creep up his neck and stain his

cheeks, but he didn't look away. "True. Initially," he insisted. "But things have changed."

Emma inclined her head. "Things have changed." She slammed the lid of her trunk, then flung the strap of her gym bag over her shoulder. "Let me take these in, then I'll be ready to go."

"Come through the mudroom off the kitchen to the garage when you're ready," he instructed. "We'll be waiting for you."

Emma deposited her bags in Kayleigh's room, then wriggled her phone into the zippered armband before yanking it up to her bicep. Anxious to leave the confines of the house and their circular discussions behind, she hurried out to the garage. There, she found Kayleigh standing next to an expensive racing bike. It looked to be a slightly smaller version of her father's sleek ride. A more clunky-looking touring bike with wide tires stood on its kickstand nearby. Emma eyed the narrow saddles on the racing bikes and sent up a silent prayer of thanks when she compared them to the more substantial seat on the cruiser.

"Okay," she said as she stepped into the garage. "I call the bike with the complete seat."

Kayleigh expelled a mirthless laugh. "It's all yours." She swung one long leg over the crossbar of the racing bike and plunked a sleek black helmet on her head.

"The only spare helmet I had was Kayleigh's old one," Max explained, nodding to the sparkling pink hard-shell dangling from the cruiser's handlebars.

Determined to play it cool, Emma shrugged off his apology. "I like sparkles." Feigning a comfort level she didn't feel, she placed the helmet on her head and tightened the strap. "It's been a while since I've ridden a bike, so I'll probably be bringing up the rear, but don't worry—I'll have your six."

"Now, remember, the right hand brake is for the rear wheel. Try not to use the front brakes on any downhill inclines," Max instructed.

Emma huffed a laugh as she secured the strap under her chin. "I said it'd been a while, but I don't think I've forgotten the fundamentals. What's the old bit about things being like riding a bike?"

Max smiled and strapped his own helmet on, then nodded to his daughter. "Lead the way," he said with a wave. "We'll head down by the park then pick up dinner on our way back. Sound good?"

"Sounds fabulous," Kayleigh said with a hint of sass. "Try to keep up," she called over her shoulder, pushing off.

Max waited until Emma raised the kickstand and pushed off herself before mounting his bike. He caught up to her before she even found her balance. They rode side by side on the quiet residential street, Emma feeling self-conscious with every downward stroke of the pedal. "I didn't mean to be rude earlier." She darted a glance in his direction. "About why you came to Simon," she clarified.

"You weren't wrong," he replied, not the least bit winded.

Emma leaned into the handlebars and pushed harder as they started up an incline. "So how do you know Simon?"

"College. We were assigned to be roommates our freshman year in the dorms."

She glanced over at him. "Really?" she huffed, her breath coming out choppy. "Random assignment?"

"Yep."

She heard the *click-click-click* of his gears changing, but was too focused on making it to the top to look over at him.

"The guy I was supposed to room with took off to be a surfer in Costa Rica over the summer. I walked into my room and there sat this scrawny guy from a town I'd never heard of, already typing away at his computer. I remember his whole half of the room was already set up. Everything in place. The clothes in the closet, books stacked on the shelf, everything in its place," he said with a laugh.

"Sounds like Simon," she huffed.

"Let's say I wasn't surprised to see how clean his office at headquarters was."

Emma smiled at the dryness of his tone. "And you two have stayed friends all these years?"

"Yeah," Max said, sounding almost as surprised as she was by the notion. "He's a different kind of guy, but he's a good guy. He says what he means, and he means what he says. You don't meet a lot of people like him in life."

Emma forced a tremulous smile as she pushed to the top of the nearly nonexistent hill. "Oh. I'm pretty sure Simon was the prototype for a straight shooter." She treated herself to three deep breaths before she attempted to speak again. "In every way," she added. "Did you know he's an expert marksman?"

"No. But I can't say I'm surprised," Max said offhandedly. "Simon's the kind of guy who strives to be an expert in anything he finds interesting."

"True." Emma stopped pumping the pedals and allowed herself to coast as the momentum carried them downhill. "I swear I'm not this out of shape," she said with a rueful laugh. "I run." Then, remembering she hadn't run for the last few months, she heaved a sigh. "Or, I guess I should say I *was* a runner. I tore my Achilles tendon a few months ago, and I haven't been great about getting back on the streets."

"I understand. I wiped out on some loose gravel a couple years ago and messed my knee up pretty bad," he said gruffly. "I didn't really get back on the bike until about eight months ago."

Emma tipped up her chin, enjoying the feel of the warm spring air on her cheeks. "What got you over the hump?"

she asked when the road flattened enough to require some effort on her part.

"Kayleigh." He tossed the answer off as if it should have been obvious to her. "She volunteered to help her friend Tia train for a triathlon. Of course, she needed a racing bike and the one I had was too tall…" He trailed off and she glanced over in time to catch his wry smile.

She laughed. "How horrified was she when you went out and bought a matched set?"

"I'd say about a seven out of ten."

Kayleigh, whom they'd caught up to on the incline, shook her head. "More like a nine, Daddy," she called out without looking over her shoulder.

Max laughed then stood up on his pedals and accelerated enough to catch up with his daughter with a few powerful pushes. "What did you say, slowpoke?"

Emma didn't have to see Kayleigh's face to know the girl responded with her usual eye roll. "I'm not racing you," she insisted, even as she leaned over her handlebars and started pedaling faster.

"You'd only lose," he taunted, then took off, his legs pumping like pistons.

The man clearly knew his child well, because Kayleigh took off after him with a shout of delighted frustration. Emma stuck to her original pace. She saw no sense in chasing after them. This wasn't a protective detail. At least, not in the sense where she was supposed to be anybody's bodyguard.

Happy to have a bit of time to herself, she leaned back, happy to enjoy a more leisurely ride to the park they'd agreed to use as their turnaround point. Her phone vibrated in her armband, but she didn't stop to check it. Whatever it was would have to wait another ten minutes.

By the time she cruised around a corner and spotted

the park a few blocks away, her natural cop paranoia had crept back in enough to make her anxious to catch sight of the Hugheses again. She spotted the father and daughter stopped near the gates marking the entrance to the walking paths. They were talking to a tall, slender woman clad in skimpy running shorts and one of those tank tops with the crisscrossing straps. Emma coasted up the curb, trying to decipher the messages telegraphed by the trio's body language.

The woman leaned forward as she spoke, her stance more insistent than aggressive. Max stood astride his bike, his face grave. He seemed to be pulling back, as if he wanted to put as much space as possible between himself and the woman. Kayleigh, bless her adolescent heart, didn't bother to mask her annoyance. Her cheeks were red. *Exertion or temper?* Emma wondered as she gently drew closer. The other woman's expression was taut as she said, "...from your account."

She squeezed the hand brake and the squeak of rubber on metal rims punctuated the threesome's tense conversation. A look of undisguised irritation flashed on the stranger's face when she realized Emma intended to stop beside them. Emma squinted in return, suddenly cursing her cavalier attitude toward missed messages on her phone. Was one of the team trying to alert her to an issue?

"Hey," she said, blandly returning the stranger's glare as she inserted herself into their conversation. "Sorry it took me so long."

"Emma, this is Amy Birch," Max said, gesturing to the spandex-clad woman. "She's a teacher at Kayleigh's school." He turned to the teacher and tipped his head to the side. "This is Emma Parker. She's—"

"My aunt," Kayleigh interjected, causing Max to jolt.

"Uh, um," he said weakly.

Emma blinked twice, but remained silent as she raised a hand to her forehead to wipe away both her perspiration and confusion.

"My mom's sister," Kayleigh explained, warming to her story. "She's staying with us for a bit."

"Oh, how, uh, nice," Amy Birch replied, glancing from the tall, willowy teen to Emma, her brow furrowed.

Irked by the other woman's natural skepticism, Emma doubled down on the teen's tale. "Yep. Kay-kay's my girl," she said in an overly chipper tone. "She inherited the Hughes height, of course. The Parker genes were totally recessive," she said, waving a hand toward her shorter, sturdier legs.

"Ms. Birch teaches Information Technology," Kayleigh informed her. Before Emma could comment on the information, she plowed ahead. "Auntie Em here is a computer genius, too."

"Is she?" Amy Birch lifted a single skeptical eyebrow.

"Oh, no," Emma replied with a scoff. "Data analysis. Nothing exciting."

"So, uh, we should let you get back to your run. Good seeing you," Max interjected. He turned to look directly at Emma and she read a clear plea in the man's eyes. "If we're going to pick up dinner on the way home, we should get to it." He moved his bike back and gestured toward the running path as if inviting her to take the lead.

"Right." She flashed a polite smile as she mentally captured the dozens of questions zipping around in her head and stuffed them into a box to be trotted out later. "Nice to meet you."

Amy Birch pressed her tongue to the inside of her upper lip as if she was having trouble holding back questions of her own, but in the end opted to swallow them. She lifted a hand in a casual wave. "Yes, I should…" She darted one more glance at Max, then turned to his daughter. "Hope to see you back in school soon, Kayleigh."

"Thanks, Ms. Birch," Kayleigh called after her in a gratingly chipper tone, as the woman took off.

"What was that?" Emma asked, trying to figure out the undercurrent of the conversation she'd interrupted. "What was she saying?"

"Let's talk at home," Max said gruffly.

Unwilling to be put off so easily, Emma turned to Kayleigh. "What happened?"

The teenager lifted one shoulder then let it fall. "Nothing." When both Emma and her father shot her exasperated stares, she huffed. "She said there'd been more posts. Accused Dad of not 'monitoring my online activities' closely enough," she said, fingers curling into air quotes and words dripping with disdain.

"Let's head home," Max said, his jaw hardening.

"I'm not going to hide for the rest of my life," Kayleigh said, her own face settling into the same hard lines as her father's. "I didn't start this drama."

"It's hardly been two days," Max reminded her. "And a girl who was once a good friend of yours tried to hurt herself over all this drama, so spare me your attitude, please." He pulled his phone from his pocket and tapped around on the screen.

"Did she say what the posts said?"

"I don't want to talk about it here," Max said through clenched teeth.

Emma glanced around at the park filled with after-work joggers, cyclists and children at play. "Fine. You order and I'll pick it up."

"I know Kay and I will be having the Paradise Bowl," he said, head down as he jabbed at the screen with a tad too much force. "Do you know what you'd like, or do you need a menu?" he asked without a glance in Emma's direction.

"What's in the Paradise Bowl?" she asked.

"Everything," Kayleigh answered, sliding into a sulk. "I'm going to head home," she said, then pushed off without waiting for a response.

Max looked up from the screen, but Emma stopped him from calling out to her with a hand on his forearm. "Let her get a head start. She needs a minute."

"I need a minute," he grumbled.

"Did she say what the messages said?" Emma asked in a low voice.

"More of the same. Picking on different kids," he answered without looking up from his phone. The device chimed, and he looked up. "There. I set it up under your name, but it's all paid for," he informed her as he settled his foot against a pedal.

"You don't have to—"

"It's done." The note of frustrated finality in his tone made her swallow the rest of her protest. "I need to at least keep her in sight," he said, preparing to push off.

Nodding her understanding. Emma leaned back, giving him plenty of room to push off. "Go. It'd be better if you don't have to see me walking this thing up the last big hill."

The corner of his mouth kicked up, but he didn't say anything else. She stood rooted to the spot, enjoying the view as he rocked the bike back and forth in an effort to gain momentum. The second he was out of sight, she unzipped her armband and pulled her phone free.

There were three message bubbles from Simon Taylor.

Dawson tells me U have a pin drop on the sender's location.

Will have to discuss next steps.

More messages on subject's alt PicturSpam account. Last post 30 mins ago. Confirm bogus. Assigning Ross to help with SM.

Emma grunted. He was assigning another agent to monitor social media? Did he think she couldn't handle this case?

She replied: Off site with H's atm, but 99% sure bogus. Will confirm on return.

Without waiting for a reply, she zipped the phone back into its pocket and turned her bike in the direction of the restaurant. When she arrived, she parked the cruiser near the entrance, feeling uneasy about her inability to secure it with a lock. The kid behind the to-go counter confirmed the order and told her it would be another few minutes. Settling into a corner of the waiting area, she alternated between watching the bike and the steady stream of athlesiure-clad diners lining up for a table.

When her phone buzzed, she jumped, then fumbled with the zipper again. She unlocked the device only to find another text from her boss.

Dawson confirmed messaged posted using browser, not mobile app. Talked to Blanton abt equip. Mainly tablets. Some tchrs have laps, but most use tabs. Abt a dzn towers in IT lab.

Emma blinked as the image of the woman she'd met in the park mere minutes before flashed into her mind. She'd been dressed for running but had not broken a sweat. And the way she looked at Max and Kayleigh Hughes niggled at her.

The tiny vestibule filled with hungry customers chatting about their days and grumbling about the wait. She closed her eyes, trying to capture the image of Amy Birch in her mind before moving back to logistics.

"Parker?" the young man who'd greeted her called above the din.

Emma jumped to her feet and threaded her way through the waiting diners to snag the brown paper to-go bag he extended in her direction. "Thanks," she called, then murmured, "Excuse me" over and over again as she beat a path to the door.

The relief she felt when she spotted the bike sitting right where she left it nearly made her laugh out loud. The last thing she wanted was pull up to the Hughes house in a ride-share. Max was trusting her with his daughter's future. It would be hard to maintain credibility if she lost his bicycle.

She threaded the handles of the bag through the handle-bars then threw her leg over. Straddling the crossbar, she took a minute to reply.

I'll pick Kayleigh's brain about which teachers use laptops, lab setup for the IT department and student access outside of class time.

After slipping the phone back into its compartment, she yanked up the zipper. Eyeing the narrow sidewalk running along the busy through street, she weighed her options for her return to the Hughes home. The thoroughfare would be more direct and slightly less hilly, but they were in the thick of evening traffic and there was no bike lane available on this particular stretch. Resigned, she pointed the bike in the direction of the residential streets.

As she huffed her way up the final hill, she had bargained her way up to four days per week lifting weights in the gym at headquarters, in addition to her vow to get back into her running routine. She coasted up the gracefully curving drive breathless and beyond dewy, only to find Max leaning against the trunk of her car, his arms crossed over his chest.

"Did you think I took off with your dinner?" she asked, brakes squeaking as she drew to a halt beside him.

"Nah. I'd hope if you were going to indulge in food theft it would be something more exciting than salad."

"You know it," she said, lifting the bag off her bike and handing it over to him.

He smiled as he took it from her. She dismounted and without another glance over her shoulder, she pushed the bike toward the garage. "I want it noted for the record I pushed through every one of those hills."

"So noted."

He followed her into the three-car garage. Once again, she marveled at the pristine polished concrete floor and perfectly organized storage containers of holiday decorations lining the back wall, wondering how people managed to keep their spaces so clean. She was lucky she had a basket of clean laundry handy when she swung by her apartment.

"Here," he said, extending the to-go bag. "Trade me."

She was all too happy to exchange the bike for the bag. "How do you do this?" she asked, unable to hold back her curiosity.

"Do what?" His biceps flexed and she tried her best not to stare as he gripped the bike by the bars and seat, then swung it easily up over his head. She gaped as he lifted it onto a couple of heavy duty hooks drilled into the garage ceiling. Only then did she notice the racing bikes hanging suspended above a white Jeep with a removable soft top.

"Your house is so clean."

He dusted his hands off on his shorts. "I have cleaners come every two weeks to do the big stuff, but it's only me and Kay, so it's not hard to keep up with stuff from one day to another."

Emma was grateful this man who made everything he did look so easy would never have cause to see her mess of a one-bedroom apartment. She rustled the bag. "Come on, I have some questions."

"Of course you do." He rolled his eyes, and father and daughter had never looked more alike.

"I'm a cop. Asking questions is what I do," she answered, happy to fall back into the comfortable pattern of police work. He gestured for her to precede him into the house and a flash of subconscious insight she'd been trying to unearth popped fully into focus.

She halted on the step leading into the mudroom and turned back to look him straight in the eyes. "You know, I couldn't help picking up on something more than a parent-teacher vibe going on back there."

"What? Back where?" he asked, brow puckering.

"In the park," she clarified, undeterred by his obfuscation. "But Kayleigh didn't seem to get it, so before we go in there, I think you'd better tell me how you know Amy Birch."

Chapter Eight

Max knew the question was coming, but her matter-of-fact approach still startled him. He was accustomed to the thrust and parry of so-called polite conversation. He should have expected it. Anyone who worked for Simon would have to be as blunt as he was.

"After dinner," he said in a near whisper.

Her eyes widened, but she walked past him into the house without pushing the point any further. For some reason her reticence made him even more nervous.

In the kitchen he busied himself with unpacking the to-go containers while Emma and Kayleigh bonded by complaining about the bike ride. He kept his back to them, pushing the packs of plastic utensils aside in favor of using the real deal, and fished the packets of dressing from the depths of the bag.

"Kay, will you get drinks, please?" he asked as he deposited a bowl in front of each of them.

"I'm having water," she announced as she slid off her stool. "Emma? Water? Milk? A Coke?"

"Water's fine," Emma replied, her gaze following him as he arranged napkins and forks.

"Me, too, please," Max said, placing his own bowl in front of the stool on the other side of Kayleigh. He wanted to maintain a buffer between him and this uncomfortable conversation as long as possible. But any thoughts he may have had about a relaxing meal evaporated as soon as his daughter started in on her meal prep.

"So have you looked?" she asked Emma as she squeezed the contents of an entire dressing packet over her bowl.

"At the new posts? Not yet, but Wyatt said he was sending over metadata on them. I'll study it after we eat."

Kayleigh gave her salad a stir with her fork, then set aside the utensil. She snapped the plastic lid back onto the bowl, flipped it over and shook it over her head, turning the artfully arranged contents into a jumble. "What will the metadata tell you?" she asked as she pried off the lid again.

"Like any data set, metadata contains all sorts of information. We'll start with the most basic stuff. Where, when and how it was posted—"

"I think you're forgetting who," Max grumbled. The easy rapport Kayleigh and Emma had developed in one day irked him. He couldn't remember the last time his daughter was this curious about anything he did, and it made him feel peevish. Petulant.

"I never forget the who," Emma answered evenly, jolting him out of his sulk. "But if I go off the data visible to the untrained eye, the 'who' is sitting right next to me," she said, pointing the tines of her fork at Kayleigh. She leaned forward to cock a victorious eyebrow at him, then sat back before continuing. "That's why we can't take data at face value. It's easily manipulated."

"Then why is gathering more of it so important?" Kayleigh persisted.

"Because gathering a whole bunch of clues is better than picking one up and running with it," Emma replied easily. "There's bound to be some garbage in the pile, fake accounts, IP masking and the like, but it's possible to build a solid foundation with even the shakiest material. Like how if you use sand and pebbles to fill in the gaps, you can build a wall out of round rocks," she said, gesturing with her fork as she spoke. "More information can make a case stronger."

The three of them lapsed into silence. Kayleigh shoveled in the food as if she was in a contest, but Max noticed Emma seemed to like to ponder as she ate. A few minutes passed before Kayleigh spoke up.

"Will you show them to me?"

The vulnerability the question exposed made him want to say "No, absolutely not," but before he could figure out a more palatable way to lay down the law with his stubborn almost-grown child, Emma Parker pulled her phone from the neoprene sleeve strapped to her arm.

"Sure. Let's look at them together." She made the suggestion with a gentleness Max knew would undercut any edict he might issue.

Peeved, he fell back to his last line of defense: house rules.

"No devices during dinner," he blurted.

Both women turned to look at him, incredulous. "Dad—" Kayleigh began, but he shook his head hard.

"I'm serious. I'd like to eat my stupid, overpriced spinach salad in peace, if you don't mind."

Emma placed her phone face down on the island, and the three of them went back to eating in silence. Kayleigh stabbed a plump olive glistening with dressing and held it up as if it was proof he was losing his mind. "There's more than spinach in here. Such drama."

"He's right. We'll look at them later. I'll show you both what we're looking at and how we dissect it all." He watched as Emma used her fork to move some of the diced tomato away from the carefully arranged line of cubed chicken before she plowed her way through the protein section of her dinner.

"It's better if you mix it all up," Kayleigh suggested helpfully.

"Not everyone shares your appreciation for food chaos, Kay," Max said as he watched his daughter decimate her dinner in record time.

"Fine," she said as she scraped together one last forkful. "You guys poke around and have your 'peaceful dinner,'" she said, using finger quotes. "I'm going to go shower," she announced, pushing her chair back without waiting for any reply.

She rinsed the plastic bowl and lid before placing them in the recycling, then dropped her fork into the dishwasher. Leaning onto the island opposite Emma, Kayleigh waited impatiently until the government agent looked up from her careful picking.

"You will show me, won't you?"

She fixed Emma with a stubborn glare so similar to his late wife's that it made his breath tangle in his chest.

Emma nodded solemnly. "I will because I think you have a right to know what's out there, but I want you to think long and hard about whether you want to see the actual posts while you shower. I'll tell you what you allegedly posted, but I don't think it would be good for you to read any of the comments," she said bluntly. "You know how bad it can be."

Kayleigh straightened and drummed the pads of her fingers lightly on the edge of the island. "Okay. I'll think about it."

The minute she left the room, Emma pushed away her bowl and swung her legs in his direction. "Okay. Give me the story."

He tried to buy some time by peering into her bowl. "Not a fan of tomatoes?"

"Not one bit."

"Aren't you going to eat your olives?"

"Not if you paid me." She pushed the bowl across the marble surface. "Take what you want."

Max reached for the remains of her salad, happy for the distraction. He scraped the tomatoes, cucumbers and olives into his own bowl, then set hers aside with a sigh. "Last summer I tried to use one of those, uh, dating apps."

"A dating app," she repeated, leveling him with a steady gaze.

Unable to meet her eyes, he focused on picking his favorite bits out of the bowl. "We matched and met up for coffee. She said she was a teacher, but we hadn't met before, so I didn't think much about it." He sighed and popped a hummus-dipped olive into his mouth, buying time as he chewed.

"You didn't know she was a teacher at Capitol Academy?" she persisted, piecing together the bits he wasn't saying while he stalled.

"She wasn't yet. We were on our second coffee, uh, date when she mentioned starting at a private school in the fall. When I found out she was going to be at CA, I ended the date."

She eyed him curiously. "Ended it how?"

"What do you mean *how*?" he asked, uncomfortable with this line of questioning.

"You know, did you get up and storm out, leaving her with the check and your half-eaten biscotti?" She held up a hand. "No, wait. You said you'd call, but then ghosted her."

He reared back, startled by the scenarios she'd cooked up and what each one seemed to say about him. "I told her my daughter was a student at Capitol Academy, and that I was heavily involved with the school. I didn't think the two of us continuing to see one another was wise. She agreed."

Emma exhaled her disappointment, then shrugged. "Boring but effective," she assessed. "Did you sense any ill will on her part? Did she try to talk you around? Try to keep the relationship going?"

"What?" He shook his head. "No. It wasn't a relationship, it was two coffee dates. One and a half, really. And she didn't want the complication any more than I did," he insisted, pointing at her with his fork before dropping it into his bowl.

"Hey, I'm only trying to look at this from every angle," she said, raising her hands in defense.

"I understand, but there's nothing more to read into it. I spent a couple hours chatting with the woman in a public place almost eight months ago."

"Gotcha." She pushed back from the counter and began gathering her things. But she wasn't done with him. Not by a long shot. "I'm only asking if there's any way she could have a different perspective on things. I mean, you're a, uh, nice-looking guy," she said as she ran water in the sink. "Nice house. Nice clothes. Nice car…"

Max blinked, taken aback by both the implication he was a catch and her repeated use of the word *nice*. Why did it sound like a condemnation when used more than twice in a sentence and never once applied to any aspect of his personality?

"You think she's been silently harboring some kind of crush on me?"

"Is it such a wild assumption?"

"It is a bit out there. You think she's trying to get my attention by ruining my daughter's prospects?" He shook his head, unable to entertain the notion. "What was posted today?"

"I haven't looked yet, but they posted after school hours from somewhere on the school property."

"Can you pull up the accounts here?" he asked, nodding to her phone.

Emma nodded and picked up her phone. With practiced ease, she swiped and tapped until she was in one of the PicturSpam accounts with his daughter's user photo. There were hundreds of comments under the photo his daughter had posted days before. Emma opened the thread and jumped expertly to the latest comments.

@MiklMomo2029: I hear @kayleighhughes08's daddy chkd her into rehab.

@LindC: You mean Zaddy Hugebucks is home alone? Hold my macchiato.

@ITgrrl7789: Rehab 4 wut? Personality transplant?

@LindC: They still live up on the hill, rite?

@MiklMomo2029: Ha! U heading over @LindC? You'll have to beat up all the PTA moms to get near him. Incl urs.

@LindC: Tell UR daddy I sed hi, @MiklMomo2029.

@ITgrrl7789: Like @kayleighhughes08's hot dad will look twice at a girl his kid's age. Guy's got ETHICS.

@LindC: *gasp* @ITgrrl7789 Noooooo! Is there a shot for that?

@ITgrrl7789: Sadly no cure

He frowned, perplexed by the commentary. "Are they talking about me?"

"Yep. You're the zaddy," she said, swiping out of the app. "These are the nicer ones. PicturSpam has pretty strict user guidelines. People are freer on sites like ChitChat, where they think their posts are protected."

"Protected from whom?"

"They have restricted audiences. The user can choose who sees their commentary in their feeds," she explained.

"How'd you get in?" He turned his curious gaze on her as she scrolled. Emma looked up, her eyes sparkling with amusement.

"I'm magic."

"You're a hacker," he countered.

"Of a sort," she admitted. "But I work for the good guys." She turned her attention back to her screen and jabbed at it a few times. "Well, would you look at…"

"What?"

She turned the phone toward him. "Our friend at-ITgrrl-seven-seven-eight-nine is on Chit, too. I need to let Wyatt know. We're cross-referencing the handles used on various platforms. Doesn't mean anything definitive. People can use different profile names and have multiple accounts, but it's worth a try. Most people are pretty lazy when it comes to usernames and passwords."

She switched to her messaging app and typed out a message with her thumbs. When she was done, she huffed a strand of hair away from her forehead and toggled back to the ChitChat screen. "Let's see what she has to say."

He peered over her shoulder as she scrolled through post after post complaining about Kayleigh, ugly things his daughter allegedly said or did to "friends" or "someone I know," and a passel of speculation about Kayleigh's car, wardrobe, spending. His cheeks flamed as he realized a number of comments referred to him bankrolling Kayleigh's lavish lifestyle and referring to him with various money-related nicknames.

"I think this user is obsessed with you," Emma murmured

as she continued to read. "Do you think her handle is 'it' girl, or 'IT' girl," she asked, turning wide, questioning eyes on him. "Maybe an IT teacher?"

"You think this is…?" He let the question trail away. "No." He stepped back, needing to put some space between himself and the notion of Amy Birch participating in—or perpetrating—this assault on Kayleigh's reputation.

"Not possible?" she challenged.

"It wasn't anything more than coffee," he insisted.

"For you." She closed out of the app. "I'm floating a theory."

"It's pretty out there."

"But worth pursuing, in my opinion. I think I'll set up a coffee date with Ms. Birch."

"I think you'd better clear it with Kayleigh first," he said, crossing his arms over his chest.

"Why?"

"Because, for some mysterious reason she decided to promote you to Aunt Emma, remember?"

She blinked twice and her forehead puckered. "Oh, yeah. Why did she?"

He shrugged. "No clue, but she must have had some reason. You'll need to talk to her."

"I will." She gave a decisive nod as she peeled the empty phone sleeve from her arm. "But even if she doesn't want me to blow her cover story for me, I can still reach out. You know, as a concerned aunt. One IT professional to another," she added with a small smirk.

EMMA SPENT THE evening holed up in Kayleigh's room. When not on the phone with other members of the Cyber Crime Division, she was quizzing his daughter about social-media handles and the intricate and interwoven connections between the teenagers mentioned in various posts. He'd lingered outside Kayleigh's door a couple times, listening to them talk. The two of them had slipped into the sort of easy back-and-forth he hadn't enjoyed with his daughter in years.

Feeling out of sorts and generally left out, he retreated to his home office and placed a call to Emma Parker's boss.

Simon answered on the first ring. "Taylor here."

"Hughes," Max countered.

"How's it going?" his old friend asked absently.

"You tell me."

"Good," Simon answered without hesitation. "Things are good."

"Really?" Max gave an incredulous snort. "Have you seen some of these posts?"

"I've seen the ones the team has flagged," Simon replied.

"How many total?"

"Uh, hang on." There was a rustling followed by the sound of keystrokes. "I think I've made it through about two hundred and sixty-seven."

Max sat up in his chair. "What?"

"Two hundred and sixty-seven," Simon repeated.

"Posts from Kayleigh's accounts?" he asked, stunned.

"From the accounts we've flagged as using her likeness or referencing her username."

Max scrubbed a hand over his eyes. He had no idea the situation had grown so out of hand. "So many?"

Simon grunted. "There are a lot more. These are the ones my team has flagged as being of particular interest."

"By what criteria?"

"We always tag any communications containing threatening, defamatory or accusatory language. Then we start looking for patterns—mentions, users, linguistic ticks."

"Linguistic ticks?" Max repeated with a scoff.

"You'd be surprised how much we can figure out by analyzing patterns of speech, colloquialisms, online shorthand.

All forms of communication contain a signature, even if they don't attach a name."

"You have never sounded nerdier," Max muttered, using his thumb and forefinger to massage the bridge of his nose.

"In this case, my nerdiness is exactly what you need."

Max smiled tiredly. Simon was right. His old friend's dispassionate analysis was exactly what he needed at the moment. "So this is progress?"

"This is leaps and bounds," Simon assured him. "Trust me."

"I do."

"Emma's doing okay with Kayleigh?"

Max slumped in his seat again, thinking about the snarky cackles of laughter he'd heard drifting into the hall. "They're getting along great."

There was a momentary pause. "Jealous?"

Max pursed his lips. The accuracy of Simon's question landed like a punch to the gut. For a man with few social skills, his old friend had a knack for cutting straight through to a person's emotional core. But Simon wasn't any good with anything that oozed out of those soft, sticky centers.

"A little," he said, knowing Simon would see through any attempt to deflect.

"You know she'll always need you," his friend said in his usual matter-of-fact tone.

"Maybe I want to be wanted, not needed."

The words escaped him before he could think them through. But Simon never judged when someone expressed their feelings. Max had long suspected it was because his friend seemed to be truly baffled by emotion.

When the silence stretched too long, Max heaved a sigh of defeat. "Are the posts bad?"

"Compared to some of the stuff we see? Nothing shocking."

Max bristled at his friend's lack of empathy. "Well,

we're not all animatronic cops. Would a human being find them shocking?"

As ever, Simon remained unperturbed by the sarcasm. "Emma thinks it may be an adult. Kids don't usually acknowledge the existence of parents, much less comment on them," he said. "She tells me you dated the Information Technology teacher last year."

"I didn't date her, I went on a date with her," he clarified. "Coffee."

"Emma said you met her twice."

"Don't you two have anything germane to the case to discuss?"

"You dated and rejected someone with what I assume would be a fairly substantial tech background to be teaching at a school like CA. I'd say it's relevant to an investigation into the pervasive hacking and spoofing of your daughter's electronics."

"I can't believe an adult would purposefully taunt teenagers into self-harm," Max insisted.

"Another reason why you're not a cop. You aren't suspicious enough," Simon concluded. "Emma's going to set up a meeting with the teacher."

"Fine." Max leaned forward in his chair, prepared to abandon it and this conversation. "I'll let you get back to your sleuthing."

"She knows what she's doing," Simon said. "Trust her. If there's anyone who can connect with Kayleigh, it's Emma."

"I know. I'll talk to you later."

"Later," Simon replied distractedly.

Muted beeps signaled the end of the conversation. Max stared at the home screen on his phone, trying to swallow the cold lump of fear lodged in his throat. What if he was the reason this was happening? He thought back to the time he and Amy Birch met for coffee, trying to recall if there'd been any red flags.

She'd seemed perfectly nice. Normal. A woman who'd burned out on the corporate rat race and opted to use her skills to help others. They'd exchanged polite greetings at the school open house. She hadn't even requested a parent-teacher conference when Kayleigh had taken her class in the fall. When they discovered she'd be a teacher at Capitol, they'd mutually agreed it was better not to continue getting together. Had he totally misread her? Was it possible she'd been plotting and planning her revenge this whole time?

No.

He shook his head as he planted a hand on his desk and rose from his chair. He was willing to entertain the possibility of an adult causing all this harm and chaos, but he refused to believe Amy Birch was the one. He might not be a cop, but he knew how to read people. His job depended on him having a finely attuned sense of when someone was on the up-and-up.

As a venture capitalist, he was approached by entrepreneurs on a daily basis. Nearly every one of them would be willing to sell their grandmother for seed money. Most were wholeheartedly convinced their business was on the brink of breaking through. Few of them actually were, and even fewer actually survived beyond the brink.

He stalked in the direction of Kayleigh's bedroom. If the investigation was going to involve him, he'd be a part of the conversation whether or not he was welcome in the girls' club they'd formed.

But when he peered in through the open door, he saw only Emma seated on the bed, her computer on her lap, a tablet on the bedspread near her hip, a phone in her hand and another plugged into one of the laptop's ports. She had on earbuds and was drumming her forefinger on the wrist rest of the computer.

He cleared his throat, but it wasn't enough. She was reading a rapidly moving feed on the phone she held, her eyes darting back and forth at a feverish pace. He was about to step into the room when she frowned, captured whatever she'd seen on the phone's screen, then started typing into the computer, her fingers hitting the keys with thumping urgency.

"What is it?" he asked, but she remained oblivious, her frown deepening. "Emma?" He stepped into the room, but she kept typing, her gaze darting to the phone she'd dropped into her lap. He hesitated for a moment, then, when her typing slowed, he dropped heavily onto the side of the bed.

Her head popped up on a gasp. She blinked twice, then yanked the cord, pulling the buds from her ears. "You scared me."

"Sorry, I tried to get your attention," he said, gesturing vaguely toward the now empty doorway. Her hand settled on her throat and he saw the pulse beneath her jaw flutter beneath fair skin. "I'm sorry," he repeated.

"'S'okay," she said, sounding breathless. "I was… I was in deep, I guess." She picked up the phone and pressed the button to lock the screen.

"What happened?" he asked, nodding to the phone to let her know he'd witnessed whatever had upset her.

"Oh, I, uh," she stammered, glancing at her laptop screen, then back up again. "I'm following some of the chatter."

"You saw something. It upset you." He pinned her with a direct stare. "Was it about Kayleigh?"

She shook her head quickly enough to convince him. "Oh, no. Not Kayleigh."

He exhaled his relief, but Emma remained stiff, her brow pleated so tightly he reached up to smooth it.

They both jumped when his thumb made contact, and Max sprang from the bed. "Sorry," he blurted, his ears flaming. "I didn't mean—" He grimaced. "Force of habit. When Kayleigh gets upset, she gets the..." He trailed off, rubbing the spot between his own eyebrows.

She offered him a half-hearted smile. "Oh. No. No problem. I understand."

He shoved his hands deep into the pockets of his shorts, backed up another step and nearly toppled over the oversize faux-fur blob Kayleigh insisted on using in place of a real chair. "Jeez," he grumbled. "This place is like an obstacle course."

Emma chuckled and pushed herself up against the headboard. "Girls like their stuff." She gestured to the fluffy footstool. "I'm thinking of getting one for my place."

He lifted an eyebrow, impressed by her ability to pivot and deflect. "Uh-huh." He crossed his arms over his chest and tucked his chin. He liked to think of it as his I-mean-business stance, but was fairly sure it would have no more effect on Emma than it did on Kayleigh. Still, he gave it a shot. "What upset you?"

"Some kids talking about another kid." She shrugged and made an attempt to wipe the worry from her face, but he held her gaze, not letting her off the hook. "Soon, I'll have an ongoing correspondence with Dr. Blanton and Ms. Guthrie, the school counselor," she said, as if she'd explained everything with a single sentence.

"An ongoing correspondence about...?" he asked, raising a querying eyebrow.

"I screenshot posts I think may contain cause for concern," she informed him, an edge of defensiveness creeping into her voice.

"What kind of cause for concern?"

"Anything we think indicates a student may be a threat."

"To others or themselves?"

"Both."

"And what happens after you flag it?" he persisted.

"Dr. Blanton and Ms. Guthrie take it from there. I want to nip it in the bud before they do something to require police involvement." She gave him a sad smile. "In other words, I'm hoping I never meet any of these kids."

"Simon says you guys are thinking an adult is behind some of this."

Her smile twisted into a smirk. "Simon says."

Max chuckled. He couldn't count the number of times he and his friends had used the prompt from the old game to taunt the man himself. "You want to meet with Amy Birch," he said, pushing the point.

"I am meeting her. We're having coffee tomorrow morning," she informed him, tipping up her chin as if expecting him to retaliate. "Apparently, she has first period free."

But Max only nodded his approval. "Good. I'll come along."

She spluttered a laugh. "No."

"Yes," he countered.

"This is a police investigation," she reminded him.

"One started at my behest," he replied. "Don't make me go camp out in your back seat. I have a vested interest, and if your theories about her supposed interest in me hold any water, she'll be more helpful with me along."

Emma eyed him warily, gnawing the inside of her cheek as she weighed his argument. After a protracted minute, she gave in with a graceless shrug. "Suit yourself. We ride at oh-seven-thirty," she said, pointedly returning her attention to her screen.

"I'll be saddled up and ready to go." He tapped twice on the doorframe as he backed out of the room. "Do you want the door closed?" he asked.

"Please." Without another glance in his direction, she picked up the phone, scowled fiercely at the screen, then fired off another missive.

He closed the door behind him, wondering which of the dozens of children he'd watch grow up alongside his daughter would be the next target.

Chapter Nine

Emma was up and ready to go early the next morning. She dressed in her usual work clothes—dark pants, a clean white shirt and her trusty loafers—and went into the attached bath to brush her hair.

Kayleigh appeared in the doorway as she was dusting her nose with powder foundation and asked, in the startling direct but genuinely curious way of teenagers, if she was trying *not* to look pretty. "I mean, you know, downplaying your best features because you work in a male-dominated field," she suggested as she propped a hip on the edge of the bathroom counter.

"Uh, no."

"Because you can help yourself to whatever," Kayleigh said, gesturing to the bounty of her cosmetics collection as if the two of them were girlfriends.

Frowning as she leaned closer to the mirror to apply a swipe of mascara, Emma shook her head. "I don't see the point of fussing with fifteen layers of stuff," Emma said with a shrug. "I'm not trying to impress anyone." She paused as she stepped back, biting her bottom lip as she inspected her reflection. "Why? You think I look bad?"

"I'm not saying you look bad," Kayleigh said in a rush. "I'm only asking because, I don't know… Maybe some lip gloss?" She pulled a tube of berry-colored lip stain from a partitioned organizer and thrust it at Emma. "A touch of color."

Emma squeezed a bit onto her finger, then slicked it onto her lips. "There. Satisfied?" She stalked out of the en suite and grabbed her computer bag.

Kayleigh grinned so wide a dimple flashed in her cheek. "A thousand percent. Do you want to borrow a purse?" She gestured to the walk-in closet like a game-show hostess. "Perhaps something in a nice, boring black?"

Emma rolled her eyes as she draped the strap of the messenger bag across her body. A quick peek confirmed she had both her laptop and the small leather case containing her credentials. She dropped Kayleigh's tablet and cell into the bag before shoving her own into the outside pocket.

"Thanks, but I'm good as I am."

"Suit yourself." Kayleigh leaned against the doorjamb, her arms wrapped tight around her torso. "You don't trust me enough to leave my phone?"

Emma flashed her a sympathetic smile. "I do trust you, but I also have read about every study known to man about the dopamine hit people get when they check their socials, and I know how hard it is to resist temptation." She pointed to the laptop closed on the desk. "Do not log on."

Kayleigh shuddered, eyeballing the computer with a sneer. "As if I'm letting that creeper peek at me."

"Hang tight." She turned to leave the room. "We won't be gone long."

"You kids have fun now," Kayleigh called after her. "Say hi to Ms. Birch, Auntie Emma."

Grimacing at the reminder of Emma's deception the day before, she clamped her lips together to keep from rising to the bait. She was pleased to find Max waiting in the kitchen, one of those pristine white coffee mugs in his hand.

"Pregame?" he asked, lifting the cup.

She shook her head. "No, I'll wait. Thanks," she added. "We're having coffee shop coffee, so I'll hold out for three pumps of caramel and extra whip."

He inclined his head. "Understood."

"Are you sure you want to do this?"

He took a sip of his coffee, unperturbed. "Why wouldn't I?"

"It could be awkward," she pointed out.

"Don't see why it should be. What do I have to say to convince you there was truly nothing between me and Amy Birch?"

"I'm not sure it matters if there was anything or not," she said, choosing her words carefully. "This could be one of those situations where reality and wishful thinking collide."

"I assure you it is not." He gave her a lopsided smile. "But I'm taking the fact you refuse to believe it as a compliment."

Tired of the byplay and ready to get to her interview, she pointed to his mug. "Take it however you like, as long as you take it to go." She hooked the thumb over her shoulder. "Do you want me to drive or are you one of those guys who feel threatened when a woman is behind the wheel."

"I don't appreciate you trying to shame me with patriarchy first thing in the morning," he returned good-naturedly. "I'll have you know I'm used to riding shotgun. Kayleigh drives nearly everywhere we go together."

"Does she think your eyesight is failing?"

"She says my reaction times are not what they ought to be," he said gravely. "I find hers to be overdeveloped, but I prefer when she errs on the side of caution." He took a deep drink of his coffee, then turned and placed the mug in the sink. "Should hold me until we can get to the main event."

"And people say cops are caffeine junkies," she scoffed.

"When you've been a single parent as long as I have,

you don't have much time for vices. I have exactly one, and you're not taking it away from me."

Emma held up both hands in surrender. "I wouldn't dream of it."

He followed her out to the driveway and made his way to the passenger side of her car without any further comment. Emma unlocked the doors with the remote, half waiting for him to come up with some excuse to drive himself, if not the both of them, the six blocks to the coffee shop where they'd be meeting Amy Birch.

Again, Max surprised her. He dropped into the passenger seat and reached for the seat belt before she deposited her messenger bag on the back floorboard.

He moved the seat back to accommodate his long legs, but made no attempt at precoffee small talk, nor did he try to adjust her radio settings. She slid him a sidelong glance.

"What's the game plan here?" he asked.

"What do you mean 'game plan'?" She glanced over at him and found him sitting upright, drumming his fingers on his knee as she navigated the twisting neighborhood streets.

"Do we do this like a good-cop, bad-cop thing?" he asked.

She snorted a laugh. "I don't see how we could, since only one of us is a cop," she replied dryly.

"You know what I mean. Am I Mr. Nice Guy and you're the tough Special Agent coming in to interrogate the suspect?"

"I'm not sure people would classify you as Mr. Nice Guy, but if you see yourself as one, who am I to debase you of the notion?"

"Ha," he said sarcastically. "I know at least three people who think I'm a nice guy. But seriously, how am I supposed to play this?"

"How about you play the concerned father, and I'll be the cop asking questions of a person of interest in an investigation," she said as she slowed to a stop at the bottom of the hill.

Turning to look at him, she gentled her tone. "This isn't a TV show, Max. My job is nothing like the way Hollywood shows it. There will be no exciting car chases or dramatic confrontations with criminal masterminds. This is real life, and in real life most investigations are boring. They involve hours of analyzing data and looking for correlations."

"We're going to interrogate a suspect," he countered.

She snorted. "I don't interrogate people, I interview them. Sometimes a subject may have something interesting to offer. A case can turn on nothing more than a slip of the tongue. Some tidbit that makes us think 'Hey, maybe I should look at this,' or 'Maybe we should revisit so-and-so as a suspect,' but nine times out of ten, it comes down to data and evidence."

"You're making me wonder why I got out of bed early," he said sardonically.

She checked the intersection then hooked her right turn, accelerating slowly. "I wish I could tell you it would be more exciting, but frankly, for my own sake, I'm happy with the way it is." Offering a wan smile, she admitted, "I like the boring cases. Surprises usually mean an investigation has gone sideways, and I don't care much for variables I can't control. My job may be dull, but it still has the potential to be dangerous."

They rode in silence for a moment, then, when she put her blinker on to signal the turn into the coffee shop's parking lot, he glanced over at her with a grin. "So you're saying I should play the good cop, right?"

She chuckled and aimed for one of the few empty spaces in the tiny lot. "Absolutely."

Capitol Café was packed. She scanned the room as they entered but failed to spot Amy Birch.

From his greater vantage point, Max spotted a table in the far corner of the room. He leaned down to speak directly into her ear. "Back corner. We may have to snag a chair from another table, though," he said, indicating the small round table nestled against the wall.

"You go grab it, I'll get our coffees," she said, standing on her toes in an effort to reach his ear.

Max shook his head. "No, I'm the one crashing this party. I promised you a triple shot of caramel and croissants," he reminded her. "I'll keep an eye out for Amy and get her order before I send her back to you."

Biting her lower lip, Emma surveyed the crowded room, then nodded her acquiescence. Gesturing for him to lean down again, she stretched to shout over the din. "Three shots of caramel and extra whip," she reminded him.

"Yes, ma'am," he answered with a cheeky salute.

Holding her bag close to her body, she wove her way through the chattering morning crowd. She had no idea there were so many perky people in this town. Most mornings, it was all Emma could do to roll out of bed in time to splurge on fast-food coffee rather than drinking the sludge at headquarters.

A couple at a nearby table relinquished their spare chair in a flurry of smiles and waves. Uncaffeinated as she was, Emma did her best to plaster a cordial expression on her face as she laid claim to the table no one wanted.

The second she sat down, she understood why. Whoever opted for the corner seat would be hemmed in. Shifting to the chair on the opposite side of the table, she made a mental note to tell Max to leave the corner seat for Amy Birch. She might not be an expert in interrogation, but even Emma understood the advantage of putting a suspect's back to the wall.

Emma groped in the pocket of her bag for a pen. The

place was too noisy to get a decent recording of their conversation, and she didn't want to spend the whole time typing notes into her laptop. She needed to get a good read on this woman, and she couldn't do so if she wasn't able to watch her as they spoke. Her fingers closed around a pen, and she sighed with relief. She placed her small notebook on the sticky tabletop, then twisted in her seat to check the line at the front.

Max was still three customers from the front of the line when Amy Birch breezed through the door. Emma watched as she drew up short and scanned the packed room. Confused recognition flashed across the other woman's face as their gazes met, but then Max must have called her name, because the other woman tore her gaze away.

Emma took the opportunity to observe the two of them together. Though Max leaned in close, like he had with her, she could tell it was merely to compensate for the noise in the room rather than any desire for intimacy. For her part, Amy Birch held her ground. She neither moved in closer nor backed away. The expression on her face and the confused glances she kept sending Emma's way told her the other woman felt she had been duped in some way. And in a way, she had.

When Emma had asked Kayleigh why she had introduced her as Aunt Emma, Kayleigh stuck with the story about explaining why Emma was staying in their house. But after today, it wouldn't be necessary. There was no reason for her to stay with the Hugheses any longer.

Besides, the whole aunt thing wouldn't hold water now. She wondered if the teacher was putting the pieces together. Emma watched as the other woman wove her way through the tables. She was pretty with her caramel-highlighted light brown hair and tortoiseshell glasses. Emma could see why any man would swipe right for a chance to meet Amy Birch.

"Special Agent Parker?" She injected each word with a healthy dose of skepticism.

Emma rose from her seat and extended her hand. As they shook, she flashed the teacher a rueful smile. "Yes. I'm Emma Parker." She pointed to the chair in the corner. "Have a seat. Is Max getting your drink order?"

Amy settled her handbag into her lap and nodded. "Yes, thank you. I don't have much time before I have to be on campus."

Emma nodded. "Understood."

"Kayleigh said you worked in data analysis," she said, a puzzled frown rippling her brow.

Emma busied herself with her notepad and pen. She'd been the one to put a truthful spin on Kayleigh's fabrication about their relationship to one another, but Emma didn't see the point in correcting the record at this point. "Yes, I'm a data analyst for the Arkansas State Police."

"Would you mind if I asked to see some ID?" the other woman asked, clearly miffed at being misled.

"Not at all." She fished her credentials from her bag, opened the leather wallet and slid her badge and identification card across the sticky table.

She sat back, giving the other woman as much time as she needed to feel satisfied. At last, Amy spoke without looking up. "I assume you've been looking into some of these social-media posts Kayleigh's been making."

"Kayleigh isn't making those posts."

The statement came from above them as both women looked to find Max towering over the table, three cardboard-sleeved cups caught between his fingers. He bent to place them on the table. He slid a cup in front of Emma. "We have reason to believe someone has cloned Kayleigh's accounts."

Emma ducked her head to hide the smile tugging at the corner of her mouth. How easily he'd picked up on the terminology. She marveled at his ability to adapt. Was it something he picked up being a single parent for so long?

"Cloned?" Amy echoed as she accepted her drink. Clutching her cup, she fell back against the wooden slats of the chair. "I can't believe I didn't think about someone hacking her accounts," she said almost to herself.

"You didn't?" Emma asked.

The other woman's eyes snapped to hers. "Of course not. I mean, I had no reason to believe they weren't legitimate."

Emma could feel Max bristle even as he settled into the chair between them, but thankfully he said nothing.

Emma picked up her pen and pretended to jot a note on her pad. "You think Kayleigh is the type to post hateful things about other students? Have you witnessed a tendency to bully others in your interactions with her?"

Amy blinked, clearly caught out by the question. "Well, no. Nothing in particular," she conceded. "I guess I meant she's one of the more popular students. You know the kind of power popular kids have. The other girls look up to her. Want to dress like her, drive a car like hers and all those things. Sometimes being the one people envy and emulate doesn't bring out the best in a person's personality." She cast an apologetic glance in Max's direction. "Kayleigh seemed to have it all. Brains, beauty, money…" She shrugged as she trailed off.

"But you haven't witnessed any behavior you would consider aggressive or derogatory on Kayleigh's part?"

The other woman shook her head. "No."

"But you had no problem believing she would bully another student," Emma said flatly.

It was Amy's turn to bristle. "I suppose it's fair to say I didn't form an opinion of my own. I'd heard about what happened and believed what I heard."

"Do you feel any ill will toward Miss Hughes?" Emma asked.

"What?" Amy shook her head. "No. Why would I?"

"I'm aware you and Mr. Hughes have a social acquaintance," Emma said, drawing Max into the conversation. Both of her guests shifted uncomfortably in their seats.

"It wasn't much of a social acquaintance. We met for coffee once or twice last summer," Amy said dismissively. "Once we realized he was the father of one of my soon-to-be students we both thought it was best to leave it at a couple of cappuccinos."

"It was mutual?" Emma leaned forward slightly. "The decision not to see each other socially again."

"Yes," both Amy and Max replied in unison.

They shared a startled glance and then Amy shifted in her seat to rest her elbows on the table, peering directly at Emma. "Are you really Kayleigh's aunt?"

Emma gave a soft snort but declined to confirm or deny Kayleigh's spin. "As we mentioned, we found evidence indicating Kayleigh's social-media accounts had been compromised. We've also determined her laptop has been hacked, and whoever did it is savvy enough to run all of these processes through various types of spyware designed to mask the user's presence as well as their activity."

Amy Birch held her gaze as she processed this information. "O-o-o-oh," she whispered, drawing the word out several beats. It was barely more than a gasp, but it undercut the hum of conversation around them. "You think I had something to do with this."

"You have a relationship with the victim. You've had social interaction with the victim's father. It may or may not have gone the way you preferred, and I would assume you have the skills to run spyware, being an industry professional."

"I can't believe this," Amy muttered.

"I checked your NetwkIn profile. You worked for Syscom

before leaving to teach at Capitol Academy," Emma said, unperturbed by the other woman's incredulity.

"I did."

"And what did you do for them?" Emma persisted.

She seemed to weigh the cost versus the benefit of answering the question, then sighed. "I developed and tested cybersecurity software for most small-to-medium-size business models," Amy admitted with a challenging lift of one eyebrow.

"Then you know about various forms of malware. How to detect them, how they get into a system and what they could do once they get a foothold," Emma said flatly.

Amy straightened her shoulders and lifted her chin. "I do, but it doesn't mean I have." She shook her head, her lip curling. "I certainly don't wormhole my way into the social-media accounts of my students. I'm a trained IT professional, not a hacker," she said, infusing the last word with a healthy dose of disdain.

"I see." Emma tapped her pen against the pad, where she'd hardly made any notes. "I was a hacker who turned into an IT professional," she said almost conversationally.

"Scared straight?" the other woman asked with a sneer.

"Something like that." Emma flashed a humorless smile. "You can understand why we'd want to speak to you, though?"

"Yes, but why would I do this? What do I have to gain?" Amy asked stiffly.

When Emma cast a pointed glance in Max's direction, the other woman waved the insinuation off.

"Yes, I had coffee with her father once or twice months ago," she said dismissively, waving a hand in Max's direction. "But nothing came of it. If you've done any internet dating before, Agent Parker, you'll know it's not unusual. A woman has to kiss a lot of frogs to find her prince."

"I think I've been called a frog," Max said, speaking into his coffee cup as he raised it to take a drink.

"I am familiar with the process," Emma assured her.

"Then you know what I mean."

"Why did you leave a lucrative corporate job to take a teaching position?" Emma asked, cocking her head to the side.

"Have you ever worked in corporate IT, Special Agent Parker?"

"No." Emma shook her head. "I went directly from university into the police academy."

"Then you may not know the salaries in the corporate world can't always make up for the sacrifices one makes in their private life. I was tired of working sixty-and seventy-hour weeks. I was up to my eyeballs in code nearly every day. I took on project after project and couldn't see where it would ever end. I wasn't enjoying my life. I didn't have a life. So I made a choice."

"It isn't as if teachers at Capitol Academy aren't making a decent living," Max interjected. "They're paid well above what most public-school teachers make, though I will say it's still not nearly as much as any teacher ought to be paid."

Amy inclined her head. "I can't believe I heard a member of the school board saying so. Do your fellow board members know you feel this way?" she asked with a knowing smirk.

Emma shot Max a glance. He hadn't mentioned being on the school board. Now she understood why Kayleigh was being granted more leniency when it came to the bullying accusations. She made a note of it on her pad, but quickly steered the conversation back to the woman across from her.

"So you left your job at Syscom for better quality of life," she said with a nod of encouragement.

"And because I want this next generation of kids to be more tech-savvy." Amy fiddled with the lid on her to-go cup.

"I was hoping to get some of the younger students in my classes so I could talk with them about digital security and social-media issues." She flashed a self-deprecating smile. "I wanted to catch them before they became so heavily invested in their phones, not really realizing I'd have to start with middle schoolers to make any real difference. Principal Blanton was the one who decided we should focus on eleventh and twelfth graders. He is of the belief they need to develop better skills before they go off to college."

"Don't most of the older kids have solid computer skills already?" Emma asked. She herself had been coding before she had a driver's license, but she knew most kids had other interests as teens.

"They do," Amy conceded. "Heck, there's an eleventh grader who is already monetizing the makeup tutorials she posts." She shrugged. "I've spoken to Dr. Blanton and we're reworking the curriculum."

Emma pursed her lips for a moment, unsure if she wanted to give voice to the thought niggling at her. In the end, she decided it would be irresponsible of her not to ask. "Do you think it's possible whoever is posting these things may have learned the skills necessary to spoof accounts in your classroom?"

Again, the teacher responded with a sad smile. "Can I say absolutely not? No. But I will readily admit most of my students are far savvier about social media than I am. I may know the technology powering the platforms, but they know how to manipulate it. They create, edit and boost two or three multimedia posts in the time it takes me to choose a GIF."

"Have you taken a closer look at any of the posts yourself?" The way the other woman lowered her gaze before answering told Emma everything she needed to know. She leaned in and lowered her voice. "You had to have noticed the posts about the other students were coming from a secondary account in Kayleigh's name."

Color rose high on the other woman's cheeks. When she looked up, she stared directly at Emma, studiously avoiding looking in Max's direction. "I did, but you know as well as I do many people maintain multiple social-media presences. I have no way of verifying which accounts are real or if someone is being impersonated."

"We've been tracking and cross-referencing all the students mentioned in posts related under Kayleigh's name."

"Then you know other accounts are popping up," Amy said, confirming Emma's suspicion this woman was also trying to crack her case.

"We do," Emma confirmed.

"And you believe the person who has hacked Kayleigh's accounts is also behind some of those?"

"It's a possibility," Emma hedged. Narrowing her eyes, she asked, "What do you think?"

Blowing out an exasperated breath, Amy checked the time on her smartwatch and inched her chair back enough for her to wriggle out of it. "What do I think? I think there's someone out there trying to get the valedictorian expelled weeks before graduation day, but I have no idea why. I also think you're not actually Kayleigh's aunt, and it's time for me to get to school."

Max stood, moving his chair aside to create a path for her. "Thanks for meeting us today," he said as she sidled past.

She paused and looked him straight in the eye. "I'm sorry this is happening. Sorry for you. Sorry for Kayleigh and the other kids. But I can assure you I have nothing to do with it. I hope you and the board will keep my cooperation in mind, as I'm sure this topic will be number one on the agenda for the next meeting."

Then she turned to give her full attention to Emma. "I

will do whatever I can to aid your investigation. If I can help, please reach out to me directly."

Max reclaimed his chair, and the two of them sat quietly in the hubbub of the busy café. At last, Max tapped the side of his cup twice, then asked, "What do you think?"

"I think Amy Birch is not the person we're looking for," she answered, considering each word as if needing to confirm his gut instinct.

"She has the knowledge and the access," he countered.

"But no motive," Emma concluded. Smirking, she lifted her coffee in a toast. "Who'da thought a guy like you could strike out so thoroughly?"

He shrugged unselfconsciously and tipped his cup against hers. "Can't win them all." He sighed. "Which means we're back to square one."

"Hardly," she said, affronted. "We're way beyond square one." Pushing her chair back, she rose. "Come on. I'll drop you off and head into the office."

Chapter Ten

Max's ego was only slightly dented by Amy Birch's indifference to him. He may have felt miffed by it if Emma Parker hadn't seemed so pleased by the other woman's lack of interest. They rode back to the house in silence, Emma quiet and deep in thought as she made the short drive. When she signaled the turn into his driveway, he cleared his throat, intending to ask her how she planned to proceed, but the words died in his mouth.

"Oh. Oh, nuh-uh—" Emma jammed the brakes so hard his seat belt caught him and threw him back so hard his head slammed into the headrest. "Stay here," she ordered, shifting the car into Park and flinging the door open. "Hey!" she shouted. "Stop right there! Police!"

He spotted a hoodie-clad figure ducking into the trees that lined the opposite side of his house, then disappearing. Emma stopped at the edge of the concrete pad, staring down at the steep downhill slope. This time of year, it would be thick with new growth and underbrush. Ignoring her command, he scrambled from the car and sprinted over to stand beside her.

"Who was—" he asked, adrenaline making him breathless. Her head whipped around. "I thought I told you to stay put."

"Did you get a look at them?" Max demanded.

"Pretty sure it was a kid. Can't say much beyond that." She turned back to survey his garage door.

Whoever their culprit was, he and Emma had interrupted them in midmessage. Rivulets of black spray paint ran from each letter scrawled across his garage door. Emma grabbed hold of a sapling and used it as a tether as she scrambled down the incline a few feet.

"What are you doing?" he demanded. "You can't chase them, it's too steep."

"I'm not chasing them," she said, sliding her hand down the thin trunk until she was able to squat and pick something up. She held a spray-paint can pinched gingerly between her thumb and middle finger. "Help me back up," she gasped as she straightened.

He leaned down and grasped her wrist. "Let go of the tree."

She looked up and met his eyes. "As long as you promise not to let go of me," she said, breathless.

"I have you."

She relinquished her hold on the tree and he dug in. He grunted with the effort of anchoring them both as she scrambled back onto the driveway. Once she was back on solid ground, she placed the can carefully on the concrete. "Don't touch."

"I won't," he promised. "You okay?"

"Yeah, it's…" She glanced back at the drop-off. "One heck of a slope. Kid must be part mountain goat."

"Or scared enough not to care," he said grimly.

Moving in unison, they turned back to the house. The message painted onto his once pristine white garage door glared back at them.

Their street artist only got as far as *LYING B* before being interrupted.

Emma pulled her phone from her pocket. "You go in and

check on Kayleigh. I'll get the Little Rock police up here to take a report."

"The Little Rock police?" He shook his head. "You can't make the report?"

"Not my jurisdiction."

"Yeah, but—"

"Max," she said, interrupting his protest. "Go in and check on Kayleigh."

She spoke the order so firmly he had no choice but to obey. Turning on his heel, he ran for the front door. He had to punch in the code twice before the dead bolt released. The alarm panel flashed a red light, indicating video surveillance was activated. Moving to the panel, he punched in his six-digit code to disarm the alarm, then pulled his phone from his pocket. He could check the security footage on the app, and maybe get a look at the punk who did this.

"Kay?" Max called into the depths of the silent house. He thumbed open the security application as he rushed down the hall toward her bedroom. "Kayleigh, answer me," he called, his demand harsh with anxiety.

A heart-stopping beat passed before he heard a watery reply coming from the back of the house. "In here…"

Forgetting all about the camera footage, Max jogged down the hall to the primary suite, where he found Kayleigh sitting sideways on the teak bench situated inside the massive shower, her knees drawn up to her chin.

Slowing his steps, he approached with caution. "Hey, are you okay?"

His daughter didn't lift her head from the cradle of her arms. "Not a good question, Dad," she answered in a choked voice.

"I know," he conceded. "What happened? Did someone try to get in?"

"Yeah… No." She turned her head away from him, as if trying to block him out of her misery.

"What happened?"

She shook her head and gasped out another sob.

He patted her back, knowing the gesture was ineffectual, but not knowing what else to do. "I'm kind of at a loss here, kid." He squatted down in front of the bench, grasping the edge to keep his balance. "I don't know what to ask you. I don't know what to say. I don't know how to handle any of this," he admitted quietly. "But I'm trying."

"I know," she whispered.

"There's no manual for being a parent," he said with a rueful smile. "I can't tell you how many times I've wished there was."

She sniffled deeply, then released a shuddering breath. "Maybe you should write one."

He scoffed. "I think we could both agree I'm hardly an expert."

"You do okay," she conceded huskily.

"Can you tell me what happened?" he asked her. She nodded without looking up. He gave her back a pat. "Come on. Sit up."

She took a deep breath before lifting her head and turning on the bench. Max pressed his hands to his aching knees and pushed up to his full height.

"Do you know who it was?" She nodded again.

"They spray-painted the garage door." Max wet his lips, uncertain of how much information he should share. "I'm gonna let you guess what kind of words."

"Oh, God," she moaned, then dropped her face into her hands again. "What did I ever do to him?"

"Do what to who, Kayleigh?" he asked gently. "Who did this?"

Kayleigh looked up, wiping her moist face with the insides

of her wrists as she shook her head in despair. "Daddy, it was Carter," she said, her voice a croak. "He came and knocked on the door, but I didn't want to answer. I heard him drive off, but a few minutes later I heard something and looked out the window." She swiped at her eyes again, then looked up, her face a mask of misery. "He was out there yelling stuff. Mean stuff. Like we haven't known each other our whole lives. How could he do this?"

"Sweetie, I think everyone is feeling really, uh, raw right now," Max said carefully. "Didn't Emma say Carter was mentioned in some of those fake posts?"

"Yeah, but he *knows* me, Daddy," she wailed.

She searched his eyes for answers and he had none. There were no traces of the self-assured teenager he'd raised, or the young woman ready to take on the world.

"I don't know what to say," Max said, opting for honesty. "I don't have an answer for any of it, sugar. I wish I did, but I don't. All we can do is help Emma and the rest of her team collect whatever evidence they need to figure out who's doing this to all of you. Then maybe, once everyone sees the truth, we can all move on."

Kayleigh switched to the backs of her hands for the mopping up under her eyes. "Move on," she said with a bitter laugh.

"Listen, Emma's calling the Little Rock police in to take the report. He dropped the spray paint. I assume they'll be able to get fingerprints from it," Max informed her.

"I don't want Carter to get in trouble," she said, unfolding her long legs in preparation for leaping to her feet. "He has a scholarship from the Jones Foundation."

Max winced. Funded by a local family obsessed with their squeaky-clean, do-gooder image, the Jones Foundation awarded scholarships based on their own definition of good character and high standards.

"He probably should have thought about his scholarship before he vandalized somebody's property," Max said stiffly. "I'll to go see what's happening outside."

Kayleigh followed him. "Please don't press charges."

"I can't let him get away with this, Kayleigh."

"But you can. We can't... If you turn him in, it will look like we're picking on someone else," she said, a plea in her tone.

He turned back to her. "We haven't picked on anyone though, have we?" He fixed her with a stern glare.

"No. Of course not," she said, taken aback.

"I believe in the truth. The evidence Emma is tracing will exonerate you, and other evidence will prove Carter Pierce vandalized our home."

She shook her head hard and grabbed on to his sleeve. "You're concerned for my future but what about Carter's?"

He stilled, his grip on taking a hard line wavering. "Carter's parents can worry about his future."

"Hasn't there been enough damage done? Can't we let it be?" she asked, her voice rising with panic. "Can't we figure out who's doing all this, make it stop, and then everything can go back to the way it was?"

He turned and took her into his arms for a hard, fast hug. "Nothing's gonna go back to the way it was," he said. When she didn't pull away, he took the opportunity to press his cheek to the top of her head like he had when she was small. "But things can only get better, right?"

"Why do I feel like you've jinxed us?" she asked with a humorless laugh.

He gave her one last squeeze then turned toward the front door. "I'm gonna go talk to Emma and see if the police are here yet. I'll let her know it was Carter. Maybe she can find a way to talk to them without getting him in too much trouble."

"But you won't press charges?"

"I won't press charges," he promised, "but I will speak with his parents." He relinquished his hold on her and gave her a gentle push toward the media room. "Go find something to watch to take your mind off this. I'll handle things out here."

"You're not going to be able to protect me forever, you know," she said solemnly.

"No, but as long as I have breath in my body, I'm going to try," he vowed.

"So dramatic."

She rolled her eyes, but Max was serious. "Protecting you is my job. The only job that matters."

Emma gave him a tremulous smile and nodded before turning away. He watched as she padded down the hall. When she disappeared into the other room, he turned to head back outside.

When he pulled open the front door, he found Emma squatting beside the can of spray paint, taking photos of it from every conceivable angle.

"I should have done this before I touched it," she said without looking up from her task. "Taylor's gonna have my hide. Total rookie mistake. You can tell they sure don't let me loose on crime scenes often. I can't even remember the most basic principles," she grumbled to herself.

"You saw it and you acted," he said reassuringly. "Besides, we don't need to worry about getting fingerprints off the can. Kayleigh recognized our culprit."

The announcement captured her full attention. She looked up at him, her eyes wide. "She did? Is she okay? Did they try to get into the house?"

Her concern for his daughter touched him. "She's okay." He sighed and ran a hand through his hair. "It was Carter Pierce," he said flatly. "He's one of Kayleigh's classmates, and—"

"The boy she went to homecoming with. The football player."

"Yes."

"Our hacker was posting about him from one of the fake Kayleigh accounts."

Max shoved his hands deep in his pockets to hide the fact that they were balled into tight fists. Never in his life had he felt as impotent as a parent as he did this week. Not even when Kayleigh was a newborn and her mother so terribly sick.

"She doesn't want me to press charges against him," he informed her. "She's worried people are going to think we'll be seen as bullying him."

"Bullying," Emma said in an undertone. "Nothing but bullies around here."

The warning blip of a police siren made them both jump.

A squad car had pulled into the driveway and stopped behind Emma's still idling car.

Max gave his head a shake, then decided to make himself useful. "I'll pull your car up and turn it off."

Emma nodded and began shooting photos of the painted garage door with its drippy letters. "Great. Thanks."

Max made his way to her car. Settled in the driver's seat, he took a closer look at the interior of her vehicle. Several empty water bottles rolled loose on the back floorboard. The console was littered with gum wrappers, loose change, a collection of mismatched fast-food napkins and a twisted-up, frayed phone cable.

The detritus didn't shock him. He'd seen her pull articles of clothing out of her trunk—he assumed she spent much of her time on the go, but from her comments it sounded like she did most of her work either at home or in the office. She was living much as he had fresh out of college. But then marriage and a baby had forced at least a semblance of order on his life. He noted the many differences between his life and hers as he pulled the car forward and shut it off.

Leaning against the fender, he hung back as Emma

greeted the officers and walked them through what they'd found when they pulled up. He watched as one of them dropped to one knee beside the paint can and pulled on a latex glove. One officer listened to Emma's description of where the can was discovered as he dropped the spray-paint can into a plastic evidence bag and stood up.

The three of them moved to the side of the driveway overlooking the slope. From their stances and the way they jostled one another, he assumed Emma was taking a ribbing for the way she'd handled crime-scene evidence. To his relief, she seemed unperturbed.

If anything, she seemed to regret having called the local police now they knew who the culprit was. Max had no doubt she was itching to dive back into her own investigation rather than answer their questions.

When the officers finally made their way over to him, it was merely to confirm his name and contact information. They made a few more notes as Emma took more photos of the damaged door, then took their leave with the promise they would be in touch.

Max strolled over to meet Emma as they climbed into the patrol car and backed out. "What did they think?"

She stared at the marred garage door, gnawing on her bottom lip. "Vandalism doesn't seem to impress them."

"They didn't need to talk to me?" he asked. "I thought in light of the other stuff—"

"I didn't tell them about the other stuff."

He raised an eyebrow. "Did you tell them you're Kayleigh's aunt?"

She shrugged. "I told them we were together when we pulled into the driveway. We saw someone spray-painting on the door, and you went in to check on your daughter as

I pursued the suspect down the hillside, where I came upon the can."

She pinned him with a pointed stare and Max held her gaze and bit back the urge to chuckle. Who was he to judge if she wanted to rewrite history a bit?

"So what's the next step?"

"I'm going to talk to Kayleigh about Carter. The LRPD is going to go speak to him and his parents. You can press charges if you want," she said, raising an inquiring eyebrow. "Criminal trespass, malicious intent to deface property, any number of things."

"But you don't think I should," he concluded, judging by her tone.

Again, she let one shoulder rise and fall before turning to face him. "I don't know many seventeen-or eighteen-year-old boys who would react any better to the things being said about him online."

"Kayleigh is hoping that if I don't press charges this whole thing will blow over and things can get back to normal."

Emma gave him a sad smile. "Oh, the optimism of youth."

"These kids," he said dryly.

"It won't ever get back to the way it was for them," Emma said, sobering instantly. "This week is going to be an inflection point for them. Everything in their young lives will be measured in before and after. For all of them. Patrice, Kayleigh, Carter and who knows how many more." Looking him in the eye, she said, "If we don't stop them, there could be others. So many others." Her mouth thinned into a grim line. "Even if they don't do anything else, it's going to get worse. They'll turn on one another. If they haven't already."

"For something none of them are actually responsible for."

"All the more reason not to make it any worse for Carter."

She gestured to the garage door. "I am sure it won't cost much to have this repaired."

"Not nearly as much as it's going to cost him…them in so many other ways," Max agreed.

"We have a plan," she said as they walked back into the house.

Surprised, he eyed her warily. "We do? How did I miss making a plan?"

"Not you-and-me we, me and my team," she explained as she brushed past him. "Let me call the boss while you go check on Kayleigh."

"I've checked on Kayleigh," he countered, watching as she walked away.

"Check again," she called without breaking stride.

She walked through his house as if she lived there. As if she belonged there. Like she hadn't appeared on his doorstep mere days before. He tore his gaze away as she disappeared into Kayleigh's room. Seeing her so at ease in his home made him nervous, but in a disturbingly pleasant way.

He wondered if she was gathering her belongings. Would she still leave today? They'd had an intruder on the premises. Should he call Simon and ask him to ask her to stay? Should he ask her himself? Did Kayleigh want her to stick around?

The last question spurred him to action.

"Hey, Kay," he called out before entering the media room—it had been his habit from her early teens. In those days, it had felt like an alien had moved into their home, and the only way he could keep the peace was to be sure neither of them made any sudden movements.

She looked up when he entered the room. "Yeah?" she said, pointing the remote at the screen and freezing the image of a morning talk show.

"So I was thinking, and it's totally up to you," he began, knowing he sounded wishy-washy. "But given everything going on I was wondering if you feel more comfortable having Special Agent Parker here?"

His daughter quirked an eyebrow. "We're back to 'Special Agent Parker' now?"

"Fine. Are you more comfortable having Emma here?" he asked with blunt exasperation.

Kayleigh cocked her head as if pondering the question. "Do you mean because she's a cop, or because of the hacking stuff?"

"Either, I guess," he said with a shrug.

"To be honest, most of the time I forget she's with the police," she said as if the notion was tinged with absurdity. He was about to question her when she continued on. "I mean, she's so cool. I never really think of adults being so cool, and certainly not police officers," she said with a laugh.

Max clamped down on the indignity urging him to ask if his kid thought he was cool. Of course, she didn't. He stepped farther into the room. "You really think she's cool?" he asked. He couldn't help wondering what qualified Emma for a status he'd never achieve in his daughter's eyes. Was it merely because she was not a parental figure? Or was it because she was a whip-smart young woman doing a job most people would assign to nerdy guys?

"She's really chill, you know?" Kayleigh set aside the remote control when he perched on the far end of the couch. "Look how far she's come," she said admiringly. "You know, Emma told me she was bullied in high school. She said at first, she was really depressed and upset about it." She glanced down at her clasped hands and wet her lips. "I imagine she was probably a lot like Patrice. She was never the type to push back, you know?"

Max nodded. "She is pretty shy and reserved."

"But Emma said she eventually got so fed up with people trying to get one over on her it made her want to be smarter and faster. She didn't crumble," Kayleigh said in conclusion. "She stood up for herself."

Max thought about the sketchy information he'd gleaned about Emma's past. "Did she tell you what it was she did to make herself feel better?"

Kayleigh ducked her head, and he caught sight of the slight curl of her lips.

"She did, didn't she?"

"Not the details," Kayleigh assured him. "She only said she made it clear to the people who were giving her a hard time she was no pushover, but in the process, she got in trouble."

"Simon told me she was arrested when she was fifteen for hacking into her school's mainframe." Max eyed his daughter warily. "She was lucky her case landed with a judge who had some empathy for her situation."

"Oh, I knew about the arrest thing," Kayleigh said dismissively. "I was talking about the other thing."

Max raised an eyebrow. "What other thing?"

"I don't know if I should say," his daughter hedged. "I mean, if she hasn't told you, I don't know if it's my place to tell you."

"You're telling me she did something worse than figuring out how to alter school records? You know she changed the grades of the students who tormented her, right? She wasn't even old enough to drive a car legally," he pointed out.

"Well, yeah, it was worse, but not like, illegal or anything."

Max exhaled long and loud. "I think maybe you and I have

two different definitions of what may be better or worse in this case."

"She's wondering if she should tell you I used to cut myself," Emma said, her tone flat and factual.

Chapter Eleven

Max's and Kayleigh's heads swiveled. She knew she should have made her presence known, but listening to them talk about her had been too tempting. Once a wallflower, always a wallflower, she supposed.

Standing in the doorway, her laundry basket propped against one hip, she flailed her arm in a vain attempt to keep the collection of bags she'd hiked onto her shoulder from sliding.

Max jumped up to help relieve her of some of the burden. "I take this to mean you're leaving," he said as he lifted the straps from her arm.

When she freed herself of the last one, she caught him staring at the crosshatch of the thin silver-white scars on the inside of her forearm. "It was a phase. My mother saw what I was doing and got me the help I needed," she assured him.

"I'm sorry. It wasn't my intention to pry."

"No, I understand," she quickly assured him. "I don't try to hide them. The scars are a part of who I am." She flashed a wan smile. "I literally wouldn't be the woman I am today if I hadn't gone through something similar to what Kayleigh is navigating now."

"I hope you realize both Kayleigh and I are grateful for all you're doing. Having you here has been a big comfort to both of us." He glanced over at his daughter. "Hasn't it, Kayleigh?"

"Oh, yeah," Kayleigh said, swinging her legs down and sitting up straighter. "I mean, do you have to go?"

"There's really no reason for me to stay. We've pinpointed a point of access, and you know not to go anywhere near the laptop until we tell you it's clear, right?"

"Yes, ma'am." Kayleigh gave an exaggerated shudder. "Doubt I'll want to ever again."

"I'll get you a new one. I was going to upgrade you before you left in the fall, anyway," Max said.

Emma nodded her approval. "Good call. We may still need to use this one for the case. I need to think it through. Either way, leave it alone. Once we're done and it's released from evidence, I can wipe it so no one can get your information from it." She directed her next comment directly to Kayleigh. "If you need me, my apartment is only about ten minutes away, depending on traffic."

"But you're still going be working on the case, right?"

Emma tried not to read too much into how confused and somewhat panicked Max seemed to be by the notion of her leaving. He was nothing more than a concerned parent trying to swim in uncharted waters.

"Of course," she replied. "Why wouldn't I be?"

"Wouldn't it be easier for you to work on it here?" Kayleigh chimed in.

When Emma hesitated, Max lifted the heavy bags from her arm entirely. Emma sighed with relief as he set them aside.

"Kayleigh has a point. If you're going to keep monitoring her devices and checking her accounts, wouldn't it be easier to do it from here?" He reached for the laundry basket, and though she wanted to thrust it at him, she clung to it like a life raft. "Unless you need to be in the office—"

"I can work from anywhere."

"So this is as good a place as any." Max gave the basket a tug and she relinquished it without protest.

"You can have the guest room." Kayleigh twisted to kneel on the couch cushion, her eagerness disarming. "You won't have to worry about me barging in and getting stuff all the time."

"I wasn't worried about you barging in," Emma said with a laugh. "I was worried about being in your way."

"You aren't in my way," Max and Kayleigh said, speaking over one another.

She laughed again. "Most people would be happy to get their space back."

"Oh, I will be," Kayleigh said in a rush. "I mean, you know, because all my stuff is in there." The girl wrinkled her nose in an apologetic grimace.

"I totally get it," Emma said easily. "But there really is no particular reason for me to stay here. I can manage all your accounts from my apartment. You don't need to have me underfoot."

"What if we feel safer having our own special agent on the premises?" Max asked.

A hot flush of pleasure coursed through Emma. She curled her hand into a ball in an effort to contain her rising excitement. The truth was, she dreaded returning to a life of sub sandwiches eaten on the sofa.

"O-o-kay," Emma said slowly. "If you're sure I'm not in the way and—"

"You're not in the way," Max said without hesitation.

"Totally not," Kayleigh chimed in. "I like having someone other than my dad to talk, too." She shot Max a side-eye glance, but Emma was no longer fooled by the teen's bluster. She was as crazy about her father as he was her.

"Yeah, well, you're not the most scintillating conversationalist either, kid," Max retorted. Turning to Emma, he said, "I'll speak to Simon if you need me to clear it with him."

Emma huffed a laugh. "He's not my father."

"Yes. No. Right. I understand." He stumbled over his words, and she loved knowing she had the power to fluster this ruthlessly put-together man. "I meant in an official capacity."

"Tell you what." She nodded to the laundry basket of folded clothes he still held. "I'll leave my stuff here for now. I'm going into the office to meet with the team. We have a plan to isolate the computer we believe some of the posts were sent from. I also have some people analyzing social-media posts for trends. I'll touch base with the others and brainstorm next steps."

"But you're going to come back here," Kayleigh persisted.

Emma shrugged, then gestured to the bags and basket. "I'll have to at least come by. You have most of my stuff."

"If this is most of your stuff, we're going to have to have a serious talk about your skin-care regimen," Kayleigh muttered, falling back into the seat again.

Emma only smiled as she turned to Max. "I think maybe it's time for you to reach out to the other parents. I'm sure by now at least some people have started figuring out there's something more complex going on here."

"I tried to reach out to Patrice's parents, but they haven't returned any of my calls," Max informed her.

She sighed. "I'm betting Carter Pierce's parents are going to take your call." Emma glanced at her watch. "Give them about an hour, then give them a try."

She bent over and pulled Kayleigh's phone from her messenger bag. Kayleigh's face brightened, but Max eyed the device warily.

"I'm leaving this with your dad. I don't want you using it to call your friends, even if your pal Tia has called twenty-seven times. And I definitely want you to stay off social media." She handed the device over to Max. "But I do not want you left alone without some form of communication again. So this is for dialing nine-one-one only. You get me?"

Kayleigh nodded, her expression sober. "I get you."

"When I get back, you and I will talk about reaching out to some of your friends to see if we can get a line on the general feelings out there and where we stand."

Kayleigh wrinkled her nose, but this time in distaste. "I don't know if I want to talk to anybody," she admitted.

"I get it." Emma flashed her a weak smile but gestured to the phone again. "But I think it would be a good strategic move. People will understand why you were incommunicado for a day or two. Most people would assume your dad has your phone and you've been cut off from all other electronics."

"Then they would assume correctly," Kayleigh said with no lack of sarcasm.

"But it's about time for us to make it look like you're sneaking around the blockade," she said with a sly smile.

"I'm not so sure I like the sound of this," Max admitted.

"What kid wouldn't take the first opportunity they had to break the embargo?" Emma asked.

"This is the part in the movie where the teenagers make the parents look like clueless idiots."

Emma laughed as she picked up her messenger bag again and left the rest of the pile at his feet. "Don't flatter yourself. The parents in those movies look like clueless idiots from the jump," she said with a smirk. "I'll be back soon. Call me if you need me."

SIMON PRESSED THE tips of his fingers into the scarred top of the conference table and they all quieted. "Tell me what you've got," he ordered as he took his seat.

Emma and Wyatt exchanged a look, as always slightly taken aback by their boss's obvious distaste for small talk. At the far end of the table, the two newest members of the Cyber Crime Division, agents Caitlin Ross and Tom Vance, looked like they would rather be anywhere else.

"If you don't mind, I'd like to listen to what everybody else has been working on first," Emma said briskly. "I have some thoughts I'm trying to put together, but I need to know if I'm missing any puzzle pieces."

Simon inclined his head. "Dawson, kick things off."

Beside her, Wyatt sat up straighter in his chair. "I've been talking with Emma and I think we're on the same page as far as the Information Technology teacher is concerned," he began. "If she were our perp, I think she'd have done a better job of masking things."

"Their tracks were covered pretty well," Simon said without hesitation.

"Pretty well," Wyatt conceded, "but well enough for a person who spent years designing security software?" He shook his head. "I don't think so."

"You're saying you think she's too good to be our hacker," the section chief concluded.

Emma and Wyatt shared a look, and then Emma spoke up. "Yes. I think she has enough experience in the field of cybersecurity to have made it much tougher on us. We know the tools we're working with aren't anywhere near the cutting edge, and up until eighteen months ago she was in the thick of it with this Syscom. If she was behind all this, I'd have to think she'd have known of a better way."

Simon gave a curt nod. "Concur."

"Aside from her experience in the field, my gut instinct when I met her was she was not our mark."

"Good enough," Simon said briskly. "Moving on."

The two newer members of their team, Tom and Caitlin, shared a look of disbelief at their end of the table.

When all eyes swiveled in their direction, Tom shifted in his seat uncomfortably. Knowing what it was like to be caught in the glare of Simon Taylor's unrelenting stare, Emma lobbed them a softball. "You find any correlations in the social-media posts?"

Caitlin responded, "I have a short list of names of people you may want to discuss with Miss Hughes. The one I'm most curious about is Tia Severin."

"Tia Severin? Why?"

Caitlin glanced over at Tom before answering. She looked distinctly uncomfortable. "I don't have any hard data. Something in my gut tells me her responses to some of the things being said about her best friend and their classmates comes across as…disingenuous?"

"We don't discount gut instincts in this room," Simon said without looking up from his notepad. "Data is king, but it's not an absolute ruler. We all know it can lie as easily as a human being controlling it."

"If you would send me a compilation of the posts you think I need to go over and flag anything of particular interest to you, I would appreciate it," Emma told the younger agent.

Caitlin straightened her shoulders, a pink flush staining her cheeks. "Sure. I've already made a ton of notes, but I'd be happy to go over them with you. Maybe things will strike you differently from how they struck me."

Emma nodded. "We'll get together after this meeting."

She turned to Wyatt. "Did you have any chance to think any further on replacing the computer tower in the IT lab?"

Simon looked up. "Good idea to swap it for one we can monitor from here."

"I'll call Amy Birch to see if they have an extra CPU of

the same brand not currently in use," Wyatt said, making a note on his pad.

"Are you sure you want to tip the teacher off?" Simon asked.

Emma and Wyatt exchanged a glance and he nodded. "We don't think she's our hacker."

"Fine." Simon made a mark on his notepad. "You two work on the CPU. Ideally, I'd like to get it set up so we can make the swap when no one else is around."

"Sounds good," Emma agreed. "I think we can get Amy Birch's help with arranging the swap."

Simon flipped the cover on his notebook and clicked his pen decisively. "Okay, we know where we're at now." He pushed his chair back from the table and stood. "Parker, I want you to stick close to the Hughes house. I don't like the thought that some kid was prowling around when his daughter was home alone."

"Yes, sir."

"As a matter of fact, I think I want you to take a patrol car."

Emma gaped at him. She hadn't ridden in a patrol car in years. "Sir?"

"We don't want any more of his friends coming around." He paused in the doorway and turned back to her. "I think it would be good to have a marked car in the driveway."

"Respectfully, I disagree," Emma said, coming to her feet. "Sir."

Simon froze for a second then zeroed in on her, one eyebrow lifting. "Oh?"

"Not yet, at least." Emma glanced at Wyatt for backup, and he nodded his agreement. "We're still gathering information, and as far as we know the only person who's aware we're involved aside from Dr. Blanton is Amy Birch. The last thing I want to do is tip people off to our presence."

Seconds seemed to tick by at a glacial pace as she waited for her boss to weigh his options. At last, Simon gave a nod and clicked his pen twice, a clear mark of concession. "You're lead on this, Parker, so you make the call."

"Thank you, sir," Emma said, anxious to call close to the meeting before he could change his mind.

Wyatt and Tom gathered their belongings and followed the boss out. The moment the men cleared the room Caitlin let out a weary breath. "He doesn't say much, but you don't really have to read between the lines with him, do you?" she asked.

Emma grinned, tickled by the other agent's assessment of their boss. "It's what I like best about him. A person always knows exactly where they stand with Simon Taylor."

She kicked back in the chair and tipped her chin up as she stared at the water-stained ceiling tiles.

"I want to echo what Simon said about not ignoring your gut instincts. If you have a feeling about something, I want you to share it with me."

"Yes, ma'am."

"And it's Emma, not ma'am," she said, shooting the other woman a sidelong glance. "So tell me, what's your gut saying?"

There was a long pause and then Caitlin replied, "I agree with you. The kids are talking. There's a lot of back-and-forth, and all the usual ugliness," she said with a sharp laugh. "But there's a kind of malicious intent behind the posts being made by Kayleigh's accounts. It seems more…mature." She winced. "Not the right word, but the best one I have at the moment."

"I get you." Emma nodded, her gaze fixed on a water mark. It looked sort of like a lion's head. "I know exactly what you mean. Whoever it is, they're an adult familiar enough with the language kids use with one another to be able to mimic it, but there's something stiff in the delivery. Is *stilted* a good word?"

"Yes. Exactly," Caitlin replied, excitement rising. "Like I said, the kid who's really throwing up any flags for me is Tia Severin. It looks like up until last week she and Kayleigh were tight. Every other post on both of their feeds is tagged with each other, and every group photo, if one was in a group photo then the other was there, too." Caitlin leaned forward.

Emma lowered her gaze to give the other woman her full attention. "And what's irking you about what she's saying?"

"More what she isn't saying. She never comes to Kayleigh's defense, or even told Kayleigh to stop. But she also never egged her on like some of the other kids did." Caitlin shook her head. "Her posts were oddly...neutral."

"Hmm."

"She took almost no stance on the entire situation. Not only on the posts Kayleigh supposedly made about Patrice, but on all the subsequent posts from the spoofed account. It's like she couldn't resist commenting, but she had nothing to add to the conversation. She wasn't supporting anyone, nor was she dragging them. She reminds me of a politician walking the line on a touchy issue."

Emma stared at the younger agent, impressed with the assessment.

Scooting forward in her chair, she slapped an open palm to the tabletop as she rose. "You've got me intrigued. Grab your notes and we'll make an attempt to decipher the coded messages of adolescents. You wanna hang out at your cubicle or mine, Agent Ross?"

THE COMPUTERS USED in the Capitol Academy information-technology lab were a common model. Wyatt was able to unearth one from the boneyard of outdated and confiscated hardware they kept locked in an evidence cage. They had it loaded with all the software Amy Birch listed for them and ready to go by midafternoon, but the teacher insisted they wait until 5:00 p.m. to deliver it, to be sure no one but Ms. Birch was still at the school.

At 4:45 p.m., they watched from a parking lot across the street as a man wearing a whistle around his neck exited the building with a mesh bag of soccer balls. The wipers swished away a fine mist of rain. Emma squinted at the guy as he moved to one of the two cars left in the staff parking lot and tossed the bag of balls into the back seat before climbing in.

"You do a lot of extracurriculars in school?" Wyatt asked, not taking his eyes off the man.

Emma scoffed. "Hardly."

"You keep trying to make me believe you've been cool your whole life, but there's too much nerd in you," he said, elbowing her across the console.

"It wasn't a matter of being cool. It was more I've never been a great team player," she said, watching as the car turned right out of the parking lot.

"You are, too," he countered.

"Now I am," she admitted as he started the engine of the state-issued SUV. "I bet you were on all the teams."

Wyatt nodded as he put the car into Drive. "Of course, I was. When you grow up in a town the size of a postage stamp, you need every warm body you can scrape together to even make a team."

"I bet you were the star player," she teased.

"Hardly," he said with a chuckle. "I did okay with baseball, though."

"Of course, you did—you're the all-American boy," she joked, mimicking his tone.

Wyatt cruised across the street and into a spot beside the lone vehicle left in the staff lot. It was a late-model cross-over with a bumper proclaiming every inch of distance its owner had conquered.

Emma gave it the side-eye as they pulled in. "I'll never understand people who run marathons for fun."

Wyatt killed the engine. "I thought you were a runner," he said with a puzzled frown.

"I ran to keep in shape, not to collect those obnoxious medals they hand out. Some of them are the size of dinner plates."

"Maybe if you had a couple of those dinner-plate medals, you wouldn't have to eat off wrappers every night."

"Har, har," she said as she reached for the door handle.

"Maybe they aren't in it for the medals. Maybe they're chasing the high. Or it was nothing more than a goal they wanted to achieve," he said, raising a single eyebrow in challenge.

"Then shouldn't the achievement be reward enough? Does the whole world need to know about it?"

"You're a sour case, Emma Parker, but something about this lady gets under your skin," he teased with a grin. "Wouldn't have anything to do with the online dating thing she had with Mr. Huge-bucks, would it?"

Emma shuddered "Please don't call him that. The creepers online are always referring to him by that name and it's weird. He's a nice guy. He has a nice house, and a nice car. I can only assume he makes a good living, but I have never asked. Regardless, it doesn't mean he or his daughter—"

Wyatt reached over and gave her a friendly pat. "Easy, Em. I was only joking around."

She swatted his hand away and flipped the hood on her windbreaker up to cover her head. "Let's get this over with."

"You got someplace better to be?" he asked as he opened his door. "Oh, right, you do."

"Anywhere away from you would be better, Dawson," she muttered, following him out of the car.

The two of them hurried across the lot, dodging puddles leftover from an afternoon rain shower. She followed Wyatt up the steps, her attention drawn to the mini CPU he said matched the units used by the school. Even the secondhand computers donated to Capitol Academy were better than most. No big, bulky towers taking up room underneath the desks for their computer lab.

"I always hated being the last person at school," Wyatt said as they approached the main doors. "So creepy."

Emma nodded. "Like a scene from one of those teen slasher movies," she said, wrinkling her nose.

Wyatt tried the handle on the door to the far right as Amy Birch had instructed, but found it was locked. He tried the other two before coming back to the one on the right. The soccer coach had exited through it only minutes before.

Emma frowned at the transom windows above the doors. There were still lights on inside, but they were clearly not at full power. Had the custodian come around and locked it already?

"I thought she said the custodian didn't lock the school until five thirty or six?" Emma went down the line, testing each door as if she hadn't watched Wyatt try them all. Not a single handle gave way.

"That's what she told me."

Emma glanced back at the parking lot. "I'd bet dollars to doughnuts she drives the marathon car. Try calling her."

Wyatt handed off the computer and pulled his phone from his back pocket. Misty drops of rain gathered on the screen as he placed the call and switched it to speaker. It rang four times before Amy Birch's chirpy voice invited them to leave a message.

"Hey, Ms. Birch, Wyatt Dawson here. We're outside, but

the doors are locked. It looks like you're still in the building. When you get a chance if you could come let us in, I promise we'll be in and out quick as a flash." He held Emma's stare for a beat, then disconnected.

Holding the computer close to her chest, Emma walked back down the steps and crossed the lawn, the rubber soles of her shoes squeaking on the wet grass. She peered around the corner of the building to the lane reserved for school-bus loading. There was an older-model compact car with a dented fender and rust spots showing through its dull gray paint parked in the lane.

"Maybe that's the custodian, parked in the bus lane?" she called as she made her way back to the entrance.

Wyatt nodded. "We'll give it a minute, and then I'll pound on the door and see if we can get someone's attention."

Emma nodded and took a moment to survey the manicured grounds of the city's most exclusive private high school. The other end of the building was flanked by the best athletic fields money could buy. The planters on either side of the carved wooden doors were brimming with freshly planted seasonal flowers. They wouldn't have lasted a day at her old school.

"Can you imagine going to a school like this?" she asked.

Beside her, Wyatt shook his head. "I'm glad I didn't. Too much competition over things that don't really matter," he said gruffly.

"No doubt," Emma concurred. "The things Kayleigh tells me." She shook her head. "All I can say is you couldn't pay me to be a teenager again."

"Amen," Wyatt said, wiping mist from his face. "Okay, time to start pounding."

He turned back to the door and gave it a series of hard thumps with the side of his fist. As they waited for a response, he checked his phone again. He gave his head a shake before shoving it back into his jeans pocket.

"You want me hold it?" he asked, gesturing to the computer.

Emma looked down at the computer. It was no bigger than a hardback novel and certainly lighter. "You think I can't hold on to this monster of a machine?"

"Nothing to do with capabilities, Parker," he said, shaking his head in slow exasperation. "You know my mama raised me to be polite."

"Oh, I know. I've got it," she assured him, then slid the computer inside her windbreaker to protect it from the damp weather.

Wyatt walked back down the steps and tramped through the grass to the side of the building.

"The car is still parked there," he said as he stomped back up the steps. "We should have come earlier."

"We couldn't risk anybody else seeing us. Only Ms. Birch and Dr. Blanton know we suspect anything more than a social-media spat."

Wyatt came back up to the doors, raised both fists and pounded on the center one for a full thirty seconds. Emma winced with each reverberating thud.

He was lowering his arms when they heard the *thunk* of the crash bar on the other side. The door flew open, sending them scurrying back to avoid being struck.

A tall, bald man in work pants and a shirt identifying him as Chuck appeared in the doorway, breathless and frantic. "Are you the police?"

Emma and Wyatt exchanged a confused glance before she stepped forward and said, "Yes. I'm Special Agent Emma Parker, Arkansas State Police. This is Agent Dawson."

The man's brow wrinkled. "The state police? Is the ambulance coming?" he asked, peering past them, breathless.

"Ambulance?" Emma looked down and saw the man had damp spots of blood on his pants leg and a smear on his hand. She stepped into his space. "Has something happened?"

"I dialed nine-one-one," he said, nodding so hard Emma was afraid he'd give himself whiplash. He craned his neck to look beyond them. "It's taking too long."

In the distance, Emma heard the wail of a siren approaching.

"We were here to meet Ms. Birch," Wyatt informed him. "What's going on?"

"Ms. Birch?" he said, his eyes darting between them.

"Yes," Wyatt confirmed. "Is she here?"

"She's the reason I called nine-one-one," Chuck explained. "I found her in the computer room. She's bleeding. And unconscious."

Emma dropped the computer and it hit the concrete steps with a sharp crack. Without waiting, she and Wyatt pushed past the other man.

"Which way?" Emma asked the custodian.

"Down the hall, take a right, third door on the left," he called back. "But wait—"

"You stay there," she ordered, turning back as Wyatt sprinted ahead. "Let the paramedics know where we are. Tell the local police what you found."

Confused, Chuck gestured to the now broken computer unit at his feet. "But what about this?"

Unwilling to be delayed a second longer, Emma shook her head and shouted, "It's trash now," then took off at a dead run.

Chapter Twelve

It was well past the dinner hour by the time Emma pulled into Max Hughes's driveway. Though it was still daylight, golden light spilled from expansive glass windows. She sat in her car for a moment, taking in the beautiful house with its perfectly maintained flower beds and precisely clipped lawn.

A coat of white paint had been applied to the garage door but was proving insufficient when it came to covering up the spray paint. No doubt, Max had made the attempt to erase the ugliness so Kayleigh didn't have to look at it.

She got out of her car and walked over to the garage to examine the not-so-perfect door.

The slapdash cover-up was clearly a temporary solution. She wouldn't be at all surprised if she woke the next day to find a professional house-painting crew hard at work restoring the door to its former glory.

But she understood why he couldn't let it stand as it was for the night. She moved back a few steps and tilted her head to the right, squinting at the faint outline of the large capital *B*.

The front door opened, and Max stepped outside dressed in a pristine white T-shirt and black joggers. His feet were bare, and his hair was damp.

"Hey," he called out to her. "I was wondering when you'd be back."

"Hey," she replied. She ran a hand through her hair. "Sorry, it's been a doozy of a day." Gesturing to the door, she asked, "I'm assuming this was you?"

"I cleared it with the LRPD first," he assured her, sounding only slightly defensive.

"Did you tell them you're not pressing charges against Carter Pierce?"

He nodded. "I did. I also spoke to Carter and his parents this afternoon. He offered to come over and paint the door himself, but I figured Kayleigh wouldn't want him around."

"Probably not." She crossed her arms over her chest and rocked back on her heels. "I bet his folks were grateful. Did you explain to them what has been happening?"

He shook his head. "I didn't go into detail because I didn't know what you would want me to say or keep quiet, but I let them know Kayleigh was not responsible for the posts on her accounts."

"Probably all they needed to hear for now," she said with a judicious frown. "Did you talk to anyone else?"

He nodded. "Patrice's mother finally returned my call."

"And?"

"They are doing okay. Patrice will make a full recovery and has started seeing a therapist." He blew out a breath. "She wanted to talk to Kayleigh."

"Did you let them?"

"Yeah." He thrust his hands into his pants pockets. "We agreed they could talk on speaker and with her mom and me in the room."

"How'd it go?"

He let his head fall back, gazing up into the deepening twilight. "It was…heartbreaking for everyone, but I think good for them?" Shaking his head, he murmured, "So much pain. And for what reason? Who's getting something out of all this?"

He turned to look at her and she could only shrug. "Max, I have to tell you, Amy Birch was attacked at the school this afternoon."

"What?" Max shook his head hard. "When? How? Why haven't I heard anything about this?"

She gave a tremulous smile. "Dr. Blanton is still speaking with the Little Rock police. I assume he'll call the school-board members and give you all an update soon."

"Is she badly hurt?"

Emma shook her head. "Someone gave her one heck of a whack on the head. She has a concussion. And the blow opened a small cut. It bled badly and scared the wits out of poor Mr. Johnson, the custodian."

"Who else was in the building?" he demanded.

"We're still gathering information, but I can tell you the soccer coach and Mr. Johnson were both on the premises in the timeframe."

"Was Blanton there? I know he usually stays late," Max said with a frown.

She shook her head. "He was not. Mr. Johnson said the administrative offices were empty, and when the LRPD reached out to him, he said he was coming from a dinner meeting."

Max rubbed his lips together as he digested this information. "And she was attacked in her classroom?"

Emma shook her head. "In the computer lab."

"Any idea what they hit her with?"

"We're not one-hundred-percent positive, but our best guess at this juncture was it was a computer."

"A computer? Like a laptop?" he asked, puzzled.

But Emma could only continue to wag her head. "No. A desktop CPU," she informed him grimly. "We found bits of the plastic casing near where Ms. Birch lay, and fragments in her hair."

"Has she regained consciousness?" Max asked, concern etched into every line of his handsome face.

"Yes. The paramedics were able to bring her around. She didn't know anyone but Mr. Johnson was in the building."

Max shook his head in disbelief. "Someone hit her with a computer?"

"Not any old computer, but *the* computer."

"The computer?" he echoed.

"We checked the serial numbers of the units left behind and none matched the one we suspected our hacker was using. We were going in to swap it out with a dummy, but now it's gone."

"It's gone."

Emma hooked a hand through his arm and pointed him in the direction of the door. "You're turning into a parrot. Let's go inside."

"I can't believe someone attacked her. In the school," he added, his voice rising. "I need to call Dr. Blanton."

"Not yet," she said, propelling him to the entrance. "I need to talk with Kayleigh."

"She's in her room," he answered, falling into step beside her. "Does this mean you're going to stay?"

Her heart quickened at the hopeful note in his question. She tried not to read too much into it. Going for nonchalance she didn't feel, she said, "Simon says stick close." But it came out sounding flippant, and she saw a cloud darken Max's hopeful expression. Instantly contrite, she tried again. "Yes, I'm going to stay. If you still want me to."

"I put your things in the guest room. Kayleigh is right— you should be more comfortable there."

"Thank you." She ducked her head to hide her smile when he gestured for her to precede him through the door. "She's probably right about my skin-care regimen, too." He stopped walking so abruptly, so she drew up, too. "What?"

"You tell me," he countered. "Is there anything else I need to know? Has your team uncovered anything else?"

She shrugged. "We mostly went over technical details for swapping the computers, but there's no point now." She pressed her lips together as she pondered how much to share with him. "One of the team has been monitoring posts other students make on social media. I'm going to talk to Kayleigh about a few of them, get her take on their personalities." She met his eyes. "We're all pretty sure it's an adult behind everything, particularly after what happened this afternoon, but have no solid evidence to back it up. A student could have snuck back into the school. It could have been another teacher, a coach, a parent…"

"So basically, we wait until something happens."

She tilted her head and gave him a wan smile. "Something has happened, Max. It's simply not the big breakthrough we all want. But we're putting pieces together. Sometimes figuring out who to look at is more about ruling people out."

"But doesn't provide solid evidence," he argued.

"We figure out who to look at, then we go looking for the evidence," she said in her most reassuring tone. "We're making progress. As we computer jockeys say, it takes a lot of bits to make a byte." She waved an arm toward Kayleigh's room. "Do you want to sit in? You might know some of the parents."

He chuckled mirthlessly, then shook his head. "I'd wager I know most of the parents, but no. You talk to Kayleigh, and if there's something the two of you think I should look at, let me know. I don't want to trample her voice in all this."

"Good call," she said approvingly. "I think in a weird way, this could turn out to be a good thing for Kayleigh. She's growing. Learning to look at things from someone else's point of view, getting a good lesson on the ripple effect words and actions can have. It will shape her choices from here on out, and from what I've seen so far, I'd say likely for the better."

"Like it did for you?" His eyes widened and he pressed his knuckle to his mouth as if to stop anything else from escaping.

He looked so shocked by the sound of his own voice, she had to laugh. Giving his arm a friendly pat, she moved past him. "Exactly."

EMMA KICKED HER shoes off and shifted her weight so she could brace one foot on the rail of Kayleigh's bed frame, but she didn't reach out to touch the girl. Reading through days' worth of social-media vitriol had left Kayleigh crying into the pastel-blue tufted throw pillow she'd held clutched to her belly for most of their conversation. She waited until Kayleigh's sobs slowed to hiccups, then spoke.

"You know most of this is all talk, don't you?" Emma asked in a voice barely above a whisper. "Everyone is scared. Everyone is pointing fingers. Not only at you, but at each other. This is the kind of chaos these creeps live for."

"I hate this," Kayleigh said, snuffling. "This is supposed to be the best time of my life, and it's not. It sucks!"

"Oh, honey, any age ending with the word *teen* is not even in contention for the best time of your life." She sighed. "This next phase...the one where you start figuring out how to live someplace other than your parents' house, and how to make twenty dollars stretch to a week's worth of food." Kayleigh's expression of blank horror made her laugh. "Okay, you probably won't have to worry about your food budget, but life beyond high school is totally different."

"Well, yeah. I sure hope so," Kayleigh said, the petulance in her tone a stark reminder of how young and insulated she was.

"You'll start picking your friends from a wider pool. People from all over the world. They'll have different clothes, and new ideas, and your world view will expand. Sure, some will be jerks, but you'll also learn to sniff them out pretty quickly." She tapped the laptop and shot her a commiserating stare. "You never outgrow the haters, but you learn not to give them a parking space, you know?"

She tapped her temple and Kayleigh nodded. "Right."

Emma gestured to her laptop, open on the bed, then the room in general. "This was all a ramp-up. And how you handle this will be a good indicator of how you handle the other stuff life throws at you." She paused then dropped her voice. "You control the narrative."

"Unless someone clones your accounts and steals your voice," Kayleigh countered.

"You still have a voice," Emma insisted. "Sure, we've been quiet for a few days while we sort some stuff out and make sure other people are okay, but this is a strategic retreat. You will get the last word. I promise you." She stared intently into the young woman's eyes. "Do you believe me?"

Kayleigh began to nod before she answered. "Yes."

She pulled the sheaf of printouts she and Caitlin had made of some of the more questionable posts from her bag and placed them on the bed. "Now, tell me about Tia Severin."

"Tia?" Kayleigh asked.

"Yes." Emma waited, watching as Kayleigh drew back as if she'd dumped a bag of snakes onto the duvet. "Do you want to see some of the things she's been posting?"

Kayleigh narrowed her eyes. "Do I?"

Emma nudged the pile of papers. "There's nothing bad here. But she didn't come rushing to your defense, either," she said, raising a single eyebrow. "Tell me about your relationship with her. She's your best friend, right?"

"We've spent a lot of time together these last couple years," Kayleigh answered with admirable caution.

"How did you become friends?"

"The usual way." The younger woman shrugged. "We had a few classes together. We started hanging out more last year, I guess. She and her parents went to Europe the summer before eleventh grade. They were over there for about seven weeks during the summer, and I was so jealous."

"They were vacationing over there?"

"I think her dad had to work some, but yeah." She frowned as she thought back. "I remember going home and asking my dad why we couldn't go, too. After all, my dad owned part of Mr. Severin's company, so it totally would have made sense for us to go, too."

Emma reared back. "Your dad owned the company Mr. Severin worked for?"

"Not owned," she amended. "You know, he invested money in it to get it going."

"As part of his venture-capital investing," Emma said to confirm.

"Yeah. I didn't understand why we couldn't have gone, too. I would have loved to go to Milan. You should have seen some of the shoes Tia had."

"You guys bonded over shoes?" Emma asked as she slowly shuffled through the printouts looking for one message in particular.

"We both really like fashion in general," Kayleigh said. "Tia totally wanted to be a model, but seriously, if it hasn't happened by now… I mean she'll be eighteen next month. She's too old to be a model."

Emma sucked air in between her teeth, but refrained from commenting on Kayleigh's hot takes on aging.

"You said the two of you would take pictures of one another to post to Foto. Has she done any modeling locally?"

"She did a thing for a couple of department stores and a TV spot for a car dealer. It was so cheesy," she said with a laugh.

"But Tia's parents won't allow her to pursue modeling seriously?"

Kayleigh shook her head. "She isn't tall enough to be a fashion model. It's one of those things girls talk about, you know?"

"I see."

"Anyhow, CA is a supercompetitive school, and Tia is really, really smart. I mean, like, top-of-the-class smart," she said with a wave of her hand. "The girl got into Brown."

Emma looked up from the papers. "She's going to Brown?"

Kayleigh bit her bottom lip then grimaced as she shook her head. "No. Actually, she's going to stay in state, but she got into Brown," she explained with a sage nod. "There was some something about money and her dad's business." She waved her hand dismissively. "I don't know the details, but I'm sure my dad could tell you. Anyway, she's heading up to Fayetteville in the fall."

"Do most of the students at your school go out of state for college?" Emma asked, truly curious.

"I'd say it's about half and half. A bunch go up to the U of A, some to private schools around here. A couple guys got football scholarships from the University of Central Arkansas, but a good chunk go out of state."

"And for those who go out of state, I assume it's a decent percentage headed to the Ivies," Emma said as she found the post she'd been looking for. "Trading an acceptance at Brown for the U of A had to be a tough decision."

"I guess." Kayleigh shrugged. "Tia has always been a big

mama's girl, though. Frankly I couldn't see her packing up her stuff and heading off to Providence."

"But you won't have any trouble packing up and going to Cambridge?" Emma asked.

Kayleigh looked up as if torn between rolling her eyes and trying not to cry. "Sure I will," she said softly. "But I think maybe it's probably the best thing for both me and my dad."

"How do you figure?"

"He and my mom got married really young. Like right-out-of-college young. And they had me right away. He's never really had a life on his own." She gave a chuckle. "He's going to be forty soon, so I guess it's about time."

"I have a feeling he'll be in the Boston area a lot more often than you think," Emma said dryly.

A slow, pleased smile spread across Kayleigh's lips. "Yeah. I know. It's okay."

Emma held up the sheet she was looking for and said, "Tia posted to ChitChat about how she was shocked you would say such horrible things to Patrice, but claims you have always had trouble distinguishing…" She consulted the paper she held. "Something authentic from a good knockoff."

Lowering the page, she looked Kayleigh straight in the eye. "What does she mean?"

"Are you kidding me?" Color rose high in Kayleigh's cheeks and she clamped her lips into a thin, angry line. Emma waited patiently as the girl drew calming breaths through flaring nostrils. "I wish she'd get over it already," she muttered.

"Get over what?"

"You know when I said her family went to Europe? Well, when she came back, she was carrying this supercute back-pack bag with the Prada emblem on it, but it wasn't a real Prada bag," she said with a sympathetic wince. "I thought she knew. I made some comment about what good knockoffs people could find overseas, and she got all bent out of shape about it."

"Because you said her backpack was fake?"

Kayleigh rolled her eyes. "She kept insisting it was an authentic Prada, but anyone who knew anything could see it wasn't. The stitching was all wrong and the lining was awful. Anyway, she swore up and down it was the real deal. I know for a fact it wasn't, but I let it go because I wasn't the one walking around with the fake backpack, she was," she said in a rush of indignation.

"I guess she's hung on to at least some of her anger over it," Emma said, quietly passing the printout across to her.

Kayleigh looked down at the screen capture they'd printed. "I guess so." She gave a short, sharp laugh then tossed the page aside. "She didn't hang on to her fake Prada backpack long," she said with an edge of snark. "I never saw it again."

"But y'all stayed friends."

"Yes."

"If you had to choose a label, would you say you were besties or frenemies?" Emma asked, genuinely curious.

"I'd say our relationship status is more like…best frenemies."

"Way to split the atom," Emma said dryly.

"Ask a simple question, get a complicated answer," Kayleigh retorted.

"Do you think she resents you?"

Kayleigh looked truly perplexed by the notion. "Resents me? For what?"

"Pick a reason," Emma replied. "You're about to be valedictorian. Off to Harvard. Your father's financial setbacks haven't directly impacted your future," she said, ticking off each option on her fingers. "Your highlights are better than hers?"

The last garnered her a soft laugh. Kayleigh reached up

and drew the length of her hair over one shoulder, finger-combing it a few times before lifting her ends close to her eyes as if to inspect them. "I don't think she hates me," she said quietly. "At least, I hope not."

"What does your gut tell you?" Emma persisted. "Do you think whoever is posting this stuff is one of your classmates, or someone else?"

Kayleigh dropped her hair, then heaved a heavy sigh, but Emma could see her closing up.

"No clue." She swung her legs over the side of the bed and stood, raising her arms toward the ceiling, then bringing them down in an exaggerated stretch. "I'm tired. I think I'll get ready for bed."

Able to take a hint when it was hurled at her like a javelin, Emma gathered her computer and the papers. "Cool. I'll be down the hall if you think of anything."

"Okay." Kayleigh strolled into the attached bath, her back straight. "Before you go, I have something for you."

Emma paused in the midst of shoving her things into her computer bag. "Something for me?"

"It's not big," Kayleigh insisted as she emerged again. "Here," she said, thrusting a clear plastic makeup bag filled to bursting with tiny tubes and itty-bitty pots of creams. When Emma hesitated, she dropped it into the open computer bag. "They're free samples I've collected here and there. You can take them. I've got my thing down," she said with an airy wave of her perfectly manicured hand.

"Thanks," Emma replied, almost certain she'd been insulted, but in the best possible way. "I'll check them out."

"'Night," Kayleigh called as she turned on her heel and headed back into the attached bath.

"'Night," Emma returned. "Door open or closed?" she asked as she stepped into the hall.

"Closed, please," Kayleigh called out, and Emma complied.

Standing in the hall, staring at the closed bedroom door, she picked the conversation apart, looking for any useful bits or pieces. At last, she latched on to one thread she needed to yank, and turned away from the guest room to go in search of her host.

She found Max in the media room, stretched out on one of the theater-style reclining loungers. "Please tell me you have a popcorn popper," she said, peering around the doorframe to take in the massive screen mounted to the wall.

Startled, he fumbled for the button to lower the leg rest, but she waved him off. "Don't get up. I only have a question or two, then I'll get out of your hair for the night."

He ignored her command and pressed the button until he was upright, his bare feet planted on the ground.

"Questions for me?"

"Yes." She swung her bag to the floor, then crossed the room to perch on the edge of one of the other massive chairs.

"Okay, but I am sad to report I do not have a popcorn machine."

"Well, now you have something to shoot for. Can you tell me what happened with Tia Severin's father's business?"

"Tia's… Steve Severin?" He looked genuinely taken aback by the change in topic.

"He had a business you helped underwrite?" she queried.

"Yes, I put together some product-development funding for him." Max shifted to look directly at her. "He's an ideas guy working with a couple of buddies who like to tinker, but none of them had a clue where to go from there. Why do you ask?"

"How did you get involved with the company?"

"The usual way." He frowned. "They needed an infusion of cash. They pitched a good product, I put together a group of investors."

"Did the company fail?"

He blinked. "Fail? Not at all," he said, bewildered by the notion. "Why do you ask?"

"Kayleigh told me Tia isn't going to Brown because her dad suffered some financial setback, so she's staying in-state."

"Oh." Max scowled as he pondered the information. "Well, he didn't lose money on our collaboration. We sold to a corporate client almost two years ago. They paid a premium for it, but it's possible he invested his portion of the deal into something else and it didn't fly."

"Are you still in contact with him?"

Max shrugged. "We're friendly when we see one another, but we were never friends."

"You were predominantly business associates," Emma mused.

"Yes."

"But Kayleigh and Tia are close?" she asked.

"They've run around together a lot the last couple years." A crease formed between his eyebrows. "Why? Do you think Tia is involved with this whole mess?"

Emma shook her head. "I don't know, really. I guess I'm picking at loose threads."

Max's phone rang and they both jumped. He picked it up and peered at the screen. "It's Amy Birch," he informed her as he accepted the call with his thumb. "Hello?"

Emma moved to the edge of the cushion and waved to get his attention. When she motioned for him to let her hear, he complied without a moment of hesitation.

"Max? It's Amy Birch."

He met Emma's eyes before answering. "Yes, I still have you in my contacts. How are you? I heard you were injured."

"I'm okay. They're keeping me overnight for observation. I was wondering if you are in contact with the agent investigating the social-media posts?"

Max glanced over at her. "Yes. Special Agent Parker. She's here actually," he said, moving to the seat beside Emma. "I'll put us on speaker."

He pulled a face as he placed the phone on the armrest between them. Emma stifled the urge to laugh at the sheer awkwardness of their situation. Max Hughes was clearly not a man comfortable with subterfuge.

"Ms. Birch?" Emma prompted. "This is Emma Parker."

"Special Agent Parker, thank you for your help this afternoon."

"It's Emma. And we didn't do much. Agent Dawson and I were only sorry we didn't try to get into the school sooner."

"I asked Agent Dawson to wait until the parking lot was clear," she said tiredly. "I had no idea anyone other than Mr. Johnson was in the building."

Emma and Max exchanged a glance. "When I spoke to the LRPD, they said you didn't see your assailant?"

"No. I was in the lab disconnecting the terminal y'all wanted to switch out. I'd gone under the desk to untangle a cable, and when I crawled out, wham!"

Emma winced and touched the top of her own head. "I'm so sorry."

"Thank you." There was a moment's pause, then Amy spoke softly. "I know I'm probably imagining this, but I could swear I heard him say 'Thank you very much.' Of course, I don't think I was fully conscious."

"A polite assailant," Max said grimly.

Emma inched closer to the phone. "You said *him*. Was the voice you heard male?"

"I may be making it all up," she conceded. "The only thing I recall for certain is waking up to find you, Agent Dawson and a paramedic staring down at me."

"Let's not discount what the subconscious mind absorbs," Emma said bluntly. "Intuition has proved to be one of the most valuable tools I have as an investigator." She pulled out her own phone and began typing notes. "Let's assume the person who assaulted you was male. We know for certain two males were in the building at the time Agent Dawson and I arrived—the custodian, Mr. Johnson, and the soccer coach—"

She paused and Amy helpfully supplied a name. "Jake Green."

"Right, thank you," Emma said. There was an awkward beat, then she prompted, "You wanted to talk to me?"

"Yes, I called because something occurred to me," Amy said hesitantly.

"About your attacker?" Emma asked.

"No, about your hacker," Amy corrected. "He—they, whoever it was—took the computer terminal, and maybe this is the knock on the head talking, but I'm not sure it matters."

Curiosity piqued, Emma leaned in. "Why do you say that?"

"Because I reworked the school's network when I came on board last fall. The connectivity was practically Stone Aged, and security nonexistent. I, uh, may have had a copy of some excellent security software acquired by Syscom at my disposal," she said, pitching her voice low and confessional. "I installed it on the school's network."

Intrigued, Emma shot Max a glance as she leaned closer to the phone. "I take it this software was not something available at our local big-box electronics store?"

"No. It was some of the best security software I'd ever come across," Amy said in a rush. "Syscom acquired it from a small company. The head guy was a programmer and really didn't know much about launching a product. I was on the preacquisition evaluation team, so I had copies on both my work and home systems. It was my job to try to break it."

"I see." Emma cocked her head. "Did you?"

"Yes. But then again, I assume you did, too." She paused before filling in the blanks. "You were able to trace the posts back to the school. When I was there yesterday, I saw your footprints in the system."

Emma dipped her head in acknowledgment. "Did you?"

"What was this software called?"

"SecuraT," Amy said. "Secure with an *A* on the end then a capital *T*."

Max stiffened. When she looked up, Emma found him staring straight at her, goggle-eyed.

She tapped the mute button. "You okay?"

"Tell her we'll come see her first thing tomorrow," he ordered.

Emma narrowed her eyes, prepared to push back, but she saw a flash of panic in his eyes, and it stopped her. "Why?"

"We can't talk about this on the phone," he insisted. "What she did was illegal."

Emma sat back, gnawing on the inside of her cheek. There was something he wasn't saying, but as much as she wanted to turn Max upside down and shake him by the ankles until all the answers spilled out, he was right.

She unmuted the call. "This sounds serious, and you may be onto something." She took a deep breath, then spoke slowly, measuring each word to sound logical and not impulsive. "But visiting hours are over, and we've all had a long day. If you don't mind, I'd like to come by the hospital and talk to you first thing tomorrow morning."

"But—"

"Amy, if we're going to stray into corporate-espionage territory, I'd prefer not to speak about it over the phone," Emma stated flatly.

The woman drew in a sharp breath. "Fine. But can you come early? I don't plan to stay in here one minute longer than the doctors say I have to."

"We'll see you first thing," Emma promised.

She ended the call, then turned to look at the man sitting stone-still in his seat. "Your product-development deal... it wouldn't have involved the sale of some software called SecuraT, would it?"

Chapter Thirteen

Emma shot Max a now-or-never glare. "What am I missing?"

"SecuraT never made it to market," Max informed her gruffly. "It was sold to Syscom as a capture-and-kill."

Emma stared at him, as if trying to absorb this new information and slot it into place. Then she locked on to the bit she needed to complete the code. "A capture-and-kill? Why?"

"Because it was too good," he said, as if his answer should have been obvious. When she stared back at him, he cracked. "It's a fairly common practice. Larger companies buy out their competition all the time."

Max's fingertips tingled but his limbs felt heavy. His whole body felt so heavy he doubted he could lift himself out of his seat if he tried. Emma stared at him, but he didn't know what else to say.

The photo of Kayleigh he used as the wallpaper on his phone caught his eye. Her smile was so wide-open and free it made his heart squeeze. Would he ever see that smile again? She'd come back from this. They all would. But none of them would be the same. Resentment welled up inside him. Frustrated, he picked up the phone and powered it down.

"Oh. Good call," Emma said, pulling out her own phone and shutting it down.

Max didn't have it in him to tell her he was turning off

his phone because he was a coward, not because they needed to be cautious.

Shifting in her chair to face him, she asked, "Do you know much about the software itself?"

He shook his head, the corners of his mouth pulling down with disgust at his own ignorance. "No. I mean, I know what it was for, what it was supposed to do, but the technical stuff?" He slowed his shake. "No."

"You saw it demonstrated?"

"Obviously," he replied, a shade too quickly. Aware he was edging into petulant-teenager territory, he shot her an apologetic wince. "I sat through numerous demos. Steve even installed it on my computer, but it's not like software a person actively uses, right? It runs in the background, and unless it throws up a flag—"

"Wait." Emma reached over and gripped his arm. "You have it?"

Max looked down at her fingers wrapped around his forearm. Her grip was urgent, but her palm was warm and comforting. When was the last time someone comforted him? He closed his eyes for a moment, absorbing her heat.

"Max?"

She gave him a gentle squeeze and it was all he could do to keep from jerking his arm from her grasp.

"Huh?"

"You have SecuraT installed on your computer? Your home computer or one at your office?"

He waved his free hand in the direction of his office. "Both."

Her hand slid down and captured his wrist. She tugged hard as she rose. "Come on. Show me."

To his surprise, she didn't let go. She kept her grip firm on his wrist as she led him from the media room, then stood aside to let him take the lead into his home office. Her fingers unfurled when he reached his desk, and he wanted to snatch back her hand. His heart hammered and his pulse thrummed in his head. They were on the edge of something, but he couldn't say whether he was scared or excited by the prospect.

"Log in," she prompted.

Max bent over the keyboard and tapped the space bar to wake the machine. He almost snickered when she looked away to allow him password privacy. "Couldn't you hack your way in?" he asked as his programs loaded.

"I could, but I'm told it isn't nice," she answered, offering him a mockingly prim smile.

Max gave a weak laugh, then stepped back, gesturing for her to take over.

She grabbed the edge of his leather desk chair and pulled the seat close. "You don't keep much on your desktop," she commented as she swirled the cursor around the screen.

"I'm a minimalist."

"I noticed." She chuckled softly as she accessed his operating system. "I'm a mess."

"I noticed," he returned.

She glanced up, shooting him a sidelong glance, a sly smile curving her lips. "We're opposites. Probably why we work well together." He opened his mouth to ask if she truly thought they made a good team, but she cut him off. "Tell me how the deal with SecuraT went. Start from the beginning. With the investment pitch," she clarified.

"Well, Steve Severin is a computer guy. He has a company here in town, SevTech. They mostly do website creation, general IT troubleshooting and some coding for smaller companies. He and a couple guys on his team had been working on SecuraT in their spare time for a couple years."

"And they came to you looking for money to...?" she asked.

He watched as her fingers flew over the keyboard. For every line of nonsense she input, a paragraph of gibberish appeared on the screen.

"Technically, it was to tie up development and ramp up to distribution. But in reality, he used it to pay his staff so he could free up more time to work on the program itself."

"Would you do me a favor and grab my laptop?"

Max went back to the media room to retrieve her bag. He carried the bag back to the office and placed it on the edge of his desk. "Here you go."

She barely looked up. Eyes glued to the screen, she typed one-handed as she fumbled to find the opening. "Thanks."

He watched her struggle for thirty seconds more, then yanked the bag open so she could grope unimpeded.

"How did the sale come about?" she asked as she pulled out her notebook.

"Steve came to me about eight months and three quarters of the funding in. He was all excited because he thought they had something really good going. They'd done some beta testing using area schools and small businesses. He hired some subcontractors to try to get into the protected systems and only one was successful. Even then, they couldn't deploy anything damaging."

She looked up with an eyebrow raised. "Who were these subcontractors?"

He shrugged. "I didn't get into the nitty-gritty, but I assume some work for larger tech firms. Sort of like headhunters."

"So he thought he had an ace and wanted to see if he could cash out?"

"Cybersecurity is a crowded field with a lot of big names. Steve knew they'd have an uphill battle trying to make a dent in the retail market, no matter how advanced the product." He angled his head to get a better look at what she was doing. She'd opened her own computer and was typing line after line of code into the prompt box. "Are you trying to get into my computer?"

"Testing," she mumbled distractedly. "How'd Syscom get involved?"

"I know the CFO. I knew they had a number of security programs out there, so I told them what we had and a meeting was scheduled."

"How long did it take to get the deal done?" she asked without looking away from her task.

"It was fast. We gave them a window of exclusivity, they did some testing, we had a preemptory offer, acceptance and a done deal within six months."

"Is the timeline unusual?"

"Most don't move so fast, but it's not unheard of," he conceded.

She met his gaze. "I assume you and everyone involved with the sale turned a nice profit?"

He shifted his weight, feeling oddly uncomfortable under her scrutinizing stare. "We're not a bunch of philanthropists, if that's what you're asking," he returned evenly.

She nodded as if his nonanswer told her everything she needed to know. "Twenty bucks says I can break into this thing before we meet up with Amy Birch tomorrow morning."

Narrowing his eyes, he held her challenging stare. "Twenty bucks?"

"Yep."

"You're on." He offered his hand to her, and they shook on the bet.

She ducked her head and began typing again, but Max was fairly sure he heard her mutter "Sucker" under her breath as she dove in.

MAX WAS TWENTY dollars poorer when they arrived at University Hospital the following morning. A plainclothes police officer greeted them at the door to Amy Birch's room.

"Are you here to see Ms. Birch?" he asked, flashing them his Little Rock Police Department detective shield.

They returned his nod of acknowledgment as Emma pulled her credentials out of her cavernous bag. "Yes. I'm Special Agent Emma Parker with the ASP Cyber Crime Division."

"Nolan Hutchinson," he replied, giving her a not-so-subtle once-over before squinting to inspect her identification.

Emma pretended not to notice, so Max bit the inside of his cheek. No doubt she dealt with guys like Hutchinson all the time. He was smart enough to know any intervention on her behalf would not be welcomed by either party.

"Anything new to report?" she asked.

"I didn't realize the state police had an interest in assault cases," he said, his voice deceptively laconic. He closed the leather wallet and offered it back to her pinned between his index and middle fingers like a playing card.

"We have an open cybercrime case Ms. Birch is helping us unravel," Emma said as she took back the wallet containing her identification.

"I see." He shook his head, his hands planted on his hips and his stance wide and defensive. "No, nothing to report yet. The crime-scene team has been over the computer lab, but they haven't had a chance to process much yet." He glanced back at the closed door. "I spoke with the victim again this morning, but there really isn't much more to add to her story than what we already had."

Max opened his mouth, about to ask whether she had updated the police on her suspicions about her assailant being male, but Emma gave the side of his shoe a kick and he clamped it shut again.

"What kind of cybersecurity issue are you having?" the detective asked.

"A hacker," Emma said in a deliberately offhand manner.

Her clear reluctance to share information with the local police concerning the case frustrated Max as a father, but since he'd been the one to go to the state police rather than the LRPD, he wasn't about to question Emma's motives in front of this other police officer.

"The school's been hacked?"

Emma nodded. "A school and a number of members of the Capitol Academy community."

Detective Hutchinson hiked up his pants and gave another nod. "I'll leave all the computer stuff to your team," he said as if he was granting them a favor. He pulled a business card out of his pocket and handed it over to Emma. "If you need more information, feel free to reach out to me directly, Special Agent Parker."

"I'll be sure to call if I need your help," she replied, graceful and noncommittal.

The detective brushed past them, and Max turned to watch him saunter down the hall.

"Jerk," Emma said under her breath.

"Yes, he is." Max turned back to her.

The mulish expression on her face told him that he'd chosen correctly on holding his tongue. Convinced the best course of action would be to let her set the tone for the day, he hung back again.

"I want to wait until he's gone before we go in," Emma said in an undertone.

"Not a problem." He leaned up against the wall outside of the hospital room and adopted a casual pose. "So what do you plan to do with your winnings? Aside from gloat over them?"

"Oh, I haven't begun to gloat yet," she answered easily, keeping one eye on the man standing at the elevator banks.

"What do you call the dance you did in the kitchen this morning?"

"Acknowledging my victory," she answered without missing a beat. "Believe me, you'll recognize the gloating when you hear it."

The ding signaling the elevator's arrival echoed down the tiled corridor. "I'll brace myself."

They both turned and watched as Hutchinson stepped into the car. When the elevator doors slid shut behind Hutchinson, Max gestured to the door.

"Shall we?"

"Yep," she replied pertly, pushing into the hospital room. She called out cautiously, "Knock, knock?"

"Come on in," a grumpy female answered in a hoarse voice.

Emma poked her head around the curtain partition. "You said to come early."

"I did," Amy replied, pushing herself up on the bed. "Come on in. It's been a veritable parade in here all night."

"I see LRPD beat me here this morning," Emma commented as she pushed the curtain back.

Max offered a sheepish wave from where he stood. It felt weird, barging into a stranger's hospital room. But Emma didn't seem fazed at all. "Good morning," he said, inclining his head in a greeting.

"Morning," Amy said briefly. "The good part remains to be seen."

Emma drew up a chair and sat down beside the bed. "How are you feeling?"

"Like I've been on a bender for three or four days," Amy

replied. "Or at least, how I imagine it would feel. I've never actually been on a bender."

"So, Detective Hutchinson…" Emma said leadingly.

"Is a real jerk?" Amy responded, closing her eyes.

"Exactly."

"Would you mind turning off the overhead lights?" she asked, waving a hand over her head. A strip of obnoxiously bright fluorescent light glared down at them. "I didn't get much sleep and my head is still pounding."

"I'll get it." Max shuffled behind Emma's chair and hit the switch. Suddenly, the room was lit only by the glow of the light spilling from the attached bathroom. "Better?"

"Loads."

"Are you sure you feel up to doing this now?" Emma asked.

"I don't think there's a lot of time to lose. I was scrolling last night, and there's some pretty ugly stuff being said. The kids are turning on each other. I think the sooner we nip this in the bud, the better."

"Agreed." Emma scooted the chair closer to the bed and lowered her voice. "I was able to get into, uh, the program you mentioned last night."

Amy's eyes flew open. "You were? How?"

"This guy." She hooked a thumb at Max and he rolled his eyes. "Guess whose venture-capital company backed SecuraT's development."

Amy looked up at him, then closed her eyes again and let out a long soft exhalation of disgust. "Of course, you did." She moved her head from side to side on the pillow. "I realize Little Rock isn't a big city, but I never found a more intertwined corner of it than I have at Capitol Academy," she said tiredly.

"It's a fairly insular world," Max agreed. "Steve Severin

of SevTech was the developer. You probably had his daughter in your class."

Amy grimaced. Cracking a single eyelid, she gave him a baleful stare. "Severin? Tia Severin?"

Max nodded. "The one and only."

"Of course, it is," she said without rancor. She blinked both eyes open and turned her attention to Emma. "What were the odds of me falling into this job."

Emma chuckled. "Probably pretty good, given your skill set and the caliber of instructor CA employs."

"Flattery will get you everywhere at the moment."

"And let me ask you this," Emma said, wearing the same sly smile from when she'd walked into his kitchen and demanded her twenty dollars. "Were you the only member of the Syscom team who was able to get through the firewalls and breach SecuraT?"

Amy closed her eyes again and simply smiled.

"I think I know what you mean about the coding," Emma told her. "Clever."

"The redundancies threw me at first," Amy said flatly. "I couldn't figure out why they bothered with them."

Max leaned down to Emma. "Some plain talk for the non-tech crowd, please?"

Emma looked up at him. "Even when someone is able to get into the network, it latches on to anyone without the correct access code. Unless they know to break the loop, it literally is like being caught in a trap."

"But whoever was doing this was able to post to various sites using the school's network," he pointed out.

"Yes. And they think they swept their footprints but they didn't," Amy explained with the patience of a natural-born teacher. "Most hackers are really good at covering their tracks, but SecuraT had some interesting scripts written into it. Keystrokes were wiped but not permanently."

Emma nodded eagerly. "They reappear again after a period of time. Kind of like writing a message in invisible ink." Her voice rose with excitement as she warmed to her subject. "Anytime the software detects any kind of attempt to do a data sweep, it captures the original and archives a snapshot. Then it will make it look like it's erasing the data, but it's not. Think of it like making footprints in the sand and wiping them away so no one can follow you."

"Only to have them captured on a map stored in a file cabinet," Amy added. "This is what made the program so valuable." Then she frowned. "Also, what marked it for death."

Max nodded as grim understanding settled in. "A company like Syscom can't sell security software built to eliminate the need for future purchase of additional security software."

"Right. Letting something like SecuraT loose on the market would have been akin to planning their own obsolescence." Amy sighed. "Software companies may only be as good as their last release, but cybersecurity relies on there being bad actors in the world constantly trying to get past it. Otherwise, no one would be scared enough to invest in it."

"And there are tons of bad guys out there. The state has been the victim of three major malware attacks in the last eighteen months," Emma informed them. "You might have heard a little about them on the news, but trust me, they were way worse than reported."

"Then there was the insurance company whose accounting system was held hostage," Amy added.

Max nodded and crossed his arms over his chest. "It seems like I'm getting a data-breach letter from one financial institution or another every week."

"They've become so commonplace people hardly pay attention to it anymore," Emma said tiredly. "Doesn't mean there isn't major damage being done."

"Exactly," Amy concurred. "SecuraT would have been a great answer for more everyday users, but it also could have been a great jumping-off point for software able to handle the larger clients."

"Were you able to trace whoever is doing these posts in the network?" Max asked, anxious to pull them back on topic. Both women looked up at him, blinking owlishly. As if he'd asked the most ridiculous question a person could conjure. "What?"

Emma took pity on him first. "No. I couldn't find any trace of the posts," she said, her voice unnervingly gentle. She turned to Amy. "Did you?"

The other woman started to shake her head, then stopped on a wince of pain. "No."

Unable to contain his frustration, Max threw up his arms. "Then what's the big deal? Why are you guys so excited, and what are you planning to do to stop this creep?" he demanded, firing his questions at Emma.

She recoiled at first, then sat up. He waited for her to blast him back, but instead, she spoke quietly and calmly. "The big deal isn't what we found, it's what we didn't find." She waited a beat. "Whoever is doing this is someone who has legitimate access to the school's network."

Max started rambling. "So we're back to every student, every teacher, all the adminis—"

"No." The single word spoken by the woman in the hospital bed stopped him mid-rant.

"No?"

"I told you I reworked all the security last fall, remember? The students, teachers and staff all have user access to the network. We could see their activity easily if it were them. We're looking at the people who have administrative access to the network."

"How many people have administrative access?"

"Only three. I sent them an encrypted email with their credentials the day I finished setting it all up."

"Who are they?"

Amy Birch held up three fingers. "Me," she said, lowering one finger. "Dr. Blanton," she said, curling the next one in. "And the president of the school board," she said, lowering the last finger and looking Max straight in the eye.

Emma must have picked up on the undercurrent in what Amy was saying because she shifted in her seat as she divided a look between them. "Who's the president of the school board?" she asked, her tone wary.

Max met her gaze directly. "I am."

He was saved from saying anything more by the attending physician breezing into the room. "Anyone in here ready to go home?"

Emma scrambled to collect her bag and practically jumped up. The chair screeched as it scooted across the tile. Max heard Emma telling Amy to rest and recover, and promising to be in touch soon. But he couldn't make out the teacher's response over the roaring in his ears.

He followed Emma from the room, down the corridor and to the bank of elevators, his mind racing.

"What does this mean?" he asked, slightly out of breath.

Emma raised a hand to halt any further questions. "Let's wait until we're out of here."

He agreed, though the trip down and through the bustling lobby seemed excruciatingly long. Outside, he regulated his long strides to match hers. Still, Emma said nothing. She kept her gaze pointed at the parking deck where they'd left his car. Her jaw was tense. Everything about her manner felt slightly too self-contained, which made him feel like something he couldn't quite grasp was unraveling.

The moment they were in the car, he turned to look at her,

his patience worn through. "Okay, we're out. Now, speak to me in short simple sentences."

"Turn your phone off," she ordered, pressing the button to switch off her own.

She waited until he complied, then started in. "Only three people could be behind all this. One of them is the woman lying in a hospital bed, one is in charge of a prestigious school and the other is sitting next to me."

Her hard stare made his breath tangle in his chest. "You think I—"

His indignant protest was strangled by a lack of oxygen. Emma didn't blink. She kept inspecting him with wide hazel eyes. It was the same expression she wore while reading and absorbing line after line of code or data. The gaze of a woman who was accustomed to staring straight at a puzzle until the pieces showed her what they were.

But he was everything he presented himself to be. A man whose life was being turned on its head. "You think I set my child up to be expelled from school weeks before graduation?"

She waited a beat too long before answering. "No."

"You've spent the last few nights sleeping under my roof. Eating meals with me and Kayleigh. Tearing our electronics apart, telling us what we can do and where we can go—"

"Now, wait a minute—" she interrupted.

"No, you wait a minute," he snapped, turning his furious stare on her. "Are you serious?"

She shook her head. "No." She cleared her throat, then spoke louder. "No, I don't think it is you."

"But you thought about it," he challenged.

"Of course, I thought about it," she retorted. "If I didn't consider every possibility, you'd be jumping down my throat for not thinking about it."

He gripped the steering wheel. "It isn't me," he said through clenched teeth.

"And you're absolutely certain there's no way Kayleigh could have intercepted the encrypted email?"

He blew out a breath. "I can't be absolutely sure, no, but come on. What does she have to gain here?"

"I have no idea."

He started the car and shifted into Reverse. "I don't know how much you know about teenagers, but I can promise you there's nothing my daughter is less interested in than my business. Why would she be checking my email?"

Emma propped her elbow on the door and dropped her head into her hand. "You're right. I know nothing about raising a child, but I know teenage girls can be shockingly resourceful when they want to be."

He braked too hard, then shifted the car into Drive. "It's not Kayleigh."

She remained silent. He could practically feel the waves of skepticism wafting off her, and he resented every one of them. He'd trusted her. They'd invited her into their home. Their lives. And now she thought—

"Barricade," she barked in warning.

He stopped inches shy of the exit gate with an angry screech of rubber on asphalt. Heat crept up his neck as he lowered the window. He waved his phone at the scanner and a second later it dinged to signal the acceptance of his payment. When the bar rose, he chanced a glance at her.

"It's not us," he told her flatly as they rolled forward.

"Okay," she said quietly.

"Okay?" He turned to her, stupefied by her abrupt acceptance of his word.

"Okay," she repeated. "I guess I need to do some digging on Dr. Blanton then, don't I?"

Chapter Fourteen

Emma had a shockingly easy time digging up dirt on Samuel Blanton. For a man who went to extraordinary lengths to cover up the trouble he was stirring among the Capitol Academy senior class, he was fairly lax when it came to guarding his own information. But maybe he did that on purpose.

Within an hour of their meeting with Amy Birch, Emma accessed the principal's personal email and from there hacked her way through his financial accounts. Though he made a decent living, the man was by no means well off.

Drumming her pen on the tabletop, Emma wondered if the disparity stuck in his craw. There had to be some children at his school with trust funds worth more than the wealth he'd accumulated over a lifetime.

She found a brokerage account with one of the state's larger firms. She was surprised by some of the transactions she found there. For a man closing in on retirement age, he played fast and loose with his finances.

Drilling down in the data, she found several large investments in emerging tech stocks, including a large buy of shares in Syscom almost three years ago.

She didn't need to look up to know Max was nearby. She could feel the tension vibrating off the man. "When would the sale of SecuraT to Syscom have first been on the table?"

He was by her side within seconds. "The vetting process would have started about three or four years ago. Why?"

"Who else would have known about this potential sale?"

"What do you mean 'who else'?" he asked, frowning.

"You weren't the only investor, right?"

"Right."

"So you and how many other angel investors?" she queried.

"There were six total to start, but only three took an active interest in the product development, aside from myself."

"So four of the six were paying attention?" she asked, clicking around on her screen.

"Yes."

"And the other two were happy to throw money into the pot hoping it paid off?" She failed at masking the edge of disdain in her statement.

"It's not unusual for investors to put money into something and then look away until it's time to cash out."

She hummed her disapproval. "Rich people."

"Why do you ask?" He moved to peer over her shoulder at the screen. "Did you find something?"

"Looks like Dr. Blanton invested heavily in Syscom stock weeks before the sale was finalized. Could be coincidence," she said in a skeptical tone. "Could it be he received a tip?"

"I can't say for certain, but I can tell you Steve Severin wasn't exactly playing it cool when word of Syscom's interest in his product became apparent."

"Do you think it's possible Samuel Blanton caught wind of this potential sale and invested in Syscom believing he was buying in to a company with a surefire hit?"

"Sure, it's possible," he conceded.

"Some people go to jail for buying and selling stock based on confidential information," she said, arching an eyebrow at him.

"Some people do," he said without taking offense. "But in reality, most of them don't."

Emma pulled a notebook close to her and picked up a pen. "Were you able to find some of his employment information?"

"I've got everything," he said flatly.

"Hit me."

"Started at CA about seven years ago. Kayleigh would have been in the lower school grades at the time. I remember him coming in, but I wasn't involved with the school board then."

"What's the general consensus about him among the parents?"

Max shrugged. "He's well-liked. A no-nonsense kind of a guy. A bit on the uptight side, but you want a principal who comes across a bit stodgy, right?"

"I suppose so. If you're a parent," she added with a smirk.

"The school board was doing the hiring, and it's made up of a bunch of parents."

"Okay, so we have a large investment in a tech stock. There hasn't been a huge loss, but also no appreciable return."

"Right now, he's stuck with it because the company has had a rocky patch and he'd lose money if he sold."

"Judging by the numbers, I'm guessing this had to be the bulk of his money. Retirement savings?" she asked, speculating.

"Most likely. But it's about to get worse," Max said darkly. "Rumor has it Syscom will be moving most of their operations overseas in the next two years. Their stock will take a hit the moment it's announced. They haven't brought anything groundbreaking to market in recent years and it could spell disaster for the whole company."

Genuinely perplexed, she asked, "Why wouldn't they pull SecuraT out of their hat and use it to save themselves?"

"There is no SecuraT anymore. They sold it for parts." He held her stunned gaze. "A lot of companies do the same with competing products. They keep what they want to use, bury some bits of it and sell off others."

Emma fixed him with a baleful stare. "I don't mind telling you hearing this hurts my heart."

"Understood." He moved to the chair beside his desk and dropped into the seat. Steepling his fingers, he asked, "So maybe Blanton is seeking revenge on the fathers he feels misled him?"

She fell back into her seat with a sigh. "It's a stretch."

"Sometimes the most implausible ideas have the most potential," he said, tossing off this bit of wisdom with a nonchalant shrug. "Possibility. It's the reason people keep trying."

She blinked at him, then shook her head. "Possibility may fly in the world of venture capital, but when it comes to convincing a judge you need a search warrant? Not so much."

"We have his financials." He pointed to her laptop as if it was the magic bullet.

"We can't use any of this." She actually laughed at his naivete. "I hacked the guy, Max. We need something clean." She sat back and dragged a hand over her face, then glared at her silent cell phone. "We need to prove Blanton was the one to take the computer from the school."

She'd given Simon Taylor the contact information for Detective Hutchinson at the LRPD. The local police had taken all of the school's security footage into custody as part of their assault investigation, but so far, they'd had no word on whether the footage had actually been reviewed yet. Emma knew all too well the department was underfunded and overworked. She could only pray they'd get to checking it sometime soon.

She glanced over at Max, who sat scrolling on his phone. At this point, she wasn't above tapping into any influence he could bring to the table. "Hey, you don't have any contacts with the Little Rock police, do you?"

Max shook his head. "No, but I know the mayor," he said distractedly.

A moment later, she watched his whole face transform as a smile lifted the corners of his mouth and crinkled his eyes. He held up the phone to show her a contact page with a phone number for the city's highest elected official.

She gestured impatiently for him to get on with it. "What are you waiting for? Make the call."

He chuckled as he did as she asked. He also stood and left the room as soon as the call connected, leaving her to stew as they spoke bigwig-to-bigwig. When he returned less than two minutes later, he gave her a brief nod. "Sorry. I didn't want you to have to listen to me grovel."

She chortled. "Did you?"

He shook his head and dropped back into the guest chair again. "Not really, but let's assume a healthy campaign donation will be expected when the next election cycle rolls around."

"How the sausage is made," she said dryly.

"And how the West was won."

They lapsed into silence as she took another look at the information she'd obtained through what her fellow CCD agents referred to as her special skill set. Max continued to fiddle with his phone as she skimmed the information. She couldn't help wondering who was next on his call sheet. The governor? The FBI?

"What do you think about me giving Steve Severin a call?" he asked, breaking the taut silence.

Emma looked up. "To what end?"

He shrugged. "See if maybe Blanton said something to him about the Syscom investment?"

She pondered the suggestion for a moment, then shook her head. "I think we need to keep things close for now. If we can find something connecting him to the assault, then we'll cast a wider net."

Max hummed, but didn't look up from his phone. "I knew a guy in school who went to work for the FBI," he said a few minutes later. "Simon knows him, too. Never would have picked him to be a Fed," he added with an amused chortle. "He wasn't the straightest arrow in college."

"Most of us weren't," she said, mindful of her own checkered past.

He huffed and dropped his phone into his lap, hauling himself up straighter in the chair. "I can't believe we're stuck here waiting on Hutchinson to do his—"

Her phone lit up. It was a local number without a contact assigned. She eyed it with suspicion before dragging her finger across the screen. "Parker," she said by way of greeting.

"Someone has friends in high places." The caller was a man. She might have had trouble placing him if it wasn't for the insolent edge in his tone.

"Detective Hutchinson," she said, shooting Max a look as she placed the call on speaker. "You're on speaker. Have you found anything useful for us?"

"As I told your boss and the guy you sicced on me from the mayor's office, the timing on the video checks out with Dr. Blanton's alibi. He left the school at four thirty-eight. He was seen at the Johnny Wilkins Steakhouse before the five-thirty meeting began."

Emma and Max shared a glance, then she grasped at her last straw. "Was he carrying anything when he left the school?"

"Briefcase and raincoat," he reported tiredly.

"And everything looked normal? Not bulging or anything?" she persisted.

Her question was met with an exasperated sigh. "I don't know. I guess so. Listen, I'm sorry the lady got knocked on the head, but we see worse—"

She cut him off before he could give her a comparative crime lecture. "I know you're busy. But would you mind sending the file with the video to me? Let us do the poking around."

"You know what? Fine. Knock yourself out," he said gruffly.

Emma didn't waste a moment. "I've got your card here. I'm sending you an email. If you would attach the file and flip it right back to me, I'd appreciate it."

"Yeah. Sure. Okay," he grumbled. "I have a dozen other things I could be doin'—"

"I know. Let me take this off your plate," Emma said solicitously as she hit Send.

"One of the desk jockeys downstairs chopped the file down to the hour before and after the incident," he informed her.

"Perfect." Emma sat back, trying to stifle the urge to grin. Or fist pump. All in all, she thought her restraint was admirable. "If I come up with anything, you'll be the first to know."

"Whatever," Hutchinson responded, then three beeps indicated the call had ended.

"He is quite the charmer," Emma said wryly.

Max flashed a full smile at her. "You'd think he'd watch himself, considering your connections."

Those enticing laugh lines fanning from his eyes melted into devastating dimples, and she almost forgot she was waiting on possible video evidence of a person who'd committed a vicious assault. She was saved from complete oblivion by the chime of her email alert.

She cleared her throat and scooted to the edge of Max's leather executive chair. He stood and came around behind her, bracing his hands on the backrest and leaning in close enough for her to catch a whiff of aftershave. The guy even smelled out of her league.

Keeping her eyes glued to the screen, she clicked the attachment and waited for the video to download.

The split-screen video image showed the interior of the school lobby as well as a wide-angle shot of the steps where she and Wyatt Dawson stood pounding on those impressive carved wooden doors.

"Did they swipe those doors from some medieval castle in Europe or something?" she asked as they watched students and teachers who, she assumed, stayed behind for various activities leave the building, some in chattering groups, others bustling out as fast as they could.

"Actually, they were carved by a group of artisans up near Mountain Home. Took them three years to complete each one, and if you look closely, you notice they share a motif, but they're all unique."

"Huh. Like snowflakes," she said distractedly. A slender dark-haired girl she recognized from Kayleigh's social-media accounts rushed through the lobby and hit the crash bar on the center door at full speed. "Whoa, someone's in a hurry," she said under her breath.

"Tia Severin," Max explained.

Emma looked up at him, shocked to have captured one of the minor players in this drama in action. "That was Tia?"

Max nodded, then pointed to the screen. "Freeze it."

She hit the space bar and the playback stopped.

He pressed his finger to the side of the monitor with the

outdoor scene. At the edge of the shot, she saw an oversize luxury SUV with pricey guards over the taillights.

"That's Steve Severin's truck. He must have been picking Tia up," he said, then leaned back.

Emma gaped up at him in disbelief. "Are you telling me they were both there—" she checked the timestamp on the playback "—ten minutes or so before Amy Birch ends up getting clocked with a computer?"

Max pulled a face, his lips now flattened into a grim line. "Not as much of a coincidence as you'd like to think it is. Tia wrecked her car last month. She'd been riding to and from school with Kayleigh every day until…"

He let the rest go unspoken, but Emma could not resist filling in the blanks. "Until Kayleigh was suspended." She restarted the playback and they lapsed into silence, the tension in the room sickening as the timestamp inched closer to 4:38 p.m.

"What if…" Max began and then stopped. "There he is."

Emma hit the button to pause the playback as he spoke. They leaned in. Dr. Blanton carried a briefcase made of black leather in one hand and had his raincoat draped over the opposite arm. He was in the process of pushing against the door, his hip pressing the bar to release the latch.

"Play it through," Max whispered.

She unpaused the video, and they watched the principal bustle through the door into the wet afternoon, his head bent and his steps quick.

The misty rain blurred the view picked up by the wide-angle camera. Emma cocked her head and peered at the footage intensely as the older man descended the steps, his head down.

"Why isn't he wearing the coat?" she asked aloud.

Beside her, Max hummed. "It wasn't raining hard."

"True, but he has it," she argued, backing the playback

up to the lobby and letting it run again. They watched his departure play through without interruption. The second the man disappeared from the frame, she skipped back again. "I had my windbreaker on. So did Wyatt," she murmured as she reset the video. "Why wouldn't he put the coat on?"

"Too warm?" Max said, hazarding a guess.

She paused the video again at the spot where he pushed against the heavy door. With a few keystrokes, she isolated the hand holding the briefcase. "Is it in there?" she murmured, trying to enhance the image enough to see if it bulged.

"Nah, wouldn't fit," Max said confidently.

She looked over her shoulder at him. "How do you know?"

"Because I have one exactly like it. It's a Karl Legstrom Palladium bag," he explained, rattling off the name.

When he saw the information meant nothing to her, he moved to the opposite side of the desk and picked up a slender leather satchel in a rich forest-green. It was identical to the one Dr. Blanton carried in every way except color.

"You can fit a laptop and maybe a few files in here, but not a desktop unit."

"They were small units," she countered, though she had to admit the CPU would have been too blocky to fit in the slim briefcase.

"Maybe he's carrying it out," Max suggested.

She backed out of the close-up and switched to the opposite arm. "Might explain why he didn't put the coat on," she grumbled.

"Why is it bothering you?" he asked, his tone amused.

"Because it does," she said with a shrug. Then she zoomed in on the coat draped over the crook of his arm and her breath caught. "Or maybe I knew all along?" she said, slowly turning to look at Max. "Do you see what I see?"

Max nodded. "Chalk one up for the lady."

She screen-captured the image and used some of the editing tools to draw red circles around the areas of interest. "I'm not a lady, I'm a cop," she mumbled as she worked.

"Or maybe you're both," he challenged.

She snorted but said nothing more as she fired off an email to Simon Taylor, attaching both the security video and the screen captures.

"Do you think it'll be enough?" Max asked as she hit the button to send the email.

"For a search warrant? It should be." She turned and looked at him full-on. "For an arrest? There are still a lot of dots to connect."

"You'll connect them."

He sounded so certain she couldn't work up enough false modesty to deny him. She would. Not only because it was the job, but also because these people—Kayleigh, Max and even Amy—had let her in on a personal level. They believed in her. They let her in. There was no way she was going to let some bitter old guy with an overdeveloped sense of entitlement and a misplaced grudge hurt them any more than he already had.

Reaching over, she covered Max's hand and squeezed. "I will. I'll connect every last one of them."

EMMA RANG DR. BLANTON'S doorbell that afternoon with Simon Taylor standing by her side, as silent and self-contained as ever.

A team of agents who specialized in the systematic search for evidence gathered behind them, unloading evidence boxes and donning the gear designed to keep their DNA from contaminating anything seized. They had a few members from the LRPD evidence-recovery team mixed in with the group, but when he heard about the issuance of the warrant, Detective Hutchinson was more than happy to let the state do the nitty-gritty work.

"What?" Samuel Blanton blustered when he opened his door to find a small law-enforcement army assembled on his porch. "What's the meaning of this?"

"Special Agent Emma Parker and Special Agent in Charge Simon Taylor, sir," she stated formally. "We have a warrant to search these premises."

"A warrant," he repeated, face reddening with outrage. "Whatever for?"

"Sir, we believe you may have evidence connected to the assault on one of the Capitol Academy teaching staff as well as the ongoing cyberbullying and stalking of a minor student."

"This is…"

He sputtered then stopped when Simon unfolded the warrant and thrust it at the man.

"You're welcome to contact your attorney," Emma informed him, "but the search will begin now."

She and Simon stood beside Dr. Blanton, search warrant in hand as the team marched into the midcentury home far from the school. Wyatt was watching over another team as they swept the man's office at Capitol Academy. Max was with him, overseeing the search as a representative of the school board. The warrant also covered searching Dr. Blanton's vehicle, but they'd all agreed the home and office took precedence.

Blanton pulled his phone from his pocket and began furiously scrolling through his contacts. Emma waved the warrant she'd refolded. "I'm sorry, sir," she said as she plucked the phone from his grasp. "I'm afraid I have to confiscate all electronic devices."

"But I need to call my attorney," he protested.

"You're welcome to use a landline, if you have one," she said, not backing down.

"I no longer have a landline," Blanton huffed.

At last, Simon spoke up. "I'll be happy to place the call for you. What's your attorney's name?"

Emma deftly bagged the man's phone, then handed it to Simon, leaving the subject of their investigation to her boss to handle. Turning to the two officers in full hazmat gear still standing on the steps, she gave them a wan smile.

"Are you my raccoons?" she asked, using the term they jokingly used for the officers assigned to going through a suspect's trash.

"Yes, ma'am," the one on the right answered.

"Better sweep the yard before it gets dark. Pick up everything. We know our assailant shattered the plastic casing on the computer, so pick up every tiny bit of whatever you find not created by Mother Nature. I'm talking old gum wrappers. Got me?"

"Yes, ma'am," they answered in unison, then took off around the side of the house.

TWO HOURS LATER, Emma was at her desk at state police headquarters, dwarfed by the contents of Samuel Blanton's desk drawers. Two banker boxes filled with tax returns and other financial documents sat at her feet. "Everything posted from the cloned socials in the last two days came from a mobile device," Caitlin called over the partition.

"An excellent place to start," Emma called back.

When Emma arrived at headquarters with her bounty, she'd asked Caitlin Ross to move to one of the empty desks closer to the cubicle she shared with Wyatt Dawson so they could talk as they worked.

Wyatt had dropped everything they'd found at the school on her desk and then taken off with Simon Taylor with a rushed apology. They'd been called to a meeting at the local offices of the Bureau of Alcohol, Tobacco, Firearms and Explosives in connection with a case they were working with the ATF as part of a joint task force.

Which left Emma and Caitlin to go through all the evidence they'd amassed in the search-and-seizure. Starting with the electronics seemed only logical to them both. Emma had Blanton's mobile and tablet, while Caitlin had his laptop, desktop from the academy and a box full of external hard drives, flash drives and outdated mobile phones.

Emma focused on the phone in her hand. Cords and cables snaked across the surface of her desk. She glanced over her shoulder, then back to her own phone, which remained maddeningly silent. She hadn't heard from Max after the search of the school office was complete. She didn't know why she expected to, but she did. And now here she was, alone again—

"Since they ditched us with all the work, we should order pizza. Or maybe Thai," Caitlin called over the wall.

Emma smiled. She wasn't alone. She was hungry and tired, that was all. "Pizza would be easier."

"What's your favorite place?" Caitlin called over the upholstered wall. "Do you eat meat?"

She'd just typed the command to run a diagnostic test on Blanton's mobile when a familiar voice cut off her answer.

"Emma?"

She frowned, planting her hands on her desk as she rose to peek around the corner of the partition. "Max?"

"Where are you?" he called above the warren of cubicles.

Part of her didn't want to answer. She'd spent hours working out of his beautifully appointed home office. The last thing she wanted was for him to see the shabby seventeenth-hand desk where she toiled like Cinderella, day in and day out.

"Emma?" he called again. "I brought dinner."

She sighed and stepped out into the narrow corridor. Caitlin rolled out her desk chair. "Who's there? He sounds cute."

Emma shot the younger agent a scornful glance. "How can someone sound cute?"

Unperturbed, Caitlin shrugged as Emma passed. "I don't know. He does."

Poking her head around the end of the set of cubicles, Emma caught sight of the man in question. He *was* cute. Or more than cute. He was Prince Charming handsome. The thought brought her right down to earth again. She was a woman who had both shoes snugly on her feet.

"We're over here," she called, waving an arm.

His face lit with a smile as he caught sight of her, and her traitorous heart did a flip. "Hey. I thought you might be hungry," he said, holding up a large carryout bag.

She was about to wave him off, but then her stomach growled loudly, blowing what cover she had left. "We are," she conceded.

"It's only subs," he said with a shrug. "I wasn't sure how many people you'd have around so I ordered a variety box." He handed over the bulging bag.

"Thank you." She heard the rumble of chair casters on a carpet mat and knew Caitlin had ducked back into the space next to hers. Smiling tiredly, she said, "Come on back. This is the really glamorous part of the job where we get to pretend we're trash pandas."

Chapter Fifteen

"Trash pandas?" Max asked, torn between bewilderment and bemusement.

"We're like raccoons—we gather everything we can, then dig through all of it."

She gave him a wan smile and he had to tuck his hand in his pocket to keep from brushing her hair back from her cheek.

"Where's Kayleigh?" Emma asked as she placed the carryout bag on an empty desk.

He frowned and looked around. Surely this couldn't be hers. "She's staying with the Marshes for dinner."

"They had a good day together?"

"Yeah. Kayleigh sounded really happy when I spoke to her."

"Did you tell her what we had going on?"

"Broad strokes," he replied. "I didn't want to bog her down with details when she was finally thinking about something else."

"Good call," Emma concurred. "I'm glad she and Patrice have been able to reconnect. I hope it will be helpful for both of them." She turned and called, "Hey, Ross, you can come out now!"

"Ross?" Max asked. "I thought you worked with that Dawson guy who was at the school."

"Wyatt Dawson and I share space here, but he's out on another assignment." She looked over her shoulder and spotted Caitlin approaching, her steps slow and her eyes wider than usual. "Special Agent Caitlin Ross, this is Max Hughes," she said, waving a hand between them. "He's a compulsive feeder."

Caitlin extended her hand. "My favorite kind of person."

Emma unwrapped a club sandwich, plucked the lettuce and tomato from it and took a voracious bite.

"Help yourself," he said, releasing the woman's hand to gesture to the bag. "I thought I'd come see if I can help."

Emma harrumphed as she chewed, eying his pristine polo shirt and perfectly faded jeans. "I could send you down to sort through the actual trash."

He raised both eyebrows. "You took his trash?"

"You'd be surprised how many people simply throw incriminating evidence in the garbage. People who commit acts of violence aren't always as clever after the fact."

"Unless they're a serial killer," Agent Ross said with a nod, plucking a bag of chips from the bag.

Emma waved the uneaten half of her sandwich as if conceding the point. "Right. Premeditated is a different animal. But most assaults are matters of circumstance."

"Wrong place at the wrong time," Agent Ross agreed, opening the bag of chips.

"You think he tossed the computer he used to hit Amy Birch in his garbage at home," Max said, unable to hide his skepticism.

"Oh. No. He had the computer in the trunk of his car," Emma informed him. She snagged a bag of chips, then gestured for him to follow. "Come with me."

Max grabbed one of the wrapped sandwiches from the box then hustled after her, flashing the other agent a quick smile. "Feel free to share those with whoever is around," he called back.

"Share them?" Caitlin scoffed. "Maybe after I load my mini fridge."

Max's chuckle died on his lips as he rounded a corner and came to an abrupt halt. Every surface of the two-person cubicle space was covered with piles of paper, files, boxes overflowing with electronics and cords and banker boxes filled with what he could only assume were hard copies of some of the financial records Emma accessed online.

"Holy cow."

"You said you wanted to help," she reminded him, leaning over the desk to check the screen of a mobile phone attached to her computer. "Clean. Damn it," she muttered, dropping into her chair.

"If you have the computer, why are you—"

"We have the remains of the computer," she informed him. "Looks like he ran over it a couple times, then tossed the remains into his trunk." She sighed. "I assume he planned to give it a couple days, then go throw it in a dumpster somewhere."

She unplugged the smartphone and set it atop a stack of files.

"So it's no good as evidence?" He wandered into her space and poked through one of the piles at random. It appeared to contain printouts of several school-board meetings. Max frowned, wondering why Blanton had bothered to print them. His own copies were all filed away in his email archives.

"It's great evidence for the assault charge," she said distractedly. "But we need to find something connecting him to the hacking."

Max pulled up short. "Have the Little Rock police arrested him?"

Emma shook her head. "Not yet. I haven't called Hutchinson yet. His case is pretty open and shut, but we need something more."

"What if Blanton tries to leave?" Max demanded, his voice rising as he envisioned the slimy old creep slipping away.

"He can try," Emma said, looking up at him, her head tilted to the side. "But the agent we have parked in front of his house will stop him." She turned back to her task. "I need some time. If I don't have it by morning, I'll let Hutchinson pick him up and we'll make our case later. But if we find a connection between Blanton and the stalking and harassment, it makes the assault case stronger."

"Piling on the charges," Max murmured. He pulled a leather portfolio he'd seen the principal carrying to board meetings and dropped into the chair behind Emma.

"We call it improving our batting average," she retorted. "Caitlin says the last few posts made to any of the cloned accounts came through mobile applications, so we're trying to locate the device."

He flipped through the lined pages of notes Blanton had jotted during various meetings. His eye was drawn to the name *Michael Pierce* scrawled on the third page. It had been underlined so vigorously Blanton had nearly torn through the paper.

"Hey," he called softly. "Do you remember seeing the name of Blanton's stockbroker anywhere?"

"No, why? I wouldn't take any tips from him if I were you," she said, flipping through apps on the tablet she had connected to her laptop.

"Does the name *Michael Pierce* mean anything to you?"

She shook her head, then raised it slowly. "Michael Pierce? Like Carter Pierce?"

"His father." Max cleared his throat and sat up, skim-

ming the piles of paper around them, hoping to spot a brokerage statement.

"Do you think he's the one Blanton used to buy the Syscom stock?"

"I don't know. I only know his name was written in the
margin of this notepad," he said, extending the portfolio
for her to see.

Emma swiveled to look. Their knees touched as she
leaned in, but if one of them was going to pull away, it
would have to be her. "Wow, written and struck through,"
she murmured.

"I think he was underlining, but yeah. Fairly emphatic,"
he concurred.

"Hey, Cait?" Emma called over the wall. "Aside from
Kayleigh Hughes, who else do we have confirmed cloned
social-media accounts?"

"Um…" There was a shuffle on the other side of the wall.
"Kayleigh Hughes and Carter Pierce are confirmed. Tia Severin and Patrice Marsh possibly," she called back.

"Huh," Emma grunted.

Max murmured a soft expletive, which she ignored as she
pointed to the banker boxes by her feet.

"Look in one of those. They're the files pulled from his
desk at home."

Max bit his lip to stifle his protest when she spun away
from him. They were working on something together. Something important. In a way, they were as connected as those
kids were. And together, they'd get to the bottom of this.
Tonight.

He tossed the portfolio on top of another pile and bent
to grab one of the boxes, but he misjudged the stability of
the pile. Gravity caught the heavy leather folder and pulled
it down with a flutter of loose pages. It hit the floor with a
thud and fell open.

"Hey, don't mess things up," Emma chided. "I know it looks like chaos to you, but it's controlled chaos."

Max cursed and abandoned his banker's box, only to freeze when he caught sight of two colorful plastic cards with the logo of a popular pay-as-you-go cellular service emblazoned on the top.

He looked up with a frown, his brain whirring as he tried to slot pieces into place. "Hey, Em?" he called, hoping his thoughts would coalesce before she answered. He needn't have worried because she didn't respond. He swallowed hard and tried again. "Emma?"

"Hmm?" she said, tapping furiously on the tablet.

He squinted at the device she'd already set aside. "What model is Blanton's phone?"

"Huh? Oh. It's the new one. Same as yours and Kayleigh's," she said, waving her hand dismissively. "But it's clean. I checked it already."

"You can get this phone on a pay-as-you-go plan," he murmured, half to himself.

"What?" She half turned, her attention snagged.

He pulled the cards from the inner pocket of the leather binder and handed them to her. "Why would he need these if that's his phone?" He nodded toward the high-end phone.

Emma flipped over the cards. "Someone has peeled off the sticker concealing the activation codes." She raised an eyebrow. "Where were these?"

He held up the portfolio. "Inside pocket."

Tossing the tablet onto her desk, Emma shot out of her seat. "Caitlin? Grab the box with the old phones," she ordered. "I think we're looking for a burner."

THEY HAD TWO PHONES, a smashed computer and more technical information regarding digital footprints of more security breaches than any judge ever wanted to see by the time Simon Taylor returned to headquarters.

Emma met her boss at the door. "We have him," she announced breathlessly. She looked beyond Simon. "Where's Wyatt?"

"I sent him home," he responded. "I didn't know he'd be needed."

Emma nodded, a frown tugging at her mouth. "He's not, really. I have everything we need. I need you to get on the phone with Detective Hutchinson's commanding officer and spell out all the reasons it would be better for them if we took the assault case off their plate."

Simon looked up from the sheaf of papers she'd thrust into his hands. "You giving the orders now, Parker?"

Her cheeks flared, but she swallowed the impulse to apologize for her strident tone. In the end, she settled for a simple reply. "No, sir."

Simon craned his neck to look past her. She didn't need to turn around to know Max had followed her, even though she specifically told him not to.

"What are you doing here?" he asked, his tone clipped.

Emma jumped in before Max could answer. "He's been helping."

Again, with the single eyebrow lift. But Emma felt no compulsion to justify Max Hughes's presence. Simon had been the one to assign her to the case. He told her to stick close. To get as much information as she could out of his old friend and do everything in her power to keep him and his daughter safe. She'd done exactly as instructed.

"He was leaving," she informed her boss. Turning back to Max with a pointed glare, she said, "I'll let you know as soon as we have him in custody."

"But—"

She cut him off with a raised hand. "You need to get home

to Kayleigh. We don't want her alone in the house until all this comes out," she reminded him.

Simon stepped up beside her, handing the paperwork she'd so carefully put together for his perusal back without another glance. "She's right. We'll handle things from here."

Max opened his mouth, but then snapped it shut. Max probably knew Simon better than she did, but they both knew there was no point in arguing when he'd decided on a course of action. He locked eyes with her.

"You'll let me know as soon as you have him?" he asked.

Emma softened his dismissal with a smile. "Agent Vance is parked outside his house, remember? We already have him."

"Emma, please," Max said, taking a step closer. "I'll… Kayleigh and I will be worried."

She caught his quick rewording. There was no doubt Simon had, too. And as twisted as it sounded, she had to admit, it felt good knowing someone would be worrying about her.

"I'll call the minute we leave his house."

AGENT VANCE ACCOMPANIED her to the door but hung back as she pressed the bell.

That Simon Taylor hadn't come out to make the arrests with her, nor had he called Wyatt to come back on duty bolstered her confidence.

This was her case.

Her collar.

Negotiations with the LRPD were remarkably smooth. They balked at first, but once they started hitting them with the technical information they had against Samuel Blanton, Emma could practically hear Hutchinson and his lieutenant's eyes rolling back over the phone.

She smiled to herself as she rang the bell a second time.

There were advantages to working in a field people preferred not to know too much about.

Samuel Blanton opened the front door. He was still dressed in the clothes he wore earlier in the day.

As a matter of formality, Emma held up her credentials even though the man had inspected them thoroughly earlier, and said, "Samuel Blanton, I'm Special Agent Emma Parker of the Arkansas State Police Cyber Crime Division. You are under arrest."

The older man rolled his shoulders back and tipped his chin up, trying to maintain the dignity he'd sacrificed the minute he cloned Kayleigh Hughes's accounts.

"On what charge?" he demanded.

"Charges," Emma corrected, emphasizing the plural. "We have evidence you assaulted Ms. Amy Birch in the computer lab of Capitol Academy yesterday afternoon."

He opened his mouth to protest, but she held up her hand.

"We also have evidence you created multiple social-media accounts using the likenesses of minor children. We also have evidence of computer hacking, unauthorized surveillance and stalking. All involving one or more minors." She tipped her head to the side. "Shall I go on? There are more, but those are the heavy hitters."

"I'll need my phone to call my attorney," he said stiffly.

Emma inclined her head, making no comment on how ineffective his attorney had been in pushing back against the search warrant.

"You can call him from headquarters," she replied curiously. "Please turn and place your hands on the wall."

"You can't be serious," Blanton said in a tone so deeply offended Emma doubted herself for a moment.

Most people who committed cybercrimes weren't the violent type, but this man had attacked Amy Birch. Was the assault on the teacher a matter of circumstance, or did he have violent tendencies?

"Sir, please place your hands on the wall," she said briskly, stepping into the foyer and pulling on his arm until he faced the wall.

Once his palms were spread flat against the plaster, she nudged his feet apart in preparation for a pat down. But his foot hit the leg of a spindly hall table, sending a stack of mail cascading to the floor and momentarily distracting her. Emma rose from her squat as Blanton spun, snatched a long-handled letter opener from the table and wielded it like a knife.

"Step back," he ordered.

Emma remained in a semicrouch, hands open to show her empty palms.

She heard Vance as he barked, "Freeze!" She didn't have to look back to know he'd drawn his weapon and had it trained on the man in front of her.

"Everyone stay calm," she cautioned, her voice deceptively steady. "Dr. Blanton, threatening me will not get you anywhere. The judge has a record of the evidence we've collected, as do the Little Rock police," she informed him. "You have nothing to gain from harming me, and everything to lose."

"I've already lost everything," he shouted, his voice trembling as violently as his hand. "I have nothing left. Nothing!"

"You have your life," she reminded him. "And I can guarantee you will not if you make a move on me. Agent Vance is an excellent shot. There's one way for you to walk away from here tonight, and it can only happen if you put your weapon down."

The older man seemed to be weighing his options. While he huffed and puffed like an exercised horse, she took the opportunity to straighten up and slid her right foot closer to the left, alleviating the burning sensation in her quads and giving Vance a cleaner shot if necessary.

"You can't possibly connect me to those horrible things those spoiled miscreants say to one another on their webchat programs. I know nothing about internet…waves."

Emma saw the sharp glint of cunning in the man's blue eyes. She didn't for one second believe he was as inept as he wanted her to believe, but if it got him talking, she was willing to play along.

"Well, I suppose it's possible someone is trying to frame you," she said, drawing each word out as if she was giving it consideration. "Someone was pitting the students against one another, and all the digital evidence points to you."

"But digital evidence can be manipulated, can it not? With artificial intelligence and all?"

He waved the letter opener, and Emma leaned back instinctively to evade any incidental contact. If he wanted to start building his defense now, she had no issue. She'd simply keep piling on the evidence. He'd used the access he'd gained through her apps to snake his way into her networked devices and invaded the privacy of a minor in myriad ways. The charges she could lay at his feet went well beyond hacking.

Then she heard a soft "Oof!" behind her, followed by an outraged Vance, who shouted, "Hey, stop!"

Before she or Blanton could react, Max Hughes barreled through the front door and shoved her suspect up against the wall, one hand on the man's throat, the other pinning the wrist of his right hand to the wall.

The letter opener clattered to the floor and Emma planted the sole of her shoe on top of it.

"What do you think you are doing?" she demanded of Max. "Have you lost what sense you were born with?"

"He was pointing a knife at you," he huffed, glaring down at the shorter man.

"It was a letter opener," Emma said through gritted teeth, "and we had it under control."

She stepped aside to give Tom Vance the room to step inside. He'd holstered his weapon and was removing a set of cuffs from his windbreaker pocket.

"Did you think you were going to make some kind of citizen's arrest?"

"I didn't think," Max admitted.

He loosened his grip on the reddening man's throat only slightly when Tom caught Blanton's flailing left arm and clapped the cuff on. Tom chuckled when Max yanked Blanton's hand across the front of his body, presenting the man's right wrist to be cuffed.

"Thank you," the agent said gruffly.

Emma watched as Blanton visibly shrank under Max's unrelenting stare. Tom had to elbow Max out of his way to get to Blanton. But Max kept his gaze locked on the older man until he was led out the door.

"He threatened your life and tried to steal Kayleigh's future," he said, breathless. "I couldn't let him…there's no way I will let him get away with any of this."

"Not your job," she said dryly. Digging her elbow into his side, she waited until he tore his gaze from Blanton and focused on her. "Protecting me is not your job."

"You've been protecting me. And Kayleigh," he added hastily.

"*Literally* my job," she retorted.

He turned to face her, gray eyes boring into hers as his chest rose and fell dramatically. She wanted to press her thumb to his wrist and feel the adrenaline pulsing through his veins, but she resisted.

"I am the one trained to protect and serve," she said quietly.

Max nodded, his Adam's apple bobbing as he swallowed hard. "And you're good at it."

"I didn't need you rushing in here like a maniac. I had it under control," she assured him.

"I know you did."

She scoffed. "And yet, here we are. Do you have any idea how much ribbing I'm—" Words fled her when he slid his hand up to cradle her nape, his fingers tangling in her hair. "What are you—"

"You might have things under control, but I saw him and I…" His gaze dropped to her mouth. "Emma."

"Max," she answered.

"I've wanted to kiss you for days," he confessed.

"What's stopping you?"

And then he was. His mouth was warm and firm. The kiss was commanding, but somehow not overbearing. He angled his head, slanting his mouth across hers for a better fit, and a small groan escaped her. It was every bit as perfect as the man himself.

"What are we doing?" she asked when they broke for air.

"What I've wanted to do since the first time you wandered into my kitchen looking for coffee," he answered gruffly. "You were a mess."

"Still am," she whispered, stretching up on her toes in a blatant invitation.

He took it, kissing her so slowly and softly she barely cared that they were standing in an open doorway spotlit by foyer and porch lights. So tenderly, she would tolerate any amount of torment Vance and the other agents wanted to dish out. This kiss was worth it.

"A beautiful mess," he whispered across her kiss-dampened lips. "Best mess I've ever seen."

* * * * *

COMING SOON!

We really hope you enjoyed reading this book.
If you're looking for more romance
be sure to head to the shops when
new books are available on

Thursday 27th
March

To see which titles are coming soon, please visit
millsandboon.co.uk/nextmonth

MILLS & BOON

LET'S TALK

Romance

For exclusive extracts, competitions and special offers, find us online:

f MillsandBoon

X @MillsandBoon

⊙ @MillsandBoonUK

♪ @MillsandBoonUK

Get in touch on 01413 063 232

afterglow BOOKS

Afterglow Books is a trend-led, trope-filled list of books with diverse, authentic and relatable characters, a wide array of voices and representations, plus real world trials and tribulations. Featuring all the tropes you could possibly want (think small-town settings, fake relationships, grumpy vs sunshine, enemies to lovers) and all with a generous dose of spice in every story.

♪ @millsandboonuk
◎ @millsandboonuk
afterglowbooks.co.uk

#AfterglowBooks

For all the latest book news, exclusive content and giveaways scan the QR code below to sign up to the Afterglow newsletter: